D0498795

"You are going blind," Doc Savage said without feeling.

The crook who called himself Blackie did an unexpected thing. He fainted. His knees folded inward, his feet slid apart, and the rest of him just collapsed on the pile of kindling that his nerveless legs became.

No sooner had he collapsed on the carpet than the draperies gave a sudden billow as from a gust of wind.

There was no wind. The pane was closed.

What there was a bullet. It sent shards of glass ripping through the heavy drapery, and after passing through the spot where Blackie had been, it dug an ugly hole in the bookcase paneling.

Doc Savage's voice crashed with urgency.

"Sniper!" he rapped. "Get down!"

The draperies began twitching and kicking with the arrival of more leaden missiles.

Other books in the Doc Savage Series
Ask your bookseller for the books you have missed.

DOC SAVAGE OMNIBUS #1 (including *The All-White Elf*, *The Angry Canary*, *The Running Skeletons*, *The Swooning Lady*)
DOC SAVAGE OMNIBUS #2 (including *The Mindless Monsters*, *The Rustling Death*, *King Joe Cay*, *The Thing That Pursued*)
DOC SAVAGE OMNIBUS #3 (including *Measures for A Coffin*, *The Three Devils*, *The Spook of Grandpa Eben*, *Strange Fish*)
DOC SAVAGE OMNIBUS #4 (including *Mystery Island*, *Men of Fear*, *Rock Sinister*, *The Pure Evil*)
DOC SAVAGE OMNIBUS #5 (including *No Light to Die By*, *The Monkey Suit*, *Let's Kill Ames*, *Once Over Lightly*, *I Died Yesterday*)
DOC SAVAGE OMNIBUS #6 (including *The Awful Dynasty*, *The Magic Forest*, *Fire and Ice*, *The Disappearing Lady*)
DOC SAVAGE OMNIBUS #7 (including *The Men Vanished*, *Five Fathoms Dead*, *The Terrible Stork*, *Danger Lies East*)
DOC SAVAGE OMNIBUS #8 (including *The Mental Monster*, *The Pink Lady*, *Weird Valley*, *Trouble on Parade*)
DOC SAVAGE OMNIBUS #9 (including *The Invisible-Box Murders*, *Birds of Death*, *The Wee Ones*, *Terror Takes 7*)
DOC SAVAGE OMNIBUS #10 (including *The Devil's Black Rock*, *Waves of Death*, *The Two-Wise Owl*, *Terror and the Lonely Widow*)
DOC SAVAGE OMNIBUS #11 (including *Se-Pah-Poo*, *Colors for Murder*, *Three Times a Corpse*, *Death Is A Round Black Spot*, *The Devil Is Jones*)
DOC SAVAGE OMNIBUS #12 (including *Bequest of Evil*, *Death in Little Houses*, *Target for Death*, *The Death Lady*, *The Exploding Lake*)
DOC SAVAGE OMNIBUS #13 (including *The Derelict of Skull Shoal*, *Terror Wears No Shoes*, *The Green Master*, *Return From Cormoral*, *Up From Earth's Center*)
ESCAPE FROM LOKI by Philip Jose Farmer
PYTHON ISLE
WHITE EYES

(*Don't miss another original Doc Savage adventure*, THE FRIGHT-ENED FISH coming in July 1992)

WHITE EYES

Kenneth Robeson

BANTAM BOOKS
NEW YORK • TORONTO • LONDON • SYDNEY • AUCKLAND

WHITE EYES
A Bantam Falcon Book / March 1992

FALCON and the portrayal of a boxed "f" are trademarks of Bantam Books, a division of Bantam Doubleday Dell Publishing Group, Inc.

Doc Savage is a registered trademark of Condé Nast Publications, Inc. Registered in U.S. Patent and Trademark Office and Elsewhere.

Interior Art by Joe DeVito.

All rights reserved.
Copyright © 1992 by Will Murray and Mrs. Lester Dent.
Cover art Copyright © 1992 by Joe DeVito.
No part of this book may be reproduced or transmitted in any form or by any means, electronic or mechanical, including photocopying, recording, or by any information storage and retrieval system, without permission in writing from the publisher.
For information address: Bantam Books

If you purchased this book without a cover you should be aware that this book is stolen property. It was reported as "unsold and destroyed" to the publisher and neither the author nor the publisher has received any payment for this "stripped book."

ISBN 0-553-29561-6

Published simultaneously in the United States and Canada

Bantam Books are published by Bantam Books, a division of Bantam Doubleday Dell Publishing Group, Inc. Its trademark, consisting of the words "Bantam Books" and the portrayal of a rooster, is Registered in U.S. Patent and Trademark Office and in other countries. Marca Registrada. Bantam Books, 666 Fifth Avenue, New York, New York 10103.

PRINTED IN THE UNITED STATES OF AMERICA

OPM   0 9 8 7 6 5 4 3 2 1

DOC

Doc Savage—born Clark Savage, Jr.—was raised from the cradle for his task in life—his job of flitting about the globe righting wrongs, helping the oppressed, smashing the guilty. He is a physician and surgeon—and a mighty good one, the tops in his line. He has the best and most modern equipment at his command, for he has limitless wealth. His main headquarters are in New York, but he has his Fortress of Solitude at a place unknown to anyone, where he goes at periodic intervals to increase his knowledge and concentrate. He's foiled countless crooks, and changed many of them into honest, useful citizens. The world would be a great place if there were more Doc Savages. But there's only one.

HAM

You'd never think a gentleman named Brigadier General Theodore Marley Brooks would be called Ham—would you? But Monk, Ham's pal, had a reason for giving him the nickname. He thought it would irritate the dapper Brigadier General Brooks—and that alone was regarded as a good reason by Monk. Ham is a knockout dresser and a knockout fighter, too. There's very little of the law that he doesn't know down to about six decimal places. But in a fight, the main law that he thinks about is the law of self-preservation, although most of his battles have been in the interest of folks too weak to fight for themselves. His slender black swordcane is something to avoid.

MONK

When you look at this picture, you can understand very well why the subject is called Monk. Hardly any other nickname would fit him as well. He's a tough hombre. His arms are six inches longer than his legs, and with this gorilla build he seldom stacks up against any opponent who's more than a brief workout for him. No one ever calls him by his real name of Andrew Blodgett Mayfair. And maybe they'd better not! There's a ring to it that Monk might not like! Yet Monk has a keen brain as well as a strong body, and is reputed to be one of the world's greatest chemists. His combination of body and brain makes him a big asset to Doc Savage's intrepid little band of crusaders.

RENNY

If you know him well, you can call him Renny. If you want to be formal, it's Colonel John Renwick. He's a giant of a man. A six-footer would have to look up at him. He weighs well over two hundred, and while he doesn't throw his weight around, he knows how to use it in a fight.

His fists—and they are very big and bony—are very bad on faces. They can actually shatter the solid panel of a heavy door. Renny is an engineer, and tops in his line.

LONG TOM

Major Thomas J. Roberts—Long Tom to his friends—is the electrical wizard of Doc Savage's little group of adventurers. In spite of his nickname, he is not so tall. Doesn't weigh so much, either, and the appearance of his skin gives the impression that he might not be in the best of health.

That skin, however, has been misleading to anybody who ever picked on Long Tom for a set-up. Try taking a cougar's cubs away, but don't ever shove around Long Tom. He's as fast as light, and a terrific socker.

JOHNNY

Few persons would take Johnny—whose real name is William Harper Littlejohn—for a scrapper. He's quite studious. He's an archæologist of worldwide reputation.

Anybody who picked up Johnny, however, would be making quite a big mistake. He can fight like a wounded panther when he's aroused. Like a great many gaunt men, he has an inexhaustible reservoir of strength. He's an important member of Doc Savage's little group.

PAT

Pat Savage is a cousin to the man of bronze. She has Doc's metallic coloring—bronze skin, flake-gold eyes—and is extremely attractive. Pat operates one of New York's most exclusive beauty salons, and constantly yearns for excitement. Though highly capable, her participation in the adventures of Doc and his aids is usually against Doc's wishes, for he believes the work of his group too dangerous for a girl.

Contents

I	BLIND AND DEAD	1
II	DANA'S TROUBLE	9
III	ANOTHER BLIND CORPSE	19
IV	DEVELOPMENT UNEXPECTED	28
V	THE TOUGH MR. JEFFERSON	41
VI	WHITE EYES SPEAKS	49
VII	WHITE EYES'S PATH	58
VIII	GIRL UNCOOPERATIVE	66
IX	THE ARGUERS	73
X	PLOT GROWING	82
XI	THE PIG RUSE	94
XII	GOOD LUCK AND BAD	99
XIII	FOILED SHADOWS	105
XIV	BLIND END	118
XV	SCHEMERS FALL OUT	126
XVI	THE HOT SEAT	131
XVII	DEAD AND GUILTY	140
XVIII	THE UBIQUITOUS RADIO	149
XIX	WHITE EYES APPEARS	157
XX	THE CHOSEN	169
XXI	THIRD DEGREE	181
XXII	ABDUCTOR IN WHITE	188
XXIII	EXPERIMENT STRANGE	195
XXIV	THE TALKING MAN	201
XXV	UPROAR	210

XXVI	EXPLANATIONS	219
XXVII	PIECES OF THE PUZZLE	226
XXVIII	GANGDOM'S LONG ARM	235
XXIX	WHITE EYES TRIUMPHANT	247
XXX	CUBAMA	255
XXXI	BLAZING CANE	264
XXXII	THE MILL	272
XXXIII	CATARACT	281
XXXIV	EYES THAT TOLD	290

I

BLIND AND DEAD

Nug Hassel was not the first to die. There were five others before him. Two were respected businessmen and three were hardened criminals like Nug Hassel. They all had fits, and their eyes turned, first brilliant red, and then milky white as they died.

Nug Hassel's death was mystifying. It was also, to express it figuratively, the match that lighted the fuse that blew up the works.

Nug Hassel died on a cold Winter day when there were a few hard snow pellets loose in the air, and his demise was not exactly a departure from the ordained scheme of things. The state had a date to strap him in the electric chair for butchering a bank cashier with a machine gun. Nug had also planned an escape, during which he would probably have been shot to death anyway. Trying a break from the Tombs is one way of committing suicide.

There was also a man posted at a distant office window with a 404-magnum rifle with a silencer and the best telescope sight on the market. The man with the rifle was a former associate of Nug Hassel's, and he was no little anxious to see his erstwhile consort in a coffin, because Nug Hassel was going to squeal, divulging the name of the big brain back of the bank job.

It happened to Nug Hassel as he was being led to the district attorney to tell what he knew. By squealing, Nug hoped to sidestep the electric chair. He would have failed, but he had no way of knowing that.

Two guards held Nug Hassel's arms as he began

1

pitching about madly. Other guards, thinking the man was trying to escape, lifted submachine guns.

Then Nug Hassel started screaming, and the guards fell to staring, for they could sense that something unseen and awful was happening to the criminal. Between shrieks, the man gnashed his own lips so that crimson leaked down into the open neck of his black-striped prison shirt. He doubled over as best he could, stamping his feet slowly, then threw back his head and made gargling sounds.

When his head was back, the guards first noticed his eyes. They were hideous, and becoming more so. It looked as if every blood vessel was bursting at once.

Someone yelled for a physician. More policemen came running. Nug Hassel continued to gargle and became limp. The guards lowered him to the cold floor, but still held his arms. They were taking no chances.

Nug Hassel ceased gargling, becoming very slack. One of the guards suddenly released the wrist he had been holding.

"I'll be damned," muttered the guard. "Whatcha know about that?"

The others stared questioningly.

"He's deader than hell," said the guard, profanely amazed.

The police lieutenant ran up, along with a physician. They took one look at the dead man's eyes, which now resembled hard-boiled eggs with the shells off. There was no hint of iris or pupil in the blank dead stare. Even the burst blood vessels, so red a moment ago, had disappeared. The entire orb was a milky white.

"He's about the sixth one," said the physician.

"What?" some one snapped.

"The others died the same way," the physician declared.

"Looked like he had a fit," a guard offered.

"So did the others," stated the medico. "They got egg-eyed like this, too."

"Good riddance," growled a hard-boiled cop.

"Don't be a sap," the physician told him. "The other five weren't all crooks. Three were, but the other two were guys who had never taken a rap. This white-eyed death seems to be getting them all over town."

The police lieutenant strained his slightly gray hair through his fingers.

"Mysterious, huh?" he asked.

"Very," the medico agreed. "I cannot tell you exactly what happened to this man. It is a puzzle."

"It won't be for long," snorted the lieutenant. "In the event of another white-eyed death, the Man of Bronze himself is to be notified. The big fellow is interested in these strange deaths."

"The Man of Bronze!" some one grunted explosively.

"Is this a break!" exclaimed the lieutenant. "I've always wanted to see that fellow work."

The physician asked sharply, "When you say the Man of Bronze, do you mean Doc Savage?"

"Who else?" asked the lieutenant. "I'll call Doc Savage now."

He hurried in the direction of a telephone.

Some blocks distant, behind the office window, the late Nug Hassel's former associate fingered his rifle doubtfully. He was tempted to put a bullet into Nug Hassel to make sure.

The sniper who had not fired a shot was extremely puzzled. He laid his telescopically equipped, silenced weapon aside and brought a pair of binoculars into play. The lenses were powerful, and the hard bits of snow in the air looked as large as white blankets.

The watcher saw the physician make tests for evidences of life in the prone form of Nug Hassel. He saw the medico shake his head wonderingly.

It was chilly in the office and the observer's laugh pushed a gush of breath steam through his clenched teeth.

"Nug must be a stiff," he chuckled. "Won't the boss feel bad about that!"

The man continued to watch with an intentness

which indicated that he had no thought of deserting his post. But after a bit he did lower the binoculars and pull thoughtfully at an ear.

Deserting the window, he opened the door a crack, waited until the corridor was deserted, then went out and found a public telephone. He dialed a number.

"Harmon Cash?" he asked.

"How exquisitely thoughtful of you to mention the name," came a smoothly sarcastic voice.

"It's all right, chief," said the sniper who had not discharged a shot. "Something happened to Nug Hassel."

"Which makes your mention of my name even more considerate," stated the other, still more sourly. "Now I will have to move my office and possibly go into hiding. Telephone calls have been traced, you know."

"I didn't have anything to do with what happened to Nug," disclaimed the other. "He had a fit and fell over dead, with his eyes rolled up into his head."

"His eyes what?"

"Rolled up into his head. At least, that's how it looked to me. All I could see was the whites. Nug's the most white-eyed corpse you ever saw."

The distant smooth voice was silent for a time, then said slowly, "This makes about the sixth."

The man who had intended to shoot Nug Hassel was slender and smartly dressed. He had a smooth face, entirely innocent looking, and there was nothing about him to indicate he was a cold-blooded killer whose services were quite regularly employed.

"Huh?" he grunted.

"This makes about the sixth man in New York City who has dropped dead with his eyeballs turned white as snow," said the distant speaker. "It is very mysterious."

"It saved us some trouble in the case of Nug Hassel, though."

The other was quiet again. "Babe."

"Yeah," replied the innocent-looking young man. "Now who's mentioning names?"

"Never mind that," advised the distant Harmon

Cash. "Go back, Babe, and keep an eye on Nug Hassel, and tell me what happens."

"Nug is a corpse, I tell you," said Babe.

"Let us hope so," Harmon Cash said fervently. "But go back, Babe, and keep me posted."

"Sure." Babe hung up.

A few seconds later, Babe was back at the window using the binoculars. His first look gave him quite a start. He jerked rigid, his youthful face lost color, and his own eyes rolled ceilingward a little, as if he had a mild touch of the mysterious affliction which had brought death to Nug Hassel.

But it was only surprise and some fear that caused Babe's eyes to roll upward. His manner was that of a man who had just seen his own private devil.

Through the binoculars, Babe was getting a look at Doc Savage.

Babe was not the only interested one observing Doc Savage. The policemen were showing unusual deference for cops. The lieutenant's manner was that of one expecting the unexpected; he watched Doc Savage as if figurative rabbits were going to be yanked out of hats, and he did not want to miss any of it.

The police physician, who had handled many corpses and dug bullets out of screaming criminals and had had crooks try to stab him with his own instruments, was in the grip of something akin to stage fright. For he was talking to an individual who was rapidly becoming akin to a legend throughout the civilized world.

"I cannot tell what happened to this man Nug Hassel," he said stiffly. "The policemen say he had some kind of a fit. I could put it in medical terminology, but it would amount to the same thing."

"Let me examine the body," vouchsafed Doc Savage.

There was vibrant, controlled power in that voice, and something else, also. It was a voice which radiated capability, resourcefulness, the power to do unusual things.

Perhaps the eyes of the Man of Bronze had something to do with the impression, too. They were weird, almost fantastic eyes—like nothing so much as pools of gold flakes continuously stirred by tiny winds. In them was a hypnotic, compelling quality.

Or maybe it was the size of this Man of Bronze. He towered above all the others present, though some of the policemen were large men. However, it was only when he was close to the others that his size really impressed, for there was a symmetrical proportion about his build that made him, standing apart, seem less Herculean than he was.

Tremendous muscular strength was apparent whenever the bronze man moved. The hands with which he made his examination were cabled with great sinews. The vertical muscles in his neck were like hawsers coated with a veneer of bronze skin.

"The Man of Bronze," breathed an officer. "No mystery about where he got that name."

Nor was there. Bronze was the giant's motif throughout—his unusually textured skin had a metallic hue imparted by long exposure to intense sunlight; his hair, straight and fitting like a metal skullcap, was of a bronze only slightly darker; the quiet brown business suit which he wore only added to the symphony in bronze which was this remarkable individual.

Doc Savage straightened from his examination.

"What killed him?" asked the physician.

Doc Savage said slowly, in his amazing voice, "It would be best not to offer an opinion just yet."

Then he moved away.

The police lieutenant looked disappointed and whispered, "Darned if I believe he has any more idea than we have about what killed Nug Hassel."

"Don't be a dope," retorted the physician. "That bronze man knows everything worth knowing. He's a wizard. They say he can excel any one of his five assistants in their special lines, and believe me, some of them are good. All of them, from reports."

"Question, please."

"Huh?"

"What five assistants?"

"Doc Savage has five men who aid him," explained the patient medico. "There is an electrician, a lawyer, an engineer, a chemist, and a combination archæologist and geologist. Each of these assistants is widely known in his particular profession. Only two of them, the lawyer and the chemist, are now in the United States. The other three are in Europe. I recall reading of their absence in the sheets, in the same articles that tell of Savage's interest in this so-called Blind Death phenomenon."

At this point, Doc Savage said distinctly, so that everyone heard, "It might be best to interview the men who escorted the prisoner from his cell."

This distinctness without rise in tone was a remarkable quality about the bronze man's voice. Not a man who heard it failed to follow the big bronze fellow, expectation writ large on their faces.

Doc Savage interviewed the guards in the privacy of the warden's office, where the latter was fiddling with the knobs of a stubborn console radio. He gave up on it when the bronze man entered.

One by one, the guards related their tales. None could explain what manner of fate had befallen Nug Hassel.

"And you say you neither saw nor heard anything unusual while this was happening to Hassel?" Doc asked after the last man had concluded his report.

To a man, the guards concurred that the only thing unusual about the incident was its devilish inexplicability.

Doc Savage thanked the guards and turned to leave.

Then, one man snapped his fingers.

"Wait!" he exclaimed. "There was one thing!"

"Yes?" Doc prompted.

"Just as Nug was going, I remember thinking how warm I felt. But the sensation went away quick and I forgot about it."

That seemed to prod the memories of the others.

They, too, suddenly remembered an inexplicable warm feeling.

"Kinda like a fever," was the way one guard put it.

The warden assumed a disbelieving tone of voice.

"Why, I thought you men had stepped from the building when the prisoner got it," he demanded.

"We did," one offered. "We were walking toward the wagon. Right outside your window, as a matter of fact." He pointed to the barred window—barred to discourage escapes, because the warden's office was situated on the first floor.

"Preposterous!" the warden blurted. "Have you any idea how cold it is out there?"

"Thirty-six degrees," Doc Savage said quietly, his flake-gold eyes thoughtful.

II

DANA'S TROUBLE

Babe, the killer who looked like a prosperous young salesman, dropped his binoculars into a pocket and sidled away from the window as if fearful of being seen. He was still quite pale. There was a frantic haste in his movements as he disassembled his rifle and inserted the parts in a large trombone case.

A few moments later, Babe again had Harmon Cash on the telephone.

"Listen, chief," he breathed. "Who do you think turned up down here?"

"I do not feel in a mood for conundrums," Harmon Cash told him over the wire.

"It was Doc Savage," said Babe.

It was fully twenty seconds before Harmon Cash made a sound. Then he swore. He did not use profanity, however, but said, "Now isn't that ducky!" and made it sound harshly wrathful.

When Harmon Cash spoke to Babe next, it was in a rapid manner which showed the man was excited.

"How did Doc Savage happen to turn up on the scene?" Cash demanded. "What did he do? How did he act? Has he any suspicion you are near?"

Babe made a whistling pucker with his lips. It was the first time he had ever heard Harmon Cash shocked out of his usual suave self. Harmon Cash was considered to be one of the most composed and coldly calculating criminal leaders in America. In fact, he never became excited, and classed himself, not as a crook, but as a businessman who had chosen not to stay inside the law.

But Harmon Cash was mightily alarmed by mention of Doc Savage.

Innocent-looking Babe told exactly what he had seen through the binoculars, and at the end of the recital, Harmon Cash got out a sigh—which, however, did not sound any too relieved.

"Get away from there," he snapped. "We do not want this Doc Savage concerning himself about us."

"You said something," Babe muttered. "What'll I do? Hide out?"

"Such a procedure seems ridiculous, but it is actually an excellent idea," said the chief.

"I'll dig in," said Babe.

"Wait," interjected the other. "There seems to be some trouble about the sugar affair."

"The sugar affair?" echoed Babe.

"Exactly. Do you understand?"

"Sure," said Babe. "I get you."

"One of them was supposed to call me this afternoon and has failed to do so," said Harmon Cash. "I want you to call at this office and see what is wrong."

"Which one is that?" asked Babe.

"Cowboy," said Harmon Cash. "Get it?"

"Sure. I'll see what's eating him."

Babe hung up, shifted his binoculars in the pocket so they would not be too noticeable, tucked his trombone case under an arm, and took his departure.

In this office building, there was a firm which dealt in musical wind instruments, both wholesale and retail, so a man going or coming with a trombone case was utterly unsuspicious. Harmon Cash had selected this building with that in mind. He overlooked few bets.

Babe did not take a taxi cab because cab drivers have memories. He walked only a few blocks, and even that was a greater distance than if he had gone directly, but he did not want to approach near the spot where he had seen Doc Savage. He entered a new and imposing modernistic pile of masonry and steel which had cost the builder more than ten millions, and which had half its offices still unfilled by tenants.

The office suite of the Cubama Sugar Importing Company occupied the fourteenth floor. A little hen of a receptionist who wore glasses stopped Babe, demanding whom he wished to see.

Babe let her bathe in the full warmth of his personality. Babe had been a high-pressure salesman before he took to killing people for so much a slaying, and he considered himself very personable.

"Kindly inform Senor Sanchez y. Annuncio de Calabero I was referred to him by H. C.," Babe imparted.

Babe's easy, confident manner seemingly did the trick, because he was soon directed toward one of the glass-fronted office doors marked with the word PRIVATE.

Above that black-lettered admonition appeared, in somewhat more elegant calligraphy, the name *Sanchez y. Annuncio de Calabero*.

Babe passed through without knocking.

"Hyah, Cowboy," Babe grinned.

Sanchez y. Annuncio de Calabero scowled at the familiarity. He was a dark, overfed man with damp, glistening eyes that looked perpetually frightened. Despite his heavy mohair suit, he shivered noticeably. A nearby steam radiator hissed, giving the modest office a tropical air. Not a droplet of perspiration pearled Sanchez y. Annuncio de Calabero's smooth complexion, which was the exact hue of lightly creamed coffee.

"What brings you here, Senor Babe?" Sanchez y. Annuncio de Calabero inquired politely. *"Eso es muy mal*. It is very bad, dangerous."

"Don't you think it's a bad idea to stand the boss up?" Babe asked shortly.

Sanchez y. Annuncio de Calabero shrugged, *"Si, si*, but I thought—"

"You had a date to call him, didn't you?"

Sanchez y. Annuncio de Calabero began again, "It is true, Senor, but I believed—"

Babe shoved out a face that was suddenly ugly.

"You wouldn't be giving the boss the run-around, would you?" he demanded.

Sanchez y. Annuncio de Calabero shoved out his own face, which assumed a hardness equal to Babe's.

"Do not get tough with me, you gringo torpedo," he warned.

Babe was engaged in giving Sanchez y. Annuncio de Calabero what he called a "horsing," a treatment which he considered beneficial when there were symptoms of some follower of Harmon Cash not following the chief's orders implicitly. He now threw in a few threats.

"Maybe you're not satisfied with the split the boss is taking out of the dough you and your partner swindled from the Cubama Sugar Importing Company," he snarled. "Maybe you're trying to worry the boss into agreeing to a bigger split."

"*Mulo!*" gritted Sanchez y. Annuncio de Calabero. "Donkey! Idiot! Some one may hear you! I think I am being watched. That is why I did not communicate with the Senor Cash."

Babe suddenly lost his tough manner. "Is that straight?"

"*Si, si,*" agreed Sanchez y. Annuncio de Calabero. "Two or three times recently, I have thought some one was shadowing me. I have not been able to see who it was, however."

Babe considered, then asked skeptically, "How's your nerve?"

"You mean—am I imagining things?" Sanchez y. Annuncio de Calabero growled. "No, senor. I am afraid some one is trailing me."

"I'll tell the chief that," said Babe, after thinking it over. "Where's your partner?"

"Partner?"

"Sure, the other guy who helped you mooch a quarter of a million in negotiable bonds from the company safe. I mean—"

"No names, Senor!" gulped Sanchez y. Annuncio de Calabero. "My partner, as you call him, is around somewhere."

"You tell him about this business of some one following you?"

"*Si, si.*"

"Anybody tailing him?"

"No."

"Okay. I'll report this to the boss." Babe waved a hand airily. "Don't take any wooden nickels, Cowboy."

"Stop calling me that," Sanchez y. Annuncio de Calabero snapped. "My name is Calabero, not Caballero. I am no pampas *gaucho*, despite what you may think."

"What I think is that you'd better keep watching your step, Cowboy," Babe grinned, and went out.

Babe grinned in an unconcerned fashion and winked at the little hen of a receptionist as he went out. Babe was not at all convinced that any one was shadowing Sanchez y. Annuncio de Calabero. He secretly believed the man had an attack of strong imagination. Inexperienced criminals frequently had such attacks.

Not that Sanchez y. Annuncio de Calabero was an inexperienced crook. Rather, the contrary. Sanchez y. Annuncio de Calabero had held a political job in Cuba for a time, and had barely escaped with his life during one of the numerous revolutions. He was an unmitigated crook. It was he who had approached Harmon Cash with the suggestion of annexing the quarter of a million dollars, approximately, which the Cubama Sugar Importing Company chanced to have in its large vault.

Harmon Cash was getting a large split of that money, which was still in Sanchez y. Annuncio de Calabero's possession. Harmon Cash always got a large split, and he had many irons in the crime bonfire. This affair was only one of them, and not the largest by any means. In this case, Harmon Cash was merely disposing of the money, which was in the form of very hot negotiable bonds.

Back in the office, Sanchez y. Annuncio de Calabero was displaying the effects of an uneasy conscience. He moved about the room nervously, pausing only to give the radiator valve a twirl. Hot steam heat poured forth. But it was not enough for the Cuban-born crook, who had yet to acclimate himself to New York in Winter. Every time he passed a snow-dusted window, he shivered violently.

He would have been still more uneasy could he have seen the unobtrusive wren of a girl who was a receptionist. It was part of the receptionist's duties to attend to the telephone switchboard. She wore the receiver headset which was a part of her equipment, and seemed to be listening with half an ear.

The rest of her attention was devoted to studying a stenographic notebook which lay open on the desk before her. She was turning the leaves, here and there finishing out a character with an expert pen stroke. She was glancing over her notes while they were fresh, making sure that she could read them later on.

Transcribed, those notes would furnish a complete record of exactly what had been said between Babe and Sanchez y. Annuncio de Calabero.

The unobtrusive girl smiled widely and put the notebook in a handbag which also held an automatic pistol, extra clips of cartridges, a tiny toylike tear-gas gun, and a private detective's badge.

Then she rang the phone which connected her with an office on another floor of the building which housed the Cubama Sugar Importing Company.

"This is Dana O'Fall," she said in a tone that was crisply unlike her usual meek voice. "I practically have the low-down on who stole those bonds. It was that human hothouse orchid, Sanchez."

"Then we'll have Sanchez de Calabero seized immediately!" snapped a sour voice at the other end of the line.

"Not much," said private detective Dana O'Fall. "Another man is helping Sanchez. I want to get him, too. And a third fellow who is not a Cubama employee seems to be disposing of the loot for them."

"Who is this third man?" asked the other unhappily.

"I didn't catch his full name," said Dana, "but if

my guessing is on the money, he's an old smoothie that the police have never been able to lay a thing on. Just let me handle this and I'll have those bonds in your hands, and land all the crooks where they belong."

"But—"

At that point, Sanchez y. Annuncio de Calabero came out of his office. He had his hat and overcoat on and seemed bound on a definite errand.

Heedless of the protestations coming through the receiver diaphragm, Dana terminated the connection.

There was a sensitive microphone in each of the sugar company's offices, and wires from all of these ran to the switchboard, where Dana O'Fall could listen in without attracting attention. Dana O'Fall was the star sleuth of one of the city's least known and most efficient private detective agencies. As a matter of precaution, she had never been seen in the offices of the agency itself.

Dana cut the secret microphone out of circuit and motioned to one of the stenographers, who, without a word, took over operation of the switchboard. Dana then followed Sanchez y. Annuncio de Calabero.

Sanchez y. Annuncio de Calabero took an elevator.

Dana let him go, then ran to the call buttons and punched a signal of a long and two short rings, then three long ones. This spelled her initials in radio code.

An elevator arrived almost at once. The elevator boy was receiving five dollars a day to be ready to bring his cage instantly when he heard the signal.

Going down the elevator, Dana O'Fall applied lipstick and rouge with expert haste. In the lobby, she first made sure that Sanchez y. Annuncio de Calabero was outside, then ducked into a telephone booth and doffed her rather threadbare coat. This proved to be reversible. The lining was actually of fine material. When she had turned it inside out, it looked like an ordinary, if expensive, bit of millinery work. After climbing into it, she exchanged her flat plain shoes for polished high heels. She added a tiny silk hat to the make-up. This only required a moment.

The result was nothing less than arresting. The Dana O'Fall who stepped out of the wooden booth and through the revolving door into the street was an entrancing creature with bright violet eyes and glossy chestnut curls. Her bearing was almost regal. The heels gave her an additional two inches of height. If Sanchez y. Annuncio de Calabero had chanced to encounter her, he would not have recognized in this fetching young girl anything of the henlike receptionist who served the Cubama Sugar Importing Company.

Sanchez y. Annuncio de Calabero did look back numerous times, but thanks to Dana's skill, noticed nothing out of the ordinary—or if he did notice anything, gave no indication. His path took him south, where the streets became dark and malodorous, and the clean white snow, which was now blowing in swirls along the pavement, eddied like crystalline stars in a wayward miniature galaxy that had happened to fall to this disreputable spot on the earth.

Few were about in this unsavory neighborhood. This made Dana's trailing comparatively easy. She did not walk directly behind Sanchez y. Annuncio de Calabero, but angled up and down side streets, sometimes walking briskly along parallel streets, and other times actually strolling ahead of her quarry. These confusing maneuvers were some of the tricks of her trade, and they served her well.

Until, coming around a corner with her fur-trimmed coat collar turned up in deference to the biting, snow-charged wind—which also helped to conceal her pretty face—Dana O'Fall failed to spot her unsuspecting quarry at the expected intersection.

She stopped, made a pretense of freshening her lipstick, but actually employed her compact mirror to canvass the converging streets. She pretended to be bothered by the wind. This enabled her to scout every direction in a very short time.

The snow lay like a fine powder on the sidewalks. Here and there, playful winds had scoured gray scablike patches clear of the sugary coating. It was too thin to take footprints for long—the wind pushed it about too much—but there was scarcely a stoop or doorway which had not captured a quantity of the stuff.

One doorway showed the unmistakable tramp of human feet. Already, fingers of wind were lifting and changing the unmistakable signs. Soon, all traces would be gone. But the snow told a clear story.

Sanchez y. Annuncio de Calabero had mounted that doorway and entered. Dana turned in without hesitation. Since she had come from the opposite direction, she did not think it likely that suspicion would be aroused.

The door was not locked. She slipped inside, listened, and detected voice mutter from above.

One of the speakers was the perpetually shivering Sanchez y. Annuncio de Calabero.

"Listen, chief," Sanchez y. Annuncio de Calabero was saying, "I need more time. This Harmon Cash is no patsy. We can't expose him without more proof."

Dana O'Fall heard Sanchez y. Annuncio de Calabero speak distinctly, but the replying tone was a nondescript murmur that defied classification, never mind understanding. It was difficult to ascertain the speaker's sex with confidence.

"You know it was an unusual procedure, my taking those bonds as a part of an elaborate plan to trap Harmon Cash," said Sanchez y. Annuncio de Calabero. "Of course, Cash did not get the genuine bonds. I still have those, and they will be returned. But Cash may discover he has fakes if we work too swiftly."

This information gave Dana O'Fall quite a start. She made a grim mouth and crept up a shabby stairway toward the voices. It was beginning to look as if she had Sanchez y. Annuncio de Calabero all wrong.

The unintelligible mutter was replying to Sanchez y. Annuncio de Calabero.

"Well, I'll admit it did help to have a genuine theft to squash any suspicions Harmon Cash may have had," returned the Cuban expatriate. "But my taking those bonds was highly unorthodox."

Dana put an ear to a rickety door. She was very interested in this.

Down on the street somewhere, an automobile horn which sounded like a bawling calf was making short blasts.

There was no speaking in the room beyond the door at which Dana listened, but she could hear some one pacing about. The pacing stopped, apparently on the far side of the room.

Dana leaned a little against the ancient panel. Without any warning sound, the door fell open. Caught off balance, Dana toppled through.

Hands, seizing her fur collar and hair, yanked forcibly and helped her through. Before she could fight back, or resist in any way, she found herself slammed up against a wall of peeling yellow wallpaper.

His polished teeth like fierce pearls, Sanchez y. Annuncio de Calabero crowded her into a corner where the paper hung in long drooping scabs.

"Senorita," he gritted, "you must be very young, because you fall for one very old trick. *No?*"

III

ANOTHER BLIND CORPSE

Dana O'Fall knew she was outclassed, both in size and strength. She could not hope to best Sanchez y. Annuncio de Calabero, the man who had turned the tables on her so cleverly. But she was not about to surrender. Not without a fight.

She promptly kicked him in the shins to start with.

Hopping on one foot, Sanchez y. Annuncio de Calabero grabbed the first barked shin with both hands. He had time to emit one warbling moan before the sudden pain in his other shin compelled him to shift feet. He continued his painful hopping without skipping a hop.

While Sanchez y. Annuncio de Calabero was so occupied, Dana O'Fall handed him a rabbit punch in the windpipe. That squelched his moans. She followed up with a thumb inserted in one of the coffee-colored deceiver's eyes. He transferred his hands from his skinned shin to the injured orb. A tendril of blood leaked along the web of skin between one thumb and forefinger.

Cursing in voluble Spanish, Sanchez y. Annuncio de Calabero launched a stiff-legged kick in Dana O'Fall's general direction.

Dana O'Fall backpedaled on her high heels as she shoved one hand into her purse. It came out clutching her small automatic. She thumbed the safety off, aimed at the swarthy man's left leg—Sanchez y. Annuncio de

Calabero was kicking with his right—and pulled the trigger.

Nothing happened.

Dana's opinion of her own capacity as a detective shot downward. She had neglected to cock the gun by jacking the slide back the last time she loaded it.

Once more, Sanchez y. Annuncio de Calabero kicked. The small automatic caromed from wall to ceiling to floor. Dana groaned. Her fingers had been bruised.

Still clutching his wounded, leaking eye, Sanchez y. Annuncio de Calabero dived for the weapon. There was murder in his one working eyeball.

Retreating to the door, Dana brought out the tiny tear-gas pistol from her purse. She brought the weapon to bear, pulled the trigger once.

The muzzle, more like a fat black tube than a pistol barrel, coughed an onion-colored cloud that spread and rolled toward Sanchez the expatriate Cuban as he laid hands on the fallen automatic.

He happened to look up as the vaporous cloud struck him. All thought of the automatic fled as he launched into a paroxysm of coughing and cursing. His uninjured eye was forced in spite of itself to close. Sanchez y. Annuncio de Calabero dropped the automatic and clapped his free hand over the inflicted optic.

Then he got down on the floor and made strangling, agonized sounds.

Dana O'Fall saw none of this last. Holding her breath against the tear gas, she stumbled down the stairs, her eyes pinched almost to the point of blindness. When she had first purchased the tear-gas gun, she had made the mistake of test-firing it in the privacy of her apartment. The lesson had stuck.

She did not open her eyes again until she had burst out into the hard, sifting snow. She started to run. Her one idea now was to get a policeman.

"Here, what's going on?" demanded a cultured voice.

Dana looked at the newcomer, then gasped, "Eduardo Luz!"

Eduardo Luz was a tanned young man who looked as if he were too well fed. He was not more than twenty-five, and his chin, which should have been clean and square at that age, was already rounded with fat. His white hat looked rather small perching atop a mop of curly black hair and he was smoking a cigarette.

He wore a tropical white linen suit that was entirely out of place in New York City during early Winter. The immaculate, ghostly lines of the suit made his dark-complected face and hands stand out like coconuts against a sun-drenched beach. The very black jewels that were his eyes seemed to jump out from the whites for that very reason, giving them a penetrating quality. For all that, he was handsome in a rather vapid way.

Eduardo Luz was head cashier for the Cubama Sugar Importing Company, and Dana, in checking up the company employees, had noted that Eduardo always arrived at work a few minutes early, and was one of the last to leave.

His jaw sagged as Eduardo Luz peered more closely at the young woman.

"I'll be darned!" he exploded. "You're that plain little receptionist from the office!"

"What are you doing here?" Dana demanded.

"I can't believe it," snorted Eduardo Luz. "Say, what have you done to yourself? You look like a million dollars."

"Answer my question," Dana ordered.

The young man ran a plump, tanned hand over the collar of Dana's expensive-looking coat.

"Say, you never bought that on a receptionist's salary," he said dryly. "Just who are you, anyway?"

"A private detective," Dana told him sharply. "And now you might explain what you are doing here."

Eduardo Luz sobered suddenly and completely. His cigarette even fell off his lip and was whisked away, spilling sparks, by the chill Winter wind.

"I followed Sanchez," he said.

"Why?"

"I've been playing your game," Luz explained. "I'm trying to find whose fingers stuck to the company's bonds. I suspect that Sanchez, and I've been trailing him."

Dana said abruptly, "Well, you're not bad at detecting. Sanchez did take the bonds."

Eduardo Luz teetered back on his heels and put his hands in his pockets. "Where are they?"

"I don't know where the bonds are," Dana told him, "but Sanchez is upstairs, nursing a dose of tear gas that I gave him. I'm going for a cop."

"You're what?"

"Going to get a policeman," Dana said, and wheeled away.

Eduardo Luz took his hands out of his pockets. One hand held one of those creations of leather and buckshot known as a sap.

The sap made a wooden sound as it came down on Dana O'Fall's head.

Dana O'Fall seemed to be awakened by the Spanish profanity of Sanchez y. Annuncio de Calabero. The words were running together in a low stream of verbal venom, and he was putting a great deal of pained feeling into them. The left side of Dana's head—the sap had hit on that side—ached with ghastly violence, so she opened her right eye.

Sanchez y. Annuncio de Calabero had a face not pleasant to behold. One eye was rimmed with red and leaking tears. The other—the one Dana had jammed her thumb into—was bloodshot and tearing crimson.

Dana tried to move. She was, she discovered, bound hand and foot. The tremendous aching in her head caused her to moan.

Sanchez y. Annuncio de Calabero snarled when he

heard her, grabbed the young woman's automatic, which lay close at hand, and hurled it with great violence at her head. His aim was very bad, and the gun hit the wall, bounced, and came to a rest so close that Dana instantly rolled in a furious effort to reach it.

Some one put a foot in the small of the young woman's back and rolled her away. Dana turned over and looked at the man who had rolled her.

It was Eduardo Luz, which did not surprise her greatly.

"Two men took the bonds," she said. "Sanchez was one. You must be the other."

"You're just too damned clever," Eduardo Luz said in a tone which conveyed that it did not greatly matter. Then he looked at Sanchez y. Annuncio de Calabero and asked, "Think you can watch her now?"

"*Si*," growled Sanchez.

"I'll go call Harmon Cash." Eduardo Luz departed.

He was gone perhaps five minutes, came back smoking a cigarette, and without a word, got down on his hands and knees and began striking matches and picking up cigarette stubs—evidently stubs which he had previously smoked.

"Well, senor?" demanded Sanchez.

It was rather dark in the room.

"The works for the dame," said Eduardo Luz, without looking up from his careful task of gathering stubs.

"The Senor Cash say that?" Sanchez demanded.

"Uh-huh." Eduardo Luz stood up and pocketed the butts. "You want the pleasure, Cowboy?"

"That name is not one I like," warned Sanchez. "*Si, si*, I will take the job."

Sanchez y. Annuncio de Calabero reached into his heavy mohair suit and brought forth a device that was hardly a pistol, but rather a barrel surrounded by a specially constructed silencer. The novelty weapon's report would be equal to the noise made by a typewriter key struck with ordinary firmness.

Eduardo Luz drifted over to a radio of the console type and switched it on.

"Better wait until the set warms up," he advised. "She looks like a screamer to me."

"*Si.*"

Luz went to the door, said while he was still walking, "Don't take too long, Cowboy."

Sanchez y. Annuncio de Calabero scowled in the direction of the closing door with one teary eye. Then, waving his curious pistol before him like a knife, he advanced on helpless Dana O'Fall.

"Don't," Dana said suddenly. "You won't get away with it."

Sanchez y. Annuncio de Calabero stopped sharply, glared, and said, "You can scream, Senorita, but it is doubtful if anyone will hear you. Still, you should have been gagged."

"You won't get away with it," Dana repeated, but her voice was breathlessly hoarse.

"No?" said Sanchez. "Watch me."

Sanchez y. Annuncio de Calabero was mistaken in his belief that the screams would go unheard. A policeman detected them. But perhaps Sanchez was not greatly wrong after all, for the cop thought the shrill, piping sounds which reached his ears so very faintly were made by the icy Winter wind. The officer was bundled to the nose in his winter overcoat, and he wore ear muffs with his uniform cap. This was the first cold snap of the season, and it had arrived prematurely, so that the representative of the law was feeling the chill to an unpleasant degree.

But the policeman did hear the next sounds. They were screams, awful, penetrating bleats, full of the grisly quality of death. The officer yanked off his ear muffs, the better to hear.

It was a man screeching. Of that, he was sure. And it was around the corner somewhere.

The frightful cries ended in something akin to a

series of gargling roars as the officer hurried in search of their source.

He hunted for some time. This old section of the city was a labyrinth, most of the buildings untenanted, and the rest occupied by wholesale shops which were deserted at this late hour.

Eventually, the officer found the doorway through which Dana O'Fall had trailed Sanchez y. Annuncio de Calabero. He made a foray inside. When he came out—which he did very promptly—he was sweating in spite of the bitter cold. He lumbered to the nearest call box.

"Isn't there an order out to call Doc Savage when we find any more of those damn blind cadavers?" he asked his superior.

"There is," agreed the superior. "Doc Savage is over at the Tombs now, I think. There was one of the white-eyed ones over there—that chopper, Nug Hassel. It's got everybody buffaloed."

"Better tell Doc Savage to come down here," advised the cop.

"Why?"

"There's a blind one here. Better send the coroner, too."

Doc Savage arrived in a few minutes, and without ostentation. He drove a roadster, a long, gloomy car with quiet power under its hood and a ghostly silence about the way it rolled along.

The strange bronze man wore neither overcoat nor hat. He seemed unaware of the chill in the air, or the icy snow that beat like fine hail.

He said nothing, and as he entered the ancient building, took a flashlight from a pocket, giving the barrel a twist. The flash was operated by a spring generator instead of a battery, and it gave forth a thin beam of exceeding brilliance.

The beam ranged for some seconds in the upstairs room, covering the corpse on the floor from head to foot. The cadaver was contorted in a gruesome fashion before a tall console radio of rich woods. Doc noted the receiver was on, although no sound came from the loud-speaker. The volume setting had been dialed down to its lowest point. He switched it off.

Stepped back, the bronze man picked up a neat feminine hand-bag, lying near a pile of severed ropes and a shattered glass-fronted portrait that had evidently come off one wall. He looked inside.

"Dana O'Fall," he said. "She seems to be a private detective. Here is the badge."

Then he stood silent, and the cop was silent, too, watching the bronze man's striking figure, awed a little by the utter inscrutability on the metallic features, and awed still more by what he had heard about the bronze man being a scientific wizard, a mental marvel, a composite genius who was almost inhuman.

The officer finally got around to leveling an arm at the corpse.

"Who is this guy?" he asked.

Doc Savage went over and examined the contents of the dead man's pockets.

"Sanchez y Annuncio de Calabero," he declaimed. "He seems to have been employed by the Cubama Sugar Importing Company, which the newspapers recently stated had lost a quarter of a million dollars in bonds from their vault."

"But what killed him?" pondered the cop aloud. "Look at his eyes. Just look at 'em, will you."

The officer was pointing, but not looking at the eyes himself, for his first glimpse of them had thrown him into a hot sweat.

The eyes were as white as fat pearls popped into the man's eye sockets. The lids lay open, giving the corpse the appearance of staring blindly into eternity.

"What do you make of it?" mumbled the cop.

Doc Savage did not answer. He spun, strode outside, and entered the roadster. He drove rapidly until he reached the first all-night drug store which displayed a telephone sign. He called a number.

"Monk?" he asked, the instant there was a receiver click at the other end.

A voice that might have belonged to a small child said, "Sure, Doc."

"Get hold of Sigmund Holmes," said Doc Savage.

"Sigmund Holmes," echoed the child-voiced Monk. "You mean the bird who—"

"Yes," said Doc Savage. "Have him on the wire when I reach headquarters. I want to talk to him."

"Sigmund Holmes," repeated Monk. "Sure, I'll get him."

IV

DEVELOPMENT UNEXPECTED

At that exact moment, less than a mile distant from Doc Savage, Eduardo Luz was listening to a suave voice which came from an adjacent room.

"Sigmund Holmes should be showing up very soon," intoned the cultured voice.

Eduardo Luz looked at boyish, pleasant-faced Babe. His vapidly handsome features registered curiosity.

"Who's Sigmund Holmes?" he asked.

Babe shrugged. He had changed his clothing and now wore natty evening garb, perfect in its every detail, and he had even less the appearance of a killer who worked for money, and who that afternoon had waited in an office with a high-powered rifle fitted with telescopic sights, his purpose being to shoot a former associate, who, however, had died very suddenly with his eyes glazed white as cake frosting, and through no aid from Babe.

"Don't worry your head over Sigmund Holmes," advised Babe. "That's another hen Harmon Cash has on, and it's none of your business."

Eduardo Luz nodded, tucked his gloves in his topcoat pocket, and then removed the coat and draped it over an arm. Under the topcoat he had worn his habitual white linen suit. Snow, melting, made jewellike globules of water on his trouser legs below the knees.

"I want to see Cash," he demanded.

Babe nodded at the room from which the suave voice had come and advised, "Go on in."

Eduardo Luz advanced hurriedly, swung through

the door, and found himself confronting the man who was probably the most astute and calm criminal mastermind in the city, the man who was wont to characterize himself as a director of criminals rather than a criminal.

Harmon Cash had a fine leonine face, and there was a distinguished smear of gray over either temple. He was smoking a pipe which used tobacco that gave off a strong, aromatic tang. He looked like a perfume salesman in an exclusive Fifth Avenue shop, for he wore an afternoon outfit of striped trousers, gray lap-over vest, and cutaway coat.

His dignified demeanor was diminished slightly by the unfortunate condition of his dark eyes. Some defect in the eye-controlling muscles caused his right eye to stare off center by a marked degree. The left, although not as extreme, likewise wandered off the true.

In the vernacular, Harmon Cash was wall-eyed.

"Who invited you here?" Harmon Cash asked Eduardo Luz dryly.

Eduardo Luz told his story, finally concluding, "Sanchez and I were going meet and talk things over. Sanchez got to the meeting place first, and a dame detective walks in on him."

Harmon Cash drew in on his pipe and let out fragment smoke when he heard finally that Sanchez y. Annuncio de Calabero had been left to take the life of Dana O'Fall. Then Cash grimaced violently.

"No honest citizen could be more horrified than I am at the necessity for such an act," he said fervently.

Eduardo Luz squinted closely at his chief. Harmon Cash was frequently heard bewailing the violence of crime, and he usually sounded as if he meant it. It was said that he often went off by himself and sobbed violently when one of the crimes he had planned resulted in the death of some innocent individual.

Harmon Cash was a rather unusual leader of criminals.

"You are sure this woman detective, Dana O'Fall, is dead by now?" he asked sadly.

"She'd better be," growled Eduardo Luz.

Harmon Cash looked as genuinely sad as if he had lost his own sister.

Four hard-faced men entered the room, cradling submachine guns of the type popularly called Tommy guns. They were minions who did Harmon Cash's bidding.

"You wanted us, boss?" one asked.

Harmon Cash took out a handkerchief and dabbed at his eyes, then applied a match to his pipe. After that, he nodded.

"I am expecting our—ah—important guest at any moment," he said. "I do not want any problems to leave this building."

"Gotcha, boss," said the man who had first spoken. He used his jaw to indicate an ornate maple bookcase whose shelves were crammed with numerous tomes bound in leather. Two men obediently stepped up and one tapped a volume that was cracked and worn with years of consultation. The faded gold-leaf title read: *The Collected Works of Wm. Shakespeare*.

No sooner had the ancient volume returned to its normal position, than the entire bookcase swung outward on soundless hinges, revealing an ordinary closet door. This opened at the turn of the brass knob. The grim pair ensconced themselves in the narrow closet space and closed the door behind them. Harmon Cash then gave the bookcase a gentle shove. It returned to the wall with a muted *click*.

A third man sidled out the door, evidently to guard the corridor approach.

The crook who was left then walked over to a long window whose tasteful floor-length drapes were closed. He stationed himself behind them. After the drapery had settled back into place, there was no sign that anyone but Harmon Cash and Eduardo Luz remained in the room.

"This Sigmund Holmes must be kinda dangerous," offered Eduardo Luz.

Harmon Cash, still looking sad, shook his leonine

head. "On the contrary, he is quite harmless." Then he gave a start.

"Who mentioned that name to you?" he demanded.

"Babe. Why?"

"Nothing," Harmon Cash said quickly. "I take it from your manner that the name means nothing to you."

"Should it?" asked Eduardo Luz in a quizzical voice.

"Perhaps not," leonine Harmon Cash said evasively, taking another pull on his pipe.

A man appeared at the door and said, "Mr. Sigmund Holmes and Mr. Robert Jefferson to see you, Mr. Cash."

Harmon Cash registered surprise. "But I only sent for Sigmund Holmes. Who is this Robert Jefferson fellow?"

With a lazy easiness, Harmon Cash took a turn about the room. He did not look greatly excited, which was one of his strong characteristics. He took things very easily, except to grieve deeply when it was necessary to take some one's life. Finally, he came to a stop in front of Eduardo Luz.

"You know where the back door is?" he asked.

"Sure," said Eduardo Luz. "I make a practice of knowing where back doors are."

"Leave by that route," Harmon Cash directed. "Get to a telephone and call this office. Ask for Robert Jefferson. Tell him you've got to see him about something important."

Luz grinned. His teeth matched his tropical suit in hue. "The idea is to get this Jefferson away while you talk to Holmes, eh?"

"Exactly."

Luz left by the back door.

After he was gone, Harmon Cash signaled the man who had announced his visitors—he was in the nature of a male secretary, although of a particularly hard-boiled type—to usher them in.

Concentrating so that his wandering eyes fell somewhat into line, Harmon Cash took turns shaking the new arrival's hands with expansive warmth and good-fellowship.

"Thank you for coming on such short notice, Mr. Holmes," Harmon Cash said effusively.

Sigmund Holmes was a tall reed of a man with an upstanding shock of prematurely white hair. His suit was conservative, the material first rate. He looked prosperous, but his dangling hands fidgeted as if he were uneasy. If his present expression was an indication, he was something of a sourpuss.

"This is my associate, Mr. Jefferson," Holmes said carefully of the man who had accompanied him.

The other man was short of stature and on the runty side. His suit was in bad shape. If it had once fit him perfectly, it did so no longer. He had the look of a Wall Street plunger who had survived the debacle of the recent stock market crash with a diminished portfolio and modest savings, and ate according to his new means. The outstanding feature about the man was his tremendous forehead. It seemed to swallow his pale, wan eyes, which peeped from the disordered strands of very black hair falling over them.

"Of course," piped Harmon Cash, lying smoothly. "Some one telephoned a few moments ago, asking for you. They said they would call later."

"That's strange," grunted the man called Robert Jefferson. "I didn't know any one was aware we were coming here."

Sigmund Holmes fidgeted with the cuffs of his shirt, as if they were too short. In fact, they fit him perfectly. His eyes grew worried.

"Perhaps it was a mistake," he offered nervously. "No one could have known you were accompanying me." He turned to Harmon Cash, explaining, "It was a spur-of-the-moment decision. We had been working late, you see, when the messenger delivered your note."

"The party who called was quite clear on the

matter," Harmon Cash interposed smoothly. "He asked to speak with Mr. Robert Jefferson."

The telephone rang.

"For Mr. Jefferson," said Harmon Cash, after answering.

The man called Robert Jefferson accepted the offered receiver and held forth for some moments, at one point asking peevishly, "Who is this?"

The answer he received was evidently not to his satisfaction, because his tremendous forehead gathered into a sea of baffled wrinkles.

"Very well," he said at last. He hung up, turned to the others, who were waiting patiently.

"This is very mysterious," he explained. "The individual has asked me to meet him in Central Park, near Cleopatra's Needle. He claims that it is urgent, but won't give his name."

"Surely it can wait," said the fidgety Sigmund Holmes, eying bland-faced Harmon Cash.

"Afraid not. This person hinted he had information of great value to us."

"I am sure we will still be here when you have concluded your mysterious assignation," Harmon Cash said quickly. He all but pushed the one called Robert Jefferson to the door with the impelling force of his cultured voice.

"Are you certain this is wise?" Sigmund Holmes asked, extracting a handkerchief and using it on his brow. Despite the season, he had begun to perspire slightly.

A quick glance passed between the two men.

"Central Park is only a few blocks from here," the other said. "I won't be long."

And with that, he allowed himself to be escorted from the room.

After Robert Jefferson was gone, Harmon Cash attempted to ply his remaining guest with the offer of a Cuban cigar and quality liquor. Both were declined, with the nervous explanation that Sigmund Holmes did not partake of either tobacco or spirits.

"I might have expected it," Harmon Cash said suavely, returning the offering to a desk drawer. "Men who work for Doc Savage are reputed to be immune to the more common vices."

Sigmund Holmes seemed extremely surprised.

"How did you know of my connection with Doc Savage?" he snapped.

Harmon Cash did not admit that he had spent some thousands of dollars in getting that information.

"I know a great many things," he smiled. "I know, for instance, that your firm, the Cubama Sugar Importing Company, is something of a misnomer."

Sigmund Holmes demanded shortly, "What do you mean?"

"I happen to know that the color of the sugar Cubama brings into this country is not white." Harmon Cash examined his unlit pipe for a dramatic moment. "It is golden."

Holmes clamped his sour lips together and said nothing.

"Not very long ago, the Cubama Sugar Importing Company was on the verge of bankruptcy," Harmon Cash continued. "The sugar crop was not good. Prices had fallen. Tariffs were high. You faced ruin. Then, quite suddenly, everything turned around. The crop remained poor, and prices low. But Cubama prospered. It was a profound mystery."

Holmes continued to say a firm-lipped nothing.

"I am a man who keeps his eyes on opportunity," Harmon Cash went on. "When I heard of Cubama's rather sudden reversal of fortune, I looked into it. And I discovered a remarkable fact, one unknown to the world at large."

Holmes moistened his lips. He seemed to be getting more tense, if that was possible. His fidgeting grew more animated.

"Doc Savage had purchased the Cubama Sugar Importing Company," Harmon Cash said flatly.

Holmes offered no denial to this statement. His nervous eyes went to the door several times, as if anxious for the return of his colleague, Robert Jefferson.

"This Doc Savage, to give him his due, is a modern marvel," said Harmon Cash. "The bronze man is also something of a mystery man. But certain facts are commonly known. They can be verified simply by reading the newspapers."

Harmon Cash paused dramatically, before launching into a long-winded recitation from memory.

"It is said that, as a child, the Man of Bronze was placed in the hands of a succession of scientists, physical culture experts, and other specialists. These notables were charged with the duty of making of the boy a combination genius and perfect physical specimen. This was done to prepare Savage for the rather droll and unprofitable life's work upon which he has embarked—of going to the far ends of the world, righting wrongs and punishing evildoers who operate beyond the law. He is quite successful in this unusual livelihood of his.

"Less well known, however," Harmon Cash went on, "is the fact that Doc Savage holds sway over a vast empire of financial holdings. The bronze man is in the habit of buying up failing companies, hotels, and railroads and turning them around, making them going concerns once more. The true extent of these holdings is unknown. All seem legitimate. Doc Savage's skills are clearly not limited to the sciences. He has a sound business head on his shoulders and a knack for selecting companies that can be put back on their feet."

In a futile attempt to gain mastery over his nervousness, Sigmund Holmes placed his hands on his knees. The long fingers trembled perceptibly.

"As I say," Harmon Cash elaborated, "all these holdings appear to be legitimate, going concerns. Except Cubama Sugar."

"If you are insinuating that Doc Savage is involved in anything crooked—" Sigmund Holmes began hotly.

"On the contrary," Harmon Cash interposed smoothly. "I have uncovered nothing untoward about

Cubama Sugar Importing. Except that it has very little to do with sugar these days. It is, rather, a blind, a mask, a holding company that conceals one of Doc Savage's greatest secrets."

Sigmund Holmes's jaw fell and he snapped forward to the edge of his chair.

"No one, not even Doc Savage, can amass such a financial empire without operating capital," Harmon Cash ventured. "It is no secret that the bronze man is a wealthy man. This, despite the inexplicable and well-known fact that Doc Savage takes no pay for his work in aiding the oppressed. It is rumored that he has a secret source of gold—a mine or something on that order—in a place known only to him. When Savage has need of funds, he taps into this gold source."

Holmes stared, open-mouthed, seemingly incapable of speech.

"This was all well and good until a few years ago, when Washington went off the gold standard. In simple terms, this meant that United States currency was no longer tied to the quantity of gold stored in the Federal Reserve. One inconvenient wrinkle of this legislation was that it became illegal for private individuals to own gold bullion. This presented a conundrum for Doc Savage, who likes to consider himself a law-abiding citizen. He had a source of gold—presumably one outside of this country—which he could not easily convert to legal tender."

Holmes still said nothing. The sourness had ebbed from his elongated face long before.

"None of this should come as a shock to you," Cash told him. "After all, you are the man whom Doc Savage put back on his financial feet in order to comply with the new federal laws. For it is your importing company which receives Doc Savage's gold bullion and converts it into bonds and negotiable securities via your Havana mill, transferring it to Cubama's offices here in New York and from there, in some almost certainly legal fashion, to the bronze man himself."

Holmes sprang to his feet. He was trembling.

"How do you know all this?" he asked hoarsely. "It is supposed to be a secret known only to Doc Savage, his five associates, and myself."

Harmon Cash seated himself, produced a rich silk tobacco pouch, and loaded his pipe with expensive weed. The perfume of his unusual tobacco hung all through the room.

"I have spent a great deal of money learning this," he said smoothly. "It has taken me some months, as well."

Sigmund Holmes sagged slowly back into his chair.

"Just what are you leading up to?" he demanded.

Cash ran aromatic tobacco through his nostrils and it boiled along the front of his overlapping tea vest.

"How would you like to have one hundred thousand dollars?" he asked.

"What are you getting at?" Holmes countered.

Harmon Cash smoked slowly. His rather aristocratic face assumed a dreamy expression. His askew eyes went out of focus and the right one drifted to the right. The left floated upward, so that they seemed to be looking at two different objects. The effect was disconcerting.

"I am a man with imagination," he murmured. "I deal with realities only because it is necessary. My greater interest is the kingdom of the mind and the realm of conjecture with reference to what would happen if certain possibilities became actualities."

"You are talking like a nut," advised Sigmund Holmes.

Wall-eyed Harmon Cash put an injured expression on his face and said, "Not at all. I am trying to tell you I am a planner."

"And I'm trying to find out what your plan is," the other snapped.

"I am a master criminal," said Harmon Cash. "Rather, I am a master of criminals. Crime itself hurts me. I hate it. But I have chosen it as a career, so it is up to me to make the most of it."

"You're a crook," said Sigmund Holmes. "So what?"

"I have money."

"You must have if you can offer me a hundred thousand dollars." Holmes pounded a knee with his fist. "But I do not see what you are getting at."

"I have a wide organization," said Harmon Cash. "But I have trouble with my men, occasionally. It is a strange fact that most crooks seem to be dumb. It is hard to find an intelligent crook."

"I am going to leave if you do not come to the point," grated Sigmund Holmes.

"All right," Harmon Cash told him abruptly. "I summoned you to this meeting on the pretext of revealing to you the identity of the thief who absconded from your firm's vault with a considerable sum in negotiable bonds. Bonds which are rightfully the property of Doc Savage."

"I was wondering when you'd get to that," Holmes growled. "So, it was just a pretext, eh?"

"No," Harmon Cash said abruptly. "As it happens I do know who stole those bonds."

Interest flicked across Sigmund Holmes's sour countenance.

"Who?"

"I did," Harmon Cash revealed. "Not personally, you understand, but through agents whom I planted in your firm."

"So you are Sanchez y. Annuncio de Calabero's mysterious accomplice," Sigmund Holmes breathed. He looked stunned.

Holmes's stricken expression suddenly migrated the handful of feet that separated the faces of the two men, alighting on the visage of the suave master crook and transforming it unpleasantly.

"You know about Sanchez?" Harmon Cash exploded. His ungovernable orbs attempted to fix upon Sigmund Holmes, with the result that one looked upward and the other regarded his left nostril in a particularly thunderstruck fashion.

Sigmund Holmes snapped, "I am not the only man of knowledge in this room."

Wall-eyed Harmon Cash got a grip on his apoplexy. He settled back in his chair. He resumed his cultured discourse.

"I know that the bonds that will shortly come into my possession represent the merest fraction of the funds that pass through the vaults of the Cubama Sugar Importing Company before they reach Doc Savage," he said, patiently. "I am not a man who is satisfied with fractions. I want it all. For aiding me, you will receive one hundred thousand dollars."

"I *have* a hundred thousand dollars," gritted Holmes.

Harmon Cash looked surprised. "Doc Savage must pay well. I might raise the ante."

"No."

"I see." Harmon Cash regarded the dim fire in his pipe bowl for some moments with his disconcerting eyes. "What would you say if I told you that my agents are capable of planting positive proof that you availed yourself of the missing bonds?"

"You go to hell," yelled Sigmund Holmes.

Then Holmes sprang to his feet and backed toward the door.

Harmon Cash seemed unperturbed by the whole affair. He blew out smoke, then nodded slightly as a man appeared in the door behind Sigmund Holmes with a pointing submachine gun. It was the individual who had earlier taken up a corridor post. He had evidently been listening.

Holmes snapped to a stop. He eyed the gun, then glared at Cash.

"You did a lot of talking about your imagination," he growled. "It must have been hot air, or you wouldn't try this."

Harmon Cash said, "I have thought it all out carefully."

"Including what Doc Savage will do to you if you harm me?" asked Holmes.

Harmon Cash looked as if some one had jabbed him unexpectedly with a pin. But the expression was fleeting.

"You are going to be persuaded to do as I wish," he advised. "Doc Savage will never know a thing about it."

Sigmund Holmes's answer was to dive suddenly at the submachine gun. The wielder of the weapon was taken by surprise and permitted the shock-haired Holmes to get a grip on it.

Holmes kicked the gunman's feet out from under him. The man, falling, let go of his weapon.

Holmes raised the gun in the direction of Harmon Cash.

A single pencil-sized red flame tongue jumped from the closed drapery. Shot sound whooped in the office. The gunman concealed behind the window drapery had an excellent aiming eye.

Holmes's shock-haired head rocked back, acquiring scarlet streaks like paint flung from a brush. The bullet had gone in through one temple, making a much larger pit opening in the back of his cranium where it came out. After he fell, Sigmund Holmes shook the entire length of his reedy body until all life and animation had departed from it.

Wall-eyed Harmon Cash bit through the stem of his pipe and wailed, "This is a hell of a note!"

V

THE TOUGH MR. JEFFERSON

Had Harmon Cash been psychic, his concern over
the accidental death of Sigmund Holmes would have
increased manyfold.

But the suave, wall-eyed crook was not psychic.
Lacking premonitory abilities, he was unaware of the
compact pick-up microphone that dangled outside of
the drapery-shielded window. The microphone hung by
a wire that shot up and angled back over a roof coping.
It ended in a small black box over which crouched a
man.

This individual wore a telephone headset clamped
to his shaggy black hair. Whirling snow danced before
his pale eyes, sometimes coming to rest on his bulging
forehead, where the flakes instantly melted. But the
individual paid the cold flakes no heed. He was listening intently to the sounds coming from Harmon Cash's
office. The closed window and the keening of wind
through city canyons made this task problematic. He
fiddled with a knurled black knob and listened worriedly.

Had Harmon Cash possessed second sight, he
would have seen that the intent man was none other
than he who had called himself Robert Jefferson. And
he would have been startled by the revelation.

For when the Sigmund Holmes associate had left
Cash's office, apparently falling for the ruse designed to
take him to Central Park, he had not actually set out for
that destination.

Instead, he had gone to a roadster parked not
many blocks distant and from it taken the electric

eavesdropping equipment whose knobs he now rotated carefully. Ensconcing himself on the roof of the building which housed Harmon Cash's office, he had been an unsuspected eavesdropper on the conversation that had ensued between Cash and Sigmund Holmes. Wind against the pick-up microphone had drowned out much of it, however.

Just now, his thin features were growing concerned. He had detected the rising shouts of argument that had ensued, and then a single loud report. Then came Harmon Cash's wail of disgust.

The wind had picked up, scooping sheets of snow from the roof to blow into the listener's eyes. The sound and white fury distracted him from his work. He muttered inaudible expletives.

Thus it was that he failed to hear a trap in the roof hoist up a few yards behind him. Heavy footsteps squeaked carefully toward him. It was the thin layer of dry snow which squeaked. The man wore rubber-soled shoes.

A liver-colored sap lifted. It crashed down, cutting across the back of his head.

The man called Robert Jefferson gave out no groan. He simply collapsed across his apparatus, whereupon the blowing snow began to whiten his back like a quick-spreading mold.

Eduardo Luz pocketed his bludgeon. Bending down, he yanked off the headset. With it, came a mop of black shaggy hair.

"Hell's bells!" Luz muttered, giving vent to a particularly American exclamation of surprise. "What's with the masquerade?"

Eduardo Luz turned over the insensate body of Robert Jefferson. He got a good look at the pale hair that the askew wig had revealed.

He stood up, as if shocked by an unexpected electrical charge. Unsteadily, he backed away from the still form, his jewel-black eyes widening in shock.

Abruptly, he turned, his feet disturbing the flat

snow of the roof with their pounding. Eduardo Luz practically dived into the waiting trap.

After he had gone, an observer might have noticed the prostrate figure begin to twitch at his extremities. Such a phenomenon sometimes presages death; or it might have been evidence of the tenacious struggle to hold on to life. Only a student of the human nervous system could have diagnosed this species of muscular activity.

The well-dressed killer called Babe was standing watch in the corridor outside of Harmon Cash's office suite when Eduardo Luz came plunging down the stairway.

Seeing the harried look on Luz's swarthy features, Babe jumped to a conclusion.

"Cops?" he squeaked.

"Worse than cops," came the reply. "I gotta see the boss."

Babe went to the office door, rapped once, and called softly, but urgently, "Hey chief! We got trouble."

Suave Harmon Cash appeared, perspiring slightly, a worried expression on his distinguished features and his perfumed pipe for once unlighted.

"What is it?" he demanded.

"I went to Central Park," Eduardo Luz said rapidly, his words tumbling like corn down a chute. "In case that Jefferson guy didn't stick around. I figured I could stall him, and give you more time with Holmes."

"Excellent thinking," said Harmon Cash.

"Except Jefferson didn't show," Luz puffed. "I got suspicious and doubled back. The snow was blowing some, and I happened to look up. And you know what I saw?"

Harmon Cash regarded his subordinate with his off-center gaze.

"I saw a microphone hanging down outside your window," Eduardo Luz said, answering his own question.

"Babe, go check," Harmon Cash rapped suddenly.

Babe plunged into the suite. He was back a moment later.

"A mike. Just like he says," Babe reported. His tone was grim.

"Go on," Harmon Cash instructed Luz.

"I could see the mike hung down from the roof, so I snuck up there. I found our friend Jefferson, working over some kind of wire-tap set." Luz withdrew his liver-colored sap. "So naturally, I smacked him one."

Harmon Cash nodded. "You did right."

Eduardo Luz licked his lips worriedly. "I'm not so sure about that."

"What do you mean?"

"When I hit him, his hair came off. A wig. I rolled him over and you know what I found?"

"Spit it out, will you?" Babe said impatiently.

"I recognized the guy. Only his name wasn't Robert Jefferson. It's Long Tom Roberts, the electrical wizard!"

Babe stared blankly. Harmon Cash's eyes wandered about the room as if in search of the meaning of Eduardo Luz's outburst. His head did not move.

"The Doc Savage associate!" Eduardo Luz exploded, at last.

Silence greeted this bit of revelation. Harmon Cash examined the bit-through stem of his pipe with an expression of forlorn regret.

Babe vented an explosive, "Oh, mother! Now we're in for it."

Harmon Cash began to smile widely.

"A bit of profound luck, gentlemen," he grinned.

Eduardo Luz absently changed the tilt of his tropical white hat atop his curly hair. "Luck!" he exploded. "What about Holmes?"

"A regrettable event has transpired," Harmon Cash said.

"Holmes went west," Babe put in. "*Far* west."

Swarthy Eduardo Luz suddenly lost a shade of color.

"Oh," he said, small-voiced.

"Possibly Long Tom Roberts is the only one who knew Holmes came here," Harmon Cash declared. "All we have to do is grab Roberts, ask him certain questions, then dispose of him. And no one will know."

"What questions?" wondered vapidly handsome Eduardo Luz.

"Never mind," said Harmon Cash. "Get up to the roof and bring him here."

Eduardo Luz and Babe hurried upstairs.

Harmon Cash returned to his office suite. He tamped aromatic tobacco into his pipe, applied tiny flame from a platinum lighter, and let out even more aromatic smoke. His face held satisfaction as he went to the window and parted the closed drapes to verify the existence of the dangling microphone. It was still there, gathering a coating of snow.

Then Harmon Cash experienced the worst mental shock of his criminal career.

A flat, clipped voice advised him to stand perfectly still.

Harmon Cash shuddered. It was the voice of the man who had called himself Robert Jefferson—Long Tom Roberts.

"Your—er—friend Holmes left a moment ago," Harmon Cash said, trying to keep the fear out of his tone—it was a fear inspired by a hard object jammed against his back, an object that felt like a gun muzzle.

"Stand still," Long Tom Roberts repeated.

Harmon Cash did not dare turn around, or even look back, although he wondered mightily if the safety of the gun might by chance be on. Hands slapped under his arms, explored his hip pockets, and finally fished a flat derringer from a chamois dust case. Long Tom Roberts then stepped back.

The embarrassing truth dawned on Harmon Cash while he was turning. Long Tom Roberts had not held a gun at first, and his only weapon was now the derringer. A fountain pen had been the hard object.

"I told you that your associate Holmes left here a while ago," Harmon Cash snapped.

"He did not," Long Tom said hollowly. "I came through the rear room."

Suave Harmon Cash suddenly felt as if he were standing in ice water. It was in the rear room that Sigmund Holmes's body lay.

Long Tom Roberts continued harshly, "I tagged along with Holmes. He and I have been looking into the missing bonds together. When you told us there had been a call for 'Robert Jefferson,' I knew you were lying. I decided to play along."

Harmon Cash gulped, "I can explain—"

"Skip it," the other snapped.

Without his wig, Long Tom Roberts presented a puny-looking appearance. He looked rather undernourished, but Harmon Cash knew that appearances were sometimes deceiving. None of Doc Savage's aids were reputed to be pushovers.

"Give me a chance," Harmon Cash exploded desperately. "It was an accident. Holmes—"

"Shut up," directed Long Tom. "Turn around and walk out of the rear door. And do not call to your men."

Harmon Cash began to shake violently. "Where are you taking m-me?"

"To Doc Savage," said Cash's captor.

Harmon Cash's shaking ceased, but not because his fear had evaporated. Complete horror had gripped him. He was paralyzed. He could hear his own heart floundering around, and small globules of sweat paraded, one after the other, down his features. His eyes careened in their sockets as if preparing to abandon ship.

Long Tom Roberts nudged the derringer. "Walk."

Harmon Cash stumbled rather than walked, having difficulty with his feet, and as they descended the rear stairs, only Long Tom Roberts's hand entangled grimly in the collar of his coat kept him from falling. They passed out into an alley full of twilight.

In a twinkling the alley became a seething confusion of humanity. Men shouted. Blows rained. Feet kicked.

Every blow was aimed at the puny figure of Long Tom Roberts, the electrical wizard.

The minions of Harmon Cash thought they would have an easy time of it. They were wrong.

Long Tom Roberts might have presented an ineffectual appearance, from his short stature to his sallow skin—which made it appear as if he had been raised in a mushroom cellar. But he had been known to whip his weight in wild cats. He proceeded to demonstrate this now.

Eduardo Luz had used his liver-colored sap to knock the derringer out of Long Tom's grasp. He raised his weapon again.

A fist lashed out. Once, and again. The blows came as with one report. Luz staggered back, his face full of consternation and his immaculate white linen suit decorated with crimson spots.

Long Tom turned on the others. His arms pumped, fists colliding with jaws, elbows blocking wrists. A knife glittered momentarily. Long Tom seized the arm behind it, and gave an excellent impression of attempting to amputate it by main strength. The attacker howled. The knife fell and clattered. The man kissed a snow pile and the hard cobbles under it with bruising force.

The puny electrical wizard was giving a good account of himself. The twilit alley soon collected a quota of sinking forms.

Harmon Cash witnessed all of this at a respectful distance. His eyes—pointing in opposite directions—roved the alley. They struggled to line up on the fallen derringer.

Taking care to avoid the flying, pummeling fists of the electrical wizard and the stamping feet of his own men, Harmon Cash got to the weapon. He jumped back, flipped the weapon around until it made a tiny club.

Then, sighting on a smear of scarlet in the back of Long Tom Roberts's pale hair, he brought the derringer stock down hard.

Long Tom Roberts folded in mid-punch. His still-traveling fist carried him into a row of ash barrels as he collapsed. The barrels upset, spilling their powdery contents over him like old brown snow.

"About damn time," a man gritted. "I thought he'd never go down."

Eduardo Luz picked himself up off the alley floor. He brushed fresh snow off his white suit before he stepped up to Long Tom's sprawled, powdery form, and kicked him lavishly about the ribs.

"What does it take to knock this bird out?" he demanded of no one in particular. "He has a head as hard as a coconut."

"Doc Savage's men are known for their toughness," put in Babe. "What do we do with him, chief?"

Suave Harmon Cash gave no answer. He leaned against the alley wall and pounded his chest slowly, as if trying to restore the normal beat of his heart. His crazy eyes seemed to be looking in all directions at once, like those of a scared, swivel-eyed lizard.

VI

WHITE EYES SPEAKS

Long Tom Roberts awoke making a low, groaning noise deep within his spare frame. The sound was not immediately heard by the others in the room.

Swarthy Eduardo Luz was saying, "Hell, boss, what were we supposed to do? We heard the guy hold you up. He would have plugged you if we had just waltzed in. Getting the drop on him as he was leaving was the best bet."

"He had a derringer in my back," Harmon Cash retorted. "I might have been killed."

"You also might have ended up in Doc Savage's hands," Babe offered, a nervous eye going to Long Tom's still form.

"Maybe," Harmon Cash admitted. An unsettled look crawled over his leonine features, indicating that that unhappy thought was only now sinking in.

"Things happen to lugs who fall into that bronze devil's hands," Babe went on grimly. "No one knows what. They just disappear. Personally, I'd rather my eyes turned white like Nug Hassel. That way, it's over quick."

Harmon Cash said fervently, "I do not want to think about either possibility."

"Don't look now," Eduardo Luz put in, jerking a thumb toward the restless form of Long Tom Roberts, lying trussed on a divan, "but I think baby is stirring."

Peeling back his eyelids, Long Tom Roberts shook his head as if to clear it. An incipient groan only beginning to emerge from his mouth turned into a yelp. He subsided.

"Remind me not to do that again," Long Tom muttered to no one in particular.

Looking up, he saw Harmon Cash puffing on his pipe, saw Eduardo Luz with a stubby cigarette clinging to his lower lip, and noticed other rough men standing about. They were all in the office suite. Long Tom Roberts, fighting the pain in his head, glanced through an open door to the larger rear room and the spot where the body of Sigmund Holmes had lain.

It was gone.

"Where's Holmes?" Long Tom croaked, his eyes shining with sudden hope.

"Babe," Harmon Cash said.

Babe went to the bookcase closet where previously two of Cash's minions had been stationed. Rolling the bookcase aside, he flung the exposed door open.

Sigmund Holmes stood revealed within. Literally stood. His upstanding shock of white hair almost brushed the niche's ceiling. His eyes were open, but there was no light in them.

Then, Sigmund Holmes sagged forward, his bristly hair scraping the door lintel. He fell on his face like a long loose bag of millet. He did not get up again.

"You thought he was still alive?" Harmon Cash asked dryly.

Long Tom Roberts seemed too engulfed by anger to answer. He relaxed in his bonds, closed his pale eyes painfully, then asked, "What do you want?"

"Doc Savage has a secret source of gold," Cash murmured. "This bullion is funneled through a holding company called—" One wandering eye jerked toward swarthy, white-coated Eduardo Luz. "Let us say it is a—ah—sweet set-up and let it go at that," Cash resumed. "The late Mr. Holmes, there, is—or should I say was—the man in charge of the concern."

"I thought no one knew that," Long Tom mumbled in a dazed voice.

"Not many do," the other man agreed. "It is only by employing expert spies that I secured my information."

"What do you want?" repeated Long Tom Roberts.

"Quite simply, I want to know where this gold is," Harmon Cash said expansively. "Or failing that, the route by which this pelf is transported to this holding company's foreign headquarters."

"Go swim in that briar," Long Tom said hoarsely.

"I warn you," snapped Harmon Cash, removing his pipe of perfumed tobacco to gesture vehemently. "Sigmund Holmes refused my generous offer to give us access to his vaults, and you saw what happened to him."

"Nuts to you, goofy eyes," Long Tom gritted.

Harmon Cash looked at the very much dressed up Babe. "See if you cannot change Mr. Roberts's mind," he said reluctantly.

Babe swung over easily and kicked Long Tom Roberts's nose. The electrical wizard groaned anew and his nostrils started oozing scarlet.

Harmon Cash shuddered violently and put a hand over his mouth.

"I shall be in the next room, gentlemen," he gulped. "Listening to soothing music."

He wheeled and walked out, carefully avoiding the prone corpse of Sigmund Holmes, which practically bisected the rug.

Babe grinned after Harmon Cash.

"Queer duck, that Cash," he said. "He can't bear to look at violence."

"Must be those cockeyed glims of his," Eduardo Luz grunted. "They don't let him look square in the face of anything."

"Still, he didn't do so bad down in that alley," Babe added. "You go downstairs, Eduardo, and help the boys keep a lookout. This might be kinda noisy."

"I am not your subordinate," Eduardo Luz said stiffly.

"Suit yourself," Babe said casually. "But it could get kinda messy in here, too, if you know what I mean."

Eduardo Luz thought about this. He did not have to think for very long. He nodded silently and took his departure down the stairs.

Babe now stripped off his dress coat, cummerbund, and removed his neatly creased trousers. He gave an order, and a doughy-complexioned underling brought a large rubber sheet from another room. This was spread on the floor.

Long Tom Roberts was rolled onto the sheet. Babe then began a series of the most exquisite tortures. His first move was to employ pliers to pluck off several of the victim's fingernails.

Long Tom Roberts moaned in agony, but made no reply to the questions which were put to him repeatedly.

Next, the puny electrical wizard was strangled into unconsciousness. This was repeated three times. Lighted cigarettes were placed on his sallow skin and allowed to burn slowly. His eyebrows, eyelashes, and snatches of his pale hair were pulled out.

"How about it, short and sallow?" Babe demanded of Long Tom during one period of lucidness.

"Do your worst," Long Tom said thickly.

"I will," Babe chuckled.

Then Long Tom Roberts was dragged over the body of Sigmund Holmes. Babe employed a foot to nudge Holmes's remains over until the glassy eyes stared ceilingward. Long Tom's face was rudely shoved into that of the dead man's.

"Spill what we want," he was advised, "or you'll end up just like this stiff."

"No," gritted Long Tom Roberts. If anything, his determination seemed to have been fortified by the sight of the slack, bloodied body of Sigmund Holmes.

Long Tom was yanked onto a modernistic divan.

Babe was proving himself to be a master of torture. He inserted a sponge in the victim's mouth, and this was slowly filled with saliva and expanded, exerting an awful strangling effect.

For almost an hour, this went on. Two of the onlookers, hardened criminals though they were, became nauseated and left the room.

Long Tom Roberts had almost lost consciousness. His eyes were glazed with pain. He ceased to speak intelligently when the sponge was removed, but only muttered, as if in a delirium.

Babe went into the other room to consult Harmon Cash. "The guy ain't going to talk, boss," he advised. "I'm just about sure of that."

Harmon Cash had been sitting in a stuffed chair, his eyes closed, his elbows on the arm rests. His hands were steepled before his face as he listened to the soothing orchestra music emanating from a table radio. He now roused out of this reverie, and marched over to the radio, as if suddenly displeased with the quality of the music it was giving forth.

"Make one final effort," he directed, twirling the tuner dial.

Babe returned and bent over the pitiful frame of Long Tom Roberts. Babe was grinning, cheerful. He rather enjoyed this sort of thing. He prepared to dissect one of the electrical wizard's fingers.

Seizing the finger, Babe pulled on it, stretching it preparatory to the first cut. He looked at the finger, as if examining it—and a weird thing happened to his eyes. They began slowly to cloud over.

Babe dropped the prisoner's hand and the knife. He leaped to his feet, threw back his head, and began to scream. His shrieks were hideous, guttering bleats of pain and terror. His head tilted far back, then came forward, and he bent almost double. He gnashed his lips so that a scarlet froth flew.

Then he fell over, convulsing, on the floor beside Sigmund Holmes. His eyes were now all but sightless white marbles, with the barest suggestion of red lying underneath—the red of exploded eye capillaries.

Spasming to the last, Babe twitched and jerked his final moments of life away.

* * *

Long Tom Roberts made his move then.

Evidently, he had been channeling his anguish into a steady struggle with his bonds, for no sooner had the gunmen in the room shrunk back to the walls before the horrible tableau of Babe's death, than the electrical wizard made a one-handed dive into Babe's natty clothes.

The single hand Long Tom had managed to work free came out again with Babe's gun.

Flourishing the weapon, Long Tom snarled, "Stay back! I mean it!"

It was difficult to say whether astonishment over Babe's death or the menace of the weapon kept those present quiet, but none of them moved.

Working with shaky haste, Long Tom Roberts freed himself and got to his feet. Unsteadily, he swept the room with the muzzle.

For a moment, it seemed that Long Tom was going to empty the gun which he held, but his eyes found the cadaver of Babe, reposing grotesquely on the floor. He noted the cloudy whiteness of the man's orbs.

He made a hoarse sound and knelt beside the form of his erstwhile torturer, Babe. He laid a hand upon it and felt the chill of death. A strange change came over his pallid, pain-wracked features.

Regaining his feet, he leveled an arm at the corpse and his voiced sounded, hollowly ominous. A knowing light came into his dulled-by-agony eyes. He addressed the cowering assemblage of gangsters.

"Look at his eyes!" he commanded of them.

Instead of obeying, Harmon Cash's men watched Long Tom Roberts with apprehension. They had already seen their fill of the grotesquely blinded eyes of the dead Babe.

"I know what killed him!" Long Tom Roberts announced. "Doc Savage, were he here, would also know."

One of the men moved a hand as if to draw a gun, then thought better of it and lifted his arms.

"Look!" Long Tom pointed again at the glazed eyes of the dead criminal. "Remember how his eyes look.

Remember it when you see your fellows drop dead around you! Remember it when you yourself find your eyes going blind in your head!"

"He's gone nuts!" one gunman breathed.

Long Tom Roberts emitted a barking laugh of derision. "You think I am insane? The truth has just dawned on me. I have realized the nature of the so-called Blind Death."

The man who had put up his arms changed his mind again and made an abrupt grab for his gun. Long Tom's weapon shifted—but there was no need for it.

The would-be killer never got his weapon out, for his eyes began to go bloodshot, and he put his hands to his face in a dazed fashion, as if to forestall the sudden explosion of blood vessels. Then he began to shriek, to double and undouble himself in frightful agony, until at last he toppled over on the floor and died.

Again, Long Tom Roberts gave expression to a derisive laugh.

"You see!" he shouted. "You could all die!"

Some one groaned, "What in blazes is happening to 'em?"

Long Tom Roberts was backing toward the door, covering his retreat by the menace of his gun. At the opening, he paused as if to make a further prediction. His mouth parted.

A voice resounded in the room. It was gargantuan, deafening, seeming to come from the very walls themselves, which shook with reverberation.

"You might call the power that is doing this White Eyes," it boomed.

"Who's that?" a crook demanded, his voice tinged with fear.

"I am—White Eyes," the voice thundered.

"Whatcha want? Why're you doing this to us?"

"Never mind that for now," proclaimed the voice calling itself White Eyes. *"Unless you want the curse of the Blind Death to fall upon your own helpless eyes, you must stop Doc Savage's man from escaping."*

The criminal minions of Harmon Cash had become

so distracted by the voice of White Eyes that all thought of Long Tom Roberts had been overlooked. Fear galvanized them now. As one, they moved toward the pallid electrical wizard.

Long Tom, poised before the door, as much in the grip of the loud, authoritative voice as any one, reached back for the doorknob. His damaged fingers brushed the brass briefly.

Almost at once, the door to the rear room burst open and swarthy Eduardo Luz, puffing from his rapid climb of the front stairs, appeared.

"You might have been more quiet about it!" he barked, then became slack-jawed at the sight of Long Tom, who, caught unawares, was slow to turn around.

Eduardo Luz was not slow. His sap came up and down in a continuous motion that owed more to nervous reflex than conscious thought.

Long Tom Roberts never completed his turn. He dropped as if his strings had been cut.

"What—what happened?" Eduardo Luz floundered, as he took in the tableau.

"White—White Eyes got—Babe and Snig," a sheet-pale man gulped. He plucked at his shirt collar as if suddenly hot.

"Who?"

"Called himself White Eyes," mumbled the other. "Just a—voice. Made them drop dead—with their eyes gone all milky."

Eduardo Luz jerked his head impatiently.

"That damned yelling stirred up things," he snapped. "Somebody heard it and turned in an alarm. The cops are coming."

That was alarm enough. One man ran to warn Harmon Cash, finding the mastermind in a cold sweat, genuinely suffering from the torture he imagined was still being inflicted on Long Tom Roberts, as he fiddled with his uncooperative radio tuner.

"I can't stand it," were Cash's first words. "Take Roberts away where I can't hear him. It gets me."

"The cops are coming!" barked the messenger.

*　　*　　*

Harmon Cash heard the story of what had happened as they fled the building. He stopped to take only three items with him. His pipe, the table radio, and Long Tom Roberts.

It took only one man to carry the insensate electrical wizard.

They had put nearly a mile between them and the death scene when some one decided to inventory the automobile in which they traveled the benighted streets, and realized they were three men short, not two.

"What happened to Blackie?" Harmon Cash demanded tensely.

No one had an answer to that question. Visions of their missing companion, his eyes blank as rounded chalk-stick heads, chilled their thoughts.

VII

WHITE EYES'S PATH

Doc Savage, man of mystery, giant of bronze, tooled his plain-colored roadster up before the establishment which had been the headquarters of Harmon Cash, half an hour later. There was a swarm of policemen about, as well as fully a dozen newspaper reporters and cameramen.

The newshawks descended on the bronze man—tried to, rather, for the metallic giant spoke in a low voice to an officer, and the latter gave orders which caused the reporters to be shoved away unceremoniously.

The scribes and photographers protested vociferously, and were not surprised when it did no good. Doc Savage, they knew from past experience, was a very difficult camera subject and almost never gave a newspaper interview. He was one celebrity who was emphatically not a publicity hound. This had the effect of making the journalists all the more determined to play his name up. The things Doc Savage did were always big news.

"There's a man named Sigmund Holmes shot to death upstairs," a police officer explained.

Doc Savage's metallic features did not change expression to a perceptible degree.

"There's also two men dead with what the tabloids are calling the Blind Death," added the officer. "That's why you were called."

Doc Savage followed the policemen inside and upstairs. There was an uncanny lightness about the bronze giant's tread.

Some one had emptied Sigmund Holmes's pockets, placing the contents on a table. The tiny lights in Doc Savage's weird flake-gold eyes seemed to become stronger as he examined the articles. He unfolded a folded square of note paper and read the lines inscribed thereon.

Unexpectedly, a low, fantastic sound came into existence and diffused itself through the room. It was musical, this note, having a weird rising and falling cadence, yet adhering to no definite tune. There was a trilling quality about it; the note might have been the product of a faint wind through a field of cold ice spires, or it might have been the sound of an exotic tropical bird. Strangest of all was the manner in which the sound seemed to come from everywhere, yet from no particular spot.

"What's that?" grunted a cop.

The sound died, however, without any of the officers comprehending from whence it had come. It was doubtful if any suspected what the sound actually was—the low, fantastic trilling which the Man of Bronze, Doc Savage, made unconsciously in moments of mental stress, a small, unthinking thing which he did when surprised, or deeply moved.

Only by that momentary trilling did Doc Savage betray emotion over the death of Sigmund Holmes, whom he had employed in his capacity of owner of the Cubama Sugar Importing Company.

Doc Savage inspected the two dead criminals, taking care to examine their sightless eyes at some length. He went to the body of Sigmund Holmes, still stretched out on the carpet, and thumbed his eyelids back.

Holmes's eyes were outwardly normal. But on closer inspection, the bronze man detected small dabs of cloudy matter over each black pupil. They were almost too faint to be seen with the naked eye.

For the briefest of moments, his fantastic trilling came into existence once more. It trailed away like a lost soul.

Returning to one of the criminal corpses, Doc removed from inside his coat—taking it from one of the multitudinous pockets of the equipment vest he habitually wore—a scalpel and tiny glass phial.

He bent over the body of the dead criminal who had gone by the name of Babe. Using the scalpel, he excised a dollop of the cloudy white matter from one of the man's eyeballs. The stuff came away on the scalpel blade like loose egg white. One of the cops turned away at the sight, going slightly green.

Doc placed this substance into the phial, capped it, and returned both items to his equipment vest.

Straightening, he next inspected the frayed cords with which Long Tom Roberts had been bound. He drew a small tube from a pocket. This had a perforated top, and he sprinkled the contents on the floor.

The tube held a powder which glowed brilliantly as it fell to the carpet; then the glowing died, except for certain spots which bore the shape of footprints. The powder was a very brittle fluorescent compound which glowed when exposed to the air; the slightest disturbance caused the stuff to expose new surfaces, which assumed a momentary fiery luster.

The weight of the men who had tramped the floor had compressed the carpet fibres, and these were still straightening, although only to a microscopic degree. The straightening, however, was sufficient to disturb the powder.

The policemen looked on, dumfounded no little, as fiery footprints sprang out where none had been visible before.

The most recent of the footprints showed with phosphorescent clarity. Those made before them were fainter. The tracks seemed to go everywhere at once, but as the bronze man circled the room under the watchful gaze of the police, the older prints soon faded, because the straightening carpet fibres were growing less active.

It quickly became apparent to all that the most recent of the footprints had made a concerted exodus of the room. Doc followed these, shaking more powder as necessary.

The trail led out into the corridor where the fiery tracks ceased entirely. It was uncarpeted.

Doc returned to the room where the bodies lay.

"Too bad," one of the cops whispered to a fellow officer, "I thought we were going to be going places."

"I wouldn't count the bronze man out just yet," the other returned.

As if to prove the second policeman's words true, the bronze man reexamined the tracks in the carpet. He sprinkled more powder, bringing out some of the older footprints. One set led to the draperied window. Doc eased these aside. His golden eyes alighted on the microphone swaying in the wind, which had collected a coating of snow. He recognized it as one of Long Tom Roberts's devices.

"Some one look to the roof," Doc suggested, returning to his examination of the carpet. A cop hurried off.

Using his eyes, Doc followed another pair of tracks to one side of the room. These passed to one side of Sigmund Holmes's corpse. They stopped abruptly at the maple barrier of a bookcase, the prints seeming to disappear under the shelving itself.

Doc tested the carved maple for secret springs and found none. His weirdly active flake-gold eyes roved the bindings. One, entitled *The Collected Works of Wm. Shakespeare*, caught his attention. He levered it inward experimentally, and was rewarded by a muted *click*.

He slid the bookcase aside, revealing what appeared an ordinary closet door.

The police made satisfied grunts as Doc reached for the knob. It refused to open.

Pocketing the container of glowing powder, Doc Savage did a strange thing. He removed one of the ornamental buttons on his brown coat sleeve. Moistening it, he slid it into the gaping keyhole.

"Step back, please," Doc directed, suiting action to words.

The keyhole spat a silvery glob of burning material. It hissed, and sparks showered. The stench of burning metal filled the room.

When the phenomenon finally died down, the entire brass plate, including doorknob, was a sagging mass of metal.

"Glory be!" a gaping cop ejaculated. "What on earth did you do to that door?"

"Thermit," Doc answered, as he gingerly plucked the closet door open by digging his strong metallic fingers into the panel's edge. The lock was too hot to touch.

There was a man inside the closet. He was cowering down on the floor, in one corner, his arms raised protectively over his head.

"You may come out now," Doc Savage told him quietly. "The danger has passed."

"Don't let him get me!" the man whimpered, not unburying his head.

"Who is trying to get you?" Doc inquired.

"White Eyes," the man whimpered. "He—he got Babe and Snig."

Doc Savage reached in, seeming only to lay one cabled hand on the man's shoulder. But the man was irresistibly extracted from his place of hiding.

He was a little unsteady on his feet, and as he drew his arms away from his head, became even more so. His face had the unnatural pallor of a habitual city criminal to whom the night was his working day. His hair was shaggy and needed combing.

"What is this," he muttered, batting at invisible cobwebs before his gaze, "some new kinda third degree? Let's have some light."

"The lights are on," Doc Savage said, studying the man intently. His regular bronze features were inscrutable.

"You kiddin' me? It's as dim as a cave in here!"

The man was blinking rapidly, squinting in his

effort to see. His myopic-looking eyes fell upon Doc Savage's imposing form.

"You're a damn big one, even for a cop," he ventured nervously.

"He *is* blind," a policeman guffawed. "He doesn't know Doc Savage when he's face to face with him!"

The blind crook blinked more rapidly and blurted, "Savage!" He made a sudden bolt. But since his eyes were not functioning correctly, he went the wrong way and smacked into the modernistic divan. He went over it like a circus acrobat who had missed snaring the flying trapeze.

The bronze man restored him to his feet.

"Listen, fellow," Doc said in a firm voice. "Get a grip on yourself."

"I don't know nothin," he said in a surly tone.

"You say you cannot see," Doc prompted.

"I can see fine," the crook returned savagely. "All I need is a little more light."

"The lights in this room," Doc Savage told him steadily, "are quite bright."

"G'wan," the crook spat.

Holding the man by one bicep, Doc used his other hand to force open the man's blinking eyelids, one after the other. The man made some attempts at resistance, but the power of the bronze man's grip defeated him.

Doc asked, "Have you experienced eye troubles before this?"

"No! What are you talking about?"

"Your eyes have a cloudy look to them."

"What do you mean—cloudy?"

"Just that. Your vision is impaired by obscuring white matter."

"White?" the man bleated. "Not the Blind Death!" He began to flounce anew in the bronze man's immutable grip. "Don't let it get me! I don't want to die blind! You gotta help me, Savage! You gotta!"

At that moment, the officer Doc had sent to the roof to investigate the microphone hanging outside the office window returned. He bore in both mittened hands a surprisingly compact eavesdropping set.

"I found this contraption on the roof," the policeman announced. "The snow was pretty well scuffed up, and there was a little blood. I'd say whoever was working this set-up got himself sapped for his pains."

"Put out a dragnet for my associate, Long Tom Roberts," Doc Savage directed.

"This his set?" the officer asked.

"It is. And he appears to be the one who had been tied with those ropes on the divan."

The cop's eyes went to the ropes.

"We figured it was Holmes they had tied up," he ventured.

"There are no rope marks of any kind on Sigmund Holmes's person," Doc Savage informed him.

"There's a call box around the corner. I'll call headquarters from there." The officer departed.

Doc's attention returned to the pale-faced criminal who was having trouble seeing. The man had been working up a sweat with his exertions, but was now subsiding. The fact that the bronze man had been holding a subdued conversation with the now-departed policeman while he had struggled to break the bronze man's grip was a considerable discouragement to him.

"What is your name, fellow?" Doc asked.

"They call me Blackie," was the sullen reply.

"You are going blind," Doc Savage said without feeling.

The crook who called himself Blackie did an unexpected thing at that juncture. He fainted. His knees folded inward, his feet slid apart, and the rest of him just collapsed on the pile of kindling that his nerveless legs became.

It was well that the Man of Bronze picked that moment to break the bad news to the weak-willed crook. For no sooner had he collapsed on the carpet than the draperies gave a sudden billow as if from a gust of wind.

There was no wind. The pane was closed.

What there was was a bullet. It sent shards of glass ripping through the heavy drapery and, after passing through the spot where the Harmon Cash minion called Blackie had been, it dug an ugly hole in the bookcase paneling.

Doc Savage's voice crashed with urgency.

"Sniper!" he rapped. "Get down!"

The draperies began twitching and kicking with the arrival of more leaden missiles.

VIII

GIRL UNCOOPERATIVE

The storm of lead quickly turned the heavy window drapes to hanging rags. Up to that point, the firing was wild. The bullets struck nothing mortal.

But as the lower portions of the drapes fell heavily to the floor, the entire interior of the room was exposed to the unseen sniper's eye. He took advantage of this. The firing grew spiteful, vicious. He was selecting his shots with care now.

Doc rectified this by crawling to a telephone table on which reposed a shaded lamp. He grabbed a leg, upsetting the table. The lamp crashed and extinguished itself with a *pop!*

One of the policemen, who had joined Doc on the floor, grinned and drew his service revolver. He sighted carefully, and turned the ceiling light into a shower of glass and one long green hissing electrical spark.

The room went dark.

"How was that?" he asked proudly. In the murk, he shed his grin when a whining bullet clipped a lock of his hair. He had lost his cap during the rush to find the floor.

"Crawl for the door!" Doc instructed.

"What about our friend, Blackie?"

"I have him," urged Doc. "Now, crawl."

The police officers then began to do uncanny imitations of riverbottom-dwelling catfish. They began inching on their stomachs for the open door.

When they were at last clear, Doc Savage set himself.

The lead continued storming. Plaster dust exploded from punctures in the wall, creating an imitation snowstorm.

Doc made his move then. Bent low, he vaulted for the open door. He crossed the length of the room in four quick strides, not seeming to pause or otherwise deviate from his path.

But when he flung himself out to the corridor floor, the crook called Blackie was tucked under one strong bronze arm.

"Mind him," Doc rapped. And before the police could reply, the bronze man had faded down the corridor.

Doc Savage whipped down the rear stairs. He banged through the back door and into an alley—the same alley where Long Tom Roberts had been ambushed earlier in the day, but the bronze man had no way of knowing this—where his peculiar flake-gold eyes roved the snow-blanketed rooftops across the street.

There had been no time during the attack for Doc to ascertain from which rooftop the sniping attack had emanated. He was doing that now.

Moonlight filtered through the swirling snow, making it sparkle like airborne diamonds. It obscured viewing somewhat, but the bronze man, after some moments, detected a dark shape floating along the coping of a brick apartment house roof.

There was a lull in the gun sounds. It might have been because the sniper lacked visible targets. If that was true, he was doubtless preoccupied with locating new quarry. And the well-illuminated street afforded the best opportunity for picking off such as appeared under the street lamps.

Doc took a chance. He raced across the street, a bronze shadow amid swirling flakes. The utter soundlessness of his passage saved him, probably, from collecting a bullet in his fine bronze hair.

Reaching the building, he went up the back stairs, mounting them to the roof with ghostlike silence. On the topmost floor, he paused under a closed trap. A ladder gave access to the trap and the roof beyond.

Doc was about to ascend when the trap lifted slightly, emitting a slanting beam of moonlight filled with spinning snow. It slapped down almost at once, shutting with a bang.

Doc retreated around a corner, and waited in the dimness. He had glimpsed the heavy trap slip from lifting fingers. He was confident that he had not been seen.

The trapdoor duly lifted again. This time it went all the way up. A figure worked itself around, and lowered legs onto the upper ladder rungs. The skulker began to climb down.

Peering around the wall edge, Doc Savage spied the dark, descending shape. It had no sooner registered on his retina than one questing heel snagged a rung. The skulker lost balance, teetered, and gravity exacted its due.

Doc, however, was already in motion.

He flashed to the ladder, his bronze arms high.

They cushioned the falling figure. Doc barely dipped with the impact. He maneuvered the figure around so the slanting, snow-scoured moonlight bathed the person's face.

The face so revealed was exquisite. Red lips parted in a surprised bow under snapping violet eyes. Chestnut curls framed an intelligent, heart-shaped face.

"Let me go!" the exquisite girl said.

When the bronze man did not immediately comply, she added, "You masher!"

Hastily, Doc Savage lowered the attractive bundle of femininity to the floor.

The girl quickly reached a slender hand downward.

Doc Savage intercepted it with his quick bronze hands. He lifted the hand to view. It was empty.

"Do you mind?" the girl said snappishly. "I was reaching for my shoe."

The bronze man colored slightly, but did not relinquish the wrist. His golden eyes roved the floor. Spying a high-heeled shoe, he snagged it with a graceful snag of his metallic fingers, and presented it to the girl.

She accepted it with a frosty "Thank you"; then, eying her captured wrist, added, "Do you mind? I should like to put on my shoe."

Doc let go. "No tricks," he warned.

The girl lifted a shapely leg and clapped the shoe on. She tested the heel. "Not broken, thank goodness," she said, frowning prettily.

"Evening footwear is not ordinarily intended for ladder climbing," Doc pointed out.

"So I've concluded," the girl said, dryly.

There was silence. The chestnut-haired girl raked Doc with her withering gaze.

"If you're standing there in silent expectation of a tip," she snapped, "you might at least put out your hand. Although most gentlemen I know would consider breaking a girl's fall reward enough."

"I was hoping," Doc Savage said at last, "that you might offer an explanation for why you are prowling this roof."

Violet eyes snapped chilly sparks. "Is it any business of yours?"

"Insofar as my being shot at by a rooftop sniper goes, it is."

The girl's bow-shaped lips compressed at that.

"Well?" Doc prompted.

"I don't talk to cops," she said thinly.

"What makes you think I am with the police?"

"Don't kid me. I recognize you. Doc Savage, aren't you?"

The bronze man admitted to his identity.

"Well, everyone knows that Doc Savage holds an honorary commission with the New York police. In my book, that makes you a cop of only a slightly different color. Am I warm?"

"In a manner of speaking, yes," Doc allowed.

"I don't talk to cops," the girl repeated. She stamped

one high-heeled foot, making an ineffectual sound. "So either arrest me or let me go."

"Right now," the bronze man said, "I am more interested in learning who has been doing all the shooting, and why."

The girl looked taken aback. "You don't think I—that is, you don't mean—"

"Let me take a stab at your identity," Doc pressed.

She lifted her chin. "Stab away."

"You are Dana O'Fall, the private investigator. Correct?"

"How did you know that?" Dana O'Fall asked, momentarily taken aback. "Have you got wanted posters out on me already?"

"I found your purse beside the body of one Sanchez y. Annuncio de Calabero, who was today stricken by what the yellower tabloids have taken to calling the Blind Death."

"I had nothing to do with that!" Dana insisted.

"I did not say that you did," the bronze man returned quietly. "Only that your hand bag was found at the murder scene. Do you mind explaining that?"

"What I have to explain, I'm saving for the man who hired me."

"And who is that?" Doc Savage asked.

"Sigmund Holmes," Dana O'Fall admitted.

The look that came into the bronze man's aureate eyes then was brittle. It might have meant surprise, disbelief, or something else entirely. His metallic features retained their impassive composure.

"You claim you are in the employ of Sigmund Holmes," he asked tightly after a moment.

"That's what I said. What's it to you?"

"The man who is president of the Cubama Sugar Importing Company?" Doc pressed.

"You're well informed," Dana said, huffily. "And my last question stands."

"We will look into your story," the bronze man said. He stepped aside to allow the attractive private investigator to precede him.

Dana O'Fall hesitated. "Don't you want to know who's been shooting at you?" she asked.

"Tell me."

Dana O'Fall tilted a dimpled chin to the open trap, down which vagrant snow continued floating.

"See for yourself. He's still up there."

The bronze man hesitated. He was a student of psychology, but women baffled him. He tried to read exquisite Dana O'Fall.

"Can I trust you to wait here?" he asked, giving up.

"You'll know when you try, and not before," Dana O'Fall offered without a hint of reassurance in her voice.

His expression grim, Doc Savage mounted the ladder, ready to jump back if fired on. Or if Dana O'Fall attempted to flee.

It was the latter. Doc had no sooner stuck his head above the level of the roof than the clatter of high heels in flight smote his ears.

Eschewing the ladder rungs, he dropped down. His powerful leg muscles cushioned the impact. He pitched around the corner after the fleeing Dana O'Fall.

She was making a dash for the stairs. Grabbing the bannister, she flung her chestnut-haired head back to see if there was any pursuit. She spotted the bronze man, and redoubled her efforts to escape.

Doc caught up with her on the first landing.

Dana whirled at the touch of metallic bronze fingers, and attempted to dig at the bronze man's golden eyes with a thumb. Doc deflected the thrust easily. Spinning her around, he pinned her elbows to her sides. Dana subsided.

"I guess you didn't find what you were looking for," Dana said unhappily.

"There was no sniper on the roof," Doc Savage informed her. "Just spent rifle cartridges and a great deal of tramped-down snow cover."

"Then I guess he must have gotten away while you were wasting your time with me," Dana said dryly.

"Who got away?" Doc asked.

"That bit of information," retorted exquisite Dana O'Fall, "I plan on saving for Sigmund Holmes."

The bronze man was silent for some moments. Abruptly, he spoke.

"Why don't I take you to him?" Doc Savage said, giving Dana O'Fall a gentle urging down the dark, ill-smelling stairwell.

"Now," Dana O'Fall shot back, "you're talking!"

IX

THE ARGUERS

Back at Harmon Cash's ruin of an office suite, the police were getting organized. Their numbers had swollen to triple their original strength. They choked the corridors and stairwells like swarming blue bees. Shouting, jostling reporters clogged the front stairs, loudly demanding access to the crime scene, but were being held in check by the annoyed bluecoats.

The officer who had gone to order a dragnet cast for the missing Long Tom Roberts chanced to hear the concentrated sniper fire and called out the riot squad instead.

They had arrived shortly after the firing had stopped.

The sergeant in charge of the riot squad was storming around the corridors, asking questions and demanding answers. His face was the color of a fresh beet from a combination of exertion and cold weather.

"Didn't anyone see the blankety-blank doing all the shooting!" he demanded of no one in particular. Or words to that effect.

He quieted down when Doc Savage, sullen Dana O'Fall in tow, emerged from the elevator cage.

"Is that the one what was doing all the shooting?" the sergeant asked Doc politely, his manner suddenly transformed.

"No," Doc Savage told him. "This is Dana O'Fall, a private investigator who maintains that she saw the sniper."

The sergeant drove a fist into a meaty palm.

"A break!" he enthused. "At last!"

73

"But she will only talk to Sigmund Holmes, whom she claims to be her employer," Doc explained.

Dana opened her mouth as if to protest the bronze man's skeptical choice of words. She evidently thought better of it. Her red lips compressed with unyielding firmness.

The riot squad sergeant caught Doc's drift. His cold-reddened features broke into smiling wrinkles. He doffed his blue cap politely.

"Step this way, then," he said airily. "Mr. Holmes awaits."

The police gave way before Doc Savage, who piloted silent Dana O'Fall by her elbow. Not a man in the bunch had any height on the bronze man. It was a rare policeman whose head came to Doc's firm chin. And New York City police are not known for their lack of stature.

Doc pushed the door leading into Harmon Cash's office before him. Dana stepped in.

The hard-boiled girl paused on the threshold, where she promptly lost her hard shell of silence. Her fingers leaped to her red mouth, which made a delectable if shocked O.

"Mr. Holmes!" she said huskily.

The body of Sigmund Holmes held her transfixed for a long moment. It was ghastly in the way the back of his shock of hair gaped like a red cavern, spilling a quantity of gray, cheeselike brain matter.

Other wounds showed, caused by sniper bullets that had gnawed at his dead flesh.

The remaining corpses were likewise riddled. The blind, dead eyes of the killer known as Babe showed like glazed marbles. They gave the impression of having rolled up in death, except that there was no thread of blood vessel or vein in the whites, as there would normally be.

Dana O'Fall turned away from the scene of carnage. She trembled from head to toe, her violet eyes disappearing behind lowered lids.

"Would you care to make a statement now, Miss O'Fall?" Doc Savage asked quietly.

Attempting to regain her shattered composure, Dana O'Fall shook her chestnut hair in the negative.

"Mighty interesting coincidence," the riot squad sergeant put in skeptically. "Claiming to work for a guy who just happens to be dead."

Dana said nothing. She faced the corridor wall, taking her ripe lower lip in white teeth. At Doc Savage's suggestion, she was escorted into a nearby empty office and held under guard. The pretty private detective offered no resistance.

Came a commotion from down the hall, where police were keeping, with difficulty, the newshounds at bay. Flash bulbs popped, whitening their angry faces. Loud voices clashed.

"Here, here," a cop admonished. "None of that now. We'll be having no more murders in this building to-day."

"I do not intend to assassinate this missing link," a well-modulated voice drawled in pear-shaped tones. "Only to puncture the beggar."

"Says who, shyster!" a squeaking, high-pitched voice shot back.

"I resent your insinuation," sniffed the one with the pear-toned voice. "I'll have you know my forebears came over on the *Mayflower*."

"Good thing," snapped the other. "The immigration laws are considerably stricter these days."

"En garde!" cried the other, and pandemonium broke out.

"They're gonna kill one another!" a reporter wailed. Flash-bulb light made more calcium explosions.

The riot squad sergeant pushed forward. "I'm going to put a stop to this, whatever it is," he vowed.

Doc intercepted him with a firm hand.

"No need," he said firmly. "Those are two of my aids."

Two figures surged down the corridor, circling one

another. One was tall, and attired in an impeccable frock coat, afternoon trousers, fawn vest, and top hat. This individual wielded a lean sword in one hand. The other hand held the hollow length of a dark cane. It was obviously the sheath for the blade—a sword cane.

The man whose face the blade hovered before looked as if he had been the victim of the quivering blade somewhere in his past. His mouth could only have been widened by artificial means. It was a very large mouth, and it was gaping now.

"Just try it, clothes-rack," the man with the wide mouth roared. "See what you get!"

The man with the blade looked intent on driving the blade into that roaring mouth. His lean, handsome features reflected indignant wrath.

Slender and wasp-waisted, it was said that Brigadier General Theodore Marley Brooks was the best lawyer Harvard ever matriculated. It was also said that tailors sometimes followed him down the street just to see how good clothes should be worn. Hence the jibe, clothes-rack.

His burly opponent lacked any weapon at all. He seemed to also lack a forehead. Yet the muscular power apparent in his long, simian arms and barrel chest made him the more formidable figure by far. Barely exceeding five feet tall, Lieutenant Andrew Blodgett Mayfair was one of the world's leading industrial chemists, but he did not look it. He did, however, resemble greatly his nickname, "Monk," which came from his apish physique. There was no fear in the twinkling eyes buried in pits of gristle set in his pleasantly homely face.

He toted a small pig under one rust-red arm. Its saillike ears lifted in alarm.

"I'll say it again," Monk warned. "I didn't invent your ancestors. I just looked 'em up."

"You take that back," said Theodore Marley Brooks, whose nickname, "Ham," he thoroughly detested.

The pair looked to be on the point of mutual slaughter.

Doc Savage's voiced lifted. "Monk. Ham."

Abruptly, the pair dropped their defensive postures. Ham sheathed his sword cane smartly. Monk lowered his furry arms, and dropped the pig to the floor, who instantly trotted up to Doc Savage and took up a position at his feet. This was Monk's pet, and Ham's bane, Habeas Corpus.

As the unlikely pair approached, Doc asked with a trace of weariness in his voice, "What is the problem this time?"

"This refugee from the monkey house claims to have gone rooting around in my family tree," complained Ham Brooks, giving his pearl stickpin a fastidious adjustment.

"I found an ebony ewe," Monk added, his voice once again as squeaky as a child's. "A black sheep," he explained. "Very black." Humor made his deep-set eyes sparkle.

"A figment of your imagination," Ham said indignantly. "There is no such person as—"

"Later," said Doc Savage, instantly ending the argument. "I have found Sigmund Holmes," he added.

"Great!" Monk said. "I came up with goose eggs. The shyster and I were driving around trying to figure our next move, when—"

"Sigmund Holmes is dead," Doc Savage said in a strange voice.

Monk instantly went quiet. Ham twisted the head of his sword cane in nervous hands.

"I was summoned here by the report of another white-eyed corpse," Doc Savage said. "It appears Long Tom has also been on the premises. I have reason to believe he was taken prisoner by a man named Harmon Cash, or by men in his employ. This is Cash's office suite."

Monk eyed the surrounding police warily. He licked his lips as if about to ask a question. His wide mouth fell shut decisively.

"I thought Long Tom was out of the country," Ham Brooks offered, puzzled.

"He was not," Doc said, not elaborating.

Curious, Monk Mayfair went to the open door and peered within.

"Blazes!" was his only comment on the grisly array of bullet-gnashed, white-eyed bodies.

"When we couldn't find Holmes," Ham Brooks was explaining, "we heard over the police radio that another blind dead man had been discovered at this address. We figured that we would find you here, Doc."

The riot squad sergeant stepped up at that point.

"Exactly what is your connection with this Holmes fellow, Mr. Savage?" he asked.

If Doc Savage heard the question, he gave no sign. Instead, he said, "I would like to take Miss O'Fall and the one called Blackie into my custody until they have answered some questions."

The sergeant scratched his jaw thoughtfully.

"It's highly irregular—" he began.

Ham Brooks, who had given the roomful of bodies only a cursory glance, addressed the reluctant sergeant.

"My good man," he began in a sharp tone of voice, "don't you know that Doc Savage holds an honorary commission with the local constabulary? If you would prefer, we can speak with headquarters about this."

"I said it was highly irregular," the sergeant said hotly. "I didn't say I wasn't going to go along. Go ahead. Take them. That's two less headaches for me, I say."

The matter settled, Doc turned to Ham Brooks.

"You will find Dana O'Fall in the next room. Watch her. As yet, we do not know how she fits into this affair."

"Righto, Doc," said Ham, striding off, cane swinging jauntily.

Doc Savage then went to collect the pale-faced crook who called himself Blackie, simian Monk and Habeas Corpus in tow.

The unconscious man was stretched out in the corridor, around the corner and out of sight. Doc dismissed the uniformed officers who were standing guard over him.

"What happened to this lug?" Monk wanted to know.

"He fainted," Doc supplied.

"No foolin'," Monk said with enthusiasm. "Well, I got just the thing for a faint heart."

He reached down with his overlong arms, and without seeming to bend much, took hold of the man's coat front and hauled him to his feet.

Standing him against a wall, the hairy chemist proceeded to slap the man into returning awareness. He seemed to enjoy the work. He put a lot of enthusiasm into each swing of his furry arms.

"Rise and shine, Blackie," he shouted lustily.

Batting and blinking his eyes, Blackie came to life. He realized he was vertical, and got his feet organized. He looked about. The man seemed to be having trouble with his vision. His pupils were as dim as a child's marbles left too long in the elements.

"Who—what—" he began in a stupid voice. "Where am I?"

"In Dutch," warned Monk.

Doc Savage explained, "You have been placed in my custody."

"No, not—that," Blackie said, aghast. If anything, his pallor increased.

Monk turned to Doc, and grinned fiercely.

"I think this lad has an idea what he's in for, huh, Doc?"

The bronze man drew up to the frightened crook.

"You work for an individual named Harmon Cash?" he said.

The man looked down at the floor, saying, "Maybe."

"That makes you complicit in the murder of Sigmund Holmes. The penalty for murder in this State is the electric chair."

"You're crazy!" the pale Blackie snarled. "I didn't bump off Holmes!"

Monk made his pleasantly homely features fierce.

"If you didn't," he gritted, "you're the next best thing."

"Have you any witnesses to testify otherwise?" Doc asked.

The man glowered at them. He drew in a deep breath of resignation.

"All right," he said. "You've got me. I'm cooked anyway. I busted jail last year. Been on the lam ever since. I'll do a long stretch up-State no matter what happens. But you gotta believe me, I didn't touch Holmes."

Then he blanched. His eyelids flew wide, making his weak eyes seem to protrude. His mouth hung open widely enough to show fillings in his teeth and a coated tongue.

He had thought of something that was like ice on his brain. He rolled his eyes and wet his lips and finally showed them an eerie grin.

"I guess I'm behind the eight ball for sure," he muttered.

"What do you mean?" Doc Savage asked.

"If I'm in the big house, I'll play hell getting along if I'm going blind, like you said, Savage."

Doc said, "When did this condition first come on?"

The man shut his eyes tightly. He stuttered a little when he spoke. "I-it musta been when the damn B-blind D-death s-struck. I guess it got me a little, too, even though I hid."

Doc was silent a moment. "You believe hiding in that closet saved you from death?" he inquired.

"You said it." The man wet his lips. "I ain't croaked, so I guess I got a slow dose, huh? The idea would be f-funny if it wasn't the d-damned truth."

"Good grief," Monk muttered. He took a step back from the man as if in fear of contagion.

"It is possible that you were exposed to the so-called Blind Death," Doc said. "But it would be very unusual if you were to succumb to the malady at this late date, given your present symptoms, which do not appear life-threatening."

The prisoner Blackie blinked. This time from surprise. "Can you make sure some way?"

Doc nodded. "A physical examination should tell."

"Brother," gasped the pale crook. "Make that examination! And if you can do something for me, I'll return the favor. You can bust up Cash's rackets mighty simple. Cash is smart, but as a gang leader he's kinda soft. Hates violence."

Monk said curiously, "It sounds as if you don't think much of your boss."

"That Harmon Cash," said the other, "is a milk-livered wonder."

X

PLOT GROWING

Doc Savage called Ham Brooks back from the adjoining office.

Monk Mayfair's homely face lit with interest when the dapper lawyer returned with entrancing Dana O'Fall in tow.

"I don't believe we've been properly introduced," he said, grinning from ear to ear.

"I know all about you," Dana said, crisply.

If possible, Monk's froglike grin widened. It threatened the gristled tufts that were his ears.

"My reputation precedes me, I take it?" he prompted.

"Mr. Brooks informs me that you are a notorious wolf," Dana said acidly.

"I've been regaling Miss O'Fall with descriptions of the Mayfair family tree," Ham inserted blandly.

"And it seems to me that you still live in it," Dana O'Fall added, eying Monk's slovenly clothes.

Monk let out a groan. It sounded like a heavy sailcloth tearing in a gale. The homely chemist whirled on Doc Savage, his rusty arms swinging.

"Doc," he implored. "Make me one promise."

"Promise?"

"Promise me you'll never set this—this—barrister to watching the women prisoners again," Monk sputtered.

"I will think about it," Doc said, dryly.

They exited the building by the back steps. For some reason the press of reporters had not discovered the rear entrance, and so had missed out on the excitement with the sniper.

While the fourth estate jostled the police around the front, Doc Savage and his party piled into Doc's roadster and drove toward the heart of the city of New York, where Doc maintained a headquarters which had as a part of its equipment a laboratory, which, for completeness, was equaled by few others.

The prisoner was talking freely now.

"How did Sigmund Holmes die?" Ham asked him.

"Snig shot him," Blackie admitted. "It was an accident. Harmon Cash nearly had a fit. He wanted to keep Holmes alive."

"Why is that?" Doc demanded from behind the wheel.

"Search me. Cash had a lot of schemes going on all at once. He didn't share much with the hired help."

"What about our pal, Long Tom?" Monk demanded, adjusting the pig, Habeas Corpus, on his lap.

"Get your dog away from me and I'll tell you," Blackie returned, shoving away from the shoat's inquisitive snout.

"Dog!" Ham snorted. "Are you blind? That's the ugliest pig in captivity."

Ham's chance remark reminded the pale crook of why he had fainted in the first place. He paled visibly. He stared out the car window as if searching for light. Snow had collected on the pane. He swabbed at it with a palm, but inasmuch as the stuff had stuck to the other side, his efforts were fruitless.

"Blind," he croaked. "I'm going blind."

"Earlier, you said some one you called White Eyes killed Snig and the one known as Babe," Doc prompted. "Tell us about that."

Blackie gulped. "Babe had the guy, Long Tom, on the floor. He was working him over good. Then he just reared back and his eyes turned to snow. He croaked."

"Did you see what agency caused this?" Doc asked, interest in his controlled voice.

"Nothing caused it that I could see. He just keeled

over. The same happened to Snig. It was after that Long Tom broke loose."

"He escaped?"

"No."

Silence filled the moving car as the group absorbed the news. On the streets, the white snow, in the form of dirty slush, had been pushed up into the curbs by passing vehicles.

"It was like this," Blackie went on. "Long Tom got the drop on us. Then, Snig went blind. Then Long Tom started up with this crazy talk."

Doc said, "Explain."

"It was wild stuff," Blackie related. "I think he was pretty far gone, on account of pain. But the trend of it was that he knew all about the Blind Death. Said you'd recognize what was back of it too, Savage." The crook swallowed. "Do you?"

"For the love of mud," Monk exploded. "That Long Tom has it all figured out!"

"Go on," Doc said to Blackie. "What happened next?"

"That was when the voice that called itself White Eyes started talking."

"What did it say?" Doc asked as he shouldered the wheel around to avoid a skidding coal delivery truck.

"It told us to stop Roberts or we'd all get what Babe and Snig got. When I heard that, I ducked into the secret closet. I guess I shoulda moved more quick, huh?"

"Did you recognize the voice?"

The pale crook nipped his lips with his teeth. "No. And that's the truth."

Monk said harshly, "Lyin' to us won't get you no cookies!"

The nervous crook leaned forward and spoke emphatically.

"Listen," he said. "That voice, it seemed to come from nowhere yet everywhere at once. It was loud— very loud. That's what brought the cops, I guess. I don't know. I was hiding by then."

"Where was Harmon Cash while all this was going on?" Doc wondered as he slid onto a crosstown street.

"In the other room listening to that longhair music he likes," Blackie said. "I told you, he hates violence. He couldn't stand to watch what Babe was going to do to your man, Long Tom. To tell you the truth, it made me a little queasy, too."

"Bless me!" muttered Monk. "This Harmon Cash sounds like one weak sister."

"Say it again, brother," Blackie said fervently. "If he wasn't so damned smart, one of the boys would have knocked him off and taken over all his rackets by now."

"What is Cash trying to accomplish?" Doc Savage put in quietly.

"Something big," said the weak-eyed criminal.

"Big—what do you mean?"

"Cash has a lot of rackets going," the other volunteered. "But he was especially interested in the Cubama Sugar Importing Company. Claimed that it was going to make us all rich. The thing is, he'd already filched a bunch of bonds from the vault. Or rather, some guy named Sanchez did."

"Sanchez y. Annuncio de Calabero?" Doc demanded in a suddenly tight voice.

"I think that's the guy," Blackie admitted. "Cash was upset with him. I got the impression he thought Sanchez was chiseling."

Doc's trilling filled the jouncing roadster for a brief moment. Both Blackie and Dana O'Fall looked about the crowded interior in puzzlement. Throughout the ride, the pretty private investigator had been a subdued passenger, but it was obvious she was absorbing every word spoken with growing interest.

"Jove!" Ham exclaimed. "That's the chap who—"

Monk elbowed the dapper lawyer in the ribs.

"Nix, shyster!" he gritted.

Ham quieted down. In the front seat, where Dana O'Fall sat, the pretty private detective eyed Doc curiously.

"Go on," Doc directed.

"That's as much as I know," Blackie returned.

"Cash has his eye on Cubama. He seemed to think it's a gold mine. Now I ask you, doesn't that sound nutty?"

"I agree with you," Monk declared. "Our timid Harmon Cash is 'hay bloomin' barmy 'eifer!' as they would say at Harvard."

"And what's wrong with Harvard?" Ham demanded belligerently.

Doc Savage said, "You do not know the exact nature of Harmon Cash's scheme?"

"No," said the crook called Blackie.

Doc indicated Dana O'Fall. "What is her connection with the gang?"

"I don't know," said Blackie promptly. "She may not have any, for all I know."

Monk snorted disgustedly. "If you ask me, I think we better turn this guy over to the police and don't do a lot of worryin' about what his prospects are. I think he's lyin' to us, and don't deserve any consideration."

The prisoner seemed to consider deeply for a time.

"Look," he said. "I can't prove I'm not lying. But I can prove that I'm trying to do the right thing."

"You might," Monk admitted. "But I doubt it."

"I can tell you where you may be able to get your hands on Harmon Cash and the rest of his gang," the other offered.

"Eh?"

"Cash is hooked up with a guy named Eduardo Luz," Blackie announced dramatically. "He's a smooth boy, not an ordinary crook. I got the idea that he was an important cog in Cash's machinery."

"The same Eduardo Luz who is employed as the head cashier of the Cubama Sugar Importing Company?" Doc interposed.

"The same, I guess," Blackie said vaguely. "He was connected with Sanchez somehow. I know that much. He was with us when that devil White Eyes got Babe and Snig—or rather, he was downstairs standing guard. Find Luz, and he'll lead you to damned Harmon Cash. He should be easy to spot. He's a dusky lad. Likes to wear white suits all the time. But don't get the idea he's

one of those tropical types. I think that's just an act.
Luz comes across as American as canned peaches."

"This may be a trap," Monk said carefully.

The dim-eyed crook shrugged. "We won't argue it.
Either you take my word or you don't."

Doc Savage spoke up.

"When you heard the voice of White Eyes," he
inquired, "was Eduardo Luz out of the room as well?"

"Yeah. He was downstairs standing guard."

That thought sunk in all around.

Pretty Dana O'Fall put aside her protracted silence
at that point, a simmering curiosity evidently reaching
its boiling point.

"Exactly," she demanded of Doc Savage, "how do
you know so much about Cubama's employees?"

The bronze man ignored the question. Monk silently
extracted a walnut from a rumpled coat pocket and
shelled it with a noisy compression of one rusty fist,
feeding the meat to his pet pig. For his part, Ham took
his sword cane apart and examined a sticky brownish
chemical adhering to the tip—an anæsthetic compound.
He decided it needed freshening, and after some cautious maneuvering, brought the point into contact with
a reservoir in a secret compartment of his wrist watch.

Dana O'Fall's violet eyes took in his suspicious
display of sudden preoccupation.

"I get the feeling," she offered to no one in particular, "I'm not the only one in present company who is
playing their cards close to their vests."

That opinion offered, she lapsed back into her
sullen silence.

Presently, Doc tooled the roadster into the sub-
basement garage of one of New York's most imposing
skyscrapers. The outer door opened automatically and
the roadster coasted down an inclined ramp to take its
place among a number of other vehicles belonging to
the bronze man, including an egg delivery truck, a
disreputable taxi cab, and a touring car of some
sumptuousness, which incidentally was constructed of
armor-plate steel.

They took a private elevator to Doc's eighty-sixth floor aerie. The ride was breathtaking. The cage ascended with such unexpected speed that all but Doc Savage were thrown to their knees. Hairy Monk grinned with fierce enjoyment. He loved riding the lift.

When the ride was over, Ham Brooks helped pretty Dana O'Fall to her feet.

The cage let them out onto a modernistic corridor at one end of which was a substantial bronze door. In tasteful letters on the face were letters in slightly darker bronze:

CLARK SAVAGE, JR.

They waded through the thick nap of the corridor rug, Doc taking the lead.

He no sooner approached the imposing bronze door than it valved open before him.

"Is this guy a magician?" Blackie whispered to Monk Mayfair.

"Naw," Monk said, pride in his bronze leader evident in his childlike voice. "Doc carries this radioactive key jigger on him at all times. It sends out what you call emanations that cause a relay to open the door like that."

"Isn't that something?" Blackie breathed in admiration.

"Stick around," the apish chemist shot back. "You ain't seen nothin' yet!"

The establishment consisted of an outer reception room and office which was sumptuously, but not gaudily, furnished. A massive inlaid desk of Oriental design dominated this room. There was also a safe large enough to swallow a person of average height, and other substantial furnishings.

Beyond this was a library which for completeness in its assortment of scientific books could be equaled perhaps by but one other library, its location unknown except to Doc Savage himself, being in a mysterious and remote spot which the bronze man termed his "Fortress of Solitude," and to which he returned at intervals to study, none knowing his whereabouts, not even his five trusted aids.

Connecting with the library was Doc's experimental laboratory, this also having an equal only in the second laboratory which the bronze man maintained at his Fortress of Solitude.

Doc turned to his aids, Monk and Ham.

"Keep Miss O'Fall entertained while I am at work," he directed.

"A pleasure," Monk said enthusiastically.

"I second that," Ham chimed in.

"Will this take long?" pretty Dana O'Fall wondered, eying Monk and his pet pig with undisguised reservation.

Wordlessly, Doc turned on his heel and led Blackie into the cavernous inner rooms.

Blackie—his last name was Doyle, he informed the bronze man—allowed himself to be subjected to a battery of tests. Of all the bronze man's scientific skills, he excelled at none more than medicine and surgery. Although he did not practice professionally, he had allowed none of his consummate skill to atrophy from infrequent use.

First, he took blood and spinal samplings, as well as a tiny bit of dermis material—which necessitated making a small wound in the nervous criminal's forearm.

Doc set the latter sample to burning and photographed the smoke that resulted through a spectroscope. While he waited for the film to develop, the bronze man subjected Blackie to an ordinary eye examination, using equipment similar to that found in any ophthalmologist's practice.

When this had been completed, Doc removed from his equipment vest—he had draped it and his coat over a handy chair—several glass phials. Each contained a gelatinous material similar to partially cooked egg white. He had taken these from the bodies of Nug Hassel, Sanchez y. Annuncio de Calabero, Babe, and other Blind Death victims the bronze man had examined during the course of this unusually active day.

Doc laid each sampling on a glass slide and popped them in and out of a high-power microscope, taking notes as he did so.

Unaware of the significance of these samples, Blackie watched the bronze man's labors with quiet intensity.

Whereas previously the crook had been almost skeptical at times as to the undeniable fact that he was suffering the effects of some incipient species of blindness, the presence of such a galaxy of scientific paraphernalia as the white-walled laboratory held had infused him with genuine terror.

"What have you learned?" he demanded anxiously.

"Sit down," Doc told him.

The criminal stumbled over to a metal table and perched upon it.

The door opened and Monk came in. He had pretty chestnut-haired Dana O'Fall in tow.

Monk began, "Doc, this girl—"

Dana shoved forward. "Mr. Savage! You've got to believe me! Eduardo Luz had nothing to do with any of this!"

"If you're wondering what brought this on," Monk offered, jerking a thumb in the girl's direction, "I just happened to tell her that she could do herself some good by talking before we went after this Luz."

Doc studied the lady detective curiously. He had studied psychology and human beings a great deal. In the case of a man, he could have told with a nearly absolute certainty whether deceit was present. But he had never met a woman whose mind he could read with any certainty by what was on her face.

"Why should we not investigate Luz?" he asked.

"I can't tell you." Dana kneaded her hands. "But you've got to believe me."

Doc watched the girl. But he found himself unable to be sure. She was too pretty.

The pale crook got off his metal table and yelled,

"You've got to stay here and find out if I'm going to croak from this damned Blind Death."

"Shut up!" Monk told him. "You don't amount to much!"

Ham appeared in the door and yelled contrarily, "I don't see why this man's life isn't just as valuable as some wild idea of this brass-plated female's, especially since she won't tell us anything solid."

"Where's your chivalry?" Monk growled. "Answer: You never had any!"

Doc said, "Out, please."

Monk, Ham, and Dana O'Fall went into the reception room, still quarreling at the top of their voices.

The pale Harmon Cash minion named Blackie grinned thinly and said, "Life would never lose its sting around them two."

The bronze man went on working. The spectroscopic plates—they were coated with a photographic solution sensitive to rays of light inside and outside the visible spectrum—were coming out of the developer, and he put them under a glass, in order to get an analytical survey of the elements present in the bit of the former convict's tissue he had burned. It was a method sometimes used by the police in searching for poison in homicide victims. It was some time before the bronze man straightened. He looked at the pale crook.

"You are not going to succumb to the Blind Death," he said.

The dim-eyed crook wet his lips. He tried twice to speak, and failed, then words popped out of him explosively.

"Is there any hope for my sight?" he demanded.

"You were not blinded, in the sense that your optic nerves have been damaged," Doc explained. "And even if that were the case, the type of blindness you have contracted possesses no deadly side effects. Rather, it is the blindness which is a side effect of the so-called Blind Death."

Blackie gasped, "But can you—"

"Your condition is not advanced, and should be reversible with the proper treatment," Doc interposed.

The bronze man went back to his scrutiny of the photographic plates and the microscopic slides.

Abruptly, without warning, Doc's small, unearthly trilling noise came into the room. Nebulous and fantastic, it ran up and down the musical scale, seeming to adhere to no definite tune, yet possessing a musical quality that was quite marked.

The crook peered about anxiously, for the trilling had some eerie essence of ventriloquism which made it almost impossible to tell from whence it came.

It meant, although the listener had no way of knowing, that the bronze man had uncovered something of importance.

Doc asked him, "Have you felt a bit queer recently?"

"Danged queer," the crook admitted.

"Since when?"

"Since that White Eyes got Babe and Snig. But I figured what happened was enough to make a man feel queer."

"Hot?"

"You mean—yeah. All over. Kinda like I had a fever. Weak, too. Like something the cat drug in."

Doc Savage nodded and took another look at the apparatus.

"What's it mean?" Blackie asked plaintively.

The bronze man did not answer the question, but went to a telephone.

The call which Doc Savage made over the telephone was brief and directed to a concern which supplied ambulances for private hauls. This company was, as a matter of fact, subsidized financially by Doc Savage. It was only one of many businesses in which he had a monetary interest.

Doc finished the telephone call. He went to the crook, grasped his wrist, led him to a filing cabinet, got out handcuffs, and manacled the man to a steel pipe.

"What's the idea?" the fellow wailed.

Doc did not answer. He went to a table, wrote for

some moments on an envelope. Much of the writing was in Latin, the language employed by doctors.

He gave the paper to the former convict.

"Hand this to the man who comes for you," Doc directed. "Be sure to do so, because it contains instructions which will insure the restoration of your sight."

"Where are you going?" howled Blackie. "Wait! Fix me up yourself!"

Doc walked out without answering.

Within half an hour, an ambulance would call for the man, and he would be taken, without knowing where he went, to a strange criminal-curing institution which Doc Savage maintained in up-State New York. There, the man's brain would undergo a delicate operation that would wipe out all knowledge of the past. He would receive a course of training which would fit him to earn a living, and in addition, instill in him a hatred for all lawbreakers. Then he would be discharged.

The world knew nothing of this strange institution which Doc Savage maintained. A surprising number of "students" had gone through the unique "college," and not one of the graduates had as yet gone back to crime.

This criminal was not the first man Doc had sent to the institution who had a prison sentence hanging over his head. To prevent the cured criminals being returned to prison, Doc had a rather unusual working agreement. The governor of the State owed the bronze man a debt of gratitude, and by way of repaying same, managed the issuance of pardons to such individuals as Doc designated.

The bronze man joined Monk, Ham, and Dana O'Fall in the reception room. Monk and Ham were on the point of coming to blows once more over the subject of their mutual ancestry. They broke off upon Doc's entrance.

"Now we will investigate this Eduardo Luz," Doc said.

Pretty Dana O'Fall did a pretty fair impression of a woman biting her tongue in frustration.

XI

THE PIG RUSE

Eduardo Luz proved easy to trace.

Consulting a Manhattan telephone directory, Doc Savage found a listing under that name. The listing gave an address in Greenwich Village, not far from Washington Square.

They took the bronze man's private speed elevator to the sub-basement garage, where Doc availed himself of the long gloomy roadster. The engine came to life with barely a sound and the long machine slid up a ramp and out into traffic. Doc pressed a dash button. A radio signal caused the garage door to open before them and then close in their wake.

Dana O'Fall sat in the back seat, between Monk and Ham. The latter had resumed their seemingly endless argument.

"I come from a good family," the dapper lawyer was insisting.

"Well, you came pretty far," Monk rejoined.

Ham's mobile orator's mouth made apoplectic shapes while he twisted his sword cane between lean fingers. He looked several times as if he was going to give vent to a choice opinion, but the silent presence of Dana O'Fall evidently made him reconsider.

Eventually, the dapper lawyer fell to examining his well-manicured fingernails critically.

"Well, well, well," Monk said broadly. "The last word at last. Hear that, Habeas? For once we got the shyster beat."

A voice seemed to come from the seat beside the

94

bronze man, where Monk's pet pig, Habeas Corpus, was busily scratching behind one long winglike ear.

"Having a black sheep in the family has made him into a lamb," the shoat seemed to say.

Ham fumed. Monk bestowed an ingratiating smile on pretty Dana O'Fall.

"That Habeas," Monk offered. "I picked him up in Arabia one time and danged if he ain't the smartest hog in the world. He already knew Arabic, and it was nothin' to teach him English."

"You do not fool me," Dana O'Fall said frostily. "I recognize a cheap ventriloquist's gag when I hear it."

This time, it was Monk's turn to fume. Seldom had his voice-throwing act failed to impress the opposite sex. Monk decided that Dana O'Fall was a hard-boiled bit of merchandise.

Doc Savage tooled the long machine south and west in silence. His flake-gold eyes were intent. From time to time, they flicked to the rear-vision mirror and the entrancing face of the chestnut-haired lady private investigator, as if attempting to read her character. If Doc Savage succeeded, the regular bronze lineaments of his face gave no sign. But then, he had been schooled to conceal his emotions.

Presently, they drew up before the address gotten from the directory. It proved to be an apartment building of some substance.

Parking, Doc turned in his seat and addressed his passengers.

"Ham, you and I will call on Eduardo Luz."

"What about me?" Monk asked plaintively, obviously fearful of missing out on any action. Monk loved action. It was the thing that drew him and the bronze man's other aids together. That, and admiration for their mighty leader.

"You," Doc Savage told him, "will remain with Miss O'Fall and see that no harm befalls her."

Monk's homely features lit up.

"Fine by me," he said.

"Mr. Savage," pretty Dana O'Fall said suddenly.

"Yes?"

"I insist upon being released," she blurted out in breathless haste. "You have no right to keep me locked up with this—this refugee from a Tarzan picture," she added hotly.

Monk scowled. Ham burst out laughing.

"As the holder of an honorary police commission," the bronze man told her, "I am empowered to hold you on suspicion, just as the police themselves would."

"Suspicion of what?" Dana flared.

"Complicity in the sniper attack of this evening."

"You can't believe I was behind that!"

"You were found on a roof from which the shooting seems to have occurred," Doc Savage said levelly. "If you did not do the shooting, you had to have seen who did. Your refusal to name this person strongly suggests that the sniper was an accomplice."

Dana O'Fall took her ripe lower lip in perfect white teeth and began worrying them.

"Would you care to make a statement?" Doc prompted.

"No."

If the bronze man was disappointed in this reply, he gave no sign. He shoved out from behind the driver's seat. Ham came out on the other side and joined him.

Together, they entered the apartment building entrance and disappeared within.

After they had gone, Monk Mayfair decided to apply some psychology on stubborn Dana O'Fall.

"If you don't cut loose with some truth pretty soon," he warned, "it's gonna go real hard on you."

"I had nothing to do with that shooting," Dana O'Fall said crisply, turning her pretty violet eyes away.

"So you say," Monk grumbled. "You also say you worked for old Sigmund Holmes. We know that's a tall one, too."

"And how exactly," Dana demanded, "do you know this?"

Monk shrugged his apish shoulders.

"We just know," he said airily. "That's all."

"A likely story," Dana huffed.

"As likely as yours," said Monk, scratching one hirsute wrist absently. The hair on it was like rusty shingle nails, and thick. Similar hair covered his nubbin of a head.

Silence filled the gloomy car interior. The hour was late. Passing traffic carried long funnels of light around nearby corners and into their faces. The lights seemed to bother the pig, Habeas Corpus, who suddenly took a notion to join Monk in the back seat.

Habeas accomplished this in a manner not unlike that of a dog. The shoat had spindly, doglike legs and he used them to climb onto the seat cushions, from there to leap onto Monk's waiting lap.

"Habeas!" the homely chemist said joyfully. "Come to papa, hog."

Habeas submitted to a vigorous scratching of his long ears. His inquisitive snout sniffed delicately in Dana O'Fall's direction.

Several minutes of this spectacle produced a softening effect on Dana O'Fall's tense features.

"Why," she said at last. "He's just like a dog."

"Habeas Corpus is smarter than most dogs," Monk said proudly.

"Is he friendly?" Dana asked.

"Sure," returned Monk, lifting the amiable shoat in her direction. "Give him a scratch and see."

Dana O'Fall reached out tapered fingers and scratched lightly. Habeas appeared to enjoy this attention, because he soon squirmed from Monk's hairy grasp and onto the lady private investigator's lap.

Dana fell to quietly scratching the contented pig about the ears with one hand. With the other, she surreptitiously reached for the door handle.

It happened that the trend of traffic invariably made bright headlight shine cross Monk's pleasantly homely features. Each time an auto passed Monk was forced to look away or shield his piglike eyes.

Hand on the door handle, Dana waited for another passing vehicle. Presently, the piled snow about the streets took on the sheen of approaching glare. It swelled, filling the car interior with hard light.

When the hairy chemist abruptly looked away, Dana O'Fall gave the door handle a downward shove. The door cracked open. Screwing up her face in anticipation, she gave the pig a hard spank on his hindquarters and the shoat, startled, took off as if a tin can had been tied to his tail.

"Habeas!" Monk squawled in alarm as the ungainly Habeas Corpus skittered into traffic. The porker slipped and slid on the slushy pavement with all the grace of a giraffe on ice skates.

"What'd you do that for?" Monk wailed.

Before Dana O'Fall could reply—if any reply was intended—twin cones of dazzling illumination swung around a corner, announcing the approach of a fast-moving automobile.

Monk's tiny eyes grew wide with horror.

"Habeas!" he howled. For the lights were bearing down on the unsteady porker.

The sight galvanized the apish chemist into action. He plunged out his door, bounded around the car, and leapt into the street. His speed was surprising, given his short, bowed legs. They pumped like pistons.

In a flash, he had scooped up the frightened pig.

But the unseen car was still coming. For a frozen moment in eternity, the hairy chemist stood impaled by the twin funnels of the juggernaut's oncoming headlamps. His wide mouth split into a shape that would have been comical had it not been for his fearful expression.

And clutched in his hairy hands, the pig, Habeas Corpus, squealed in utter fright.

XII

GOOD LUCK AND BAD

Swarthy Eduardo Luz was a man in a hurry.

He was also a man trying desperately not to be tailed.

He drove through the thoroughfares of Manhattan as if fearful of pursuit. He turned often, doubled back frequently, and recrossed busy intersections over and over.

When he was finally satisfied that he had collected no followers, he directed his auto—it was a sporty make with a top that could be lowered in good weather—toward Washington Square. Since it was a bitterly cold evening, the top was up. The car was white as polished ivory. It almost matched his suit, which was soggy and soiled from much crouching in the snow.

On the floorboards in back, covered by a blanket, lay a high-powered rifle. The same rifle had been used earlier in the day by the late killer called Babe, and would have been employed to snuff out the life of Nug Hassel had a more grisly fate not overtaken him.

It had finally been fired in a futile attempt to take the life of a Harmon Cash minion known as Blackie.

In that, vapidly handsome Eduardo Luz had failed. His anger showed in the set of his pearly teeth. From time to time, he sucked in a breath through them, as if they hurt.

A stubby cigarette smoldered in one hand, but the dark-complected crook seemed not to notice.

He watched the bouncing calcium-white oblongs his headlamps carved in the streets before them. The faster he drove, the more they seemed to retreat from his on Rushin's machine.

Scurrying before him, they were like twin eyes of light questing hungrily. Blind and baleful, they reminded Eduardo Luz of the dead, staring eyes of the deceased Harmon Cash underlings, Babe and Snig, and he grunted out loud.

"White Eyes..." he muttered.

They seemed hypnotic, those headlight orbs, as Eduardo Luz chased them up and down slick Manhattan streets. Soon, he was lost in thought.

The lights went around a corner, bouncing in time with the white machine's springs.

Suddenly, they lifted, illuminating a bizarre sight.

"Hell's bells!" he choked.

It looked for all the world as if a full-grown gorilla straddled the street. The gorilla wore a baggy suit, and clutched another animal—it looked to be a pig—in his hands.

Eduardo Luz had excellent reflexes. He stabbed the brake pedal. The car went into a long sideways skid. The gorilla jumped away with alacrity. Eduardo Luz had a momentary impression that it had dived into a snowbank, but then his attention was focused on avoiding an imminent collision.

He did not succeed. Sliding, the car swapped ends several times. The snout clipped a fire hydrant, tearing loose the grille, and, rocking, the front wheels climbed the curb.

The exposed radiator ran smack into a brick wall. It cracked. A Vesuvius-like shover of hot water erupted. When it touched the snow under the chassis, it made more water.

Eduardo Luz took the brunt of the impact on his chest. The steering wheel broke when he was thrown forward. He lost his still-lit cigarette stub.

The driver's side door happened to fling itself open with the last jolt of movement, and Eduardo Luz slipped out like a handful of cigarettes from a cellophane pack.

He crawled through the lukewarm mixture of radiator water and melting snow until he reached the curb. Getting himself organized, he looked back and saw that his machine was a wreck.

He groaned, perhaps more at the expense of the loss than from actual pain. He looked around with his penetrating black eyes.

A cracked grin split his pained features. For he recognized the entrance hall to his apartment house.

Then, the grin melted like a snowman's smile.

Emerging from the entrance, alert and wary, were two men. One was well dressed and carried a slim dark cane.

But it was the sight of the other that made the Latin blood in Eduardo Luz's veins freeze.

For there could be no mistaking the tall bronze figure that rushed to the snowbank where the badly dressed gorilla had ended up.

"Doc Savage!" Eduardo Luz gritted. "He's on to me!"

Panic seized the smooth crook then.

His auto useless, his apartment no longer a safe haven, he leaped for the long plain-colored roadster that was parked nearby.

The driver's door was unlocked. A key reposed in the ignition. Eduardo gave it a twist. The engine sprang to life. Eduardo Luz fed the engine gas and the machine slid from the curb with a smooth authority that was unexpected.

This brought an immediate reaction from those on the street.

The man with the cane seemed not to know what to do. He stood torn between the fleeing car and concern over the fallen gorilla. Finally, he knelt beside the beast.

Doc Savage, on the other hand, pitched after the swarthy crook.

The bronze man was moving like a metallic beam of light. Head up, arms pumping, legs churning, he volleyed after Eduardo Luz like a grim Nemesis.

Luz, watching in the rear-vision mirror, felt his heart quail a little. The bronze man was actually gaining on him!

"Can't let him get me," Luz bit out. He pressed the gas to the floor. The roadster surged ahead. The intersections flashed by. The bronze man·began to fall behind. But something in the metallic determination of his face told Eduardo Luz that Doc Savage would not give up easily.

Coming up in a busy cross street, Luz saw the signal begin to change. He accelerated, barely making it.

Opposing traffic hummed into life. The bronze man whipped over onto the sidewalk, looking for an opening, but could not pass.

The last Eduardo Luz saw of him, Doc Savage had cut down a side street in a futile attempt to circumvent the flow of traffic.

Luz piloted the unexpectedly powerful roadster down a street that would put more distance between him and the bronze man.

"Let him try to catch me now!" he chortled loudly.

A voice from the rear seat gasped suddenly.

Eduardo Luz showed he had nerve. He kept the roadster on its path. Carefully, he switched on the overhead light.

Sunken in the rear cushions, the light found a slim form.

"Holy smokes!" exclaimed Eduardo Luz at the sight of violet-eyed Dana O'Fall. "I thought Sanchez did for you."

Dana O'Fall made a dive for the right side door.

Eduardo Luz shouldered the steering wheel in the same direction, saying, "Oh no you don't, sister!"

The roadster jounced up on the sidewalk to scrape its right flank against a building facade.

The opening door caught on brick. Dana reversed in her seat and made a grab for the other door. Her fingers brushed at the handle. But it eluded her. The door had been opened from without.

Dana O'Fall found herself looking up into the vapidly handsome features of Eduardo Luz.

"You and I," he said darkly, "have a great deal to talk about."

"I have nothing to say to you," Dana retorted.

"Maybe not now," Eduardo Luz remarked, extracting his liver-colored sap from a pocket and wrapping a white silk handkerchief around it several times, "but the time will surely come."

Dana screamed. The padded sap plunged for her chestnut curls, connected with an audible *bonk*, and she gave out a breathy sigh as she crumpled to the cold floorboards.

Looking up and down the street anxiously, swarthy Eduardo Luz slammed the rear door shut and reclaimed the front seat.

The long roadster rocketed from the sidewalk like a dim comet.

Eduardo Luz wasted no time in quitting Manhattan Island.

He sent the long, powerful roadster coursing across the Holland Tunnel and into New Jersey. In Jersey City, he pulled off the Skyway into a filling station, and availed himself of a public telephone.

When he got a connection, he made his voice low and careful.

"Boss?" he asked.

"Luz?" asked the cautious voice of Harmon Cash.

"The same," Eduardo Luz admitted.

"I have," Harmon Cash allowed, "been sweating figurative icicles anticipating your call."

"Couldn't be helped," Luz put in quickly. "I've been on one hell of a sleigh ride. I went back to the office for Blackie, like you said, but—"

"I am not referring to Blackie," interrupted Harmon Cash. "The radio has been abuzz with the reports of Blind Death victims all night. The identity of one of those victims should be of interest to you."

The line crackled silence.

"I'm listening," Eduardo Luz said warily.

"It seems that our mutual friend Sanchez y. Annuncio de Calabero has joined the departed ones of ivory-eyed distinction," revealed Harmon Cash.

"That explains the girl!" Eduardo Luz gritted, one piercing eye going to the waiting roadster.

"Girl?"

"The private peeper, Dana O'Fall," Eduardo supplied. "I got her stashed in the back seat of my car."

"This is arresting news," Harmon Cash mused over the telephone connection. "Especially inasmuch as only today, you assured me that this Dana O'Fall was dead and Sanchez alive."

"What're you saying?" Luz snapped. "Spit it out!"

"I am not saying anything," Harmon Cash returned smoothly. "I am merely musing out loud. And my musings naturally lead me to wonder if, as Sanchez's partner, you are privy to the location of the Cubama bonds, a certain portion of which are due me in return for my services in disposing of the remainder?"

"I don't have them with me, if that's what you're driving at," Eduardo Luz said testily. "And do you want to hear about Blackie, or not?"

"I think," Harmon Cash said after a long pause punctuated by the draw and exhalation of his ever-present pipe, "that you and Miss O'Fall should join me in this relaxing spot, and it might be a good idea if you bring the bonds with you, as well."

"I'll be there," Eduardo Luz promised.

"Do not keep me waiting," Harmon Cash implored in a suddenly tight voice. Then, as if catching himself, his cultured voice softened. "All this frightful waiting is getting on my poor, shattered nerves. And you know how excitement tries me so."

On that wearisome note, the line went dead.

XIII

FOILED SHADOWS

Swarthy Eduardo Luz trudged back to the Doc Savage roadster like a forlorn white ghost. The snow had stopped falling, although the way the wind blew flakes of it around, that was not immediately apparent. The sky above was very, very black, like a hovering dark mass that brooded over a benighted world.

The only light came from passing cars. There were not many. The hour was very late. It lacked but two or three hours to the cold, cheerless approach of dawn.

It transpired that a truck happened to pass the filling station just as Eduardo Luz approached the waiting roadster. It was such an unprepossessing machine that Luz felt safe driving it. It appeared built to not attract attention.

But a splash of furtive headlight gleam fell upon the license plate. The number read: DOC 1.

"Good grief!" Eduardo Luz sputtered to himself. "I should've known!"

He sprinted to the machine, gave sleeping Dana O'Fall a cursory glance, and industriously kicked dirty snow onto the plate, smoothing it down by hand so it resembled a vagary of wind-blown precipitation.

Satisfied, Eduardo Luz got the engine going, backed out of the filling station with alacrity.

For as inconspicuous as the roadster was, its license plate was not. Any passing police officer would know by the plate that this was a Doc Savage machine.

The low number was a courtesy New York State bequeathed upon certain notables. It signified prestige.

And without doubt, the bronze man had set the forces of the law to watching the roads for his lost machine.

It was apparent, however, that no one had chanced to notice the roadster, Eduardo Luz decided. He had not been molested at any time. He drove back in the direction of New York City, where, he knew, the cache of bonds filched from the Cubama Sugar Importing Company safe lay.

He grinned tightly as he piloted the roadster. News of the death of his partner in crime, Sanchez, had been a shock. But as the full meaning sank in, he realized it meant more swag for him.

"Sure," he grinned. "Let Cash have the stuff now. The sooner he moves them, the quicker I get mine. And Sanchez's share, too!"

His pearly teeth shone in the dashboard lights. Idly, he fished two fingers into a coat pocket, spearing out an elongated white tube of a cigarette. The act of extracting this caused a well-smoked cigarette butt to tumble from the pocket and roll to the floorboard, out of sight.

Frowning, Luz braked the machine and felt around under the seat. This took many minutes, but the swarthy crook stubbornly refused to abandon the hunt.

Finally, after much muttered cursing, his questing fingers located the fugitive butt under the seat. Luz restored the fag to his coat pocket, and resumed driving, his features evincing great relief.

His frown returned, however, obscuring his perfect teeth, when he noticed a dark sedan in the rear-vision mirror. He thought he had seen it before. During the ride over the bridge. But he could not be certain.

It was not a radio prowl car, Luz knew. But Manhattan detectives sometimes resorted to unmarked cars. This could be one of those.

Putting his theory to the test, the swarthy crook

took a sudden turn-off and picked up speed. The sedan duplicated the maneuver.

"Hell!" Luz said bitterly. "Looks like I collected a shadow."

He fed the cylinders all the gas they could ingest. Expecting the sedan driver to do the same, Eduardo Luz's intensely black eyes flicked between the road and the rear-vision mirror.

To his surprise, the pursuing driver did not. Instead, the sedan slithered into a side street and vanished.

"Maybe I was wrong," he muttered.

The swarthy crook meandered back to the main road and resumed his New York-bound course.

A coupe caught his attention next. It, too, seemed to be shadowing him. There were no other cars on this stretch of road.

"We'll see about this!" he growled.

Deliberately, Eduardo Luz eased up on the gas. The trailing coupe had no choice but to overhaul the roadster. Luz was driving conspicuously under the posted speed limit.

When the two cars were abreast, Eduardo Luz gave the steering wheel a hard wrench to the left.

Fenders bumped and locked. The coupe fought to hold the road, but the blacktop was too slick. Tires squealed in rubber agony. The soft shoulder was creeping inexorably up on the other machine.

"Follow me, will you!" Eduardo Luz sneered, pressing the other car harder.

It was no contest. The roadster was the heavier machine. The unseen coupe driver fought expertly to hold the road. In the end, he realized his predicament.

Surrendering to fate, he steered into the waiting soft shoulder. The coupe gave a little bounce and plunged its nose into a furrow of heavy plowed snow.

It landed with a mushy *whump!* The rear tires, poised a good yard off the ground, spun freely and uselessly.

Eduardo Luz laughed cruelly as he sped away.

He did not laugh long, for he began to imagine that he was once again being followed, this time by an early-bird delivery truck. Many had started to appear on the road, carrying fresh-baked bread and milk to market.

This was an egg truck. Its headlights blazed after him like twin maws of hungry luminance.

"To hell with this!" Eduardo Luz bawled. "Cash can wait for his cut!"

He broke three laws getting the roadster turned around and going in the opposite direction, away from the city.

The egg truck did not follow.

The noble experiment that was Prohibition produced a number of ignoble results. The speakeasy being one. At one time, such establishments were to be found in all large cities, often in unlikely spots.

With the coming of Repeal, the speakeasy went legitimate. Those "speaks" fortunate enough to be placed in excellent locations became, virtually overnight, legal saloons. Others, in more remote localities, withered and died.

The speak Eduardo Luz pulled up before was one of the latter. Situated near the Jersey flats, it had once been a magnet for the illicit thirsts of the Garden State. Now it was a decaying shell settling into a patch of weeds.

Eduardo Luz coasted to the rear of this establishment, a long, peak-roofed affair of rude wood, listening to the unplowed snow scrape and squeak against the roadster's undercarriage. He killed the motor, got out.

Going to the rear door, he pulled it open.

A woman's shoe abruptly sailed out and knocked off his hat.

"Damn you!" Luz howled in surprise. This brought a companion shoe arrowing in his direction, hurled by pretty Dana O'Fall, who had come awake.

Dana had better luck with this second shoe. It struck, heel-first, smack between Eduardo Luz's penetrating eyes. He recoiled, momentarily stunned. His knees wobbled, and he fell on his fallen white hat, crushing it into the dirty snow.

Dana O'Fall bounded out of the roadster. She wasted no time getting behind the wheel. In the darkness, she groped for the ignition key.

"Oh, where is that darned key?" she exclaimed, fumbling. Her violet eyes were wide, anxious.

In the snow, Eduardo Luz shook his vapidly handsome head. Cursing, he reached frantically into his white tropical suit.

Dana saw this out of the tail of one eye and, thinking she was about to be fired on, redoubled her efforts to locate the ignition key.

"Where is it?" she moaned again.

Luz found what he was looking for. It was his trademark sap. Evidently, he was not accustomed to carrying common firearms.

Still on his back, he hauled off and threw the weighted object.

Dana saw it coming. She ducked expertly. The projectile sailed past her chestnut curls and ricocheted off the windshield. Oddly, the glass did not crack or pit.

The liver-colored sap bounced on the seat beside the pretty private investigator. She snatched it up, and stepped out from the car to stand in her stocking feet.

Crouching beside the stretched-out white figure that was Eduardo Luz, she shook the skull-cracker before his nose and warned, "Produce those keys, buster, or get a dose of your own bad medicine."

"Coat . . . pocket," Eduardo Luz said tightly.

Tapered fingers dived into a side pocket of the linen coat, scrounged around some, and came out as a fist—full of smoked cigarette butts.

"What are you," Dana snapped, "a collector?"

She made a move for the opposite pocket. The hand froze as a suave voice from behind her cut in like a dagger of ice.

"Be good enough to step away from Mr. Luz," it drawled, "or I shall be forced to have my underlings get rough with you. It is, I might say, a fate I would rather spare you of—if for no other reason than it would trouble my sleep for some weeks to come."

The sound of a man's voice, more than his words—they were too world-weary to be considered menacing, Dana decided—convinced the violet-eyed lady private detective to surrender.

A moment later, Eduardo Luz recovered his sap by virtue of plucking it loose from Dana's unresisting fingers. He placed his other hand against her face. He gave a hard shove.

Expelling a gusty "Oof," Dana fell back into the snow.

Eduardo Luz next proved he was no gentleman. Snarling, he clambered to his feet. He drew one shoe back, preparatory to delivering a carefully aimed kick.

"No!" Harmon Cash shouted. "No violence!"

"This skirt has it coming!" Luz insisted, his foot poised.

Dana O'Fall drew in a sharp breath. This sound was followed by the thunderous report of a pistol. Saffron gun-flame momentarily colored the snow.

Eduardo Luz and Dana O'Fall craned their heads around, their features bearing nearly identical expressions. Expressions which seemed to wonder: "Where did the bullet go?"

As it happened, straight up.

Leonine-headed Harmon Cash stood there, surrounded by minions, whose weaponry—an assortment of pistols and submachine guns—were held loosely, pointed in no particular direction.

The same could not be said for the crime boss's right hand. It lifted straight as a jackstaff. Almost swallowed in his upraised fist was his tiny derringer. A curl of smoke lifted from it.

"I do hope I haven't startled either of you," he said, his suave voice filling with apparently genuine concern for their well-being. He wore a yellowish camel's-hair topcoat that looked very warm.

Luz brushed snow off his very abused suit. He had trouble finding any, owing to the blending effect snow had against white linen.

"I'm all right," he said, grimly. "Considering what I've been through tonight."

"She does not appear very tough," Harmon Cash said, cocking an eye—the left—in Dana O'Fall's direction.

Ribald laughter came from Cash's minions.

"I didn't mean her," Luz snarled. "You got problems, Cash."

"What do you mean?"

"Doc Savage is on your trail."

The effect this piece of news had on the suave criminal mastermind was marked. His face went three shades paler, and as if suddenly magnetized, his eyes drew together until Harmon Cash became momentarily cross-eyed.

This display would have been comical had it not managed to convey to each onlooker stark fright.

"Inside," Harmon Cash rapped. "Quickly!"

Two men fell on the girl and hauled Dana to her stockinged feet. They dragged her inside. Harmon Cash followed. Eduardo Luz brought up the rear.

The interior of the former speakeasy boasted the same rude furnishings of its recent heyday. The floor was awash with sawdust. Tables were of rough wood; some were simply empty kegs upended and ringed with high wooden stools. The bar—such as it was—was simply a line of benches against a long wall.

Illumination was furnished by brass lamps, whose wan light failed to reach up to the high exposed rafters.

Harmon Cash directed the girl be placed in a chair before the makeshift bar. Two men stood guard over her.

Harmon Cash turned to Eduardo Luz and spoke a single harsh word:

"Talk."

Luz took a deep breath and plunged in.

"I went back for Blackie, just like you asked," he related, his breath steaming, for it was very cold in the speakeasy. "The place was swarming with cops. I couldn't get near the place."

"You had instructions for that eventuality," Harmon Cash said, freshening his pipe.

"Sure," Luz allowed. "That's why I took along Babe's rifle. I set myself up on a roof across the street and used the telescope sight. The drapes were open a crack. I sighted on that. That's how I knew Doc Savage was on the scene."

"This is not good," Harmon Cash gritted through his clenched pipe stem. "This is not good at all. Go on."

"Savage had Blackie. The minute I saw that, I opened up."

"You—ah—dispatched Blackie, I trust?"

"Couldn't tell," Eduardo Luz admitted. "I was firing through those damn drapes. I don't know who I hit."

"You mean you failed to ascertain whether or not you got the job done?" Harmon Cash asked, distressed.

"What do you expect?" Luz returned hotly. "I ran out of bullets. The cops were sure to comb the neighborhood. While I was trying to see through the shot-up window, I heard someone pushing against the roof trap. I went down the fire escape, and that's all I know."

"You did not see who it was?"

"With all those flatfoots around, I wasn't about to stick around to find out," Eduardo Luz said sourly.

"Then it might have been Doc Savage?"

"Possibly," Luz admitted.

"And," suave Harmon Cash drawled on, "Savage might have followed you here."

"That's why I kept driving around before calling," Luz retorted. "I'm no babe in the woods, you know. Once I was sure I wasn't being shadowed, I figured to call you from my place." Luz swallowed.

"Go on."

"Only when I got there, I spotted Savage coming out."

Harmon Cash groaned. The exhalation went down his pipe stem and sent glimmery sparks rising from the fragrant bowl.

"I had a crash, and stole a car to get here." Luz indicated silent Dana O'Fall with his slightly plump chin. "That one happened to be in the back. I got away O.K. and called you."

Harmon Cash considered this. His swivelly, lizardlike eyes gravitated toward Dana O'Fall.

"Perhaps you might explain your role in this affair, my dear," he suggested smoothly.

"Take that question for a long walk," Dana O'Fall snapped, "and lose it."

The two guardian Harmon Cash minions seized the pretty detective by her fur-trimmed coat collar roughly.

"You might," Cash directed, "reconsider that reply."

"And you might reconsider the rest of your life, goofy eyes," Dana blazed. "Doc Savage knows of your interest in Cubama Sugar. If you ask me, he knows an awful lot about Cubama and its people. Including tall, dark, and smooth-as-poison there."

This last reference was to Eduardo Luz, who demanded, "What do you mean?"

Dana said, "When your man Blackie mentioned Luz to Doc Savage, he immediately knew the name. Knew you were Cubama's cashier without being told."

"Savage is on to us," Harmon Cash wailed. "Damn!"

"Wait a minute!" Eduardo Luz pressed. "How would Savage know about me and Cubama? It doesn't make sense."

"I told you," Cash repeated. "Savage is on to us."

"Something," Eduardo Luz said tightly, "is not adding up here. You're the bird who's cooking up a scheme to fleece that bronze devil, not me."

Harmon Cash removed his pipe from his mouth.

"I suppose," he sighed grimly, "now would be a good time to take you into my confidence."

"I'm all ears," Luz said, cautiously.

Cash looked to the pair guarding Dana O'Fall. "The back room," he suggested, "would be a better place for that two-faced snoop-for-hire."

Kicking and thrashing, Dana O'Fall was unceremoniously dragged into the rear, her stocking feet making twin trails in the sawdust. A heavy door slammed.

Harmon Cash addressed Eduardo Luz once more.

"Perhaps you have wondered about my knowledge of Cubama Sugar's fat coffers," he said.

Luz plucked at his dimpled chin. "It had crossed my mind—why?"

"It was your late friend, Sanchez y. Annuncio de Calabero, who brought Cubama to my attention," Harmon Cash revealed. "Sánchez had picked up certain rumors surrounding Cubama during his last days in Cuba—before he was so unceremoniously evicted from that pleasantly lazy little isle."

"I know he got in Dutch with the new government down there," Luz said carelessly. "So what?"

"So this. He got himself hired as Cubama's New York office manager. There, he made your acquaintance. And together, the two of you cooked up your little scheme to plunder Cubama's New York vault. But once you accomplished this clever feat, you discovered that disposing of hot bonds was not easily done. And knowing of my reputation in these matters, you came to me."

"If you're going somewhere I've never been with this," Eduardo Luz suggested, "you might shake the reins a little."

Harmon Cash's leonine features gathered into an indignant frown.

"Sanchez told me of the rumors he heard during his Cuban days," he continued stiffly. "As it so happens, I had contacts down there. I looked into this and learned a great deal."

"Yeah?"

"I learned that no less than Doc Savage is the angel behind Cubama Sugar's rising fortunes."

Eduardo Luz's jaw dropped a half foot.

"Savage owns Cubama!" he croaked, his swarthy features going as flat and washed-out as bone.

"Not only owns it," Harmon Cash went on, "but employs it as a front for the transfer of certain foreign gold reserves into negotiable bonds."

Luz's jaw dropped farther. His eyes bugged out in shock.

"You mean," he gulped, "those bonds we took—"

"Belong to Doc Savage himself," Harmon Cash finished.

Eduardo Luz took two steps backward, as if from a blow. He was breathing through his slack mouth, and it was coming hard. There was little warmth in the kerosene-lamp-lit speakeasy interior and his breath steamed. Great was the average crook's terror of the mighty bronze man. Eduardo Luz was no exception.

Then it dawned on him.

"Wait a minute!" he shouted. "What about that hullabaloo with Sigmund Holmes back at your office? What's his connection with Doc Savage?"

"Sigmund Holmes just happened to be in charge on Cubama's Havana mill," Harmon Cash supplied. "He came to the United States to look into those bonds you highjacked. I am astonished you did not know that."

"My line is cashier," Luz said defensively. "I reported to Sanchez. What went on in the Havana office didn't concern me."

"Well, it concerned me," Harmon Cash said coolly. "Now it concerns us all. Since Savage is after you as well as me, I see no avenue open to us except to split our ill-gotten gains and—ah—take it on the lam, as they say."

Luz compressed his too-pretty lips.

"You *did* bring the bonds?" Cash inquired coolly.

"I tried to," Luz said slowly. "On the way back to the city, I got the idea I was being followed, so I gave it up."

Harmon Cash started. "Followed? What makes you say that?"

"That roadster outside?"

"Yes?"

"I stole it. Turned out, it belonged to the bronze guy himself."

"My stars!" Harmon Cash gritted. "Why didn't you just lay a trail of radium paint behind you?" The suave mastermind turned to his minions. "Get the girl. We're making tracks. Savage could show up any minute."

"If I was being tailed, I shook them," Luz insisted.

"Savage is three-quarters magician," Harmon Cash retorted. "He is an inveterate inventor of the most infernal gadgets. Suppose he had that roadster fitted out with a radio transmitter, or some such contrivance?"

"What of it?"

"Radio transmitters can be located by other transmitters. It is called triangulation, or something like that."

"I don't—"

Just then two of Harmon Cash's minions returned from the back room, wearing crestfallen expressions.

"Chief!" one croaked. "The girl, she's gone!"

"Gone!" bleated Cash, his wandering eyes growing to the size of fried eggs. "What happened to Sid and Ike?"

"Out cold without a mark on 'em. And we can't wake 'em, either!"

Harmon Cash and Eduardo Luz exchanged glances.

"You fool!" Cash stormed. "You may have brought Doc Savage down on our heads!"

"Me!" Luz snarled back. "You're the guy who's chiseling Cubama on the side. Sanchez and I brought Cubama to you."

"You're one to talk. I have yet to see those bonds."

"I told you—Sanchez was laying low because he thought he was being watched," Luz protested hotly. "It must have been that lady dick."

Harmon Cash made a pretense of reaching into a coat pocket for his tobacco pouch. He came out with his tiny derringer instead.

"I think we had best settle this to my satisfaction," Cash related sharply.

"You don't fool me," Luz snapped back. "You haven't the moxie to pull that trigger."

"Do not be too sure of that," Harmon Cash said flatly. He waved to his two machine-gun-toting minions. "Gentlemen, relieve Mr. Luz of any weapons he may have about his person. And while you are at it, frisk him for other items. Such as negotiable bonds. And be quick about it—I have a feeling that Doc Savage is not far from here."

The gunmen started forward.

Just then, the front of the speakeasy caved inward, propelled by the sharp snout of a powerful sedan.

XIV

BLIND END

The heavy sedan swept the front door ahead of it, along with pieces of the adjoining walls, and lurched to a stop, engine racing, its long hood coated with splinters.

The sudden clamor paralyzed every man in the building for what seemed a very long interval of time, but actually encompassed scant seconds.

The speakeasy was obviously in worse repair than it had appeared from outside. No supporting timbers were struck. Yet, debris—principally dirt, caulking, and the dusty, gossamer tendrils of ancient cobwebs—began filtering down from the rafters almost at once. Then a rafter itself tore loose with a groan. It creaked loudly, hanging there like a precarious bludgeon.

That broke the momentary paralysis gripping the room.

"Cave-in!" Eduardo Luz shouted.

Harmon Cash's off-center orbs lifted. He spied the sagging timber. It let out a second groan and slid another foot. Dust poured down from chinks opening in the roof itself.

Cash pointed to the settling sedan, shouted, "Cover me, boys!"

On command, two of the gunmen trained their Tommy guns on the sedan. They hauled back on the firing levers.

Gory gun flame lipped from stuttering muzzles as they hosed lead against the sedan's windshield. The racket was unbelievable, deafening. The windshield glass whitened with myriad cracks. But the glass held, sagging inward perceptibly.

The gunmen redirected their fire. Bullets bounced off the hood, which shed paint chips but acquired no holes.

"Hell, this bus is bulletproof!" a gunman complained.

They paused in their firing. And just as quickly, resumed it.

For the driver had cranked one closed window up higher, revealing a shielded loophole built into the glass. The muzzle of a weapon resembling an oversized automatic shoved out in their direction. It cut loose. The sound was like a bullfiddle string plucked, and one gunman fell, alive but unconscious, with his weapon still chattering.

It chattered his head off his shoulders before the trigger finger finally relaxed in death.

Bracing himself, the remaining gunman continued his barrage. He was aiming at the small opening the loophole provided. Glass all around it turned white, threatening the loophole anchorage.

The sedan driver hastily withdrew his weapon, rolling down the window to defeat the gunman's murderous intent. He gave the engine gas. It lurched ahead, rolled toward the Tommy jockey.

The gunman faded back. He gave a quick glance over his shoulder, calling, "Boss! What do I do!"

In the rear room, Harmon Cash was shoving a beer keg aside. This evidently exposed an uncovered escape tunnel—few speakeasies lacked this simple precaution against the police raids—because the suave crook simply jumped down, and was lost to sight.

Eduardo Luz dived after him, followed by the remaining Harmon Cash underlings, who carried their mysteriously unconscious cohorts.

This was enough for the Tommy jockey. He swung about to give the crawling, inexorable sedan a last burst of leaden abuse before fleeing himself.

The machine gun refused to fire. Swearing, the gunman brought the weapon up and gave the heavy ammunition drum a hard spank. This apparently dislodged the jam.

He had neglected to ease back on the trigger, because the stubborn weapon obliged with a sudden spray of lead.

Bullets thudded into the damaged roof. They chewed the length of the sagging, groaning rafter. It let go.

The far end of the heavy beam struck the sedan roof with a colossal thud. Probably it only startled the driver into stopping. Certainly it had not damaged the machine. The roof was not even dented.

The near end, however, did do some significant injury.

This was the end that had been anchored to a crossbeam. The weight of the rafter had torn and twisted the stout wood fibres into a chewed ruin, finally pulling it free.

This was the end that struck down the remaining gunman.

He ended up on the floor with an obviously broken neck and what little life remained in him going away with each rapid shake of his limbs.

Emerging from the heavy sedan, a short, angry figure plunged into the next room, clutching his oversized automatic, and giving vent to a bellowing war cry.

In the dark, he collided with another figure.

The bullfiddle roar came again. Another, similar extended note joined in. Muzzle flashes made peppery lights. Enough to be seen by.

"You hairy gossoon!" a refined voice snarled.

"You walking writ of hocus-pocus!" came the squeaky-voiced reply.

A flashlight sprang into life, and Monk Mayfair and Ham Brooks found themselves glaring across its dusty beam.

"You were supposed to wait for my signal!" Ham howled wrathfully. "Not charge in like a bull ape!"

"I couldn't help it," Monk retorted. "The sedan got away from me."

"Nonsense. You just wanted to hog all the action for yourself."

"Where's Doc?" Monk asked suddenly, looking around.

"Getting that Dana to safety, of course. But never mind that. Where is this Eduardo Luz person?"

"I think he went down a hole in the floor. Spray that flash around, shyster."

Ham obliged. The light hunted around, finally coming to rest on a round hole in the sawdust-covered floorboards.

"They went down there," Monk pointed out.

"After all that showing off, you let them get away?" Ham accused.

"Not all. There's a couple of dead ones back by the sedan."

Ham's prim mouth thinned. "Doc will not enjoy hearing about that," he warned.

"Couldn't be helped," Monk vowed, innocent-voiced. "They shot themselves up. I had nothin' to do with it."

"Just as you are not responsible for letting the rest of our quarry escape. Well, come on," the dapper lawyer said, waving his flashlight for Monk to enter the escape tunnel.

Monk was a cautious soul. No jumping into dark holes for him. He first pointed his oversized automatic— it was a supermachine pistol, invented by Doc Savage and capable of an enormous rate of fire—and hosed shells into the hole as a precaution. The shells were of the type called "mercy bullets," being hollow and filled with a quick-acting potion that brought unconsciousness.

The bullfiddle moan came again. Empty cartridges spewed from the ejector mechanism like a solid brass wire.

When Monk eased off the trigger, he heard no cries of any kind, so he jumped feet-first down the hole. Ham clambered after him, taking pains not to injure his immaculate evening dress.

Once below, Ham took the lead, using the flash.

"See anything?" Monk breathed.

"Yes," Ham hissed back. "About a mile of tunnel."

They picked their way along it. The walls were packed dirt. Here and there, ground roots poked through like petrified veins.

"That was a fool stunt you pulled," Ham muttered as they inched forward. "What were you trying to do, impress Dana O'Fall?"

"Did Doc get her out okay?"

"Would I have given you the signal to get ready if he hadn't, simplewits?" Ham said acidly.

Monk said nothing.

"I saw it all," Ham went on. "Doc slipped in the back way, and came out with Dana. He was taking her back to the truck when I signaled."

The tunnel petered out just ahead. Ham's flash showed a blank wall. They stood around, looking for some sign of egress.

"Suppose we missed a turn along the way?" Monk wondered in his small voice.

"Impossible!" Ham snapped. "Ah," he added. He steadied his light on a network of stout roots that virtually covered one section of wall. The light picked out exposed bits of fresh wood where the dirty outer root bark had been scraped away.

"A natural ladder," Monk offered, craning his bullet-shaped head upward.

"Follow your instincts," Ham suggested.

"Huh?"

"Climb, monkey, climb."

Monk glowered at the dapper lawyer. But he clambered up the root network. It took his weight handily. He shouldered the ceiling roof up by main strength. It gave like a trapdoor.

Monk poked his nubbin head into the fresh air above.

"Ye-o-ow!" he squawled.

"What is it?" Ham called anxiously, maneuvering around to get a clear shot past the hairy chemist. He had drawn a supermachine pistol of his own from a padded underarm holster.

"Doc beat us to the punch, looks like."

"Is that all?" Ham complained loudly. "You had me scared half to death." Which, if anything, revealed the true feelings these two adventurers had for one another. For despite their perpetual squabbling, either man would have cheerfully laid down his life for the other.

They emerged from the tunnel into the salmon-pink light of dawn.

As Monk Mayfair had indicated, Doc Savage was there.

The bronze man was on one knee, attempting to read sign.

"I heard a car start," Doc informed them, "and rushed to this spot. But our quarry had already departed."

"The place was an old speakeasy," Monk supplied.

Doc straightened. His metallic expression was grim.

"Did you take any prisoners?" he asked Monk and Ham.

"None of any disposition to talk," Monk said awkwardly.

Doc's golden eyes fixed on the hairy chemist.

Monk swung careless, overlong arms like a baseball pitcher limbering up before a game. His unlovely features were sheepish.

"What this overeager ape is trying to say, Doc," Ham broke in, "is that he got carried away and murdered a few people."

"I did not!" Monk said indignantly.

"Monk!" Doc's voice was grim. It was the bronze man's policy never to take human life if it could possibly be avoided—an injunction the apish chemist had, on more than one occasion in the past, violated.

"Honest, Doc," Monk squeaked in a plaintive voice, "I didn't do nothin' like that. After I busted in, a couple of them went crazy. One shot himself. The other guy stared blowin' holes in the sky and brought the roof down on himself. I was an innocent bystander."

"Men have been hung for murder on flimsier evidence," Ham scoffed.

Monk spun on the dapper lawyer, growling, "You stay out of this, shyster!"

"The car our quarry escaped in," Doc said, "was not one of our machines, so we have no hope of tracing it by radio triangulation. Let us see what the hideout tells us."

They trudged back to the partially demolished speakeasy. On the way, Doc collected Dana O'Fall from the back of the egg delivery truck, where he had locked her. It was the same conveyance that Eduardo Luz had—correctly, as it turned out—suspected of following him.

Monk had been driving the sedan, and Ham had been behind the wheel of the coupe that had ended up in a snowbank after Luz had forced it off the road. By this maneuvering, they had managed to keep the roadster—which carried a constantly operating battery-powered radio transmitter bolted to the chassis—in sight at all times.

Doc unlocked the rear of the truck, saying, "You may come out now."

Dana O'Fall's voice caroled out, not unmusically.

"Not," she said stiffly, "until someone finds my shoes."

"I say that's excuse enough to keep her out of our hair, Doc," Ham Brooks offered.

The bronze man evidently agreed, because he relocked the truck without another word.

They returned to the demolished speakeasy, where Doc Savage made a quick inspection of the dead Harmon Cash underlings. It took but a moment for him to ascertain that the hairy chemist's protestations had been truthful. Both crooks had succumbed to the misfortunes of combat.

"See?" Monk squeaked. "Not my fault."

"If you had waited for the attack signal," Ham interjected, "we might have at least one talking prisoner, and some idea of where Long Tom is."

"Another country heard from," Monk returned glumly.

Doc Savage offered no comment. He was moving about the speakeasy, which was filling with dawn. His examination was brief, and included pointing a black box—much like an old-fashioned magic lantern, with a lense that was nearly black—at every uncovered wall and floor surface. No light seemed to shine from this contrivance, and no result was gained. He switched it off.

The bronze man returned to the quarreling pair with a palpable air of disappointment.

"The ultra-violet light didn't pick up any messages Long Tom mighta left behind?" Monk inquired worriedly.

Monk was referring to a trick they often employed— that of leaving messages written with a chalk that left no visible marks, but which fluoresced eerily under application of the ultra-violet light projector Doc carried.

"It is obvious to me," Doc said, "that this place was an emergency hideout, and not used for several months before to-night."

"The trail is cold then, Doc?" Ham asked, worrying his ever-present sword cane in his hands.

"There is still the girl, Dana O'Fall," Doc pointed out. "Her story has yet to be heard."

"She's a tough nut," Monk warned.

"Then we will employ a nutcracker capable of penetrating her shell," the bronze man said grimly, abruptly quitting the ruined building through the gaping hole Monk had created.

Monk and Ham exchanged worried glances.

"Wonder what Doc's got in mind," Monk muttered.

"I don't know," Ham returned, "but I think Dana O'Fall better change her tune quick."

They followed the bronze man out into the breaking dawn.

XV

SCHEMERS FALL OUT

Harmon Cash did not reduce speed to under seventy until the gleaming forest of spires that was New York City appeared in his auto windshield.

It had been an unpleasant drive. Fear of Doc Savage had trailed after the fleeing machine like a ragged spook. And Harmon Cash's driving left much to be desired. Several times he had nearly lost control negotiating sharp corners, only to pull out at the last possible instant. Once, he had nearly driven into the back of a stalled bus, having evidently misjudged its distance.

Eduardo Luz, clutching a strap in the rear, suspected that the suave criminal mastermind's eye condition contributed to his difficulty in navigating the machine. He had said nothing, fear of the bronze man having stilled his tongue.

Finally, he recovered his nerve enough to speak.

"I've been thinking," he ventured.

"If you have an idea about how to make Doc Savage disappear," Harmon Cash said levelly, "be good enough to share it with me."

"It's not Doc Savage who's going to disappear," Luz muttered, stubbing a cigarette out in the door ashtray. Instead of leaving it in the pan, he carefully pocketed it. "It's me."

"That is probably a wise idea," Harmon Cash said, noting the other's pack-rat idiosyncracy. "I am thinking along those lines myself."

"Yeah? What about this Cubama scheme you have cooking?"

Harmon Cash shook his leonine head sadly. "I think Cubama is out, unfortunately. Savage knows—or suspects—something, thanks to that loose-mouthed Blackie. We're too hot now."

"Too bad," Eduardo Luz suggested. "It sounded like there was money to be had."

"There is—for the man brave enough to take on Savage."

Luz wondered, "Are you saying you're backing down?"

"What do you think?"

"What I mean," Eduardo Luz said casually, "is if one of us decided to follow up on the Cubama angle after this cooled down, who's got squatter's rights?"

Harmon Cash considered this a moment.

"My thoughts on this brisk morning," he said at last, "are on survival. And those Cubama bonds, which I gather are not currently on your person."

"You gather right," Luz returned. "They are not. But you haven't answered my question."

"What gives you the right to preempt me on Cubama, assuming I go through with my plans?" Harmon Cash demanded.

"Because I brought Cubama to you in the first place. If it wasn't for you holding out on me and Sanchez, I wouldn't have Savage after me."

Harmon Cash shifted his unlit pipe between clenched teeth.

"Not exactly," he said. "Savage appears to be after you, not me. For all I know, he has no solid inkling of my interest in Cubama. His concern is for the bonds already stolen, not further theft. That particular felony can be laid squarely at your doorstep, not mine."

"Until and unless you take your share of the bonds," Eduardo Luz noted.

Harmon Cash permitted a tight smile to wreathe his face.

"Ah, now we come to the crux of the matter," he

murmured. "Are you perhaps suggesting that I refrain from taking my cut?"

"Your cut," Luz retorted, "comes after you fence the bonds. Maybe I'll just hold on to them for a while."

"I do not think I like that idea. It smacks of welshing."

"And I don't like the way mugs who hook up with you end up dead," Luz retorted hotly.

"How do you mean?"

"Take Nug Hassel. He did a bank job for you. Gets himself pinched. The next thing, he keels over, blind and dead."

"The Blind Death has been claiming lives rather indiscriminately all over the city," Harmon Cash offered.

"Then Sanchez gets it the same way."

"Might I remind you," Harmon Cash interjected smoothly, "that you were the last to see Sanchez alive?"

Eduardo Luz rubbed his slightly fattish jaw thoughtfully.

"I still haven't figured that out," he muttered slowly. "When I left him, he was fine."

"Assuming you did leave him when you say," Harmon Cash said meaningly.

The remaining Harmon Cash minions—which included the two who had been borne off insensate and were only now rousing to wakefulness—had been taking in this tense exchange wrapped in stony silence. Now, worry crowded their hard faces.

They looked to white-coated Eduardo Luz as if suddenly in the presence of a tarantula unwrapped from innocent muslin.

"I left him," Eduardo Luz repeated firmly. "And then Babe and Snig got theirs."

"As I recall," Harmon Cash said, pulling over to the side of the road and turning around to fix Luz with his disorganized optics, "you were downstairs when they perished, ostensibly standing guard."

"Are you saying that I'm White Eyes?" Eduardo Luz gritted.

"Are you suggesting that White Eyes is myself?" Harmon Cash inquired solicitously.

"Seems to me," Luz retorted, "the more of your mob who kick the bucket, the bigger your share."

"Just as the untimely demise of your friend, Sanchez, assures you of a larger cut of your ill-gotten loot," Cash pointed out. "Welsher."

This conversation was not conducive to soothing ruffled nerves, as the faces of Harmon Cash's remaining gunmen proved. They were crawling with sweat, their eyes jumping back and forth between their suave leader and vapidly handsome Eduardo Luz.

"If I am White Eyes," Luz said suddenly, "then everyone in this automobile is in mortal peril." His intensely black eyes glittered with menace.

The Harmon Cash underling seated beside Luz abruptly shoved closer to the door, away from the white-coated crook. One hand rested on the door handle. His body tensed.

Harmon Cash took all this in without seeming to.

"Are you admitting to your identity?" he inquired softly.

"What I'm saying is that I'm through with you and I don't plan on using your services to fence those bonds," Eduardo Luz said flatly. "What do you say about that?"

"I say—" Harmon Cash began, then seeing Luz's hand go to his door handle, he exclaimed, *"Stop him!"*

Eduardo Luz flung himself out of the car. He ducked his lithe, white-clad body and began to run.

"Don't just sit there," Harmon Cash shouted at his petrified underlings. "He's getting away!"

"No thanks," one man in the back seat said. "I like my eyes the color they are."

"Me, too," the other rejoined. "Doc Savage is one thing, but White Eyes is poison."

Both men remained seated.

Savagely, Harmon Cash dug out the tiny chamois dust case that contained his derringer. Then, he suddenly recalled that he had neglected to reload it since last discharging the flat little weapon. There was no time for such a time-consuming nicety.

"A gun! One of you give me a gun!" he sputtered, turning.

A long-barreled revolver was slapped into his hands. Cash took it and jumped from the car. Laying the barrel atop the auto's roof, he drew a bead on Eduardo Luz's fleeing figure.

Swarthy Luz was running across an open meadow, which was like a glittering expanse of powdered sugar. His white attire blended perfectly with the landscape.

Nevertheless, Harmon Cash worked his eyes around until he had the fleeing crook squarely in his gun sight.

He pulled the trigger once. Twice. Nothing happened. Not even a click.

Then the opportunity was lost as Eduardo Luz disappeared over a hump of snow.

Giving vent to several genteel curses, Harmon Cash bounced back into his seat.

"Couldn't do it, huh, boss?" a gunman asked.

"Do not be ridiculous!" Harmon Cash exploded. "I was unable to find the safety latch."

He threw the useless pistol onto the floorboards with a bitter gesture and got the car under way.

"A fine lot of hardcases you boys turned out to be!" he complained.

"Hell, boss. What could we do? You heard the guy. He practically admitted to being White Eyes."

"Bosh!" snapped Harmon Cash. "Eduardo Luz is no more White Eyes than am I!"

Every man in the careening auto noticed that their chief's voice held a note of doubt that belied the vehemence of his words.

XVI

THE HOT SEAT

Dana O'Fall did not much like the manner in which events were proceeding.

First, Doc Savage had rescued her from the clutches of Harmon Cash. It had happened with breath-stealing speed. One moment she was seated in the semidarkness and the next, her guards were falling to the floor about her, asleep.

The first simply keeled over. Dana had a bad moment thinking that it was another attack of the Blind Death. But this man simply stretched out on the floor and no longer moved.

Dana swung her head around then. It was just in time to see a human tower of bronze emerge from the shadows to seize the remaining gunman by the back of the neck. Corded bronze fingers performed some arcane manipulation and that man, too, went down on the floor, overcome by Doc Savage's strong hands.

Dana had not been bound. She stood up.

"Mr. Savage!" she breathed.

The bronze man wasted no time. He scooped her up in his cabled arms and bore her to a rear door, and out to a waiting egg delivery truck.

As he moved, his stealth that of an Indian, he made a sound not unlike a whippoorwill calling. Dana realized it was a signal of some sort.

A moment later, there came the din of an automobile engine howling in acceleration and, in a twinkling, the speakeasy seemed to cave in.

Dana was unceremoniously placed in the back of

131

the truck, and the door slammed. That was the last she saw of any one until Doc and his men returned, and she hotly demanded her shoes. The footgear sailed in a few minutes later, and she was again locked in amid a profusion of empty egg crates.

That had been over an hour ago.

Since then, they had done quite a bit of traveling. Not until they had reached Manhattan—unmistakable traffic sounds suggested the big metropolis to her keen ears—was she removed from the dark back of the truck, finally.

Ham Brooks performed the honor, assisting her to her newly shod feet.

"Where am I?" she asked, blinking at the blinding light.

The sedan and stolen roadster stood nearby, Doc Savage and Monk Mayfair emerging from their respective machines. Dana recognized a familiar sub-basement garage.

They had returned to Doc Savage headquarters.

"Oh," Dana O'Fall said disappointedly. "I guess this is where I get the third degree."

The remark was intended as a species of hard-boiled bravado, but the grim faces of the three men made Dana swallow her game smile.

They escorted her to Doc's high-speed elevator in ominous silence.

"You can't hold me forever, you know," Dana pointed out in an edgy tone.

"Miss O'Fall," Ham Brooks offered, "you must realize how serious we are about getting to the bottom of this affair."

"Yeah," Monk added. "This is where you come clean—or else!"

Dana could think of no retort that did justice to that sobering declaration, so she settled for swallowing several times, as the cage shot upward at high speed.

She found herself escorted through Doc's reception room and shelf-crammed library, finally to the huge experimental laboratory that occupied most the eighty-sixth floor.

"We'll be outside," Ham said soberly.

"Where we can't hear the awful sounds," Monk added.

They took their leave, bestowing mournfully sympathetic looks upon the pretty private investigator.

The door closed. Doc Savage immediately busied himself extracting an array of strange devices from a storage closet.

The bronze man appeared preoccupied with his work, so Dana made a stab at the door. It refused to budge.

"Escape is a waste of time," Doc Savage said absently, still digging out equipment, "but you are welcome to try."

The bronze man's assured tone was such that Dana instantly put all thought of escape from her mind. Instead, she hunted for a comfortable chair, selecting a simple wooden stool.

"The big oaken chair would be preferable," Doc suggested, without turning.

Dana's eyes raked the room, coming to rest on a squat affair of rude wood hung with broad leather straps in one corner.

"No, thank you," she said frostily. "It reminds me of an electric chair."

"That," Doc said, coming back with armfuls of electrical equipment, "is exactly what it is."

Dana O'Fall jumped a foot.

"And you expect me to sit in it!" she exclaimed.

"If you do not mind," the bronze man stated, laying a stack of battery boxes beside the medieval-looking chair. He returned to the closet, coming back with a pair of large cases. These were festooned with calibrated dials and minute inspection ports, which gleamed with myriad vacuum tubes.

Doc Savage straightened, noted Dana O'Fall still standing, white-faced, her violet eyes a little sick.

"You—" she began. Dana swallowed, tried again.

"You're not, I mean—Say, don't I get a trial by jury first?"

"No," said Doc Savage, one arm drifting up to take Dana O'Fall by the neck. His metallic fingers might have been cast of cold forged bronze. They dug in.

Dana screamed. The sound she emitted was barely a mouse squeak, it was choked off so quickly. She felt her muscles go stiff, and powerless. She allowed the bronze man—she had no choice really—to guide her to the heavy oaken seat.

As a grim-faced Doc Savage strapped her wrists and ankles to the arm rests and chair legs, Dana O'Fall experienced a glimmer of understanding of what had befallen her guards back at the Jersey speakeasy.

In an inflectionless voice that chilled her blood, the bronze man began explaining the scientific principals behind the hideous equipment he was assembling.

"Science has known for some time that the human organism generates tiny electrical currents," Doc was saying, as he adjusted a wrist strap. It was wide and heavy.

"The brain is one source—transmitter is not too strong a term for it—of these weak currents," Doc added. "Sensitive galvanometers have been known to register the presence of human-generated electrical power in minuscule voltages."

Dana remembered that penitentiary electric chairs performed their grisly work, in part, by disrupting the electrical regulators of the human body. She wanted to scream, but the spell Doc Savage had wrought over her left her powerless to speak.

Doc Savage withdrew. He came back a moment later, saying, "The exact nature of these electrical emanations is unknown."

Unable to even turn her head, Dana caught a blood-freezing glimpse of a bulky helmet of an affair that was not much more than a cage of wires and glass tubes.

This was lowered onto her head. The device was

heavy. It crushed Dana's lustrous chestnut curls to her scalp.

Doc was saying, "I acquired this contrivance some months ago, during the course of an adventure."* He stepped back, inserting an insulated connector cable that trailed from the helmet into one box. "The headset you are wearing might be termed a sender," Doc explained.

Then, to Dana O'Fall's utter astonishment—because she next expected Doc Savage to pull a knife-blade electrical contact switch, shocking her into oblivion— the bronze man placed a similar helmet on his own head. This one virtually covered his skull, much like a fencer's mesh face guard.

He threw switches on the main box. Nothing appeared to happen. There was no sound of voltage, no weird corona of electrical display. For a moment, Dana wondered if the complicated contrivance was not correctly assembled.

Then, Doc Savage spoke. "Cast your mind back to your encounter with Sanchez y. Annuncio de Calabero," he requested.

Although she could not imagine what Doc Savage had up his sleeve, Dana O'Fall strove mightily not to think back on Sanchez's death.

"Were you present when the Blind Death struck him?" Doc pressed.

The human mind is very susceptible to suggestion. Warn a person not to think of a specific image—a purple cow, for example—and invariably the imagination will conjure up an appropriately lavender bovine. Dana O'Fall was not immune to this quirk of human psychology.

The memories came back then. Dana saw in her mind's eye the figures of Sanchez, perspiring in his heavy mohair coat, and Eduardo Luz, attired in white linen, as she lay helpless, bound on the floor of Sanchez's hideout.

----
*The Midas Man

Luz was returning from his phone call. As he turned on a console radio to cover the sound of impending mayhem, he informed Sanchez to give her the works. Then he departed.

Dana O'Fall considered herself hard-boiled. But the returning memory of Sanchez coming after her with a pistol made her squirm mentally.

Doc Savage's voice intruded upon this recollection with a question that, had she been able to move a muscle, would have propelled Dana O'Fall out of the electric chair as if jolted by agonizing juice.

"The individual in the tropical suit," Doc inquired calmly. "That is Eduardo Luz?"

Dana could not answer, naturally. But a moment later, Doc Savage's helmeted head was nodding as if she had. Dana's eyes registered her frozen start.

Then Doc said, "Yes, I am reading your mind. The theory behind this device is quite simple. Electrical brain waves are thought carriers of a sort. I am merely receiving yours through this helmet."

Dana thought a question.

Despite what was happening, she was still startled when the bronze man replied, "The reason I am employing this device upon you and did not on Blackie, is that I was quickly convinced that he was speaking the truth. I am less certain of you. Further, this device is not, strictly speaking, a perfect mind reader. It receives mental images after a fashion. This includes figments of the imagination, without regard to their truthfulness."

Dana tried to make her mind a blank.

"The human brain," Doc admonished, "cannot sustain such a nonthinking state as you have created for very long. This will be over soon if you allow your memories to flow. Now, did you witness Sanchez succumb to the Blind Death?"

Dana attempted further resistance, but the bronze man repeated the question several times, in different variations. Before long, memories of Sanchez y. Annuncio de Calabero in his death agonies came flooding back.

Sanchez had the novelty pistol that was mostly

barrel. Then, he dropped it, as his perspiring brow became a flood. He looked hot, very hot. He pawed at his eyes, which blinked rapidly. He stormed around the room, Dana forgotten.

The speed at which his eyes turned crimson where they had been white and white where they had hitherto been composed of pupil and iris was appalling.

It seemed that one moment, he was twisting around on his feet, complaining of intolerable heat, and the next his eyes were blind pearls of death.

Sanchez y. Annuncio de Calabero shuddered on his feet and at once collapsed.

Dana remembered inching for the pistol and, after some maneuverings, shooting a framed picture off one wall. The glass shards that resulted had proved effective against her bonds.

Stubbornly, she made her mind a blank once more.

"Please continue," Doc pressed.

In her mind's eye, Dana recalled evacuating the room in such haste she forgot to retrieve her purse. Anything to get away from the awful power that had overtaken Sanchez. She made a point of thinking that thought by way of explanation for her forgetfulness.

Doc Savage told her, "I have your purse, and it will be returned to you in due course."

Dana transmitted her surprise. She could not get used to having her mind laid bare like this—and not be able to complain about it.

"Harmon Cash," Doc prompted. "I would like to see what he looks like, please."

Continuing her contrariness, Dana resisted. Again, to no avail. Wall-eyed Harmon Cash paraded around in her brain and quiet satisfaction came into the bronze man's metallic voice.

"One last question," Doc said.

Dana knew what was coming and prepared herself. If she had the power to do so, she would have squeezed her violet eyes in concentration.

"Who are you really working for?" Doc asked.

Dana knew she could not keep this information

from the bronze man's mind-reading machine for long, so she took another tack, harking her memory back to the last time she had taken in a movie. It had been a romantic comedy, and the main actor—he was known to all fan magazine readers—had struck her fancy.

She imagined herself in the movie, accepting a kiss from the movie idol. In her imaginings, it was quite a kiss. Dana made the next one even more passionate.

Doc Savage abruptly colored uncomfortably. His bronze hands removed his helmet with alacrity. With a thumb, he snapped off various switches, cutting juice to the mind reader.

If Dana O'Fall had the power to smile, she would have grinned from ear to ear. She had defeated the bronze man at his own game, had actually embarrassed him into quitting his mental probings.

In silence, Doc began repacking his mental machine. The helmet of wires and tubes came off Dana's head at the end. Bronze fingers undid the chair straps and finally, they went to work on her spine.

Dana felt mobility return to her limbs. She jumped to her feet.

"That was a dirty rotten trick you pulled!" she flared. "Making me think you were going to fry me in this phony hot seat. There are laws against torturing people, you know!"

"You were not tortured," Doc pointed out quietly.

"And that—that brain eavesdropper contraption!" she added. "If there isn't a law against invading a person's mind, there ought to be!"

Doc said nothing. The mind reader had proven, once again, to be less than reliable. It was unlikely, he realized, that it would ever become a useful tool in his work. Yet it was too dangerous to keep around. Doc decided that it would best be stored in his Fortress of Solitude, along with other such inventions as had fallen into his hands for which the world was not yet ready.

Going to a wall annunciator, he spoke to Monk and Ham, still waiting in the reception room.

"We are done in here," he said.

Monk and Ham appeared presently.

Both feigned profound surprise that Dana O'Fall was still among the living.

"Doc must be slipping," Monk clucked.

"I assume this female has been separated of all her secrets," Ham inquired of the bronze man.

"There remain a few to be extracted," Doc said unhappily. "But we do have something to go on."

"You do?" Dana asked in surprise.

"It would repay effort," Doc Savage announced, "if we were to investigate the apartment where Sanchez y. Annuncio de Calabero met his end."

"But what are we gonna find there?" Monk squeaked.

"Perhaps," Doc said, eying Dana O'Fall steadily, "the secret of the Blind Death."

XVII

DEAD AND GUILTY

There was only one uniformed policeman stationed at the unsavory hole of an apartment where Sanchez y Annuncio de Calabero met his grisly demise. When Doc Savage appeared on the scene, he practically saluted the bronze man.

Doc asked, "Has anything been removed from this room?"

"Only the departed victim," the policeman returned smartly. "A detective is supposed to give this dump the once-over later on."

Doc nodded. "I would like to examine the room for clues."

The policeman did not have to think twice. He knew of Doc's high standing with the police department. He said, "Go right ahead, Mr. Savage."

Doc Savage made a careful circuit of the room, noting the shabby furnishings, the state of disrepair that included cracked paint and peeling, ancient wall paper. Someone had swept into a corner the pile of severed ropes that had bound Dana O'Fall and the broken wall portrait she had made use of in freeing herself.

Monk Mayfair and Ham Brooks were off to one side, watching with interest. Pretty Dana O'Fall, looking very lost, stood between them. As if contemplating flight, her violet eyes went to the door often, but that was where the policeman had happened to station himself.

After subjecting virtually every inch of the room to the scrutiny of his flake-gold eyes, Doc Savage abruptly concentrated on the big console radio standing in one corner.

It seemed to be an ordinary set, not new. Doc took hold of it by its molded frame, upended it slightly, as if testing its weight. The radio moved easily in his hands, which meant very little. The bronze man possessed incalculable strength, the result of a two-hour routine of exercises which he undertook every day, and had since he had been placed in the hands of a succession of experts when a child.

Doc returned the radio to its base. He noted that the knobs were in the off position, the dial indicator tuned to a local station. Stooping, he removed the electrical plug from the wallboard plate.

Then Doc Savage turned the radio around with his strong hands until he was looking at the back. Removing a folding knife from his carryall gadget vest, Doc attacked the screws holding a ventilator grille to the back of the radio.

The grille came away in his hands and his powerful spring-generated flashlight came out. It licked out a ray of light. Doc washed the interior with it, picking out individual vacuum tubes, capacitors, and resistor coils. He was at this several minutes, his metallic features intent.

Finally, he straightened.

"Whatcha find, Doc?" squeaky-voiced Monk asked hopefully.

Doc did not reply. Instead, he turned to the policeman.

"In whose name is this apartment rented?" Doc asked.

"Sanchez, the dead guy," the cop replied.

"Sanchez y. Annuncio de Calabero," Doc Savage said aloud to no one in particular, "held a high position with the Cubama Sugar Importing Company. This could not possibly be his main place of residence."

"It's not," the cop returned helpfully. "I hear he's got an apartment over on Sutton Place. Swanky digs, too. The detectives already went through it."

"Find anything?"

"Not that I heard," the cop stated.

Doc directed his next question to Dana O'Fall.

"Do you remember if this is the same radio that was here when Sanchez perished?"

"Why ask me?" Dana O'Fall said snappishly. "You saw the whole thing yourself, remember?"

This information appeared to startle the police sentry not a little. But he did not challenge it. All of Manhattan's finest were under orders to cooperate with the bronze man in every way.

And that was that. Thanking the officer, the bronze man took his leave, the others in tow.

As they piled into Doc's roadster, Ham Brooks broke the silence.

"That radio, Doc," he said as the automobile eased into traffic. "What was it?"

"An ordinary radio," Doc said. He sounded very disappointed about his discovery—or lack of one. He sent the roadster out into traffic.

"Where to next?" Monk piped up, ever the optimist.

Doc was silent a moment, as if thinking.

"Seven persons have so far fallen victim to the so-called Blind Death," Doc said quietly. "Two, known as Babe and Snig, were working for Harmon Cash. A third, Sanchez, was an associate of both Cash and Eduardo Luz, and a Cubama employee. But the others were a mixture of known criminals and honorable businessmen."

"That's the part that's got me buffaloed," Monk admitted. "What's this White Eyes bird after?"

"Why don't we ask her?" Ham put in.

"Her?" Monk exclaimed, small eyes starting from his head.

Ham Brooks used his sheathed cane to indicate silent Dana O'Fall, sitting up front beside Doc Savage.

"I am referring to our mysterious female prevaricator here," he said smugly.

"I resent that!" Dana said, turning around to glare at the dapper lawyer. "You have nothing on me!"

"She's right," said Monk, who made a policy of never agreeing with the sartorially perfect lawyer, even when they actually saw eye to eye. "Where's your proof, ambulance chaser?"

"Quite simply this," Ham said crisply. "She claims to be an employee of Sigmund Holmes, which she most assuredly is not. Ergo, she is lying. Further, Doc discovered her lurking in the vicinity where the Blind Death last struck. If that does not make her the chief suspect, I will eat my best hat."

"How do you know I didn't work for Mr. Holmes?" Dana flared. "Did you check the employee records?"

"If we did," Ham shot back, "would we find your name?"

Dana swallowed. "No," she admitted glumly. "I used an assumed name. Penelope Fret."

Ham made a scoffing noise deep in his throat.

"I'd still like to know how you characters know so much about Cubama," Dana muttered, scrutinizing Doc's metallic profile.

Mention of the Cubama Sugar Importing Company seemed to remind Monk Mayfair of something.

"Say, Doc, the way this is goin', don't you think we should ring in Renny and Johnny? Maybe have them work some other angles? With Long Tom missin', we're spread pretty thin as it is."

"No," Doc replied. "They are engaged in demanding work at present. It would be better to leave them to it."

The pair mentioned were the remaining members of Doc's little band. Renny was Colonel John Renwick, one of the world's foremost civil engineers. Johnny was better known as William Harper Littlejohn, the renowned archæologist and geologist. They were currently pursuing their respective professions in different European capitals.

"I guess that means more action for us, then," Monk said cheerfully.

Ham noticed they were tooling through the sector of lower Manhattan dominated by Wall Street and its imposing houses of finance.

Before the dapper lawyer could remark on this, Doc slid the roadster into a parking slot in front of a squat tower of granite with the name "Rock of Ages Mutual Insurance Corporation" chipped out of the stone lintel over the brass-trimmed entrance way.

"Say, isn't this where—?" Ham began.

"Yes," Doc said, shutting off the motor. "This is where C. Perley Swain was found dead."

Doc got out, the others following him through a revolving door that went *whisk-whisk-whisk* as they pushed into the spacious, many-columned lobby.

"Who's C. Perley Swain?" Dana O'Fall wondered aloud.

"The third guy," Monk offered, "that the Blind Death got."

"Oh," said Dana in a small voice.

The office of the president of the Rock of Ages Mutual Insurance Corporation was on the fifth floor. The name on the door said: RANDOLPH PACKER. It was fresh. Randolph Packer had been appointed president of Rock of Ages by a unanimous vote of the staid firm's board of directors, replacing the late C. Perley Swain, who had been found seated before his desk with his august face pressed into the ink blotter.

When the company doctor had lifted his head, the corpse's jaw had dropped open to reveal a cavern of blood and a pair of eyes that might have been glazed confections. In his death throes, C. Perley Swain had bitten his tongue nearly in two.

When the receptionist announced the arrival of Doc Savage, Randolph Packer came out of his office like a cannonball. He practically wrung his hands together.

"Mr. Savage!" he exclaimed. "I am very surprised, although pleased, to see you again. But I expected the police."

"Police?" Doc asked.

"They have just been called. We are beside ourselves here. First, poor Mr. Swain, and now this!"

"Blazes," Monk croaked. "Not another blind one!"

Randolph Packer looked aghast. "No, not at all," he said, giving his hands another vigorous wring. "I have just this minute come from the company vault. As you know, Rock of Ages retains a large quantity of securities and other negotiables as investments."

"I do not think I like the sound of this," Ham said unhappily.

"Go on," Doc urged.

"The bonds," Randolph Packer groaned, "have just been discovered to be counterfeit!"

Doc Savage was escorted to the Rock of Ages vault. It was a massive affair, fully as large as that of a commercial bank. Randolph Packer personally spun the dial. Tumblers clicked. He gave the spoked wheel a nervous twirl, and the big steel door rolled open like a shiny mausoleum.

Doc stepped in. His golden eyes glanced over neat stacks of securities piled on stainless-steel shelving. Pausing, he took up a sheaf of bonds. They were Liberty bonds. Examining the top sheet briefly, he riffled through the stack.

"They look O.K. to me," said Monk, who was peering over Doc's shoulder.

"Let me see," Ham said, shoving forward.

"These bonds are clearly counterfeit," Doc Savage pronounced. "Although it would take an expert eye to verify this as fact."

Turning to Randolph Packer, he asked, "Who had access to this vault?"

"Only myself," Randolph Packer moaned unhappily. "These bonds were certified authentic before they were placed in our vault. They must have been switched at some point, but I did not do it. How will I convince the board? I shall be fired."

"And before you?" Doc pressed.

"Before—" Randolph Packer's teary eyes narrowed,

then exploded in shock. A startling thought had occurred to him.

"My word!" he whispered in a strange voice. "The only other possible culprit would be poor C. Perley."

This was the theory the police heard when they showed up not long after. Everyone had gathered in the office of Randolph Packer—the former office of the late but no-longer-lamented president of Rock of Ages, C. Perley Swain.

While the police were taking statements from everyone, Doc Savage went about the office. He had been here before, when he had first looked into the mysterious death of C. Perley Swain. Strange occurrences like the Blind Death invariably interested the bronze man.

The first time he had been here, Doc had found nothing untoward. This time, however, he showed definite interest in a modest radio reposing on a typewriter stand.

The modern businessman has more and more gotten into the habit of stationing broadcast radios in his office, not for entertainment purposes, but to keep tabs on hourly financial and news broadcasts. So there was nothing unusual about the radio being here, per se.

Doc lifted the radio. It was not heavy. Nor was it, he recalled, the same model that he remembered from his previous visit.

Randolph Packer was saying, "I do not mean to besmirch the good name—the formerly good name—of my late colleague, Mr. Swain, but there simply is no other possible explanation. Only the company president is permitted to open the vault. And I take oath that I did not tamper with those bonds."

"This is not C. Perley Swain's office radio," Doc announced suddenly.

Packer turned, flustered. "Eh?"

"The other was a radio clock."

This apparent non sequitur seemed not to penetrate Randolph Packer's agitated brain.

"Where is the radio that was here before?" Doc inquired, returning the set to its place.

Randolph Packer blinked at the question. Then it sunk in.

"Why," he remarked, "it was Mr. Swain's personal property. Naturally, the firm could not keep it, and so it was returned to Mr. Swain's next of kin."

"And who is that?"

Randolph Packer went through some papers on his desk. He lifted a bill of lading from an express company.

"According to this, it was shipped to a Homer Ding of 8904 Thirty-fourth Avenue, Jackson Heights."

There was no Homer Ding at the address in Jackson Heights, a quick telephone call revealed. Instead, there was a vacant apartment, lately rented, and no furnishings. The person who had claimed to be Homer Ding could not be found.

"Obviously, this Ding person rented the apartment for the sole purpose of receiving the radio," Ham Brooks ventured as they evacuated the Rock of Ages building and reclaimed the roadster.

"I don't get it, Doc," Monk asked once they were in traffic. "What's so danged important about the guy's radio?"

Doc expressed no opinion.

"Are you deaf?" Dana O'Fall asked in exasperation. "He asked you a question."

Again, Doc made no comment. It was a habit of his when he did not wish to express a definite theory to feign deafness. Often aggravating to outsiders, Monk and Ham in the back seat took quiet encouragement from Doc's silence. It meant, they knew, that the bronze man had developed a theory to explain the Blind Death.

Doc drove uptown several blocks, coming to a stop near an office building which, while substantial, was considerably more modest than the pile of granite that had been Rock of Ages.

A brass plaque by the door read: STELLAR CO-OPERATIVE INSURANCE.

Doc was greeted with a hearty handshake by the company's president.

"So nice to see you again, Mr. Savage," the man grinned. His grin faded at the bronze man's next words.

"I would like to examine your firm's bond holdings."

"Whatever for?"

"To determine whether or not certain bonds have been replaced with counterfeit issues."

The president's face fell. It kept on falling in progressive stages, as he led Doc to the Stellar safe—a sturdy cast-iron box—and removed stacks of bonds for Doc Savage's inspection.

His jaw wasn't quite dragging on the floor when the bronze man pronounced two stacks of Liberties as counterfeit, but his manner indicated otherwise.

Doc summoned the police on his behalf.

As they were leaving, Dana O'Fall put a question to the bronze man.

"How is it you knew to come here?" she demanded.

"Until two weeks ago, Stellar Cooperative Insurance was presided over by Joseph Sultan."

"And who," Dana asked, "is Joseph Sultan?"

"The first victim of the Blind Death," Doc told her.

XVIII

THE UBIQUITOUS RADIO

The hour had approached noon by the time Doc Savage and his party repaired to Doc's skyscraper headquarters. The sun was high and the skies clear. Snow began melting in the streets below, turning the gutters of the city into rivers of sliding slush.

Up on the eighty-sixth floor, it might have been a spring day. Bright sunlight slanted in through the long windows on three sides of the massive experimental laboratory where Doc Savage toiled amid a profusion of equipment. An expert—the missing Long Tom Roberts, for instance—would have recognized that the bronze man spent much of his time tinkering with a wide array of experimental radio devices. He wore an unusual protective garment of some metallic material that made him look as if he were draped in shiny tinfoil. This was fitted with a hood of similar material, which the bronze man resorted to infrequently.

The afternoon lengthened. Frequently, Monk or Ham would saunter in to report on their own progress. Doc had set them to work on certain tasks.

Monk came in now. He was accompanied by his pet pig, Habeas Corpus, who had remained in the building during their recent sojourn downtown.

"I just talked to the cops, Doc," Monk reported. "They've got that dragnet spread into Connecticut and Jersey now, but still no sign of Long Tom."

Twirling matched dials on two different sets of apparatus, Doc nodded silently.

149

"You don't think—" Monk began. "I mean, Long Tom couldn't be—"

"No," Doc said firmly. "I do not believe that Long Tom is dead."

Monk let a gust of relief escape his barrel chest. Complete was his faith in his leader's judgment.

"The evidence at Harmon Cash's office indicates Long Tom was being interrogated rather vigorously," Doc explained. "We know from the testimony of Cash's man, Blackie, that it was unsuccessful. He may be kept alive until he reveals certain secrets."

"Knowin' that ornery cuss," Monk ventured, "he could live to be a hundred." The apish chemist made thoughtful shapes with his wide accident of a mouth. "You know," he added worriedly, "this is startin' to shape up like Cubama is smack in the middle of all these doin's."

"We do not know that as yet," Doc said absently, abruptly changing his calibrations. "Remember, the bonds missing from the insurance company vaults were switched. No such imposture was attempted at Cubama."

"Still, I don't like it," Monk said. "Accordin' to that Blackie, Harmon Cash has his eye on Cubama. You don't think he knows what it really is, do you?"

"I do not know," Doc admitted.

Monk blinked. It was rare for Doc to admit he was stumped.

"Come to think of it," Monk said, settling onto a stool and worrying Habeas's ribs with a friendly toe, "you never did explain what Long Tom was doin' in town, when everybody thought he was in Europe."

"Long Tom," Doc Savage explained, "was never abroad. I set him to working under cover with Sigmund Holmes on the matter of the missing Cubama bonds. He was using the alias Robert Jefferson."

Realization gleamed in Monk's gimlet eyes. He smacked a fist into a calloused palm.

"So that's why you wanted us to keep hands off the Cubama investigation!" he exclaimed. "If we showed up, it would tip people off to your interest in the place. Slick."

"Now that we know the Cubama theft somehow ties in with the odd business of this unseen killer, White Eyes, and his Blind Death, which I had already been investigating, no such subterfuge is necessary."

"That reminds me," Monk said suddenly. "It's high noon."

"So it is," the bronze man said, shaking off his metallic gloves. He crossed the room to a glass booth where stood an ordinary short-wave radio set. He switched this on, and adjusted the wavelength. After several moments of low talk in a dialect that seemed to consist of mostly clucks and gobbles, he broke contact.

Doc returned to his apparatus, and resumed his work.

"You called for another shipment, huh?" Monk asked. "Think it's a safe move with all this ruckus goin' on?"

"With our operating funds depleted by the Cubama theft," Doc stated quietly, "we have no choice in the matter."

During the exchange, the homely chemist had left off scratching his pet pig. The ungainly shoat ambled expectantly in Doc Savage's direction, unnoticed.

It happened that Habeas caught his doglike legs in a tangle of insulated wiring while crossing the laboratory. He emitted a surprised squeal.

Doc Savage's response was violent. He whirled, his flake-gold eyes hard with concern.

"Habeas!" he barked. The shoat froze. He was accustomed to obeying the bronze man's voice.

Monk leaped from his stool. "Doc!" he squeaked. "What is it? What's wrong?"

"Monk," Doc said with forceful intentness. "Call Habeas back to you."

"Why?"

"Just do it."

Doc Savage's brittle tone was all the motivation the apish chemist required.

"Here, Habeas," he called. "Here, boy. Have a walnut."

Habeas looked over his shoulder, hesitated. Monk extracted a walnut from a coat pocket and popped it in two with a great squeeze of his fingers.

Habeas came running. He leaped into the furry beams that were Monk's arms, whereupon he began munching on chewy walnut pieces.

"I don't get it," Monk said.

"This apparatus," Doc Savage said, returning to his experiment, "is highly dangerous to be around, hence the protective clothing I am wearing."

"Oh yeah? It have anything to do with the Blind Death?"

Instead of answering, Doc asked a question. "Has Ham returned from his investigations as yet?"

"Any minute now," Monk predicted. "But five bucks says that ambulance chaser comes back with egg on his pretty kisser."

In fact, Ham Brooks came back with a tabletop radio clock under one arm and a peculiar animal balanced on the other, not an hour later.

"Success!" he crowed.

He placed the radio on an unused workbench and released the animal—it was a small tailless ape of some sort—which immediately gave vent to a tiny howl and went chasing the pig, Habeas Corpus, around in manic circles.

Doc Savage immediately shut off his experiment.

"You unmitigated clothes horse!" Monk howled over the din. "Why'd you bring that—that unclassifiable here?"

"My good man," Ham sniffed, "Chemistry is not unclassifiable. In fact, there is every reason to suspect you and he share a common ancestry."

Which was certainly plausible, if outer appearances alone were a yardstick of biology.

For the creature busily bedeviling Monk's pig was a rust-hued miniature version of the simian chemist himself. Ham had acquired him during a recent adventure in a South American jungle, and smitten by the unknown anthropoid's resemblance to Monk, had adopted him.*

Chemistry had only entered the country a few months before, and had not yet adjusted to his first Winter. Hence, Ham had taken to leaving him, for his own good, at the exclusive Park Avenue club where the dapper lawyer resided.

"You're one to talk about ancestors," Monk retorted hotly, "considering that you have a pirate in your woodpile."

"I do not!" Ham insisted, shaking his dark cane in Monk's homely visage.

"Black Jack Brooks," Monk recited. "Born in London, 1799, and hung as a pirate on his birthday, in 1842, in Norfolk, Virginia. He was a cutthroat, a pillager, and a rogue." Monk grinned widely. "In short, a Brooks through and through."

"A slander!" Ham howled. "I'll sue!"

"They had the right idea in those days," Monk went on. "Hanging the really bad ones. Too bad the modern-day version of the pirate, the lawyer, can't be treated to the same medicine."

Ham Brooks shut his mobile orator's mouth with bear-trap suddenness. He looked like a man chewing his own tongue. His face slowly purpled.

"You—you!" he sputtered.

Doc Savage broke in.

"Ham, this radio?"

"Yes, Doc?" Ham said with effort, his empurpled features slowly returning to their natural coloring.

"Where did you get it?"

"At the residence of Joseph Sultan, the late president of Stellar Cooperative Insurance," Ham explained.

---

*Dust of Death

"It was in his parlor, which was where they found him the night the so-called Blind Death claimed him. His butler was only too happy to donate it to our investigation. Why? Is that not what you wanted?"

"This radio," Doc stated flatly, "is the one that was in C. Perley Swain's office. The one that had been shipped to the fictitious Homer Ding."

"The same model, you mean?" Monk asked.

"No," Doc returned, taking a box of tools from a cabinet. "This is the identical radio itself. I recognize distinctive scratches on the grille carvings."

Monk and Ham crowded around the radio in interest, their argument forgotten. Even the two pets settled down.

Doc worked quickly, removing the screws that held the base of the radio in place.

Doc asked Ham, "Did you notice how heavy this radio is?"

"Certainly. But I assumed that was due to its fine construction. Joseph Sultan could afford the best."

Doc had the radio upended, preparatory to removing the base plate. He still wore his metallic protective garment. He took the precaution of drawing the silvery hood over his bronze head.

"Perhaps you two might wish to withdraw to a safe distance," he suggested.

Monk and Ham scooped up their pets and took up a position of safety behind an oversized televisor device.

With careful bronze fingers, Doc Savage lifted the base plate. There came a sudden report, exactly like a mousetrap being sprung. It was not loud, but it was enough to scare Monk and Ham into ducking.

Doc Savage jumped back, releasing the radio. It was well that he did. The report signaled that a pressure trigger of some kind had been tripped.

Before the radio could crash to the table, it jumped apart in a flash that hurt their ears and sent fragments of polished wood, glass bits, and copper wire flying in all directions. Fire flew like bright stuffing.

* * *

When the last echoes stopped hurting their ears, Monk and Ham peered out from behind the televisor. They saw Doc Savage, a spectre in silver, come to his feet, unharmed, and approach the blackened pit that the exploding radio had made in the workbench. He threw back his protective hood.

"Blazes!" Monk said in a small voice.

Ham asked, "Are you all right, Doc?"

"I am fine," Doc told him, as he picked through the remnants of the destroyed radio, "but the person who constructed this device was clever. Nothing remains of its inner mechanism now."

"Booby-trapped, huh?" Monk ventured.

"Of course it was booby-trapped, you nitwit," Ham complained. "You saw it blow up with your own eyes, didn't you?"

A frantic knocking at the laboratory door interrupted the beginning of another argument.

Ham answered it.

Dana O'Fall stormed in, complaining, "How long am I supposed to stew in that confounded library? I'm a career girl, you know. I need to earn my keep every so many days."

"Care to enlighten us regarding the identity of your employer?" Doc Savage asked, looking up from the crater on the bench top.

Dana compressed her red mouth stubbornly. "No," she said, "I do not."

"Then you are free to go," Doc said, returning to his examination.

Dana O'Fall stood there wearing the stunned look of a person who had witnessed a thunderbolt strike frighteningly close.

"What?" she asked, dumfounded.

"Doc, you cannot mean to let this—this—culprit go!" Ham exploded.

"Monk, please escort Miss O'Fall from the building," Doc directed.

"Sure thing," Monk said. "C'mon, sister."

After they had gone, Ham scowled darkly.

The dapper lawyer made his mouth prim. "I say, I must protest. That vixen is up to no—"

Doc said quietly, "Follow her. See where she goes. If she won't reveal the truth behind her activities, perhaps she will lead us to an explanation unawares."

Ham brightened. Testing the ease with which his sword cane separated, he said, "Righto, Doc."

The dapper lawyer left Doc Savage to his quiet scrutiny. After a while, he gave it up and returned to his radio experiment.

In solitude, the bronze man toiled until the bleak Winter sun went down, and long after.

XIX

WHITE EYES APPEARS

That night, as Doc Savage delved into the riddle of
the Blind Death, a convocation unlike any ever to take
place in New York City began at eleven minutes to
midnight in a vaudeville house on the lower east side.

This was unusual for several reasons, not the least
of which was the undeniable fact that the theater was,
and had been for some time, abandoned.

There was a palpable air of disuse hanging about
the place. Its garish marquee was a sagging ruin. The
once-bright windows were planked over. A sheet of thin
veneer covered the entrance door. Not even the name
of the establishment could be read, only a letter here
and there.

Yet all night they had been arriving.

The first to arrive did so in a long, curtained town
car. It slithered down the wide, slushy length of First
Avenue and pulled up before the forlorn establishment.
Two men got out. They wore evening dress of the "soup
and fish" variety, and they carried violin cases tucked
under their arms.

After giving the boarded-up entrance a quick once-
over, they scuttled into an adjacent alley. There they
stopped before a side door, over which hung another
sheet of veneer. It could be seen that this rectangle of
wood had recently been hammered into place. It was a
clumsy job. Only one corner—the upper right—was
actually secured, and that by only a stout, broadhead
nail. This made it movable in an awkward manner.

It could also be seen that two oblate white blots

were daubed on the veneer. They had been carefully applied with common whitewash so that they resembled a pair of sightless eyes.

White eyes.

"Brrr," muttered one of the violin carriers. "Guess dis is de joint."

"Them peepers is givin' me the willies," the other added, his own orbs scouring the slush-choked alley.

"Guess we go in, den." This reluctant utterance had come from the first man, who proved—if his poor English had not—that he was no musician by the simple act of extracting a Tommy gun from his case. The other displayed an identical weapon. They drew back on the cocking levers. This required serious effort, and their breaths gushed like steam from tugboat whistles as they fought the heavy spring mechanisms.

When their submachine guns were properly cocked, they pushed the askew panel aside and up, quickly ducking into the dark theater.

The panel flopped back into place on its single nail and the opaque whitewashed eyes righted themselves after a moment's macabre swinging.

Several minutes dragged by. The panel swung up once more and the pair, still cradling their cocked weapons, struggled out into the dim alley. They pelted back to the waiting town car. One rapped on a rear window. It rolled down.

"It checks out, boss," one of the gunmen reported. "Looks like we got here first."

"This is damned strange," a wary voice from deep within the car grunted. "You sure it ain't a trap?"

"If it is," the other gunman said, hiking his Tommy gun up into the moonlight, "we got the drop on this bird, whoever he is."

The door clicked open after a pause. A tall man stepped out, wearing immaculate evening dress and a top hat tilted rakishly on his rather narrow head.

"Let's mosey," he said gruffly.

The trio—the pair with the heavy armament leading the way—disappeared into the darksome alley.

Thus did Topper Tweed, one of Manhattan's worst racketeers, arrive. An alumnus of the noble experiment that was Prohibition, Tweed had poured the profits of his rum-running days into other illicit activities. It was said that he commanded the largest mob in the city. Yet so cleverly did he operate, that the law had failed to apprehend him.

Not very long after, Jim James Garben put in an appearance.

Jim James Garben looked like nothing so much as a down-and-out wrestler. He wore shapeless pants of no easily determined color and a pullover jersey that was as green as fresh limes. When he walked, his legs bent at the knees with the weight of his powerfully muscled torso. His head might have been a freak muscle with an immobile face glued to it.

He arrived by nighthawk taxi. After paying the driver, he sauntered into the alley without any evidence of trepidation in his rolling gait.

Jim James Garben ducked behind the hanging panel, walking smack into the trained muzzles of twin Tommy guns wielded by the two Topper Tweed hoodlums.

Disdaining the menace of the weapons, he fingered an ivory-hued business card from a pocket.

"I give this invite to you clowns?" he wondered in a gravel-and-sand voice.

One of the Tommy jockeys took the card. He glanced at it briefly. It bore a simple message inscribed in fountain-pen ink. The message read:

YOU ARE CORDIALLY INVITED TO ATTEND A MEETING IN YOUR INTEREST AT MIDNIGHT AT THE OLD HAROLD THEATER.

Beneath it was an inky pair of eyes. Mere outlines, they looked as blind as stones. And under these flat orbs was a continuation of the ink script, reading:

FAILURE TO APPEAR MAY CAUSE YOU TO GO FOREVER BLIND.

The signature at the bottom was a flowing: *White Eyes*.

The Tommy chopper returned the ivory card, saying,

"Our boss got one, too." He turned, calling, "Topper! Look who's here. That dock walloper, Garben."

Which was an understatement. Burly Jim James Garben, for all his hulking appearance, virtually controlled the wharves of Manhattan. He made his money by diverting goods as they were unloaded from ships of commerce. Thousands of dollars in pilferage went into his coffers each annum.

"So what?" barked Topper Tweed, who considered himself a cut or two above a ruffian of the caliber of Jim James Garben. He was seated in the middle section of the seat rows, just back of the first row.

Jim James Garben looked past the dim top-hatted figure. He saw the stage. It was dark. A spindly vertical shape stood in the middle of the stage, faintly visible against the backdrop of a white curtain. Only the keenest of eyes could make this shape out as a standing microphone of the "spider" type.

No one lurked behind it.

"You heard the boss," the other chopper sneered to Jim James Garben. "So what? Now, go park yourself."

Jim James Garben gathered his cauliflowered muscle of a head into an annoyed knot. He took another look at the business card with its not-so-subtle warning and, evidently experiencing second thoughts, lumbered past the pair.

He selected a seat some distance from the top-hatted form of Topper Tweed and occupied it forcefully. The seat groaned.

After that, they began arriving in twos and threes. Seats soon filled. Hoarse questions, some shouted, others only whispered, volleyed back and forth in the cavernous and musty-smelling vaudeville emporium. No one had any answers.

The New York Police would have been very interested in this assemblage. Had any agents of the Federal Bureau of Investigation been present, they might well have been tempted to rub their hands together in anticipation of a headline-grabbing pinch or two.

For these were the cream of the underworld. They had come from both ends of Manhattan, from the other four boroughs, as well as from Long Island and the State of New Jersey. They were pickpockets and stick-up men. Safecrackers and swindlers. Second-story artists and murderers for hire.

And the name on everyone's lips was the same: "White Eyes."

"I don't like this place," a whiney voice complained. "It's spooky."

"I wouldn't be here myself, but I've been reading about this Blind Death business," another stated.

"I wasn't plannin' to come, but I heard that a guy who got one of them white cards went around tellin' everyone he wouldn't be buffaloed into any midnight meeting. He keeled over cryin' for his mother to save him. Dead. They said that when it was all over, his eyes were like white grapes stickin' outta his skull."

"I heard that, too."

Silence settled over the room. Eyes studied watches in the murk. The hour of midnight approached. Tension thickened the gloom like a shroud.

Abruptly, a solitary spotlight jumped into life.

Because they had been so long sitting in darkness, the optic nerves of the assembled of crookdom rebelled at the sudden illumination. Hands went to faces. Eyes blinked. Heads turned away.

When the spots had evaporated from the last man's eyes, they began to notice that the stage was no longer empty.

The solitary spotlight had picked out the spider mike.

A spectral apparition stood before it now. The ring-mounted microphone blocked the unexpected figure's mouth from view.

Not that there was a great deal to be discerned.

The apparition was a vision in white. It wore an immaculate white suit whose accessories—shirt, tie, socks, even shoes—were a leprous white. A broad-brimmed white hat of the type popular in the banana republics perched atop the apparition's head. A Panama hat.

The blaze of footlights coming up from the orchestra pit bleached this manlike figure of any shadow. They illuminated the creature's face.

Every man in the audience strained to behold the exposed lineaments.

Oddly, the face, too, was white as a bone. Its delicate features were like fine, immobile china. The contours of each eye suggested the Orient. The throat below the pointed chin and the close-set ears appeared whitened by a powder—talcum powder or perhaps cornstarch—to further defeat identification.

"Hell, he's got some kind of get-up on his kisser," a gruff voice complained over the growing hubbub.

"Forget that," another chimed in. "Lamp his glims."

Almost as one, the assembled crooks leaned forward in their chairs, blinking to more clearly make out the too-white apparition's features.

A gasp was followed by low profanity. Those too vain to wear eye glasses had to have it explained to them.

"His eyes," one hissed. "They're as white as cue balls!"

It was true. The white-garbed entity had no eyes to speak of. That is, he possessed only the white meat of a normal human eye. Iris and pupil were lacking. The footlights struck blind glimmers off those unseeing optics.

Yet neither the harsh lights nor the lack of optical apparatus seemed to bother the tall white figure. He stood, a pillar of ivory flame, as the nervous muttering settled down.

Then a hand gloved in white kid reached up to take the microphone standard, and a voice like white thunder rolled out over the aisles.

"*I am . . . White Eyes!*" it announced.

The loudness of his voice was near to deafening. It

came from two radio speakers, set in opposite wings of the stage.

"O.K., we came," a voice shouted back. "So what?"

The creature calling itself White Eyes cocked a powdered ear as if to catch the challenging voice.

"*Topper Tweed?*" it boomed.

"What of it?" returned the surly tones of Topper Tweed.

"*Thank you for coming to this, undoubtedly the greatest gathering of the lawless element to take place in history,*" the voice of White Eyes said grandly. "*You are no doubt wondering why I summoned you all here.*"

"Are you the guy what's been blasting down guys with that white-eyed bunk?" another voice challenged.

The blank, reflective orbs of White Eyes seemed to sweep the room. They came to rest on one individual in particular, as if they possessed the power of sight despite the obvious lack of natural optical mechanism.

"*I am,*" White Eyes returned without concern. "*Do you object to this, Mr. Jim James Garben?*"

"I might," Jim James Garben grunted. "If you try any of that monkey business on me and my mob."

"Yeah, what's the idea of threatening us?" a voice lifted angrily, emboldened by the first challenge.

"*I threaten you with impunity,*" proclaimed White Eyes, "*because the power that the newspapers have dubbed the Blind Death is unstoppable. You have all read of the Blind Death, how it has struck down men of high station and low, without regard. How they expired in miserable agony, sightless and uncomprehending. Some of you have heard it whispered that the voice of White Eyes—my voice—was heard during the last incident. And how those who fail to obey the commands of White Eyes pay the ultimate penalty.*"

White Eyes waited until the last reverberations of his amplified voice had died away before he resumed speaking.

"*Many have wondered about the power of White Eyes,*" he thundered. "*I will reveal it to you. It is akin to that of the basilisk of ancient legend. For those of you whose schooling is lacking in the classics, I will explain. The basilisk was a reptilian creature whose eyes possessed the uncanny power to slay men at a mere glance."*

"You mean you look at guys and they just drop dead?" This anonymous query was lost in the booming echoes, and was not answered.

"I have discovered the secret of the basilisk!" White Eyes announced. *"I have only to look at a man in a certain way and his eyes become as mine. Death is the unavoidable result."*

"Bushwa!" yelled a man.

The uncanny white orbs searched the room. They came to rest on the figure of Jim James Garben, who had jumped to his feet, defiantly.

"You do not believe me?" asked White Eyes.

"I'll tell a man!" Jim James Garben hurled back. He stabbed the air with a blunt finger that was like fat sausage. His tone was challenging. "I not only don't believe you, I'm gonna wring your starched neck in front of all these mugs to prove it!"

Big burly Jim James Garben started shoving out to the side aisle. He all but cleared the row in his haste.

Storming up the aisle, he mounted the stairs to the stage.

"Remain in your seats, all of you!" White Eyes boomed out. *"Mr. Garben has a point he wishes to make. As do I."*

Big Jim James Garben stalked past the booming radio loud-speaker on that end of the stage and advanced toward White Eyes, who stood calmly holding the microphone stand in one white-gloved hand. The other remained at his side.

Every man in the theater saw clearly what next transpired.

Jim James Garben was rolling up his jersey sleeves as he advanced.

Slowly, methodically, the head of White Eyes swiveled in his direction. It was an unhurried movement. Behind the suspended spider mike, he tilted back his porcelain face so that his uncanny eyes showed clearly under the wide brim of his Panama.

The intensely white footlights struck diamondlike gleams off those unflinching orbs.

White Eyes seemed to be mustering every iota of power in his being, as if to expel it through his blank, yet seeing, orbs.

Then it happened!

Jim James Garben stopped in mid-step. He was in the act of rolling up his other sleeve. Abruptly, he forgot all about it.

"Behold!" White Eyes shrieked.

Jim James Garben's meaty hands flew to his eyes. *"Witness the power of White Eyes!"*

Jim James Garben fell to his knees as if poleaxed. His falling shook the stage. He writhed, still clutching his eyes.

"I—can't—see!" he moaned.

One hand, groping for the floor, came away from his left eye. Everyone could see the orb clearly. It was horribly bloodshot. Then, like a fried egg cooking, it began to turn white.

The whiteness started deep in the black center of Jim James Garben's exposed optic, it seemed. It crept out until it had obliterated all color. Then it rolled over the bloodshot white of the eyes, returning it to its former natural whiteness.

Jim James Garben was tough. Except for his first strangled cry, he had said nothing. Now he was crawling blindly on hands and knees to the edge of the stage—as if to escape the awful power that had seized him. His muscular face worked, a picture of agony.

And behind him, his impossible orbs following the tortured man's progress, stood White Eyes, head tilted back like a master mesmerist casting a spell. One hand grasped the microphone standard. The other hung loose and unmoving at his side.

Jim James Garben had fallen to taking in gulps of air through his open mouth. Spotlights clearly showed rows of strong teeth, a few back molars with filled cavities.

One by one, these filled teeth began popping. They were like dried corn in a fire. Bits of tooth enamel flew out, to land amid the audience.

"Holy smokes!" some one said, aghast. "His damn teeth are exploding!"

It was a testament to the burly dock walloper's stamina that Jim James Garben eventually made it to the orchestra pit. Twisting, he threw himself off the stage, landing with sufficient force that it brought a discordant thrum and tinkling from the piano below. Evidently, one leg was in a weakened state, because the impact caused the piano to collapse on one side.

A man gingerly approached the orchestra pit. He looked down.

"Is he moving?" a voice from near the front row demanded hoarsely. It was the horrified voice of Harmon Cash.

"No," the investigator gulped.

"Dead?" bleated Harmon Cash, sounding very, very sick.

"Not only that," said the man, withdrawing to his seat, "but his eyes are just like that guy up there."

"Now you understand the power of White Eyes!" thundered the calm figure on the stage. *"If I so desire, I could render you all blind and very dead."*

Here and there, automatics were cocked with the ominous sound of clockwork crocodiles testing their jaws.

"But that is not why I called you here," White Eyes added.

"Why did you?" This from Topper Tweed. There was newfound respect in the prominent gangster's tone.

"I brought you here to make an important announcement."

Silence blanketed the theater.

"Henceforth, you all work for White Eyes!"

"Fat chance!" a sulky voice called from in back of

the house. A person familiar with it would have recognized it as belonging to Eduardo Luz.

"Under my command, I will weld you all into the greatest army of criminal power ever seen in mankind's bloody history!"

Dark mutterings greeted this amplified utterance.

"And your first target will be the individual we all fear."

The house went very, very quiet.

"I intend to declare war on the man known as Clark Savage, Junior," White Eyes proclaimed. *"Doc Savage!"*

"Hell's bells," a man grunted explosively.

"That's it for me," another spat. "I'm leaving. Guys who go up against Savage have a funny way of never being heard of again."

There was a concerted rush for the exit. Not every one bolted. Not even a majority of the audience members. But many did.

"I warn you!" White Eyes thundered.

A few stopped in their tracks. Others quickened their pace. The veneer panel was violently shoved out of the way.

"The eyes of White Eyes are everywhere! I possess the power to throw my vision to any point on the globe, much as a ventriloquist appears to throw his voice. There is no safe place to run to. I will strike down any who do not join my underworld alliance!"

A few superstitious souls reluctantly reclaimed their seats. Others continued pouring out into the cold blackness. The house settled down. Once again, all attention was given to the being that called itself White Eyes.

"You're out to get Savage," came the interested voice of Topper Tweed. "How come?"

"I am glad you asked that question," returned White Eyes. *"Let me pose to you a question. Namely, if you could execute one great crime, what would it be?"*

"That's easy," said Topper Tweed. "I'd knock over Fort Knox—where the G keeps all the country's gold."

Murmurs of agreement raced around the room.

"Fort Knox," came the booming voice of White Eyes, "is a candy store compared to the opportunity I am about to present to you."

"Baloney!"

"You all know that Doc Savage is a wealthy man. What you do not know is that the bronze man has access to a source of wealth I believe beggars all the gold in Fort Knox. A staggering trove." White Eyes paused dramatically. "And the only obstacle that stands in our way to this trove—is the Man of Bronze himself!"

"Why don't you just cast your damn spell over that bronze devil, if you got the power to do it, like you say?" a voice inquired.

"Because dead, the bronze man cannot give up his secrets. He must be taken alive. That is where you gentlemen come in."

"How are we gonna do this?" wondered Topper Tweed.

"I propose," came the deafening voice of White Eyes, "to assault the very headquarters of Doc Savage itself!"

"It's been done. And the guys who done it are still on the missing-persons list."

"That is because these forays were attempted on a picayune scale. We will attack in overwhelming numbers. Even the bronze man's mighty defenses will fall before us. Are you with me?"

Booming echoes bounced off the ornate walls as this sunk in.

"Okay," said Topper Tweed. "I'm in."

"Me, too."

"Count me in."

"Gentlemen of crime," said White Eyes broadly, "I promise you will never rue this decision."

XX

THE CHOSEN

Criminals are notoriously suspicious gentry as a class.

Even though the remaining crooks who had been held spellbound by the power of the being known as White Eyes had just sworn fealty to the white-garbed crime magician, they were not entirely satisfied by his explanations.

It was true that, for the most part, they feared this new leader of crookdom. But these were men who could not be catalogued as soft and easy to sway, and when they wanted a thing, they had formed the habit of taking it by force, provided such a course was feasible. Right now, they wanted answers.

"How do we know there'll be enough swag to go around?" was one version of the question most asked in the aftermath of the demise of big Jim James Garben.

"If by that you are asking me how many millions the Man of Bronze actually controls," boomed out White Eyes, *"I admit that I do not possess the answer to that question."*

The room grew ominously quiet.

"Take a wild guess," a cynical voice piped out.

"I would guess," White Eyes said dramatically, *"that the final tally could only be arrived at by the changing of a consonant."*

"Huh?"

"Not millions," White Eyes said. *"But billions."*

A rumble of approval shook the chandeliers over the heads of the criminal army. Most of them had never before thought in such numbers. It staggered them. It excited them. It also appealed to their innate sense of greed.

For White Eyes had chosen his potential army well. They were, from the standpoint of a crime boss, not a bad gang of subordinates. Every one of them had proven himself bad. Moreover, there was not a dumb killer among them. They were men who possessed brains of a certain twisted sort. Only the most imaginative had received the white-business-card summons.

White Eyes began to prove this now.

"*I am going to call out certain names,*" White Eyes thundered. "*These men will receive special instructions. The remainder of you will return to your homes and places of business to await the next summons.*"

White Eyes paused to let this edict sink in.

"*I call upon—Mortimer MacGillicuddy!*"

"That's me!" a thin voice called from the wings.

White Eyes turned his bone-china face toward the sound of the voice. It was evident that, however his blank eyes operated, it required the turning of his head in order for him to see peripherally.

"*Are you Mortimer MacGillicuddy, better known as 'Cyanic' MacGillicuddy?*" he demanded.

"Y-yes."

"*You are wanted for partaking of a kidnaping in which you disposed of your victim's body with chemicals,*" White Eyes stated flatly.

"No need to broadcast it," Cyanic MacGillicuddy grumbled. "Hell, yes. We didn't figure they could prove anything without a corpus delicti."

White Eyes boomed out satisfied laughter. "*They could not prove a murder very well, but they could prove a kidnaping. Will you turn your skills to the goal I have set for this organization?*"

"I'm here, aren't I?"

"*Excellent. Next—*"

Cyanic MacGillicuddy said swiftly, "Say, I got a brother who is as tough as they make them. He'd be a handy one to have along."

"I know the men I want," the spectral White Eyes retorted sharply. "You were chosen because you were a chemist. The others have been chosen for various very good reasons. I want only men I have selected."

Cyanic MacGillicuddy frowned in disappointment, but made no protest.

White Eyes cast his blank orbs around the hall like a dimestore fan turning on a rotary gear.

"Next, I call upon—Slinky Sid Slocum!"

"M-me?" croaked a man in the front row. He was a wizened wart of a fellow with shifty eyes and a sour mouth. His fingers were unusually long and fretted nervously in his lap.

"They say that you are the top safecracker east of the Mississippi?"

"They're lying," retorted Slinky Sid.

"Oh?"

"I'm the best box man—period. Show me a safe, and I'll bust it open for you. Cold chisel. Nitro. Or by finger music. I'm tops."

"You will have to be, for the safe I wish you to crack belongs to Doc Savage himself."

"A piece of cake," Slinky Sid Slocum boasted.

"That is the spirit I want my criminal army to have," White Eyes boomed enthusiastically.

"We're gonna need more than spirit to keep us motivated while we're waiting for the go-ahead to attack Savage," a reedy voice called out.

"Meaning?"

"I'm talkin' about scratch, moolah, jake, berries. Get me?"

"Ah, of course. Thank you for reminding me. I have anticipated the need for seed money."

"I don't work for chicken feed," another bold voice announced.

"Men who work for me," White Eyes said, drawing a sheaf of large engraved sheets from his immaculately white coat, *"will never want!"*

White Eyes flung the papers. They shot up into the air, fluttering down like exhausted pigeons. One landed in the lap of Slinky Sid Slocum. He blinked ratlike eyes at the engraved face.

"This here's a bond!" he shouted. "A twenty-five-dollar Liberty!"

White Eyes extracted more of these. They were scattered into the aisles. Some scrambled for them. Others, of greater means, like Topper Tweed, did not deign to leave their seats.

When the excitement had died down, and seats had been resumed, the voice from behind the porcelain face said, *"Now that proof of my good faith has been established to your satisfaction, let us conclude our agenda."*

Other criminal names were called by White Eyes. It was a tribute to the power of the white-garbed criminal mastermind that no one failed to answer his call. Evidently, the crooks who had fled the theater despite his earlier warning had not amounted to much. Only the boldest remained.

Last to be called was Topper Tweed, who growled, "I was wondering when you'd get to me."

"I have very special plans for you, Topper," White Eyes announced. *"For you, as the head of the largest, most prosperous gang in the city, shall be my general."*

"Suits me just fine," Topper Tweed grunted.

"All whose names I have not called out will henceforth take their orders from Mr. Tweed."

Topper Tweed beamed. His narrow face gleamed under the hot lights. He turned his top hat around thoughtfully by manipulating the brim with his fingers.

"And Mr. Tweed shall take his orders from White Eyes!"

"When do we move?" asked Topper Tweed.

"Soon. Very, very soon," promised White Eyes. *"Certain preparations must be undertaken first. But our next order of business will be to evacuate these premises, which I need not remind you must be done in a controlled and orderly fashion in order not to arouse police interest."*

"It is a little late to be worrying about the flat-foots," a too-calm voice called from somewhere in the cavernous theater.

"What do you mean?" demanded White Eyes, head rotating.

"I mean I just called the riot squad," replied the voice. "If I were you gents, I'd keep my pants plastered to your seats and your hands where they can be seen."

Voices lifted like a million angry bees buzzing.

"And who," wondered the booming voice of White Eyes, *"might you be?"*

"I might be a concerned citizen," came the satisfied reply, "but I'm not. Just call me one of the boys who doesn't like to be threatened."

Some one had the presence of mind to thumb on a flashlight. It hunted out the speaker, who was standing by the makeshift door.

"That's Ned Stone!" a voice shouted hoarsely.

"Ned Stone," explained White Eyes, *"vacated this hall when I made my generous offer which will make you all billionaires."*

That reminder had no sooner bounced off the ceiling than the caterwauling of radio cars sounded in the near distance.

A man jumped up in his seat, bawling, "Get that guy! He's put the kibosh on our strolling down Easy Street!"

Bedlam broke out then. The first thing that happened was that fully a score or more of weapons were drawn and pointed in Ned Stone's general direction.

The unfortunate crook had but a moment to contemplate his error in announcing his betrayal. Bleating in fear, he made a hasty dash for the door. He must have forgotten that it pushed aside—not out—because he bounced off the veneer.

Then gun thunder filled the hall. The shooting was not of marksman quality. More bullets clouted the scrolled plaster walls than penetrated their target. But with so much lead flying, it hardly mattered. Ned Stone

was riddled into unrecognizability before he hit the
floor.

Then every one was out of their seats and surging
for this lone exit. Hard, uncaring feet further desecrat-
ed Ned Stone's mortal remains. The veneer door was
slammed loose and knocked aside during the first part
of the stampede.

Cars started outside. Men scrambled for hiding
places or ducked into subway entrances. Taxis were
commandeered, their drivers pistol-whipped out from
behind steering wheels.

The radio cars—there were four of them, and the
night air was filled with the keening promise of more en
route—slewed into this pandemonium. The first shots
fired went into the air. Warning shots.

These were answered by spiteful return fire. Blue
uniforms splashed slush as they fell, and the slush grew
pinkish and then increasingly scarlet.

Riot guns blasted back. Cars knocked one another.
Tires exploded from bullet punctures. Somewhere a
fire hydrant cracked before a heavy sedan, sending up a
gusher of water, which began to freeze almost as soon as
it touched pavement.

Soon, a pitched battle was under way. The police
were handily outnumbered, but their foes were more
intent upon escape than fight, and this unquestionably
preserved many bluecoat lives.

The alleys and byways of this disreputable section
of town became choked with fleeing badmen.

Attempts to cordon off area streets met with mixed
success.

A roadblock consisting of two radio prowl cars
parked with front bumpers locked and rear wheels up
on opposite sidewalks lasted only as long as it took
Topper Tweed to organize a string of cars to attack it.

A heavy phaëton took the lead. It plowed through
the road block by the simple expedient of striking at the
most vulnerable point—the locked bumpers.

With a loud crash and a squealing of tires, the radio
cars were knocked aside, clearing a narrow path. Wheels

bent, the heavy phaëton slithered out of control and lost half its length to a solid brick wall. But the other gang cars got through the blockade.

The police stubbornly poured lead into the mad train in the hope of stopping it. But this was not to be.

"Burn 'em down, boys!" Topper Tweed shouted exultantly from the second car as glass jangled around his narrow head.

Gun flame spiked from almost every window of the caravan. More than one gunner had a submachine gun.

The police ran for cover after one of their number was literally chopped in equal halves by a Tommy gun.

Elsewhere, the bluecoats were having better luck. They collared quite a number of fleeing felons.

"What a feast!" one exulted. "This is gonna set the big boys back a year!"

The speaker would have been disheartened had he been made aware of the total number of Manhattan's underworld that had congregated on this frigid night. They had pinched barely a fraction of the total number. Still, it made for merry thoughts of Christmas bonuses to come.

When the din had settled, a detachment stumbled across the mutilated corpse of Ned Stone, and made a foray into the seemingly deserted Harold Theater.

The stage footlights were still illuminated. So was the lone spotlight which pointed at the tall spider microphone like an accusing finger.

"What have we here?" demanded the man in charge, a veteran sergeant.

Behind the microphone stood a figure that might have been composed of pure light. Everything about him was white, even his immobile face.

"Put 'em high," the veteran sergeant ordered. "And keep 'em there!"

The white figure lifted his leprous hands into view.

"*I am at your command,*" a thunderous voice assured him.

"Take him," the sergeant said gruffly. "Some corny stage magician, I guess."

There was a concerted rush for the stage.

"I don't want them hands to so much as wiggle," the sergeant warned, following his men up the steps, his riot gun trained unerringly at the strangely white phantasm of light.

"*My hands, rest assured,*" White Eyes promised, "*will not move one iota.*"

It happened when the entire detachment stepped onto the stage.

First, one man dropped his revolver.

"Clumsy oaf!" the sergeant barked. "Pick it up!"

Then, the man who had lost his firearm started to moan. He sank to his knees, his hands going to his eyes. He wailed something unintelligible.

Then, another man cried out. And another. They simply got down on the stage and went into convulsive contortions.

Poised on the short steps leading to the stage, the veteran sergeant could not believe his own eyes. They went from the stricken bluecoats to the white figure like an out-of-control metronome.

"What're you doing to them?" he demanded, dumfounded.

The white figure answered calmly. "*Nothing. As you can see, my hands are in plain view.*"

The veteran sergeant watched a man roll toward him. The sergeant mounted to the top step. He reached out to pry a clutching hand away from his comrade's eyes.

He saw it clearly, then. The white of the exposed eye was gruesome in its swelling of blood vessels.

"Bill!" he choked. "Speak to me! What's happening to you?"

"My eyes! They're burning up!"

The exposed orb quickly clouded over with what looked like a spreading fungus.

"Saints preserve us!" the sergeant ejaculated. "It's the damn Blind Death."

Noticing the blank eyes of the figure behind the microphone, the sergeant made a connection.

"You!" he gritted. "You're gonna pay for what you done to my men."

He vaulted the last step onto the stage. His riot gun pointed menacingly at the white figure's midriff, the sergeant advanced, cold vengeance on his weathered face.

"I don't know how you're doing it," he said through set teeth, "but I know this is your work, damn you!"

He realized his mistake when his eyes simply stopped working.

The riot gun slipped from his hands, going instead to his suddenly hot face.

"Mother of mercy!" the sergeant moaned. "Now it's got me, too!"

Convulsing like an impaled insect, he joined his fellows on the bare stage floor. The only difference was that the others had finished the worst part of their dying, and the sergeant was just beginning his.

Soon, he was a stretched-out corpse at the outer fringes of the very white spotlight, which made his blind eyes gleam, along with those of his dead comrades, like phosphorescent mushrooms.

The silent, spectral figure of White Eyes ignored the dead as he gathered up his radio sets and disappeared behind the white curtain.

Not long after this, a figure in a white suit slithered down a snow-whitened alley a dozen blocks east of the Harold Theater.

It crouched in the snow, eyes darting up and down the benighted street with anxious rapidity.

An automobile came around a corner, gathering speed. The man in white set himself.

As the car passed, he vaulted from the alley and leapt onto the running board of the passing machine.

The car weaved as the driver realized he had acquired an unexpected passenger.

"Luz!" he squawled, rolling down his window.

Clinging to the door frame, swarthy Eduardo Luz ducked his head to better see the driver he had imposed on.

"Harmon Cash!" he howled. "What the hell are you doing here!"

"The same thing you are!" Cash wailed, his cock-eyed gaze going to the rear-vision mirror. "Trying to evade the Hydralike heads of the law."

"Step on it, then!" Luz shouted.

The auto took the next corner on two wheels. Luz barely retained his precarious grip.

By a series of evasive turns, Harmon Cash managed to depart the zone of police activity unchallenged. He slowed to a decorous pace.

"*Whew!*" he said heartily. "I should never have responded to that invitation."

"You got one too, huh?" Luz asked nervously, still glancing about.

"Do not tell me that White Eyes also demanded your presence," Harmon Cash said sourly.

"I took a chance and breezed by my place," Luz admitted. "There was one of those white cards stuffed in the mail box, sure. Why not?"

"Because," Harmon Cash said, braking the car with jolting suddenness and whipping out his tiny derringer, "we both know that you are White Eyes."

Eduardo Luz barely held on. He stepped off as soon as the car stopped bouncing on its springs.

"Let me point out that this handy item is loaded this time," Cash said flintily.

"It's the white coat, isn't it?" Luz demanded, stepping back from the car but not taking his dark, liquid eyes off the round maw of the derringer. "That's what's planted that nutty thought in your head."

"On the contrary," Harmon Cash returned smoothly. "I had you pegged for White Eyes before that worthy—before you—showed your masked face. You practically admitted it during our last encounter. Distributing the Cubama bonds so freely to your criminal army simply clinched the matter."

"What makes you think they were Liberties?" Luz asked.

"Supposition."

"If I'm White Eyes," Eduardo Luz said levelly, "then you had better watch where you point that belly-buster. I might just strike you dead where you sit."

"I do not profess to understand how you performed that sleight of hand they call the Blind Death, but I am not afraid of any man I have in my sights. And I am greatly perturbed that you have usurped my grand scheme to separate Doc Savage from his vast wealth."

Eduardo Luz looked into the wayward eyes of his former employer, Harmon Cash. It was as if he were attempting to read the man's resolve.

"You know," he said at last, "I've got it in my mind that maybe *you're* this White Eyes fellow."

"Ridiculous," Cash scoffed. "I was in the audience. As the true White Eyes would know, for my voice could plainly be heard from the house, asking questions."

"Now that you mention it," Luz said, rubbing his swarthy jaw, "I do recall hearing a voice that sounded like yours. It was coming from the front. Seems to me that a bit of clever voice-throwing could explain that."

"I assure you that cheap ventriloquism is not among my repertoire of talents," Harmon Cash said in an injured tone.

"Wouldn't have to be," Luz countered. "All you'd have to have done is switch off that mike and speak up in your normal voice. That weird china mask would cover any lip movement. No one would guess the voice was coming from White Eyes." Luz paused. "Funny you didn't notice *my* voice, though."

"A great many voices were raised to-night. And your rather pat voice-throwing theory could apply to a great many individuals present tonight."

"Maybe," Luz said slowly, "maybe neither one of us is White Eyes."

"All things are possible on a night such as this," Harmon Cash said blandly.

"But there's one way to prove if you're White Eyes, or if you're not," Luz said slowly.

"That is the kind of logic," Harmon Cash allowed, "that I would most happily imbibe of."

"Every one knows you wouldn't harm a fly—by your own hand."

"So?"

"But White Eyes has killed almost a dozen so far."

Harmon Cash's strange orbs grew reflective. "True."

"If you're White Eyes, you won't hesitate to plug me," Luz said, taking a cautious step backward. "But if you're not, and this timidness of yours isn't some kind of act, you won't."

"That is a perilous gamble to take," Harmon Cash cautioned. "For your life is forfeit if you are mistaken."

"I'm going to walk away now," Eduardo Luz said after a calculating moment.

And he did. But only so far as a lamp-post. As soon as he got to it, he ducked around it, and flung himself into the shelter of an alley.

Harmon Cash followed the white figure with his derringer. He thumbed back the hammer. His leonine features contorted, his eyes attempting to line up on the derringer's tiny gun sight.

In the end, he flung the weapon aside, saying, "I just cannot do it! For the life of me, I cannot kill a man in cold blood like that." Harmon Cash sounded very disgusted with himself.

He got the machine going and made his way out of the vicinity, driving in a wayward pattern as if slightly inebriated.

XXI

THIRD DEGREE

Doc Savage arrived at the Harold Theater while it still lacked several hours to dawn.

By that time, fully half of Manhattan's contingent of police officers milled about the six-or-seven-block cordoned area. The police commissioner was there, taking charge and issuing grim orders. Morgue wagons were carting away the dead.

Doc accosted the police commissioner, saying, "I understand that there has been another occurrence of the Blind Death."

"Occurrence!" the commissioner spat disgustedly. "It was a bloody massacre. C'mon. Follow me."

The police commissioner was no political appointee. He had risen through the ranks. He shoved his way through his own bluecoats with the same impatient bluster that had marked his early career as a beat cop.

"Make way! Make way!" he called, and a river of blue parted before him.

Doc Savage found himself examining the slain officers sprinkled around the bare stage like so many contorted dolls. For want of sheets—there were too many dead for the common niceties to be observed—handkerchiefs had been laid over the faces of the dead. Doc lifted one of these, noted briefly the staring, blind eyes, the expression of horror that rictus had marked on the unmoving face, and replaced it without a word. His metallic expression was grim.

"I didn't mind the Blind Death so much when it was just taking criminals," the commissioner muttered.

"But this! Let me tell you, Savage, there'll be hell to pay for sure."

Doc made no answer. He noted the solitary spider microphone ringed by spotlight glare and discerned two electrical leads that trailed from its flat base to either wing of the stage.

Doc followed one of these. It ended in an open splice. He knelt, examining the exposed copper wiring briefly, and noticed scrape marks striating the thin layer of dust where the wire petered out.

"These leads were recently connected to some sort of loud-speaker apparatus," Doc ventured. "Evidently a meeting of some kind was held in this place."

"We caught a few of the ones that were in on this," the commissioner offered. "They're sweating them down at the Tombs now."

Doc rose, saying, "I would like to be present at the interrogation."

"I'll arrange it," said the police commissioner, looking away from the bodies of his officers. His eyes happened to light on the darkness of the orchestra pit.

"Well, well, well," he said, pushing back his hat. "What have we here?"

Doc floated to his side. His weird flake-gold eyes discerned a body sprawled amid the wreckage of an old piano.

"Recognize him?" the commissioner asked the bronze man.

Doc nodded. "Jim James Garben."

"The same. Looks like the Blind Death took a big one for a change."

"He will have few mourners."

Noting the condition of the teeth in the dead Garben's gaping mouth, Doc added, "I would like to perform the autopsy on this man myself."

"Done," said the police commissioner. He stomped off to make arrangements.

Benny the Bust was, in the parlance of the underworld, a dip. That is, he picked pockets. He had the general air of a weasel about him as he sat under the lights in a dank room in the Tombs. He jerked spasmodically. Sweat rolling down from his scalp made his scrawny throat slick and moistened his open collar.

"I ain't done nothin', I tell you!" he protested.

"Come on, Benny," a cop said as two shadowy figures entered the cramped room, "we got you dead to rights. Now for the last time, what was going on in that meeting?"

Benny the Bust cringed under the lash of the cop's voice. He blinked stupid eyes into the lights, was unable to see past their hot glare, and so was unaware of the new arrivals' identities.

"I ain't tellin', I say!" he snarled.

The cop punished the side of Benny's stool with his nightstick. Benny recoiled, hunkering down on his perch.

"Talk, you cheap dip."

"I can't!" Benny said miserably. "White Eyes will strike me blind with those blank peepers of his."

A controlled voice asked a question.

"You saw this person called White Eyes?" it asked.

"Who's asking? You don't sound like no copper."

"I am Doc Savage," said the controlled voice.

Benny the dip swallowed tightly. His shifty eyes darted this way and that.

"Answer the question!" a cop shouted.

"Yeah, maybe," Benny admitted in a miserable voice.

The voice of Doc Savage asked, "Describe him."

"White, he was all in white. White coat, white hat, white face, and white—eyes." Despite the brutal lamp heat, Benny shivered uncontrollably.

"His eyes were white?" the bronze man demanded. His voice was closer, but his features remained beyond the reach of Benny the Bust's dazzled eyes.

Benny swallowed again. "That's what I said. They gleamed like pearls. And when he looked at that dock guy, Garben, he went down, struck blind and dead. Never saw nothin' like it, I tell you."

"What was White Eyes's purpose in calling a meeting of underworld figures?" the bronze man inquired.

Benny the Bust hesitated.

"Give us a few minutes alone with him, Mr. Savage," a cop growled. "We'll drag some words from him."

"Savage," Benny said quickly. "I hear you're a right guy. If I tell you, will—will you protect me from this Blind Death whammy?"

Beyond the hot radiance of light, the resonant voice of Doc Savage was directed away from the shivering pickpocket. "Commissioner," it said, "I can give this man protection only if I am given his parole."

"We found him slinking around the cordon area," the commissioner said, as if thinking aloud. "He hasn't been charged with anything, and may not be if he had nothing to do with my boys being killed."

"I'm no killer!" Benny bleated. "Honest. What say?"

"Aw, he's only a cheap dip," a cop interjected.

"He's yours," the commissioner said at last.

Benny the Bust's ratty face visibly relaxed. As much as he might have ordinarily feared the bronze man, it was the wrath of the police he feared most now. No jailbird suffered more than the cop killer, and Benny was savvy enough to realize this.

The metallic features of Doc Savage pushed out of the glare, fixing Benny with his weird golden eyes that seemed always to be in motion.

Doc asked, "What did White Eyes say to you?"

Benny the Bust tried to look away. It was as if he were a frightened rabbit transfixed by a predatory viper's eyes. Irresistibly, his gaze was drawn back to meet the bronze man's compelling, hypnotic orbs.

"He—he's after you, Savage," Benny vouchsafed.

A cop swore profanely.

"What do you mean?" Doc demanded.

"He thinks he has a line on where you get your loot from," Benny went on in a cracking voice. "Wants it all for himself. He promised every one of us mugs a share."

"This White Eyes has mighty tall notions," a cop muttered in disbelief.

"And they agreed?" Doc asked, not sounding at all concerned.

Benny shrugged thin shoulders. "Why not? He was throwing money at us like it was water." Apparently overtaken by an urge to unburden himself, the frightened dip plucked a folded square of heavy paper from the concealment of one shirt sleeve. "See?"

Doc accepted the offering, unfolded it. His eyes took in the ornate face of a Liberty bond. He memorized the serial number at a glance.

"He had many of these?" the bronze man prompted.

Eagerly, Benny the Bust replied, "Like confetti, they was. If I was faster, I would have gotten more."

"I'll wager if we frisk this one," came a hard cop voice, "we'll find a couple more."

The aghast look that settled over Benny the Bust's face all but confirmed this guess.

Doc Savage turned away from the crestfallen crook.

"I would like to visit the spot where Nug Hassel perished," he requested.

"Hadn't you gone over it once before?" the commissioner asked, perplexed.

Doc nodded. "I would like to do so again."

Leaving the cowering crook for the moment, Doc Savage retraced the path Nug Hassel had walked—the last mile that had resulted in his premature demise.

It was not really a mile. Barely five hundred feet stretched between the solitary cell that had been Nug Hassel's last abode and the side door where he had fallen—in blind, ignominious death.

Doc traversed this path twice, once in each direction, seeming to take in everything there was to see.

"As I recall," Doc said to the police commissioner, as they were completing their second circuit, "Nug Hassel was being transported to the district attorney for the purpose of identifying the man who masterminded the bank robbery for which Hassel was convicted."

"That's correct," the commissioner admitted.

"Did Nug Hassel ever mention this man's name?"

"Yeah, he did. But without a signed affidavit, we couldn't arrest him. It was too bad, too. We'd been trying to pin something on that slick operator for a long time."

"The name?"

"Harmon Cash," said the commissioner of police.

Doc's eerie trilling sounded briefly. He suppressed it.

"I think, Commissioner, that if you look into the backgrounds of the other criminals who succumbed to the Blind Death, you will find that they are, or were at one time, all associates of Harmon Cash."

"Damn right I'll look into it."

"Before you do, I would like to examine every radio in this building."

The commissioner blinked. "That's not very many."

"We should begin with only those that can be found along the path that Nug Hassel walked."

"That really narrows it down, then."

Doc looked at him.

"The warden's radio," he said, "is the only one that fits your description."

The warden's radio was a tall console model. It stood up against an outside wall of his office—a wall by which Nug Hassel had to have passed as he had exited the Tombs under guard. In fact, it stood only a handful of feet from the site of his demise.

The warden was called from his bed. Blinking sleepy eyes, he submitted to the bronze man's questioning.

"No," he told Doc Savage, "this isn't the radio that was here the day Nug Hassel died."

Interest flickered in the bronze man's weird flake-gold eyes. "Explain, please."

"Well, it is like this," the warden began. "I received the gift of a new console model some days before." He looked to the commissioner with guilt growing on his tired features. "Naturally, I had it searched for contraband before I allowed it past the gates. We opened it up and examined the works."

"Go on," Doc urged.

"I suspect we damaged the receiving tubes somehow, because after it was placed here, it only worked for a few days. I had it shipped back to the donor. This model you see was the one I had set aside when the gift radio came in."

"When did the radio cease to function?" Doc asked, looking away from the console.

The warden rubbed his blocky jaw in thought. "It was—" he began. He looked up, shocked. "Why, it was the very day Hassel met his Maker."

"Before or after?" Doc asked.

"After. I remember turning it on not an hour after they carted Hassel away. I was curious as to whether his death would make the news."

"This donor," Doc asked. "Was his name by chance Homer Ding?"

"Why, yes," exclaimed the sleepy warden. "He claimed to have a keen interest in penal reform. However did you know?"

The bronze man simply thanked the warden and he and the police commissioner left him to his befuddlement.

"On behalf of the police department of this city," said the commissioner as they retraced their steps, "I can promise you our full protection against this threat to your safety."

"That," Doc Savage said flatly, "will not be necessary."

XXII

ABDUCTOR IN WHITE

Dawn brought new snow.

It was the light, powdery quality of the previous fall. For the first hour, the flakes struck exposed surfaces of building and ground alike and were speedily absorbed into the cold moistness, leaving no trace.

As the day progressed, the papery precipitation continued undiminished, eventually winning its silent conflict with the damp environment. Flakes began to stick. They accumulated in a thin sugary layer, slowly clumping into a coating like the rough nap of a great garment.

Dapper Ham Brooks cursed the weather bitterly.

He was shivering behind the wheel of the identical coupe he had been driving two nights previous, when Eduardo Luz had forced him into a New Jersey snowbank. The coupe had been retrieved from Harmon Cash's speakeasy hideout, where the dapper lawyer had left it.

It was now parked outside of Cash's erstwhile Manhattan office.

"Blast it!" Ham snapped as stubborn snow powdered the coupe's windows. He got out and gave each window a vigorous rub with a bit of waste rag. This forced him to lean over the coupe's hood to reach certain spots, soiling his elegant morning coat in the process. His trouser crease had already been ruined by the necessity of remaining in the cramped car for many hours.

Ham had been performing this chore all morning. He had been stuck in the coupe since following exquisite Dana O'Fall from Doc Savage headquarters the day before. For reasons known only to herself, the lady private investigator had secured the empty suite next to the one formerly occupied by Harmon Cash.

She had remained inside all night, preventing the dapper lawyer from leaving.

Ham had taken up a position where, by employing binoculars, he could see after a fashion into the office windows, which were on the second floor of the building.

"Drat!" he fumed, bringing the binoculars to bear once more. The sticky snow was beginning to obscure the row of panes.

There was a compact short-wave set mounted under the coupe's dash. Ham switched it on, waited for the carrier-wave hiss, and began speaking into the microphone.

"Calling Doc Savage," he said crisply.

"Go ahead, Ham," came the bronze man's vibrant voice, only a little distorted by the loud-speaker.

"I've been monitoring this duplicitous female's activities as best I can," Ham said wearily. "But so far nobody suspicious has entered or left the building. I don't mind admitting that I'm bally tired of all this inaction."

"Stay with it. Obviously, she has some purpose in renting that suite. It is better not to interfere."

"I just wish I knew what her game is," Ham complained. "This is a confounded nuisance, this waiting." His tone grew interested. "How is Monk coming along?"

"Monk is attempting to locate Eduardo Luz and Harmon Cash," Doc declared.

"From what you were telling me, Doc, it sounds like this Luz fellow must be White Eyes."

"That is simply conjecture," the bronze man cautioned.

"Perhaps. But who else wears white clothing, has ample bonds to throw about, and possesses reasons for wishing ruin upon Harmon Cash? From what we know of this Cash, he is an up-and-coming criminal power.

Just the sort White Eyes would see as a threat to his plans."

"*Let me know if any action impends,*" the bronze man directed. The carrier-wave hiss died. Ham shut off the set, and clapped his binoculars back over his dark eyes.

"I'll just wager," the dapper lawyer muttered in the cold coupe interior, "that this Dana O'Fall is on White Eyes's pay roll."

Whether Dana O'Fall was a tool of the mysterious White Eyes or not, she was clearly a believer in taking an early lunch—or perhaps she had endured too many hours without food to remain in her newly acquired office any longer.

At quarter past eleven, she emerged from the building, bundled up in her expensive fur-trimmed coat. She positioned herself on a snow-blown street corner and commandeered a taxi cab with a two-finger whistle that would have done credit to a traffic cop.

"A break at last!" Ham chortled, tossing the binoculars aside and scrambling to get the coupe in motion.

The taxi scooted down Lexington Avenue, angled across town at Fifty-first Street, and let Dana O'Fall off before a simple diner. She went in.

Ham found a parking space and deftly inserted the coupe. Through blowing snow, he watched Dana take a booth and appear to order lunch.

Frowning, Ham got on the short wave.

"Doc," he said when the bronze man came on the air, "I've followed Dana O'Fall to a diner. This would be a perfect opportunity to poke about that office of hers, if you can break away."

"*I cannot. Why don't you do it?*"

"What if this is a ruse to smoke out trailers?"

"*Dana O'Fall is a very perceptive young lady,*" Doc said. "If you loiter in plain view, she will undoubtedly catch on that you are shadowing her. There is more to be gained by investigating that office."

"Righto, Doc," Ham said, sending the coupe back the way it came.

The office was a furnished one, Ham found after picking the lock. There was a plain desk, no blotter, and an assortment of simple chairs, a few of which actually matched.

There was also a telephone on the desk top, and beside it a wire-tap device, along with a telephone headset.

The wire-tap was not connected to the desk telephone, Ham quickly discovered. The wire instead led to an inner wall and through a hole in the baseboard no bigger than a pencil lead. Wood shavings on the floor before it told Ham that the hole had been recently drilled.

Recalling that Harmon Cash's office was adjacent, Ham picked up the desk telephone, jiggled the hook until he got the local operator.

"Please connect me," Ham requested, "with Mr. Harmon Cash at the following address." Ham recited the street address from memory.

Presently, a muffled telephone bell could be heard jangling beyond the wall.

"There is no answer," the operator told him after several rings.

"Keep trying," Ham urged. Then, laying aside the receiver, the dapper lawyer hurried out into the corridor and picked the lock. He rushed in to scoop up the ringing telephone.

Disguising his voice, he said querulously, "Hello? Who is it?"

He dropped the phone and hurried back to the other office. Disdaining the telephone, he clapped the headset over his ears.

The operator's annoyed tone came through the headset saying, "Go ahead, sir. Your party has answered."

Having ascertained that Dana O'Fall had indeed tapped Harmon Cash's line, Ham Brooks grabbed the nearby telephone and, reverting to his natural voice, asked, "Mr. Cash, please."

Ham allowed a few seconds to pass for the operator to disconnect, intending to hang up immediately after.

To his utter astonishment, an unfamiliar voice came through the receiver diaphragm and asked, "Is some one there?"

Quitting Dana O'Fall's office, Ham Brooks flashed next door to Harmon Cash's suite.

The door was still open. Recklessly, he plunged through.

A universe of angry red stars burst before his vision, the result of a very solid object descending on the back of his expensively tonsured skull.

Ham went down hard, fighting to hold onto consciousness.

Through pain-seared eyes, he saw the trouser legs of his assailant. They were as white as the snow falling outside the window.

Then the valiant lawyer surrendered consciousness.

An unguessable interval later, Ham Brooks woke up in an unexpected place. The front seat of his coupe.

Snow lay in opaque sheets on the windows, which explained why he had not been noticed slumped over the wheel.

The dapper lawyer groaned.

"I would advise silence," a hard male voice intoned from the rear seat.

Ham started to turn. A heavy metallic object nudged the back of his head, bringing instant, piercing pain.

"Owww!" Ham groaned.

"I suspect that this curious pistol which I found in your coat would completely obliterate your five-dollar haircut if I pulled the trigger," the voice warned.

With an elbow, Ham felt for his supermachine pistol. The padded armpit holster was empty. His eyes went to the rear-vision mirror. It had been snapped off its mount, obviously to thwart identification of his mysterious passenger.

"I imagine you know that you are holding what is called a mercy pistol," Ham stated. "It fires bullets which do not kill."

"Any time you feel the need of a nap," the unfamiliar voice said tightly, "feel free to turn around."

Ham declined the offer. Although there was an excellent chance that his captor had not divined the intricate series of safety latches the supermachine pistol boasted, he was in no mood to put that theory to a test.

"I do not understand the need for secrecy," Ham said. "I already have a fair idea of your identity."

"Educate me."

"You are Eduardo Luz," guessed the dapper lawyer. "Your unseasonable apparel is a dead give-away."

"And who would know better than the Beau Brummell of the legal profession?" the other grunted. There was a pause. "You know, I *could* be White Eyes."

"Perhaps you are both," Ham said carefully, staring at the whitened windshield as if searching for reflective spots.

"A number of people think that's true," the voice said, "but unless I am mistaken, you would not recognize the natural voice of either person."

It was true, but Ham was loath to admit it. He only knew what Doc Savage had gleaned from his probings of Dana O'Fall's recollections.

"You might be interested in knowing that Dana O'Fall has returned to her office. You *were* watching her, weren't you?"

When the dapper lawyer failed to respond, the voice continued.

"And Dana O'Fall is monitoring Harmon Cash's office. Why do you think that is?"

"I have no idea," Ham sniffed.

"Maybe Dana will give us some answers, if we wait long enough."

Ham Brooks stifled a groan. The unfamiliar voice emitted a humorless laugh, as they settled down to what promised to be an extended wait.

*   *   *

Much to the dapper lawyer's relief, Dana O'Fall came running out of the office building within the hour. She flagged down a taxi in obvious excitement. It whisked her away.

"As they say in the flickers," the voice of Ham's captor put in, "follow that car."

Grimacing, the dapper lawyer obeyed.

Without benefit of a rear-vision mirror, he was forced to negotiate the snow-slickened streets of Manhattan with extreme care, keeping the taxi in sight at all times. It led to some hair-raising moments involving pedestrians, but much to Ham's chagrin, there was no police interference. The special plates of the Doc Savage machine assured that undesired courtesy.

"Watch your damn driving!" the voice of his unknown passenger gritted, as they narrowly circumvented a slow milk wagon returning to the stable from its morning rounds.

"What do you expect?" Ham complained, shrill-voiced. "I'm driving half blind without that mirror."

"You'll have a worse time of it if I unloosen some slugs from this complicated cannon."

Ham swallowed a hot retort and concentrated on his driving.

The lack of a rear mirror meant that the dapper lawyer had no inkling of the ghostly quiet sedan that had picked up his trail not long after he left the vicinity of the former office of Harmon Cash.

XXIII

EXPERIMENT STRANGE

In his skyscraper laboratory, Doc Savage, giant man of bronze, man of mystery, and muscular superman, was bent over the complicated radio apparatus that had occupied his attention since the day before.

He wore the silvery shroud that enveloped him from head to toe. The hooded portion of the garment was over his bronze head, concealing everything except his dust-fine golden eyes which peered through tiny apertures. They were obviously cut for protection, not comfort. The bronze man's eyes were barely visible behind the transparent lenses of heavy goggles fitted over the eye holes.

From time to time, he threw off this rig to answer a ringing telephone or to respond to the short-wave band his aids habitually used.

Monk, combing the city, had reported sighting Eduardo Luz in the neighborhood of his apartment. He had given chase, losing the man in the near white-out conditions.

Mysteriously, Ham Brooks had stopped calling in, and Doc was unable to raise him. Doc had dispatched the homely chemist to the Harmon Cash office address, and Monk had reported no sign of the lawyer, or Dana O'Fall.

"I cannot leave my work at this stage," Doc explained. "Ham's coupe is equipped with a hidden radio transmitter that is always operating. Attempt to track its signal."

"Gotcha, Doc."

Doc returned to his experiment.

The calls continued to pour in all day. A few were the work of news-hungry reporters who had learned of the threat to Doc Savage himself. Doc declined all comment. The remaining calls came from the police commissioner, telling of the progress in sweating some of the criminals that had been arrested the night before.

There was precious little. A few names had surfaced during the arduous third degrees—names of criminals who had come to the White Eyes meeting and had spurned the spectral criminal's offer to band together in a massive crime enterprise.

These independent souls had begun turning up all over town, quite dead.

"It was like somebody just rolled their eyes clean around," was the way the police commissioner had put it.

"White Eyes is moving to tighten his grip on the underworld," Doc pronounced grimly, "by eradicating all dissenters."

"I'm not weeping over dead crooks," the tough commissioner allowed. "None of the white-eyed stiffs match the description of your missing aid, Roberts," he added in a more sympathetic voice.

"Long Tom is more valuable to whoever has him alive than dead," Doc said.

"If he's a prisoner of Harmon Cash, I wouldn't lay odds on his future. Two of the stiffs have been identified as Cash torpedoes. White Eyes must have it really in for Cash."

"We do not know who has Long Tom at this point."

The police commissioner made no mention of Benny the Bust, the pickpocket whom Doc had taken from the Tombs. Nor did Doc volunteer the man's fate. He had gone to join Blackie Doyle in a new start at Doc's up-State crime college.

"The coroner says you can autopsy Jim James Garben's corpse any time you like," the commissioner offered.

"I would like to perform that work here, if there are no objections," Doc said.

"I'll send Garben express," the commissioner chuckled, by way of a macabre jest.

Doc terminated the call and resumed his experiment. He had brought a scoop of fresh snow from the observation platform above his headquarters floor. It partially filled a glass beaker.

Restoring the silvery hood and goggles, Doc threw switches. Nothing seemed to happen. Then, almost magically, the snow turned to water. One moment, it was a flaky opaque heap. The next, clear water stood in the container.

It grew disturbed, came to a furious boil. Steam rose.

Doc leapt for a cutoff switch. He was too late by seconds. The water simply vanished, and the beaker shattered, falling in on itself.

The apparatus shut off, Doc examined the glass shards intently. He was careful not to touch them, even with his gloved hands.

Then he went to a refrigeration chamber, and extracted another snow-filled beaker. It gave off supercold vapor.

Doc placed this amid the shattered remains of the first beaker. Then he draped it with a small blanket of the same silvery material which comprised the garment he wore.

This time, he let the apparatus run for five minutes. The vapor ceased leaking from under the silvery blanket, but there was no steam, no sound of boiling, no breaking of glass.

Doc snapped the cutoff switch and lifted the blanket. White snow filled the beaker, showing only the approximate amount of liquefaction that would stem from snow sitting at room temperature for five minutes.

However, Doc felt of various objects around the beaker. These were metal tools, and were unusually warm to the touch.

A flashing light on the nearby short-wave set distracted Doc from further study.

"Doc!" came the squeaky voice of Monk Mayfair, the hairy chemist.

"Go ahead, Monk."

"I been shaggin' the hidden transmitter in Ham's coupe, like you asked. I spotted the car."

"Is Ham all right?"

"I think so. We're out on Long Island. Looks like Ham is followin' a taxi. I'm hangin' back, so whoever's in the cab won't get spooked."

"Good. It sounds like Ham is on to something important."

"Maybe not so good," Monk said worriedly.

"What do you mean?" asked Doc.

"I've been tryin' like the dickens to raise him on the short wave, but he don't answer. And I think I spy somebody in his back seat. Get this, the guy's all tricked out in white."

"Follow Ham to his destination," Doc directed. "Report in as soon as you have that information."

"Sure thing," Monk squeaked. "I just hope that shyster ain't in any trouble."

Monk switched off.

Miles away, the homely chemist hunkered down behind the wheel of his quiet-running sedan. The caravan consisting of the taxi in the lead, Ham's coupe in the middle, and Monk's sedan bringing up a cautious rear, was wending its way to the outer tip of Long Island.

They were running along the coast line, where winds coming off the oyster-colored ocean pushed the moist air relatively free of snow.

Monk wondered if Ham was aware of his presence. The sharp-eyed lawyer could hardly fail to spot him in his windshield mirror, but so far Ham had given no sign of having done so.

Worry wrinkles made the homely chemist's unlovely visage even more homely than usual. He fingered one cauliflowered ear absently.

The journey took them to Southampton, an area of fine homes and expensive seaside manses, overlooking the heaving slate expanse of the Atlantic Ocean.

The grounds of the home the taxi cab arrived at did not exactly qualify as a mansion, but it was large and quietly dignified, boasting a many-columned portico with a view of a neat private dock at the rear.

Ham's coupe slowed after the taxi turned up the driveway to the sloping apron of snow between white house and gray water, then continued on.

Monk decided to turn off the road well before reaching the white house. He took the liberty of parking in a private driveway and came out of his machine, hunkered down in the hopes of not being seen.

Presently, the taxi blew past him without its fare, on its way back to the city.

Minutes dragged past. There was no other visible activity that Monk could discern. He decided that the absence of movement required investigation.

Unlimbering his supermachine pistol from its armpit holster, he went in search of Ham's coupe. His big feet made crunching noises in the snow cover.

Monk found the car empty. A cursory glance showed the homely chemist that Ham had left his elegant sword cane propped against the steering wheel.

Monk's jaw dropped to comical proportions at the sight of the abandoned stick.

"Blazes!" he gulped hoarsely. For he knew his comrade in arms—knew he never went anywhere without his trademark affectation.

Monk got the door open, warmed up the short wave.

"Doc!" he squawled into the microphone. "I followed everyone to number 334 Pond Lane, in Southampton. Ham's in trouble for sure. I'm in his car. He left his fool cane behind!"

Before the bronze man could reply, the bullfiddle moan of a supermachine pistol sounded nearby.

"Doc, I gotta go!" howled Monk, pitching from the coupe. He ran for the house as fast as his bandy legs could carry him.

The bullfiddle moaning came again, and this time blended into it was the spiteful crack of pistol shots. Then the supermachine pistol ceased sounding. The spiteful shots continued, however.

A woman screamed once, shrilly.

"Blazes!" Monk croaked, his voice sick.

XXIV

THE TALKING MAN

Had Doc Savage remained in the sanctity of his skyscraper headquarters, he would have had a full two-hour drive to Southampton, on the outer reaches of Long Island.

But the bronze man, impelled perhaps by some premonition of trouble, had taken to his long somber roadster shortly after receiving the first word that Monk had followed Ham Brook's coupe onto Long Island.

He was speeding through the Shinnecock Hills now. A siren concealed under his hood wailed, making traffic melt before him. Doc had engaged the siren with a flip of a dash switch when Monk's last frantic call—warning of Ham's peril—had come.

Doc was twenty minutes away from Southampton. The speedometer needle crawled toward sixty, then seventy, and beyond. Doc negotiated sharp turns with the skill of a Barney Oldfield.

Ten minutes of quietly furious, intent driving brought him to the vicinity of 334 Pond Lane. He had cut the siren during the last stretch, for the sake of a stealthy approach.

Parking the car beside Monk's abandoned sedan, the bronze man reconnoitered the palatial house on the water.

In the snow back of the porticoed house, he came upon a sprinkling of tiny supermachine pistol cartridges amid a stamping of footprints. Doc recognized Ham's tapered soles, and nearby, tracks made by Monk's wide

201

feet. There were other prints as well, one set of which dwarfed those of the simian chemist's.

Doc attempted to read the signs. They were too confused, the product of too many frantic feet. That there had been a tussle in the snow, including an apparently brief trading of gunfire, was clear, but no more than that could be gleaned.

Doc floated up to the house, lingered under a bay window from which warm light spilled.

He peered in.

The room was choked with people, Doc was surprised to see. Most had guns, and these weapons were pointed at two very white-faced individuals, who stood with their hands upraised. Chestnut-haired Dana O'Fall was one of them. The other was a tall hulk of a fellow with absolutely no hair atop his massive head and a bad case of the squints.

Through a knot of gunmen Doc spied a figure entirely clothed in white. The angle was too acute to determine this person's identity. His face was obscured by other heads.

Doc ducked back with haste, fearful of being spotted. He eased around the side of the house, keeping low to avoid detection through ground-floor windows.

Careful stalking brought him around to the ocean-facing entrance door, where a modest brass nameplate said simply: MAXIMUS LAVENDER.

The name meant nothing to the bronze man, but inasmuch as the bald-headed man had been attired in a comfortable smoking jacket, Doc concluded that he must be the homeowner, Lavender.

Right now, the bronze man was more concerned over the fate of Monk and Ham. There had been no sign of them in the room.

He noticed, however, a trail of disturbance going away from the door. It cut a furrow in the snow leading down to a dock, where—unusual in this season—a flashy speedboat was moored. Footsteps. Recent. Smoke seemed to drift up from the engine of the sturdy craft, indicating it had only lately arrived.

Crouched before the front door, the bronze man reached into his gadget vest and removed from one of its innumerable pockets a slim steel tool. He inserted this into the lock, manipulated it for several moments.

The lock surrendered. Slowly, taking extreme care, Doc eased the knob around until he felt the tongue disengage.

The bronze man faced a difficult choice, now. So far, he had managed to approach undetected. But if there were guards posted on the other side, he could not hope to ease the door open unseen.

He set himself, his metallic features grim. One hand rested on the knob, holding it open. The other was empty. It was Doc Savage's policy never to carry firearms—not even his compact, extremely efficient mercy pistols—because he felt a man could grow dependent upon such weapons and correspondingly be made helpless if deprived of them.

Doc Savage flung open the door.

He hit the ground, rolled, coming to one knee in a far corner, ready to react to any threat.

He found, somewhat to his relief, that his precautions were unnecessary. The room—a walnut-paneled foyer—was deserted. A grandfather clock ticked loudly in one corner.

Doc whipped to the nearest room, peered in. He saw a well-appointed parlor, also untenanted. Doc returned to the foyer, which devolved into a long corridor.

Voices floated up this.

"I will ask you again, Miss O'Fall," one said. "What is your interest in this man, Lavender?" The voice was male and muffled. Doc did not recognize it.

"I told you," Dana O'Fall shot back. "I was eavesdropping on Harmon Cash's telephone line. This man Lavender called, asking to speak with Cash. I picked up the line and got him to agree to see me. So here I am."

"It bane truth be," a queerly accented voice chimed in.

"Quiet, Lavender," came the muffled voice. "I'll get to you later."

"I warn you must," the queer voice pressed. "Mine friend Harmon Cash, coming he is. He is big shoot—"

Harsh, cruel laughter greeted this last.

"Shot," the muffled voice could not resist correcting. "You mean shot."

"Like you say, big shot. He will make mincemeat of you, and your fonny white trick suit."

"I am not afraid of Harmon Cash," the muffled voice insisted. "Now, be quiet! It is Miss O'Fall I am addressing."

"I told you everything you wanted to know," Dana said in a sullen tone.

"Not," returned the muffled voice, "who you work for."

"Isn't it obvious?" Dana said with a trace of vinegar in her voice.

"Make it clear to us," the other suggested.

"My employer is Doc Savage. Why do you think his men were following me?"

A chorus of curses rolled down the corridor—obviously the assembled gunmen expressing themselves in the typically profane fashion of their breed.

They went quiet after a hissing sound pierced the hubbub.

"If that is true," came the muffled voice, "then I would wipe that supercilious expression off your face, Miss O'Fall. After all, I have two of the bronze man's men prisoner in the cellar."

That was all Doc Savage needed to hear. He went in search of the kitchen—the typical indoor room from which a cellar could be reached.

Doc tested a door. It opened on a well-stocked pantry. He tried another. This gave up impenetrable darkness and a cold, musty odor common to basements of homes close enough to water to be vulnerable to flooding.

Doc went down the stairs in darkness, using one hand on a sloping wall to guide him.

There was light below. It came through boxy foundation windows. Smoky gray fingers streamed from the open vents of a roaring coal furnace. It was quite warm down here.

The basement was sectioned into paneled rooms. Doc went to the first door he found. He had picked up a drinking glass from the kitchen sink. He placed the open end of this against the door and one bronze ear to the base. He listened.

The glass made a fair sound conductor. Doc picked up muffled scrapings and the occasional distressed grunt.

A harsh voice said, "If you don't stop squirming around like that, monkey-face, I'm gonna bop you one."

Placing the glass out of the way on the concrete floor, the bronze man grasped the knob. He gave the door a hard shove.

He was in luck. The guard—it was he who had spoken—happened to be standing directly before the door. Impelled by the muscular strength of Doc's cabled right arm pushing the door, he lost his footing and his gun both at the same time.

Doc gave him no time to recover either. He fell on the man like a bronze vengeance. His sinewy fingers took the man's throat from the back. He exerted sudden pressure, adding a sharp twist.

Nerve paralysis induced by Doc's manipulation of spinal centers caused the guard to go as limp as a rain-soaked scarecrow.

Doc heaved erect. The room, he was surprised to see, was a modest laboratory. Workbenches were overflowing with electrical apparatus.

The bronze man gave these only a cursory glance. For in one corner, bouncing on the floor, was the hairy chemist, Monk Mayfair. He was trussed like a Christmas goose with heavy copper wires. Electrical tape had been wound over his lower face, effectively gagging him. His tiny eyes were screwed up in anger. A buzzing sound, like angry bees, came through his nostrils.

Doc sank to one knee, and went to work. His bronze fingers found the points where a tool had been used to twist the ends of the copper wire into makeshift knots.

Using only the obdurate power of his bronze fingers, Doc untwisted the copper knots at the hairy chemist's bound wrists and ankles.

Monk flung off the wiring and bounced to his feet. After he yanked his tape gag free and spat out a balled-up handkerchief, he resembled an enraged bull ape.

"Doc!" he whooped. "Am I glad to see you!"

"Quiet!" Doc cautioned. "Where is Ham?"

"I dunno," Monk admitted, windmilling his furry arms to regain circulation flow. "By the time I got to this joint, the fighting was over. I saw footprints going in the front door. I was on my way to shake the rafters when this speedboat charges up, and all these guys pile out, loaded for bear. I put a few to sleep with my mercy pistol, but there were more than I could handle. I lit back for the house. The door opened and someone conked me on the head. I woke up here."

"Did you see who commanded the boat crew?" Doc asked.

"Not so's you'd notice. He was wearin' white, though."

Doc nodded. "Either White Eyes or Eduardo Luz."

"Maybe both," Monk said hopefully. "I feel like knockin' a few skulls together."

"Not yet. I overheard a voice say that both you and Ham were down here. We must find Ham before we can take action."

"If that shyster's down here, I ain't seen him."

As if on cue, a muted thumping came from under a workbench. It was weak, tentative.

Doc went to the source, and slid out from under

the workbench a long steamer trunk, about six feet long and three square. It was secured by a series of latches. Doc threw these, and flung up the lid.

"Blazes!" Monk croaked.

For lying within the steamer trunk was a pitiful figure. At first glance, it appeared to be a corpse. The extreme pallor of the face suggested this. Too, there were small burn marks here and there on exposed portions of the skin. The absence of eyebrows and eyelashes was remindful of a corpse mummifying in death.

Except for the eyes. They were open, emitting pale fury.

Monk blinked stupidly. "Long Tom!" he howled.

It was an unfortunate outburst. For a man suddenly appeared, gun in hand, at the laboratory door.

He blurted, "What's all this racket—*hell!*"

The gunman's eyes went wide at the sight of the bronze man and the apish chemist. Although he had an automatic in his fist, he did not avail himself of it. Instead, he turned tail and pounded up the steps to the first floor, shouting at the top of his lungs.

"Doc Savage!" he bawled. "He's down in the basement!"

"Now we're in for it!" Monk muttered.

With grim speed, the bronze man reached into the steamer trunk and plucked out the pallid electrical wizard, Long Tom Roberts, simultaneously pulling down a simple handkerchief gag.

Doc set Long Tom on his feet. He was not bound. But Long Tom immediately began to weave unsteadily.

"Bug—" he muttered through cracked lips. "The bug—made them—blind."

"Monk," Doc rapped urgently. "Long Tom is in no condition to travel on his own. Get him to safety. I'll hold the stairs."

"But, Doc—" Monk protested.

Feet pounded above. There were shouts.

The bronze man lifted Long Tom in both arms, and

handed him to the hairy chemist. Monk accepted the burden, following Doc outside.

The bronze man went to the handiest window, undid a simple hook-and-eye fastener. Instantly, the jangling of an alarm bell started up.

"Must be a capacity alarm hooked up to the windows," Monk commented.

Grimly, Doc shoved up the window. Together, they eased Long Tom through the opening. It was comparatively easy, thanks to the electrical wizard's undersized physique.

Monk began to squeeze through. He barely made it. Doc refastened the window, but stayed by it.

A moment later, a voice shrilled from above.

"It's that Monk guy! He's escaping!"

Doc launched himself to the opposite side of the cellar. He unlatched a window. Digging into his equipment vest, he extracted a metallic sphere about the diameter of a cherry with a tiny lever on one side.

He gave the lever a flick and pitched the device out onto the snow-covered sloping back lawn, and got down just in time.

Came an eardrum-busting crack of a sound.

Upstairs, glass jangled. Feet skidded.

"Some one threw a grenade!" a frantic voice advised.

Doc pitched to another window, this one on the opposite side. He threw another of the silver cherries— they were actually compact grenades of awful potency.

Another explosion. Doc moved among the windows, opening them and flinging grenades. He took care to send them all in directions away from that taken by the fleeing Monk.

Concussion sound shook the house. Bodies could be heard hitting the floor, upending furniture in an effort to avoid feared shrapnel. There was none. Doc took care to toss the grenades too far away to jeopardize innocent lives—if anyone in the house could be so categorized.

When he had exhausted his supply of grenades, and before the last concussions had ceased to echo, Doc

Savage floated up the cellar steps with the eerie silence of a possum ascending a tree.

At the top of the stairs, he encountered a lone gunman in the act of picking himself off the floor.

The man gave out a yelp of surprise and pointed a short-barreled revolver directly at the man of metal. His finger clamped down on the trigger.

"Better say your prayers, bronze guy!" he hissed. "'Cause you're about to go to sleep!"

XXV

UPROAR

Doc Savage moved with all the trained power in his mighty frame. Before the gunman could properly squeeze the trigger, the bronze man clamped fingers of awful metallic strength over the cylinder.

The gunman pulled the trigger. Nothing happened. The trigger refused to come back, the cylinder to revolve.

"What the hell!" he bleated. He tried to cock the weapon with his thumb. The hammer, too, declined to obey him. It might have been welded to the firing pin.

Doc's free hand drifted up to his neck. It dawned on the astonished gunman, an instant before he lost all awareness, that Doc Savage had been exerting so much force through his other hand that he held the bullet-bearing cylinder in place, effectively freezing the mechanism into uselessness.

Doc eased him to the floor and, heedless of his own peril, went to a kitchen window which overlooked the front lawn.

Monk Mayfair was making his bandy-legged way to the main road, and the waiting cars, Long Tom Roberts limp in his burly arms.

When it was evident that the simian chemist was safe, Doc faded back from the window and began going through the house in search of Ham Brooks and whatever else he could find. The place was almost weirdly quiet now. The quietness had come suddenly. Even the alarm bell seemed to settle down some.

210

Then a muffled, queer voice rang out.

"Frisk the place and get Doc Savage and his other man," it directed.

It was the same queer voice that had earlier interrogated Dana O'Fall and Maximus Lavender, the voice that might have belonged to Eduardo Luz—or the mysterious White Eyes. Doc gravitated toward the voice.

He heard an uproar. Two shots. Blows. A cry. The cry was in Ham's voice.

Doc hurtled forward. Carpet was underfoot; there seemed to be carpet on all of the corridor floors. This one was not tacked down and it slipped a little on the hard wood. Then, as Doc stopped suddenly, it split, slid badly, added to his troubles.

Men had appeared ahead, with guns. They were not fast enough, and Doc got back around the corner of the corridor.

Yelling, the men charged.

Doc dug from a pocket of his vest some of the tiny anæsthetic bombs which he habitually carried. They resembled glass marbles with a liquid interior, and were thin shells filled with a chemical concoction which vaporized instantly, produced abrupt unconsciousness when inhaled, and which became harmless after mingling with the air for somewhat less than sixty seconds.

The anæsthetic bombs broke almost soundlessly down the corridor. Their effect was immediate, striking. The yelling stopped as if throats had been cut. Bodies fell.

There was a brief silence.

"Doc Savage is using some kind of gas," said the strange muffled voice. "Be careful. Get back."

That command to get back warned Doc. He retreated, and not an instant too soon, for there was a crash, and a major portion of the corridor came to pieces around a kernel of fire and smoke.

They were using ordinary hand grenades which perhaps had been bought from some bootlegger of war paraphernalia.

Reasoning they would use other grenades, Doc retreated rapidly. Came another explosion. The house was full of crashing, the alarm bell was still jangling patiently, and the air reeked of powder that had been burned.

Doc, watching over his shoulder, eased around a corner. And he put too much confidence in his ability to detect the near-presence of an enemy. He sometimes did that. He had trained his ears, his olfactory organs, and his other senses from childhood. But there was a lot of noise and smell in the house, and he ran straight into trouble.

Two guns crammed against his back. The holders of the weapons did not waste time in preliminary talk.

They pulled the triggers of their weapons.

Doc's bulletproof vest, while it would stop revolver lead, was flexible, and had he not twisted furiously, the impact of the shots, with the pistol muzzles shoved into his back, would probably have broken ribs and left unpleasant bruises. As it was, the slugs smashed across the chain mail, delivering glancing blows. He was knocked back. Then he went forward.

His fists plunged, bronze blocks, at the two gunmen. No business of pressing spinal nerve centers now. He simply hit them.

They fell senseless several feet from where they had been standing.

Doc took two steps after them, turned right through the most convenient door, and stumbled over a body. There was light in these rooms. He looked down.

The body was that of bald, too-tall Maximus Lavender. A heaving of the chest, a writhing of fingers showed that it was not a dead body.

Doc scooped the man up. When he was moved, Lavender groaned, got one eye opened, shut it, groaned more loudly, then ventured to open both eyes.

"I been mangled, positively," he groaned. "I am next to dead or maybe there."

Doc said, "Where are the others?" and hurled two more of his anæsthetic bombs down the hallway.

"I wouldn't know," groaned Lavender. "When the booming start up, I try to break away. My head, poor him! They knock on him with a damned gun. Once, twice. A lotta damn times. I would know what happened, not so you could notice it."

He waved his big arms, indicating he could stand, and did so when Doc stood him on his ample feet. His massive face was wreathed with pain. There was a scrape of raw skin near the point of his bald scalp.

"Me, why did I ever go from Missouri!" he groaned.

"Missouri?"

"Sure. Me, I was born in a red-oak brush patch out by there."

Just how a native-born Missourian should happen to slaughter English as Maximus Lavender did was a subject for conversation, but not one pressing enough to warrant it being discussed at the moment. There was more shooting.

"Damned gas!" the muffled voice whanged from another part of the building. "We'll have to get out of here!"

"What about the prisoners?"

"Take them along—alive," ordered the muffled voice.

There was noise, movement. Doc Savage went to a window. Glass fell out of the window and a bullet came in. He got back swiftly with Maximus Lavender and went to another room—a bookshelf-lined study—and approached the window there. He did not peer outside directly, but used a tiny periscope of a device, the tube of which was hardly larger than a match stick and unlikely to be seen.

Men were running out of the house and down toward the dock, with its bobbing speedboat, running awkwardly as men will do going downhill. Two appeared, carrying a prisoner.

The captive was Ham Brooks.

Other men appeared carrying two other prisoners, who apparently had been gagged, and who were wrapped around and around with long window drapes to prevent use of their arms. The gags, the drape windings, made it difficult to identify them.

Squinting Maximus Lavender looked over Doc's shoulder, boldly thrusting his bald egg of a head in front of the window.

"Der girl, Dana, and mine pal, Harmon Cash, dat must be," Lavender said. "And they are tied up like rummers—like lummers—mummers—like bandages. No, like—aw, hell!"

"Harmon Cash—here?" Doc demanded sharply.

"Sure, Harmon, he was coming me to see. They take him prisoner, I hear it from another room. They lock a closet around him, I think."

"The leader in white—was he a man known as Eduardo Luz?"

Bald Maximus Lavender blinked. "How should anyone know? Der feller, he was masked from toe to hat."

A bullet nudged itself a neat round hole in the glass of the window at that point.

"Better get down!" Doc rapped.

"Sure tootin'," said Lavender.

He got down. Lead came through not only the windows, but the walls.

"Zin-n-g!" said Lavender. "Rifles, if me would you ask."

Doc took a chair, threw it through the window. He threw another chair through. The glass and crosspieces of the window were heavy, but so were the chairs, and the bronze man made a sizable opening. He began to hurl his anæsthetic grenades. It was not much use, for they were not heavy enough to carry to the men, and there was no breeze to waft the vapor toward the gang. In fact, the prevailing wind was coming off the water.

"Hold your breath," Doc urged Lavender.

"Excuse it, please?"

"You cannot see it, but there is an invisible gas out there," the bronze man explained. "It will become harmless after sixty seconds. Holding the breath will keep it from overcoming us."

They held their breaths.

The shooting went on, and the voices continued shouting for a time; then there was silence, except for the steady clanging of the alarm bell.

Then the muffled voice called, *"Doc Savage!"*

Doc did not reply.

"Savage!" the voice called. *"This is no trick to get you to show your position!"*

"Then what is it?" Doc asked. His voice did not seem lifted, but it had acquired a marked carrying quality.

"I have your man Ham and Dana O'Fall and another person, whose identity would interest you, prisoners," said the voice. It said something more, which was lost in the steady clanging of the alarm bell.

"That bell, darn me," said Lavender angrily. "Give her a minute and I shut me off."

He scuttled out into the hall, and the bell noise shortly stopped, after which he returned. "I put in dat alarm to keep a burglar away. Am I indignant."

Doc called, "Now maybe you can make yourself heard."

"We have your man Ham, Dana O'Fall, and Harmon Cash," said the strained muffled voice. *"They will be killed if you interfere further in this matter. If any of you interfere, in fact."*

"Us interfere!" Lavender howled angrily at the unseen person speaking with the mouth covered. "Us interfere! She is you interfering with you, I mean, with us! Me, I do nothing. But am I let alone? Hell, no! Me, I know not one damn little thing about anything. Hell, no! I should say I like it, not much!"

"Shut up," said the muffled voice, *"and let Savage talk."*

"To you, squirrel food!" yelled Lavender.

Doc had crawled over to the window. That their foes should start speaking was suspicious. It might mean that they were trying to keep Doc occupied while they made a flanking attack. The bronze man used his tiny periscope.

There was nothing phony afoot. The raiders were down by the dock. They were loading their unconscious comrades and the prisoners aboard the flashy speedboat.

A man in white was doing the speaking. The ghostly, all-in-white leader was holding a megaphone which must have been taken off the speedboat. Megaphones for speaking to other craft on the water are common boat equipment. The megaphone enabled the muffled voice of the white-clad personage to carry.

Doc called, "What is it you want to say?"

"A warning!" twanged the man in white. *"I am all set to embark on quest of something never before attempted. It is a tremendous task, probably the largest job of theft any one man in the world has ever undertaken. I will not stand for interference."*

"What is it?" Doc called.

"I am after your legendary gold supply. This is a perfect opportunity for you to divulge its location to me."

"Ho, ho!" exploded Lavender sarcastically. "He is laughing up our sleeves!"

The white-garbed man said, *"You, Lavender, are a sensible man. Sensible enough to let things ride as they are and not get involved deeper."*

Lavender squawked in a big voice, "Why am I picking on you? I mean—why are you picking on me?"

"You're in this thing but you don't know it, you big tongue-twister," said the figure in white.

Doc Savage had been maneuvering the periscope in an effort to get a better look at the gang leader. The lens, while it magnified somewhat, did not bring the individual close enough to make details especially clear. Doc made a mental note to add a set of magnifying lenses of great power to the periscope eyepiece.

The bronze man took a chance and lifted his head, peering out of the window. They did not shoot at him.

He lifted a pocket telescope and hastily focused the lenses. Then they shot at him. He was forced to duck down.

"You seen how much?" Lavender wanted to know.

"Not much," Doc said.

He was, as a matter of fact, disappointed. He could not tell whether the immaculately attired figure was swarthy Eduardo Luz or the masked White Eyes. The Panama hat the man wore concealed a major portion of his features, and the white gloves helped cover skin tone. The white of the gloves was exactly the hue of dead fish flesh.

Lavender had been looking worried. Now he howled, "What you mean it, I am in this?"

"*I hope it doesn't get through your thick head,*" called the figure in white.

Doc rapped suddenly, "Lavender!"

"Sure, fella."

"There is something queer about their stopping to talk." The bronze man got up from where he had been crouching, rapped, "Come on!"

He dived headlong through the window. An instant afterward, Lavender landed alongside with a loud spat, as if an elephant's liver had been dropped.

The man in white began cursing. Guns went off, and bullets made mouse-squeak noises over their heads, but could not reach them because of the bulge of the slope down to the water of the frigid Atlantic, which afforded a distant rampart.

Doc crawled swiftly, and Lavender trailed him. They gained a clump of shrubbery and crawled on. They could hear men running up the slope from the water, slipping and sliding in the snow.

Then the earth lifted like a great humped camel under them. The side of the house came sliding along the ground, devouring bare shrubbery with a great crackling. It was like a big white monster trying to get them.

Doc grasped Lavender, flung him madly, leaped himself, and the house did not lie down on them.

"Thank me!" gulped Lavender. "You didn't move quick, or I would now be holding up a house."

He said that after the explosion, and while the earth was still convulsing and debris, dust, smoke, and flame were climbing high into the air. In the uproar, it was doubtful if his words were heard, even by himself.

"They forgot and left a bomb, I don't think," said Lavender. "Yes, sir, and they were talking us to death, almost."

The men coming up from the ocean appeared, circling the house wreckage, peering through the smoke and dust for Doc and Lavender. Steam rose, too. For the heat of the flames was causing the carpet of fallen snow to retreat from the house in a growing circle.

Doc threw an anæsthetic bomb. One of the men laid down and went to sleep. The others did not see him immediately, and when they did, the gas had become harmless. They ran up and grasped their fallen, snoring comrade.

There was some shouting by the white-clad gang leader. The men picked up the unconscious fellow and ran him down the steep melting slope to the river. They fell down twice, owing to the slushiness of the terrain.

They all made it back to the flashy speedboat, flung away springlines; and with a sputtering roar of motors, the boat carried them out into the bleak gray expanse of the Atlantic Ocean.

The calm and quiet of the shore returned.

"Daggone me for a son of a gun," gasped Maximus Lavender. "That sure happen in what you call no time at all."

XXVI

EXPLANATIONS

Behind them, the furiously burning pile that had been Maximus Lavender's house suddenly settled, sending skyward a boiling blotch of black smoke shot with spitting sparks.

"My poor shack!" the bald-headed man moaned, squinting before a rolling blast of heat. "She is ruined, like me!"

"There is nothing we can do about it now," Doc said urgently, giving the man a firm shove. "We can talk on the way."

"On the where way?" Lavender demanded in the tangled manner that was his style.

"Later," Doc rapped, starting off for the black road that ran before the fiery ruin.

Maximus Lavender gave a last squint at the consuming fury that had been his palatial dwelling, and loped after the bronze man.

Lavender did not keep up with Doc. He tried, and he was a fairly good runner, except that his big feet flew about a little as he ran. Almost at once, he started huffing and puffing, as if in imitation of a steam engine.

"Boy, oh boy, are you Olympic!" he gulped at one point.

Doc was not using all of the great speed of which he was capable; he kept just far enough ahead of Lavender to encourage the big man to keep up, but not far enough ahead to discourage the oversized lummox of a fellow.

Doc reached his roadster, where Monk Mayfair stood, practically jumping up and down in the road, Ham Brooks's elegant cane in one hirsute paw. He gave a tremendous whoop at the sight of Doc Savage.

"Doc!" he squawled. "Are you okay? What happened? Where's Ham?"

Doc barely broke his stride upon reaching the sedan and the roadster. He yanked open doors on one side of the latter, pushed Monk behind the wheel, and got in back, where Long Tom Roberts lay stretched out the length of the rear seat.

Breathing with noisy exertion, Maximus Lavender jumped around and piled in next to the hairy chemist.

Monk sent the roadster racing toward New York City, his foot heavy on the accelerator pedal.

"The fire," Maximus Lavender remarked, squinty eyes widening at the recklessness of Monk's driving, "she is back that way, don't you think?"

Anxiously, Monk asked, "How is he, Doc?"

In the back seat, the bronze man was working over the body of Long Tom Roberts. From his equipment vest, came a hypodermic needle and a phial of stimulant. Doc administered this, and while waiting for it to take effect, gave clipped orders.

"Monk, get on the radio. Inform the harbor police that a speedboat carrying several criminals, with Dana O'Fall, Ham, and possibly others aboard as captors, is at large."

Reaching for the microphone, the apish chemist gave out a gusty sigh of relief.

"*Whew!*" he said, hoarsely. "That news ain't exactly sunshine, but it was better than what I was thinkin'. I was afraid that overdressed shyster got caught in that conflagration back there."

"Hey!" Lavender exclaimed in an injured voice. "That'sa no way to talk about my pride anna joy. That shack, she costa me fort' thousand round iron men. She's no fragcon—confrat—what you said, dummox."

"And who," Monk growled, taking a corner on two screaming tires, "are you, tall and knobby?"

"Call me Max."

"Why?"

"Why you think, short and hairy?" Lavender snapped back. "Because Max, she's my name, 'at's why."

"Oh, brother," Monk groaned. They were on a straightaway now, and Monk held the wheel steady with one hand as he communicated with the New York harbor police. After a few minutes, he switched off the set and called into the back seat.

"They're sending out boats now," he reported. "How's Long Tom doing?"

"He is coming around," Doc advised.

The pallid electrical wizard—pallid was an understatement at this particular point—was fluttering his eyelids like tiny insect wings. His cracked lips parted stickily.

"Who dot feller?" Maximus Lavender asked, squinting curiously.

"This," Doc Savage informed him, "is the man who had been held a prisoner in your basement laboratory for what appears the last two days."

Maximus Lavender blinked his squinty eyes furiously.

"You spoofing us all, I don't think. Yes, mabbe?"

"I discovered him locked in a steamer trunk in your laboratory set-up," Doc said flatly.

The bald man's huge jaw sagged, and the resulting play of hinge muscles actually made his oversized ears tip forward.

"The laugh, by Gar, she is on me," he murmured weakly.

Doc Savage looked up from his ministrations. "That was your lab, was it not?"

"Was, I don't think, is an understatement, don't you?" big Maximus Lavender said thickly.

Doc regarded him with his hypnotic golden eyes.

"You normally wear glasses?" he inquired.

"They bother me lately," Lavender admitted. "Burn my nose and ears allatime."

Monk snorted. "Listen to this big goof!" he said.

"He's so mixed up, he can't talk straight. His eye glasses burn his nose and ears. What a laugh!"

"She's true!" Lavender protested.

"Just why," Doc Savage asked suddenly, "do you speak so unusually?"

"I am a kid and my pop takes me from Missouri to China," explained Lavender. "He take me to Africa, Italy, Sweden, Madagascar. He so damn busy he forget to educate me, and I'm a son of a gun, I pick up this English thing wherever I find her. I must do a hot job, because everybody who hear me, they bust down and cry, like hell. They laugh all over the place."

Doc made no comment.

Lavender grinned. "My English is good, not a bit of it. Mabbe you think I don't know him. But she is good trademark, see. Anybody who hear me slaughter the words, he not forget me, and that in my business is too bad, I don't think."

"What is your business?" Doc queried curiously.

"Radio."

"Hah!" Monk exploded. "I shoulda known! He's one of them radio comedian actors. It's all an act!"

"Excuse it, please," Maximus Lavender said indignantly. "Barking up the wrong pew, mabbe you be."

"Whoever writes your material," Monk said dryly, "oughta be shot for grammarcide."

"Get it crooked," Lavender persisted. "I do not work on der air, but in der vacuum."

"Huh?"

"In the tubes," Maximus Lavender explained. "I tinker. A radio tinkerer, I am. Savvy?"

Doc said, "Tinkering did not build an estate like the one you just lost, Lavender."

Lavender sighed. "Mabbeso, I sell an invention now and then," he admitted.

"Exactly what," Doc demanded, "is your connection with Harmon Cash?"

"A good friend of him, Cash is me."

"I feel like repeating that old soldier's challenge," Monk growled, eyes on the road. They were approaching the city.

"Challenge away," Lavender suggested.

"Friend or foe?"

Just then, Long Tom started speaking.

"Doc—" he croaked. "He knows—about Cubama—and gold—"

"Do not exert yourself, Long Tom," the bronze man said quietly.

The puny electrical genius reached up and laid a hand whose fingertips were scabbed over and without nails against the bronze man's coat front.

"Cash—Harmon Cash—Cubama—" he croaked weakly, squeezing the dark-brown cloth spasmodically. His pale-blue eyes were unfocused and bleary.

"What's dis about mine friend, Cash?" Maximus Lavender asked intently.

"Never mind, tongue-tied," Monk growled.

"Doc—" Long Tom persisted. "The—Blind Death—I know—how—how—" With a sigh like a releasing valve, the electrical wizard closed his eyes. His head lolled back onto the seat cushions, and began shaking from side to side with the bumps in the road.

Monk let out an anguished groan. His tiny eyes flicked to the rear-vision mirror. They were full of fear.

Carefully, the bronze man unclenched Long Tom's fingers and said, "He will need rest, and some minor plastic-surgery repairs to his burns and wounds, but otherwise he is in good shape, considering his ordeal."

Monk released a relieved breath.

"He one tough baby, that's a fact," Maximus Lavender said with approval. "But the moniker I still do not capture."

"This is Long Tom Roberts," Doc Savage advised, "the noted electrical expert, and a member of our group of adventurers."

At that bit of intelligence, the bald-headed man with the permanent squint went through a remarkable transformation of physiognomy. His eyes seemed to explode under beetling brows until they were as round as nickels. Wrinkles of astonishment crawled up his brow, creating furrows as far back as the crown of his bald-as-a-goose-egg skull.

Turning as pale as the snow pecking against the windshield, Maximus Lavender suddenly faced forward.

"Hot dog!" he said weakly. "Is everybody happy!"

His expression belied his words.

Doc said, "Lavender, what can you tell us about Harmon Cash and the individual who calls himself White Eyes?"

"Is White Eyes der feller what has snow-blind eyes and dresses for courting Eskimo squaws?"

"The same."

"About dat one," Maximus Lavender admitted, "I know less than I do about der King's English."

"And Harmon Cash?"

"I think this is one time untying my tongue could get me into heap big trouble."

"In other words," Monk questioned, "you're clamming up?"

"Bet their boots."

And that was the last thing the strange-talking Maximus Lavender said for the remainder of the trip.

As they approached the city, the snow intensified. It was assuming blizzard proportions. Traffic on the Queensboro Bridge had slowed to a sedate crawl.

On the bridge, Doc Savage asked Monk Mayfair, "Check with the harbor police. They may have results by now."

All the harbor police had to offer, they were disappointed to learn, were sedate apologies.

"We found the boat," an official reported. "Some one must have a lot of dough to throw around. Either that, or he was really tired of that hooker. It was scuttled on the Jersey side of the Hudson, near Hoboken."

Doc reached forward and took the microphone from the apish chemist's hairy paw.

"Any bodies?" he asked.

"No. Should there have been?"

"No." The bronze man thanked the official and returned the mike to Monk, who hung it up.

"That," Monk said grimly, "about sinks us, too."

XXVII

PIECES OF THE PUZZLE

The mood on the eighty-sixth floor of Doc Savage's skyscraper headquarters for the remainder of the day could best be summed up in one word.

Glum.

The pets—Habeas Corpus and Chemistry—sat dispiritedly off in one corner, as if acutely aware that one of their masters was missing. After a short time, Monk's personal secretary—generally believed to be one of the most attractive members of her profession in all New York—showed up to take charge of them. She left for Monk's Wall Street laboratory, the two animals following with uncharacteristic docility.

Immediately upon his return, Doc Savage had thrown himself into caring for Long Tom Roberts, the electrical wizard who had suffered such horrendous abuse at the hands of his captors.

There was a small but amazingly complete operating room in one corner of the big laboratory, and the bronze man worked over his injured comrade there.

Hard, metallic lights came into the constantly whirling pools that were his flake-gold eyes as he surveyed the damage done. Those lights promised grim retribution for any responsible parties who fell into the bronze man's hands.

Doc worked on Long Tom's maimed fingers first, cleansing them in a series of antiseptic solutions and then carefully bandaging them. They would soon heal, he saw, the fingernails eventually regrowing to their normal length.

Doc next administered various medicines and nutrient solutions to the puny electrical wizard's wracked, undernourished body.

During these ministrations, Long Tom once again opened his pale, pain-filled eyes. He recognized Doc, began speaking.

"Doc—" he gasped. "Bug—killer—cat—"

"I know," Doc said quickly.

Long Tom closed his eyes, a ghost of a smile creasing his thin features. "Good," he breathed.

"I have one question, if you are up to answering it," the bronze man continued.

At the faint nod from the electrical wizard, Doc asked, "I know you were abducted by Harmon Cash, but who put you in the steamer trunk in which you were found?"

"Don't—know," came the halting reply. "Woke—up—in box."

Doc Savage accepted this answer without visible expression. He completed his care and administered a sedative that soon caused the exhausted electrical wizard to drop off into a peaceful slumber.

The bronze man then put in a call to the Southampton fire department.

"The house owned by Maximus Lavender is a complete loss," the chief told Doc. "We also found a body in the rubble."

"His identity?"

"That's a good question," the fire chief returned. "Whoever he is, the fire burned him beyond recognition."

Doc thanked the man and hung up.

A call came in from the city morgue, promising the dead body of the late crime boss of the docks, Jim James Garben, within the hour.

Since Monk had gone to investigate the site where the fugitive speedboat had been scuttled, Doc took the opportunity to indulge in his daily routine of exercises,

which were responsible for his fabulous physical strength
and abnormally keen faculties.

This began with a complicated regimen of muscular contortions which brought a thin sheen of perspiration to his Samson-like physique, and progressed to a
variety of senses-attuning experiments, which included
reading Braille writing by touch, listening to a device
which reproduced sound waves just beyond the audible
range, and identifying various scents contained in
stoppered bottles by olfactory skill alone.

Doc was deep into his routine when Monk ambled
in, contributing to the general air of glumness.

"Nobody," he said ungrammatically, "saw nothin'."

Doc nodded. The abductors of Ham and Dana
O'Fall had already proven themselves too clever to
leave an obvious trail.

Monk commented, "I see our overgrown guest has
his nose buried in the radio section of the library,
Doc."

"Now might be a good time for him to see the
laboratory set-up," Doc remarked.

"I'll fetch him," Monk said, shuffling off.

Tall, bald Maximus Lavender entered the huge
laboratory with his eyes squinting as if against harsh
light.

By the time he reached the work area where Doc
Savage had repaired after toweling perspiration off his
massive muscles, they were practically popping from
their bony sockets.

"Gun of a son!" he exploded. "This is one fine
damn toy box."

"Hah!" Monk snorted. "Listen to him. He's
impressed."

"You say your line is radio," Doc remarked. "Perhaps
you would care to examine an experiment I am currently
conducting?"

"Sure as tooting," Maximus Lavender said heartily.

Doc Savage stepped aside to allow the bald giant to
see the apparatus that lay on a workbench. It was the

same one over which he had been toiling earlier in the day.

Lavender leaned over the apparatus, his eyes returning to their perpetual squint.

"I make it out not," he muttered.

"Perhaps you might don your eye glasses," Doc prompted.

"Stormy brain wave, that," Lavender said, fishing into his pockets. He brought forth a pair of round spectacles with plain steel rims. He put them on as if they hurt, but instantly, his squint disappeared.

Peering closer, he took in the apparatus. His ungainly face puckered like a dried lemon. A tongue like a pinkish slug crawled from his gullet of a mouth to nudge at the corners of his lips, wetting them.

"Understand it I do not," he said at last. "Ahead of me, you way are, I think."

"Here," Doc said helpfully, reaching for a switch. "Let me demonstrate it for you."

Big Maximus Lavender reacted to this simple statement with unexpected animation.

One huge hand whipped to his steel-rimmed glasses, as if to fling them from his face. The other made a stab at intercepting the bronze man's hand from reaching the switch. Simultaneously, his boatlike feet started to backpedal, away from the apparent object of his fear.

As a consequence, he accomplished none of his goals. Instead, he flopped onto the brick flooring, terror riding his features.

"No! No!" he moaned. He batted at his glasses, as if they were on fire. They went flying, owing to a clumsy but lucky swipe.

"What's eatin' him?" Monk demanded, slack-jawed.

Doc reached down and claimed the glasses.

"You seem," he told the agitated radio inventor, "to be quite terrified of something."

"My glasses," Lavender said, subsiding, "she hurt

my face like hell. I think maybe I was having another attack."

"There he goes again," Monk guffawed. "Sayin' his specs hurt his nose and ears."

"She do!" Lavender insisted. "I mean, they does! No, it do."

"There are faint burn marks at the bridge of your nose and behind your ears," Doc noted.

Monk bent down, to see this for himself.

"So there are!" he muttered.

Maximus Lavender came to his feet like a jointed yardstick unfolding itself. He squinted in hairy Monk's direction. "See, short and homely?"

"They correspond very closely to pressure indentations these glasses might make," Doc added. His golden eyes searched the big inventor's long, drawn plug of a face.

Lavender cleared his throat. "Like I say, them specs help my eyes, but are murder on the nose and ears. I mabbe need a new set, no?"

"You need a language teacher," Monk inserted derisively.

Doc went on, "I know from my previous experiments that if I had turned on this radio apparatus, the metal rims of these glasses would have begun conducting heat, and likely caused burns similar to those you have already suffered."

"Good thing you not fire her up, huh?" Lavender said nervously. "We not have hot time, yes?"

Doc pointed at the silent apparatus. "You claim not to recognize this apparatus, yet you seemed to understand its effects. How?"

"Radio instincts," Lavender said quickly. "I got 'em bad. Kinda like a seventh sense."

"Baloney," Monk growled. "You've got a secret tangled up in them words of yours. Doc, how about I yank some parts off this walking soupbone? Maybe that knot in his tongue will unravel."

"You and my mother," Lavender scoffed. "Together they can't whip you—I mean, me." He put up his dukes in the manner of John L. Sullivan and began shadow-boxing around the simian chemist.

"Is he serious?" Monk wondered.

"Why don't you find out?" Doc suggested.

Grinning, Monk obliged. His furry arms came up. He moved in. Although the hairy chemist stood only a few inches over five feet tall, he tipped the scales at two hundred and sixty pounds.

Big Maximus Lavender towered over him by better than a foot, but was disadvantaged as to height. He realized this almost at once. Still, he took a wild swing.

Nimbly, Monk ducked under the traveling fist. He slid in, one rusty fist sweeping ceilingward in a classic uppercut.

Maximus Lavender's blocky jaw took the full brunt of the apish chemist's traveling knuckles. His mouth had been open. It shut suddenly, teeth clicking solidly, and his big feet actually left the floor in the instant before Monk's punch laid him out cold.

"Well, whaddya know about that?" Monk said, happily dusting his knuckles. "The overgrown oaf had no technique and a glass jaw to boot!"

Doc Savage turned away unconcernedly, saying, "Find a comfortable place to park him."

"You got it," Monk said, gathering up the ungainly radio inventor.

"And alert me the moment the city morgue attendants show up," the bronze man added, returning to the stoppered bottles with which he had been involved when he had left off his exercises.

Monk turned. "Who died?" he asked.

"Jim James Garben," Doc supplied. "You are welcome to assist during the autopsy."

"Might be fun at that," Monk remarked cheerfully as he carried limp Maximus Lavender to a comfortable library divan.

The cold corpse of Jim James Garben arrived, covered with a dusting of snow, well before dusk.

The morgue attendants—there were two of them—
stood about the laboratory, blowing cold air out of their
lungs and stamping snow off their feet, as Doc Savage
signed for the body.

"It's sure blowin' out there," one offered, as the
other cast amazed eyes over the laboratory, with its
profusion of glittering equipment.

At that, Monk went to a window and looked out.
Up this high, they were often oblivious to the changing
weather. The unbroken stretch of clouds that were
visible beyond the windows made the snow outside
hard to detect.

Up close, however, the true situation was clear.
The air was literally charged with furious flakes. None
stuck to the big windows, however, thanks to a special
coating of the bronze man's devising. Down in the
man-made canyons, the white stuff already lay better
than a foot deep. Snowplows, like rooting hogs, were
busy. There was hardly any other traffic otherwise.

"Hey, Doc," Monk announced, ambling back, "we
got a regular Nor'easter percolatin' out there."

By this time, the morgue attendants had taken
their departure and Doc Savage was transferring the
sheet-covered body of Jim James Garben to a marble-
topped operating table. Near by, Long Tom Roberts
slept on a comfortable bed.

Doc handed Monk a hospital gown. While the
apish chemist climbed into this, the bronze man set to
examining Garben's mouth with a dentist's probe.

Monk maneuvered an overhead lamp into line,
bringing out the sad state of the wharf crook's molars.

"I've seen some dock fights that took their toll in
teeth," he said wonderingly, "but I'd like to meet the
guy who could wreck a man's back molars like that."

"Notice that only the filled teeth are shattered,"
Doc pointed out.

Monk blinked. "So they are. How come?"

Doc withdrew his probe, saying, "They seem to
have exploded from expanding pressure of the metal
fillings against tooth enamel."

"Huh! What coulda caused that?"

"Heat," replied the bronze man, next examining Jim James Garben's eyes.

They remained as white as the moment when the burly crook had expired in agony. Under the glassy white slickness of each orb, a sullen red coloring hinted at a network of burst eye capillaries beneath.

Doc checked each eye in turn, saying nothing.

Then, he quickly shaved the hair off Garben's pate. There was not much of it, so it did not take long.

With a scalpel, the bronze man opened the corpse's newly shaven scalp, laying bare the entire crown of bone that comprised the top of his skull.

Doc took a buzzing circular-saw tool to this, running it around the bone from forehead to the base of the skull. It was grisly work, and even Monk, who was sometimes accused of being a bit on the blood-thirsty side, screwed up his homely face in distaste. Still, not once did he look away.

When he was done, the bronze man laid aside the saw, and with gloved hands took hold of the portion of Jim James Garben's skull above the circular cut. He lifted. The crown of bone came away clean, exposing the convoluted twistings of the dead man's cerebrum.

Under the light, Doc examined the brain critically, touching it here and there. He took up a scalpel and plunged it into the dead gray matter at the spots he had previously touched.

Monk noticed the ease with which the scalpel blade penetrated the substance of the exposed brain.

"Goin' in awful easy, ain't it?" he croaked.

"Too easily," the bronze man pronounced. "Notice the unusual texture of the cerebrum?"

"Yeah. It's loose. Kinda like scrambled eggs. Why's that, Doc?"

"This man's brain," Doc Savage decided, "has been cooked like an egg in its shell."

"Blazes!" Monk gulped, for want of a better comment.

The hairy chemist was about to ask what power could do that to a living being when, throughout the massive laboratory, several automatic devices came into play.

Some were simple alarms. They whooped or jangled, each according to its unique purpose. Others were protective devices engaging in response to these warnings.

"What the blazes?" Monk howled. "Did every electrical line in the building decide to short-circuit all at once?"

"No," Doc Savage said grimly, shucking off his surgeon's gown. "The skyscraper is under attack. White Eyes is making his move."

XXVIII

GANGDOM'S LONG ARM

There were warning indicator lights placed for convenience at points all around the vast white-enameled laboratory of Doc Savage headquarters.

Every one of these was blazing now. The various alarms put up quite a din besides.

"Must be an army of 'em!" Monk bawled. He jumped to a televisor device and threw switches that brought a remarkably distinct moving image of the modernistic skyscraper lobby to the frosted-glass screen.

"It *is* an army!" Monk howled. "They've taken over the whole dang lobby."

Doc, stationed at another televisor, was madly throwing switches. This device displayed the concrete floor of his sub-basement garage. It swarmed with armed men. Quite a few military-style machine guns bristled from the moving pack.

The raiders took up an ambush position at the doors of the lowest terminus of Doc's high-speed elevator, cutting off that avenue of departure.

But that was the least of the bronze man's worries, he saw as he touched a switch that showed him the interior of the cage itself. There were hidden televisor cameras at dozens of strategic places throughout the skyscraper.

The ascending cage was packed to the walls with men. Doc recognized one in particular by his high headgear.

It was the crime boss named Topper Tweed.

Each of the intruders, he was unhappy to see,

wore Army-style gas masks over their faces. They had obviously been well prepared.

"Continue monitoring activities!" Doc clipped, pitching from the televisor. He hurtled the length of the library to the reception room, where he slammed into the seat behind the ornate Oriental table that dominated the room.

The top of this article of furniture was studded with exquisite inlays. Many of these were concealed studs which actuated specific defenses the bronze man had installed throughout the imposing edifice.

One caused every passenger elevator in the building to stop in place. Another controlled the high-speed elevator, and a third would, if pressed, flood the cage with anæsthetic gas. Doc let those be. The last was rendered useless by the raiders' gas-mask precaution, and Doc preferred to deal with them in the corridor when they disembarked. Doc pressed the inlay stud that shut down the regular banks of elevators, which numbered greater than fifty.

While waiting for the speed elevator to reach the eighty-sixth floor, Doc Savage manipulated other inlays, causing steel gates to close off the stairways on the eighty-fifth floor level and sending an alarm to the chief elevator starter.

Almost at once, Monk's shrill voice came over a desk annunciator.

"Doc!" he yelled. "I got the elevator captain on the phone. He says if you lock any of the elevators, they're gonna blow his head clean off!"

A rare frown crossed the bronze man's metallic countenance. The existence of the elevator-stopping control was unknown to the starter captain. Solving that puzzle would have to await developments, Doc knew.

Having no choice, he depressed the control. An indicator light in the form of an inlay turned from red to white, indicating the cages had resumed their upward toil.

"Tell the captain the elevators are working," Doc said into the annunciator, his tone grim.

Another glowing indicator told that the speed lift had come level with this floor.

Doc tapped an inlay. Nothing seemed to happen. He hit another. Surprisingly, this caused the massive bronze door that opened on the corridor to valve open, as if in welcome.

Doc set himself behind the big table, his bronze features inscrutable, his hands resting on the table top. The cables on the backs of those strong members, even in repose, played like silent harp strings.

Feet tramped down the corridor.

A face poked into view. It wore a gas mask and the eyes behind the insectlike lenses seemed to goggle comically, as if in disbelief. It withdrew.

Another appeared, took in the sight of the bronze man calm behind the inlaid table, and brought up a Tommy gun defensively.

"Come in," Doc Savage told him in a voice that was steady and devoid of fear.

They all came in, bristling with weaponry. One pushed through to the forefront. His silken top hat proclaimed him to be Topper Tweed. The juxtaposition of the topper and the gas mask made for an absurd picture.

The sound of his voice coming through the device indicated that the gang leader had no inkling of his ridiculous appearance. The voice was bitter and metallic.

"Savage," it said, "White Eyes sent us."

"So I deduced," Doc imparted. "I imagine you have come to deliver an ultimatum."

"We have your man Ham, and that lady gumshoe," Topper Tweed spat. "We got this joint surrounded, too. You can't get out."

"What do you want?"

"You know," Topper bit out. "Every damn ounce of gold you got to your name."

"That is," Doc said, "quite a sum. I assume you brought enough men with you to carry it all off?"

Behind round lenses, a dozen hard eyes went very wide.

"It's here!" a voice croaked. "The gold's here!"

"That's enough for me!" Topper Tweed snarled. "Blast the bronze devil!"

Doc Savage very rarely miscalculated. He took pride in taking every conceivable precaution, in being prepared for all possible contingencies. Such foresight had saved his life many times during the course of his strange career of righting wrongs and punishing evildoers beyond the law.

Before he had engaged the inlay that had opened the door, apparently exposing himself to danger, he had first pressed one which silently lowered a broad sheet of bulletproof, nearly invisible, glass before the massive table.

This was usually of sufficient size to thwart any attempt on his life.

Not now.

A line of gunmen brought up their rapid-firers. They began hosing lead. But instead of aiming at Doc, they directed their lead around him.

The submachine guns stuttered. Lead blobs splashed the invisible pane, hung in the air momentarily. Those that did not *spang* away, began slipping to the floor. None reached the bronze man.

"It's wider than we thought!" Topper Tweed shouted. "Spread your lead, boys!"

That told Doc the raiders knew all about his protective barrier.

Hastily, Doc pulled an egg-shaped sphere of metal from his pocket as lead began chewing up the walls where the redirected streams of metal circumvented the bulletproof shield.

Gauging the furious handiwork of their rapid-firers, the gunmen started to work toward the outer edges of the protective pane, plainly intent upon doing murder.

Doc flung his grenade then. It was not an explosive, nor a gas projectile, but one which generated intensely black smoke.

The smoke erupted like a boiling black dragon, quickly filling the reception room. More lead blasted, peppering the walls.

Under cover of the smoke, the bronze man eased by touch for the library door. It responded to his radioactive pocket token, opening and closing without a sound.

A quantity of the black smoke drifted in with him. He touched a wall panel control and concealed fans whirred into life, swallowing the black stuff like so much evil cotton candy.

Grimly, Doc Savage traversed the length of the library. He paused to gather up sleeping Maximus Lavender from the divan on which Monk had placed him, and bore him into the safety of the big laboratory.

Monk Mayfair's face was a study in slack-jawed shock when Doc stepped in. He looked up from the frosted-glass televisor screen, from which he had been monitoring the fracas in the reception room.

"They knew about the elevators and the bullet-proof glass gimmick," Monk blurted. "How?"

"Do not forget," Doc said, placing Lavender in a chair, where he promptly began to snore, "they have Ham."

"Ham wouldn't talk!"

"Sodium pentothal has a way of making men talk against their wills," Doc pointed out.

"Truth serum!" Monk said explosively. "Yeah, that would explain it, all right." He seemed relieved—contrary to his seemingly intolerant attitude toward the dapper barrister—that Ham Brooks had not willfully betrayed them.

Doc drifted up to the televisor, asking, "What are they doing?"

"I can't tell what's goin' on in the reception room," the hairy chemist reported, "but they're swarmin' all over the stairwells and corridors. There must be more than a hundred of 'em! They got cuttin' torches and they're using 'em on the gates."

Doc absorbed the sight of the cutting torches at work and went to a wall panel, carefully reading stylus indicators. He threw another switch. This showed the interior of the main loading dock far below. A snowplow with a badly dented blade had struck a supporting pillar. In between blade and post hung the mangled loading-dock door.

Open moving vans were strewn about, also. So were a number of bodies—loading-dock workers.

The image on the screen told them all they had to know about the method employed to breach the skyscraper in such overwhelming numbers.

"Won't be long before the riot squad pulls in," Monk called in encouragement.

"They cannot help us," Doc said. "It would take a pitched battle simply to clear the lobby and basements."

Doc thumbed a wall annunciator. This one picked up sounds in the reception room.

Voices crashed. Above the din came Topper Tweed's gas-mask-muffled tones.

"This damn smoke is starting to thin. Where's Slinky Sid?"

"Here," a nervous voice piped up.

"Slocum, there's your safe. Get to cracking!"

Monk let out a groan. "They're going for the safe, Doc!"

"They will be disappointed to learn it contains no gold or valuables," Doc said. He resumed listening.

Topper's frantic voice came again. *"Cyanic! Where are you, MacGillicuddy?"*

"Over here. I'm at the library door."

"You got that hydrochloric acid ready to go?"

"Yeah."

"Well, use it!"

Hearing this, Doc flashed to a cabinet and removed one of his supermachine pistols and an extra ammunition drum. He flung these to the hairy chemist.

"That door is not proof against acid in large quantities," Doc rapped. "Use your mercy pistol to hold them at bay as long as you can."

"Sure, Doc," Monk said, moving for the door. "But what are you going to do?"

"No time!" Doc clipped. "Do it!"

Monk hastened to obey. He plunged into the library, set his machine pistol on continuous firing, and waited anxiously.

The inner veneer of the door began to smoke around the edges. It bubbled and a river of smoking liquid—hydrochloric acid—began pooling from under the riser.

Monk was a chemist. He knew the awful potency of hydrochloric acid. He took a cautious step backward.

Beyond the bubbling door, a muffled voice could be heard saying, "The hinges are melting!"

"Don't touch the door, you idiot! That stuff'll eat your hands clean to the bone!" This was the voice of Cyanic MacGillicuddy.

"Somebody grab that filing cabinet and give it the old heave-ho," Topper Tweed bellowed.

The panel began to shake soon after. It stood up to two blows, then it just fell inward.

Monk cut loose then. The machine pistol fired an unbelievable number of rounds per second. He got the first three raiders who jumped over the smoking door.

They fell onto the acid-splashed panel, unconscious. Their bodies began to smoke, too. Bone showed here and there. Hydrochloric acid is terrible stuff.

"Anybody else wanna come chargin' in," Monk howled gleefully, "I'm ready for 'em."

This proved more boast than fact.

Through the thin acid smoke, the apish chemist could see a heavy military machine gun angle its muzzle around the jamb like a huge, whiskerless rat sniffing for cheese. It was very low to the floor. One leg of a tripod could be seen poking into view, like a leg poised to pounce.

Monk understood what he was up against then.

Like all of Doc's men, he wore a flexible undergarment of chain mail that was proof against most bullets. Not, however, the larger military calibers. It was a sobering realization.

Monk dived behind a bookcase. Just in time. Heavy-caliber slugs began knocking rare tomes from shelves, and chewing wood like voracious beavers.

"*Yeeow!*" Monk howled. He got down on the floor and pulled books from a lower shelf. This gave him a firing port of sorts.

He cut loose with more mercy bullets. The drum ran empty almost immediately. Quickly, he withdrew to change drums.

This took but seconds. By that time, fully a half dozen gunmen had spilled over the fallen door to take up firing positions.

Monk set his pistol to single shot, began to pick them off one at a time.

After two raiders fell, the others responded with a withering fire, forcing the hairy chemist to crawl the length of the bookcase, just ahead of a line of tumbling, slug-propelled scientific volumes.

When Monk's bullet head hit the wall, he knew he was out of cover. He squeezed himself into the smallest space possible and returned fire through a new firing port he hastily excavated.

He had some luck, but several raiders simply withdrew and got the filing cabinet upended. They pushed this along the main library corridor like a moving shield.

The mercy bullets were designed to break upon impact with human skin, introducing the quick-acting anæsthetic through the shallow wound thus created. They were not meant for penetration.

Monk saw his shots break and splash futilely against the cabinet as it scraped along the floor.

The gunmen behind it were not so handicapped. They fired as they came.

Paper and leather binding shreds flew all around

Monk Mayfair's gristled ears. He tried to make himself even smaller.

He was saved when one of the skyscraper's many protective devices engaged.

There was a spot in the floor which masked a pressure plate. It was smack in the middle of the corridor, where the unwary could not help but tread on it.

Doc and his men were trained to avoid it.

The Topper Tweed raiders were not. They tripped the plate. Instantly, four sheets of bulletproof glass descended from the ceiling. It enclosed the astonished gunmen in a neat trap.

One man tried to shoot his way out. Fortunately for the hairy chemist, he had only an automatic pistol. He fired one shot. It ricocheted off two of the panes and took another raider in the throat, killing him instantly.

After that, no more shots were fired. But other gunmen were boiling into the library.

Monk took that opportunity to make a break for the laboratory.

He made it, much to his surprise. For the library was rapidly filling with other attackers.

When the lab door closed behind him, Monk was surprised to see Doc Savage again attired in the silvery protective garment he had worn during his earlier radio experimentations.

The bronze man threw one to Monk, saying, "Put this on."

Monk climbed into the suit, finding that it fit after a baggy fashion.

"Blazes!" Monk muttered. "They're wrecking the joint! How we gonna stop 'em, Doc?"

"I have been in touch with the governor," Doc said quickly. "He reports that the police are unable to storm the lobby due to innocent persons these raiders have taken hostage. An army unit has been mobilized, but they are over an hour away."

"Does that mean we gotta surrender?"

Before the bronze man could reply, a voice jumped out of a nearby annunciator.

"Savage!" it crackled. It was the voice of Topper Tweed.

"Yes?"

"I got a message from White Eyes for you."

"I am listening."

"You got exactly five minutes to surrender. Got that?"

"And if we do not?" the bronze man wanted to know.

"The Blind Death gets you and every one with you!"

"Do I understand you to say that White Eyes is with you?" Doc asked.

"You got my message," Topper Tweed snarled. *"Five minutes!"*

"What do we do?" Monk asked anxiously.

"These garments will protect us for a short period," Doc said, moving for the bed on which Long Tom Roberts still slumbered. "But our predicament would remain unchanged."

He had another garment draped over one bronze arm. Cradling the puny electrical wizard, he endeavored to pull this over Long Tom's small frame.

"There is another garment on the bench," the bronze man called, tight-voiced. "It should fit Lavender."

Monk grabbed this. He spent several awkward minutes getting the too-tall radio inventor into the tinfoil-like shroud.

Evidently Topper Tweed was no great judge of passing time. Or possibly he was merely impatient. Long before the five minutes had elapsed, his voice, harsh and terrible, came again.

"You asked for it, Savage!"

Almost at once, chemicals standing in glass retorts and tubes throughout the laboratory became agitated. Some commenced a merry bubbling. Others changed color due to chemical reaction. A solution-filled beaker popped apart with a loud report.

Most distressing of all, there came an unpleasant odor from the exposed skull of the late Jim James Garben.

"Doc!" Monk called in a horrified voice. His eyes were on a Bakelite control wall panel near the door, which began a slow, tortured melting process. "If the Blind Death don't get us, all these boilin' chemicals sure will!"

"Bring Lavender," Doc directed. He was carrying Long Tom, and moving toward a store room situated behind the center of one wall.

Lugging Maximus Lavender across his broad shoulders, the simian chemist followed on bowed legs. Lavender was not light.

Inside the store room, Doc opened a secret panel.

It revealed a small bullet-shaped car, which was padded and equipped with numerous straps similar to those found on New York subway cars. It was very compact, despite having room for four persons inside.

"I don't like retreatin'," Monk growled.

"We stand a better chance of success if we can regroup," Doc rapped, placing Long Tom inside the car. Accepting big Maximus Lavender, he placed him beside the insensate electrical wizard.

Then, he and Monk stepped in.

Doc closed a hatch. The interior of the car went suddenly dark. Doc threw a lever.

Like a plummet, the car simply fell, to the accompaniment of toiling machinery and compressed-air hiss. They held on by the shuddering straps.

The car seemed to fall a mile, suddenly level off, and continue on its way like a mail-carrying cylinder through a pneumatic tube—which was exactly what the strange conveyance was, although on a much greater scale. The cacophony of sound was punishing to the eardrums.

Deceleration took hold of their stomachs first, signaling that they neared the climax of the wild ride.

Then, more air hissed and with a jar, the bullet of a

car stopped. Safety latches clacked. A red light signaled that it was safe to exit, and Doc Savage threw the hatch up.

The bronze man was the first to step into the light, and so he was the first to realize that the clever abandonment of his besieged headquarters was all for naught.

For standing before him, attired in spectral white raiment, was the being who had so boldly challenged him.

"*Welcome*," thundered the voice of White Eyes. "*You have played directly into my hands.*"

XXIX

WHITE EYES TRIUMPHANT

The being who styled himself White Eyes certainly lived up to his sobriquet, Doc Savage saw.

His suit was cut from a bolt of some intensely bleached but rich fabric. As far as it was possible, every article of clothing this individual wore was a matching hue, down to the kid gloves and shoes of white buck.

A gay touch, a white carnation, sprouted from a lapel boutonniere. It did not take away from the effect of a leprous mushroom in the shape of a man the full ensemble suggested.

But Doc Savage was not looking at White Eyes's apparel. His flake-gold eyes were taking in the crime master's face.

It seemed to be cast from porcelain, the slanted Oriental eyes like bleached almonds. The fixed expression held the inscrutability of the East.

The gleaming visage was a mask, of course, the eyes but slits in the china. And from behind the oblique eye holes, stared orbs that could not possibly see, for they lacked every feature of sighted eyes, being entirely white.

"*Welcome, Doc Savage,*" repeated the booming voice of White Eyes, proving at once that his bold ivory optics somehow possessed sight. "*I have been expecting you.*"

He spoke into a velocity microphone held up to his face by one gloved hand. A thin wire led from this to a simple radio receiver standing off a little ways. Its speaker face was pointed in their direction.

Monk Mayfair stepped from the bullet car, his manner clearly belligerent despite his being swathed in an all-enveloping suit of silvery foil.

"So you're the guy that's been givin' us so much trouble," he bellowed angrily. "Now sounds like a good time to fix your wagon."

Monk started forward.

Doc Savage's voice lifted, hard and brittle. "Wait!"

"What for?" Monk grumbled, hesitating. "He's all by himself."

"He is too sure of himself," Doc said steadily.

"*You are very wise,*" thundered White Eyes. "*For you face one whose eyes possess the death-dealing gaze of the fabled basilisk.*"

At that, White Eyes tilted back his head, causing the shadow created by his wide-brimmed Panama hat to retreat. A sparkle seemed to leap into his slick orbs. His free hand went into one coat pocket, thumb out, in a confident gesture.

"*One more step and I will, to coin a phrase, strike you blind!*"

"Nuts to you, spooky!" Monk growled. "These suits are proof against your blind hoodoo!" He set himself to leap.

Doc Savage moved then. Using all the trained speed of which he was capable, he got in the way of the hairy chemist, blocking his charge like a human wall of quicksilver.

"No, Monk," he repeated. "Look around you."

Apish Monk cast his gimlet eyes around the great vault of a building they had found themselves in. It was a long, windowless structure of brick, not well lit.

But in the murk could be discerned the shapes of several airplanes, ranging from a tiny speed plane to a great tri-motor capable of long flights. A small dirigible seemed to bump the roof over their heads. To one side, a submarine like a razorback pig of steel wallowed in a trough. There was also a fair assortment of boats.

This was Doc's combination boathouse and aircraft

hangar, built on a pier overlooking the Hudson River. A faded sign over the outside entrance read, "Hidalgo Trading Company." There was no such concern. The mythical Hidalgo Trading Company was Doc Savage himself.

"Recall what transpired in our laboratory," the bronze man said. "Every gas tank in the warehouse could explode if enough heat is generated."

Monk blinked owlishly. He subsided, his face screwed up in frustration.

Doc Savage turned to the apparition in white, saying simply, "We surrender."

"*A wise decision,*" intoned White Eyes. "*Very wise.*"

He carefully removed a gloved hand from a coat pocket. Unbeknownst to White Eyes, several cigarette stubs fell to the concrete flooring.

If Doc Savage noticed the butts, he gave no sign.

"My aid, Ham," Doc demanded. "Where is he?"

White Eyes directed his voice over his shoulder.

"*All right, men, bring out the prisoners.*"

At the command, gunmen began appearing from behind assorted aërial conveyances. Two brought a battered, black-and-blue Ham Brooks—he hardly lived up to his sartorial reputation now—and exquisite Dana O'Fall at the point of guns.

Ham staggered as if inebriated, his clothing in rags.

"I'm sorry, Doc," he said in a slurred voice. He looked so miserable that Monk Mayfair eschewed any jibe at his expense.

Dana O'Fall looked at the bronze man—his size gave him away—and remarked acidly, "You almost got me killed at Lavender's estate, you know."

White Eyes lifted his microphone to his stylized mouth.

"*Would you be good enough to present your back to these gentlemen?*"

Dana demanded, "Why?"

"*Because,*" White Eyes explained, "*I am about to ask them to step out of their clothing.*"

"Oh," said Dana O'Fall, abruptly turning around.

"*Gentlemen,*" White Eyes said, giving Doc Savage and his men a casual wave of one kid glove.

Doc and Monk silently shed their silvery protective garments. They paused.

"*Do not stop there,*" said White Eyes. "*I am aware of your reputation for secreting tricky devices about your persons.*"

Doc and Monk stripped down to their skins. More than one nervous crook's eyes bugged out at the sight of the bronze man's rippling muscles, which, even in repose, were remindful of bundles of bronze-coated piano wire.

When a casual inspection seemed to reveal no hidden devices, White Eyes directed them to don their clothes.

"*No, not those,*" White Eyes said quickly as they reached for their outer garments. "*These silver items would be preferable.*"

Nodding in the direction of Ham Brooks, who was holding his tattered trousers up by one hand, Doc said, "There is a garment suitable for Ham in the device behind us."

White Eyes gave a signal. Gingerly, a gunman slid behind Doc and Monk and stuck a head into the bullet car, which had come to a stop inside a huge concrete block set in the floor.

"Chief!" he blurted. "There's two others in here. Looks like they're out cold."

"*Haul them out,*" White Eyes ordered. "*And pass Mr. Brooks his garment.*"

While Ham Brooks changed clothes, the silver shrouds that contained Long Tom Roberts and Maximus Lavender were excavated. Their hoods were rudely yanked off.

White Eyes regarded them with his blank basilisk stare for several silent moments.

"*They go, too,*" he clipped.

"Go where?" Doc Savage asked, zipping up his coverall garment, but leaving the hood down.

"We are flying south," White Eyes explained. *"All of us."*

The white-garbed criminal rotated his head about the room, evidently the better to see with his odd optics. They came to rest on the big tri-motored plane.

"That ship looks worthy of the journey," he decided. *"We will take that one."*

A man broke away from the cluster of gunmen, and climbed up on the tri-motor's wing. He worked at the hatch. When it came open, he fell back with such violence that the wing vibrated like a monster saw. He slipped off slowly, made a heap on the floor, and began snoring loudly.

"Gas!" a voice yelled.

A moment of frozen panic ensued. Fingers tightened on triggers. White Eyes's hand went back to his pocket.

Every one held his breath.

Doc Savage broke the tension with his controlled voice.

"Each of my planes is equipped with safety devices to prevent theft."

"You might," White Eyes said darkly, *"have mentioned that slight fact."*

Doc Savage offered no rebuttal.

"I assume your famous vest of surprises lies at your feet," White Eyes thundered in a brighter voice. *"Be good enough to remove from it as many of those anæsthetic balls as it carries."*

Kneeling, Doc obeyed. He straightened, his fingers full of the grape-sized glass globules.

Dana O'Fall was pushed into their midst. She looked ready to kick the shins of every gunman around her, but wisely refrained.

"Gas masks on, all of you!" White Eyes proclaimed.

"Uh-oh, Doc," Monk muttered. "I think I see what's comin'."

The gunmen donned their masks. One assisted White Eyes into his.

"When I tell you to," White Eyes told Doc Savage

in a voice that was so muffled that even the makeshift radio loud-speaker could not reproduce it with anything resembling clarity, "*you will crush those ornaments and inhale very deeply.*"

"How do we know you will not simply slaughter us afterward?" Doc demanded.

"*You do not. But if it will ease your minds, understand that I cannot obtain any of your fabulous gold if you are not alive to show me where it is.*"

"Gold?" Dana O'Fall asked in surprise. "And where exactly are we going?"

She was completely ignored.

Another voice piped up. "But, chief," it complained, "what about Topper and the rest?"

"Yeah! The cops got the place completely surrounded. We can't just leave them!"

White Eyes brought the microphone closer to his set, porcelain visage so that his words were very clear.

"*Any of you who wish to go to the rescue of our besieged friends,*" he said, "*may do so at this time. Those who prefer to partake of the bronze man's gold had better follow me into that airplane.*"

A cold silence settled over the great warehouse.

"Sounds like somebody just got double-crossed," Monk said pointedly.

No one moved for the doors.

After it was clear that this represented a unanimous decision, White Eyes strode over to the radio lying on the floor and picked it up in a manner that revealed it was unusually heavy for a common radio.

"*A simple device to disguise my voice,*" he remarked, apparently for every one's benefit. "*For obvious reasons, I prefer that my identity remain undisclosed.*"

"I already know who you are," Doc Savage told him flatly.

The being who styled himself White Eyes reacted to this unequivocal statement with a noticeable start.

"*You do?*"

"I do."

"*Well, isn't that ducky?*" White Eyes boomed.

"Why don't you take that bit of knowledge into the land of Nod with you?"

No one moved.

"Crush those damn grenades!" White Eyes thundered.

Doc did as he was bid. His bronze fingers constricted. Glass crunched. Gunmen, forgetting their masks or perhaps not trusting them, retreated slightly.

The liquid anæsthetic made tiny splashes which vaporized instantly into invisible gas.

Oddly, in as much as he had learned to hold his breath for extended intervals from the pearl divers of the South Seas, Doc Savage was the first to collapse to the concrete, falling on one arm, which cushioned his great body.

Dana O'Fall succumbed then. With a slow sigh, she made a pretty heap at Monk Mayfair's feet. Ham went next. He fell across the body of his bronze leader as if dead.

Last to go was Monk, who strove to hold his breath until the anæsthetic gas mixed with the air and became harmless.

He was thwarted in this by the simple remedy of being brained from behind with the substantial stock of a Tommy gun. Expelling a gusty breath, the simian chemist completed the pile.

"That's that!" a gunman said with obvious relief.

"Not quite," said White Eyes, stepping up to the human pile. Several of the tiny grenades had slipped from Doc's fingers unbroken.

Methodically, White Eyes planted his white-buck shoes on each of these, pausing for a minute here and there, until they had all given up their volatile mixture.

"Not even this bronze devil can hold his breath through all that," White Eyes explained. *"Now, load them into the plane."*

"You ain't told us where we're goin' yet," a man pointed out.

"Where we're going," White Eyes boomed out in

an immensely pleased voice, *"the snow tastes sweet and the sun always shines."*

Several minutes later, the great doors of the warehouse hangar rolled open and the lumbering tri-motor—it was equipped with floats for water take-offs—slid down into the cold water.

The powerful engines thundered into life, propeller blades clawing wind-blown snow, and creating slip-stream glitter. Conditions had become blizzardlike.

The tri-motor volleyed down the river, got on step, and vaulted into the incredibly white sky.

Dragging a tail of sparks and snow behind, it climbed out over the Atlantic and turned south.

XXX

CUBAMA

A big red cow was dancing.

She had bells on her neck, bells on her legs, bells on her tail. She even had a particularly big bell on a ring in her nose. The bell made a painfully ear-splitting sound, somewhat like the noise a large plate-glass window would make if dropped off the Woolworth Building. Every time the cow danced, a lot of glass broke.

Ham sat up. He groaned loudly as all the bells on the big red cow exploded with a deafening roar and the bovine herself vanished amid a great display of colored lightning. She had been entirely imaginary—a nightmare.

"Holy cow!" moaned Ham, plagiarizing the absent Renny Renwick's pet expression. "Am I blind, or in hell?"

"Neither," came Doc Savage's quiet voice from the impenetrable blackness. "Unless I am very much mistaken, we are being held in the vault of the Cubama Sugar Importing Company."

"This is all my fault," Ham said miserably. The slurring that had twisted his words before was absent.

"Must be that pirate blood coursing through your veins," Monk Mayfair's childlike voice sounded.

"I resent that!" Ham snapped, with a trace of his old vinegar. "Besides, they used truth serum on me. I could not help myself."

"I can vouch for that," Dana O'Fall put in. "I watched the whole thing. They beat Mr. Brooks mercilessly. He refused to tell them anything. Then they used the truth serum, demanding every secret of your headquarters."

"One liar," Monk said unkindly, "vouching for another."

"Will you two dry up?" a quarrelsome voice interjected—Long Tom Roberts adding his two cents to the disembodied exchange.

"Who is dot?" another voice asked, worriedly.

"I might ask the same of you," Long Tom snapped.

"I bane be Maximus Lavender," the voice admitted.

"Never heard of you," Long Tom said sourly.

"Dot is goot."

"Huh?"

"Never mind that now," Doc Savage said. "I estimate that we've been out for several hours. The air in this vault cannot last forever. Let me suggest that conversation be kept to a minimum until we figure a way out of our present predicament."

"Got any suggestions, Doc?" Monk asked hopefully.

"Yes. We wait."

And so they waited in the darkness, breathing shallowly, until at length, the sound of tumblers clicking warned them that the great vault door was about to open.

They shut their eyes against the first bright crack of daylight.

"*I am disappointed,*" came the amplified voice that they had come to know as White Eyes. "*There is not a shred of gold to be found on these sultry premises.*"

As they blinked their vision back to normal, White Eyes became visible, velocity microphone clutched in one hand. He was flanked by cold-eyed gunmen.

"What made you believe that there was?" Doc Savage asked.

"*Informants. News cuttings. Deduction. I am no ordinary criminal of the breed you are used to dealing with, Savage.*"

"As you can see, the vault is empty," Doc pointed out.

"In that case," said White Eyes, *"there is nothing for it but to close this air-tight door and leave you all to the slow, unhappy end of your days. I am told that suffocation is an exceedingly ugly way to depart this life."*

The steel door began closing.

"If you are interested," Doc Savage said quickly, "the gold is on its way."

The door stopped.

"A flimsy deceit," sneered White Eyes.

"I am speaking the truth. A recent theft of bonds you may know something about forced me to replenish my supply of the stuff."

"How much gold?" White Eyes asked carefully.

"Four millions."

White Eyes stuck one gloved hand into his coat pocket and rocked back on his heels in thought.

"I do not," he said at last, *"know whether to believe you or not."*

Abruptly, he signaled with his velocity mike and the ponderous steel door finished rolling back into place. Darkness returned like a curse.

"That accomplished a lot," Dana O'Fall said bitterly.

Monk offered, "It gave us another hour of air, I'll bet."

"Another hour longer to suffocate in, you mean."

"I'll take it," Monk said amiably.

Doc Savage said, "We have little time. The gold shipment should be arriving before long. I reckon there are only a few hours of light left."

"What gold shipment?" Dana O'Fall demanded.

"The one that is destined for these vaults," Ham said crisply.

"And that's another thing!" Dana exclaimed. "How is it you know we're locked in the Cubama vault? For all we know, this could be the Black Hole of Calcutta!"

Despite the pitch blackness, this tirade was obviously aimed at Doc Savage.

*   *   *

What reply the bronze man would have vouchsafed went undisclosed, however, for the tumblers began their dicelike rattle once again.

The prisoners were better prepared for the light this time. They got a glimpse of two thugs hurling a third man into the vault. The man stumbled in backward, so they never got a glimpse at his features before the dark clamped down on them once more.

"Who's this?" Monk demanded.

"I am embarrassed to say," a cultured voice said bitterly.

"Let me at him!" Long Tom said with snarling vehemence. "That smooth devil tried to kill me!"

"No," came Doc Savage's controlled voice. "We will hear him out." The excited electrical wizard settled down in the darkness.

"I bane know!" Maximus Lavender blurted out. "I recognize der voice, not to mention der tobacco-smoke bouquet."

Everybody smelled it then—a rich, aromatic blend that flavored the close, warm air in the vault rather quickly.

"Mine friend, Harmon Cash!" Lavender said joyously. "I vas afraid dead you were, mabbe."

"We may all be dead soon if that damn White Eyes doesn't get what he wants," the voice of Harmon Cash warned.

"Exactly what do you mean?" Doc Savage demanded.

"I've been a prisoner ever since I was carried away from Max's house by that raiding party," Cash explained.

"I knew it vas you dey betook away in der mummy wrappings dot time," Lavender said.

"White Eyes has been keeping me on ice until now, saying he had a place for some one with my brains in his organization," the smooth crook continued. "Evidently, he has changed his mind. He thinks this Cubama heist is a dud."

"So far he's right," Monk growled.

"So now we're all going to be left to die," Cash finished.

Dana O'Fall let out a gasp that was anything but hard-boiled.

"Savage," Harmon Cash said plaintively, "if you have anything up your sleeve, the time in which to produce a miracle is rapidly dwindling."

Instead of answering, Doc Savage said, "I am puzzled by one thing."

"What is that?"

"Your connection with Maximus Lavender. Care to explain it?"

"Let Max tell it."

"To I got do?" asked the big, knobby man. "I mean, do I got to?"

"We're at the end of our ropes," Cash sighed. "Might as well share every hempen strand."

Big Maximus Lavender made an uncouth sound through his lips. This was what passed for a sigh, apparently.

"I am radio man, no?" he began. "I tickle the tubes and they do like I say. One day I build a tube that when tickled, gives out with what they call ultra-short waves. Micros. Not much good for broadcast, but the flies, it drive them buggy."

"Come again?" Ham asked. This was his first extended exposure to Maximus Lavender's tongue-twister sentences, and they were getting the dapper lawyer down.

"I turned on the micro-wave tube and all over the room, the bugs turn themselves off. Poof! They croak like frogbulls—I mean bullfrogs."

"Do I take it to mean that you built a radio device that killed insects?" Ham Brooks inquired.

"You betcha. I call her my bug banisher. On account she makes them vanish, almost."

"Wait a minute!" Long Tom Roberts said in a flustered voice. "That was my idea!"

"What you mean?" Lavender said thickly.

Long Tom could be heard crawling across the vault flooring in the direction of Lavender's voice. The big man made scooting sounds of escape.

Long Tom evidently corralled the big man, because the latter could be heard to say, "It vas mistook—mistick—mistake—"

"Take," Long Tom gritted, "is the operative word. I don't suppose you know I took out a patent on a micro-wave insect killer over a year ago?"

"What you know about that?" Lavender exclaimed. "Heh heh. She's a small world. Coincidence, no?"

"Coincidence, definitely not," Long Tom said angrily.

Dana O'Fall spoke up, "Why are they fighting over patents when we should be thinking about escape? Or is everyone too goofy from that knock-out gas to worry about the situation?"

"The Blind Death that has been terrorizing New York City," Doc Savage explained for every one's benefit, "is caused by a radio transmitter that emits so-called micro-wavelengths."

"That's right," Long Tom gritted. "I figured it out when I saw that devil, Babe, keel over. I could feel the heat. You see, I've experimented with a number of bug killers over the years. The micro-wave version was the most promising, but it had a number of side effects that were injurious to people as well as insects. I patented it anyway and went on to other approaches." The puny electrical wizard's sour voice sank into gravel. "I never thought any one would stoop low enough to steal the patent."

"I not steal," Maximus Lavender protested. "I improve! Mine bug banisher, she'sa work like a dream. That'sa why I give her to mine friend, Harmon, to promote. Only when I read about der Blind Death, I get the idea in my noggin my bug banisher, she'sa gone haywire. Instead of flies dropping like people, it be vice versa! I try to warn Cash. I call all over town. Instead, I reach this hot number, Dana. Excuse the French."

Dana offered, "I was merely following a lead to Harmon Cash and the stolen bonds."

"Cash, what have you to say about this?" Doc Savage asked.

"It's all true. I accepted the bug banishers—there were five in all—and I distributed them to persons I trusted for evaluation. If it flew—or rather, if the bugs stopped flying—I intended to finance production of the devices. I stood to make a killing. For once, a legal killing. Despite what you may think of me, I am not averse to an honest dollar."

"What happened?"

"Winter came. Without insects to kill, I put the idea aside until Spring."

"Doc meant if these bug blasters are behind the Blind Death," Monk Mayfair suggested, "that kinda points the finger at you."

"Hardly," Harmon Cash said dryly. "I mentioned that I distributed these devices among my underlings. I am reluctant to admit that my trust was misplaced in regard to one in particular. That man obviously learned of its potential for mischief."

"Would that man be Eduardo Luz?" Doc Savage asked quietly.

"It would."

"I knew it!" Monk snorted. "I knew it all along."

"You know Luz is White Eyes for a fact?" Doc pressed. His voice was very interested.

"I have never seen him unmasked," Cash admitted. "But Luz is infamous for wearing white linen suits, even in the dead of Winter, as now. The man has a positive mania for the color white. His imaginative disguise is clearly intended to conceal his somewhat dusky complexion, which is a dead give-away. It fits. I never did believe all that bosh about basilisk eyes and throwing the vision."

"A judge would call that circumstantial," Ham Brooks, ever the lawyer, pointed out.

"That's right," Dana added. "I'm about the only one in here besides yourself who's seen them both up close. They could be the same man, but White Eyes's suits are not cut of tropical material. And Luz may wear a white hat, but it's not a panama."

"There is another piece of evidence that is even more pat," Harmon Cash announced.

"Yeah, what's that?" Monk demanded.

"Eduardo Luz is possessed by another mania," Cash said flatly. "He zealously collects the stubs of cigarettes he has smoked. Like many new to the game of crime, he had an inordinate fear of leaving fingerprints for the police to find. So he keeps the stubs in his pockets until such times as he can dispose of them by fire or other means."

"What's that got to do with anything?" Long Tom asked sourly.

"Just this," Harmon Cash said proudly. "I myself beheld this murdering monster, White Eyes, remove a hand from a coat pocket in an idle moment." He paused dramatically. "Out came a veritable avalanche of butts."

"That clinches it!" Monk said, practically smacking his lips. "He musta been the guy in white who grabbed Ham!"

Contrarily, Ham Brooks declared, "I myself would prefer more proof than the word of a known criminal."

"Look," Harmon Cash said quickly. "I'm no angel, but I'm not a killer either. Luz—I mean, White Eyes—is. And from the way I heard him talking, he's planning to kill us all if he doesn't lay his hands on some gold soon. Savage, if you're holding out on him, you're putting all our necks in the noose."

"Lavender," Doc asked. "The steamer trunk in which Long Tom was found—how did it get into your basement?"

"Mine friend, Cash, he give her to me. For safekeeping, he claim. I not know a man inside. Honest Injun."

Doc's voice changed direction. "Cash?"

"I admit it," the cultured voice replied. "I abducted your friend in a moment of confusion. My terror of this White Eyes compelled me to do so. But I was, as they say, hot. I gave him to Max until I could figure out what to do with him. As a matter of fact I had decided that Mr. Roberts should be released and had returned to

Max's place to make that happen when I was set upon by White Eyes and his band of cutthroats."

"I seem to remember," Long Tom said bitterly, "something about your interest in Doc's gold."

"A plan I abandoned when White Eyes began terrorizing the underworld," Cash retorted quickly. "I am afraid, Mr. Savage, that in a weak moment, I shared my—er—ambitions with Eduardo Luz. The rogue stole my plan out from under me, killing off my hirelings so that I could no longer pursue it."

"You are afraid of this White Eyes?" Doc asked steadily.

"White Eyes," said Harmon Cash fervently, "is either as crazy as a loon, or the devil straight from the hot place."

"I don't believe him," Long Tom snapped.

"I do not believe any of you," Dana O'Fall added sharply.

Monk piped up, "What do you say to all this, Doc?"

Silence filled the blackness like a warm, rich ink.

At last, Doc Savage spoke.

"When they open the vault door," he said, "it will be time for the truth."

They could not get a word out of the bronze man after that.

XXXI

BLAZING CANE

At the first click of the vault door tumblers, Doc Savage hissed in the murk, "Hold your breaths, all of you!"

Doc's men were well trained. They obeyed instantly.

Harmon Cash, however, sounded near panic.

"Savage! What are you trying to pull? Don't try anything! Please! We'll all be slaughtered!"

Doc hit him.

In the dark, it was a difficult thing to pull off. But the bronze man had maneuvered himself to a seated position beside the smooth crook. His silver-wrapped fist made contact with the working point of Cash's jaw.

Doc pulled his punch, otherwise Harmon Cash's jaw might have been torn loose at the hinges. As it was, his head rocked back, rebounded off the steel wall, and sagged over his immaculate attire.

The vault door opened then, spilling light.

The faint sound of crunching glass was covered by the ratlike squeal of the big hinges.

The two White Eyes minions who had opened the door poked their heads in and promptly went to sleep.

Still holding his breath, Doc scooped up a machine gun before it clattered to the floor. Monk, crawling on hands and knees, scrambled for the other rapid-firer.

The hairy chemist then showed a reckless disregard for his own life by jumping out into the vault foyer and pointing his weapon in all directions. His disappointment in the lack of targets was evident in his face when he urged the others from the vault with a long silvery arm.

Doc and his party poured out of the vault. Doc lugged limp Harmon Cash across one shoulder.

"Will some one please explain what happened back there?" Dana said, hoarsely.

"I palmed a few of my anæsthetic grenades back at the warehouse," Doc said swiftly, his alert golden eyes roving for signs of trouble. "They were secreted in my suit."

"I wondered why you succumbed first," Ham said approvingly. "You obviously wanted White Eyes and his men watching the rest of us fall asleep while you pulled off the gag."

Monk took the lead. He led the tiny band down a whitewashed corridor that seemed an inappropriate setting for the massive steel vault.

The reason why was clear as they mounted a flight of simple steps to the floor above.

They were in a long hacienda-style house that had been converted into an office set-up. The floor was littered with desks and other office accoutrements.

It was also, Monk Mayfair was pleased to discover, crawling with armed criminals.

Monk set himself. The submachine gun began vomiting bullets, noise, and flame in incredible volume.

The modern Thompson submachine gun is a powerful instrument for dispensing lead. It also has a tendency to rear up during heavy use.

Monk was doing all he could to empty the drum. And the weapon was bucking. He fought with all his burly might to keep it level.

As a consequence, he did a great deal of damage to assorted office furniture and the long ceiling with its lazily turning fans, but not to persons.

There was no return fire. Every one was too busy seeking shelter from the storm of lead.

Under this cover, Doc Savage led the others out the nearest exit.

Monk followed them to the door, paused briefly.

A few shocked faces poked into view, like human gophers.

Monk sent them back into their holes with a last burst of lead. Then he plunged out the door after the others.

The office, Doc Savage knew, was situated near the extensive sugar fields of the Cubama Sugar Importing Company—it was called "Cubama Sugar Exporting Company" on the modest sign over the door—which would offer extensive shelter.

Doc led them into this.

The earth under their feet was deep and rich, the consistency of a freshly plowed field. It was very red. It also afforded only a little more traction than clay.

They had to strain their legs to reach the nearest stand of cane.

It was tall stuff, jointed like green bamboo, and waved in the sultry breeze. Long, droopy leaves, remindful of elongated corn ears, hung at points along the stalks. The manner in which the cane was planted in rows brought to mind a fantastic cornfield.

They plunged in.

"Be careful of those leaves," Doc cautioned. "They are sharp."

Experimentally, Ham Brooks brushed one. It felt rough to the touch. He did not feel any pain, but when his hand came away, it was bleeding from a thin cut.

"Ouch!" he said, sucking the cut.

"Serves you right, shyster!" Monk growled.

"Don't you two ever get along?" Dana O'Fall snapped.

"Keep moving!" Doc Savage urged.

The bullets began arriving then.

The cane was thick, having been planted in close rows so as not to waste any fertile soil. It was also very tall, topping a dozen feet in some places. It provided excellent concealment, but the thin, waving stalks were not meant to turn lead.

Bullets chased them into the cane, whacking off the lazy leaves like a sickle cutting hay. Stalks split. The stuff broke all around them, expectorating foamy brown juice that was incredibly sweet to the taste. Monk paused to lick some that had spattered across his homely face. He made lip-smacking sounds after swallowing.

Shouts of men in pursuit filtered through the cane rows.

Doc halted, letting insensate Harmon Cash slide off his broad shoulder. The smooth crook landed face-first.

"Keep running!" the bronze man called to the others. "These garments we are wearing are not exactly suitable camouflage."

The others pushed on, collected tiny cuts where their faces—the only exposed parts of their bodies except for unprotected Dana O'Fall—brushed the thin, razor-sharp cane leaves.

Doc crouched down, pulled back on the cocking lever of his Thompson, and aimed high. It was the bronze man's policy not to carry a deadly weapon, but he was not averse to using one if the circumstances were dire enough.

These were.

The gun began blasting lead. Hot brass casings spewed from the ejector mechanism.

The bronze man sheared off the tops of a row of green cane at the point he judged many of the pursuers to be.

The cries of fright and frantic calls to beat a hasty retreat proved him correct. Not wanting to exhaust all his ammunition, Doc Savage released the trigger and bore Harmon Cash away.

He caught up with the others as if not encumbered by the double weight of the heavy weapon and the unconscious crook.

Blood-thirsty as always, Monk asked, "Get any?"

"They are temporarily discouraged," Doc replied.

"Temporary," Monk muttered, "ain't gonna get us out of this fix."

"It will be dark soon," Doc supplied. "That should buy us some time."

"Time for what?" Dana demanded. "Isn't there a police station around here somewhere?"

Ham Brooks laughed derisively. "My dear Miss O'Fall, this is a sugar plantation. It extends for miles in every direction. The nearest authority is forty miles due north, in Havana."

"I'm for all heading north," she said, puffing. It was very warm, even sultry. Compared to the invigorating cold of Manhattan, the air was like a moist blanket around them. They found their strength sapping away. A sweet, musty odor hung in the air.

"Our best bet is the airfield," Doc Savage said.

"Now you're talking!" Dana crowed. "We'll steal your plane back!"

"If we time it right," Doc added, "we'll arrive before the gold."

"There's that mysterious gold again," Dana muttered. "How about a clue?"

"You're a detective," Monk snorted. "Figger it out yourself."

"Doc, I just thought of something," Ham Brooks said suddenly. "This is the cutting season. Where are the workers?"

A partial answer came in the form of a grisly discovery they made a few minutes later.

When sugar cane is cut, the workers hack off the sharp leaves with a small sickle on the ends of their long cane knives. Then they employ the big blades to remove the top joints for later replanting and hack off the remaining length a few inches off the ground. The cane is then stacked in windrows for transportation to the mills by wooden ox cart or rail.

It is hard, taxing work, but a good cane worker could reduce a quarter acre to cut cane in a typical twelve-hour working day.

The native workers had completed perhaps half a normal day's work when they were gunned down. Fully a ton of cane had been cleared and neatly stacked in nearby windrows.

They were of many complexions, these workers. Some were white, some brown, others as dark as the blackest African savage. Cuba was an island of inter-mingled races living in harmony.

All had been slaughtered by various means—bullet, bludgeon, and blade. A few gazed skyward with blind white eyes standing out against their dusky faces.

"Dead as macaronis," was the indelicate way big Maximus Lavender expressed it.

"No doubt White Eyes's men killed them when they would not—or could not—show them the gold," Doc Savage said grimly. There was grief in the bronze man's golden eyes. Grief—and a rare anger.

Monk excavated one of the long cane knives, called *mochas*, and eyed its steel edge lovingly.

"I'm for paying these birds back in their own currency," he suggested tightly.

Ham and Long Tom found cane knives as well. Ham seemed particularly pleased with his, inasmuch as his habitual sword cane had been left behind. He made a few clumsy passes in the air with the blade, once accidentally snagging his metallic coverall suit with the wicked sickle back of the haft.

They pressed on.

Big Maximus Lavender seemed to become aware of his strange garment for the first time. He lifted silvery paws, remarking, "A candy bar I am, mabbe?"

"These suits will protect us from the radio effect that produces the Blind Death," Doc Savage explained, not winded at all. "It is composed of layers of metallic foil, whose reflective properties cause the micro-waves to bounce harmlessly away."

"What about me?" Dana asked, small-voiced. "I have no such protection. What happens if we're attacked by these awful radio waves?"

"Let us hope that is a bridge we never have to cross," was all the comfort the bronze man offered.

Ham Brooks put in a question.

"I still do not understand," he admitted. "How does this Blind Death business work?"

Long Tom answered.

"Ultra-short waves such as micro-waves have many

properties," the puny electrical wizard said, puffing. "In the frequencies I used in my insect eradicator, they excited the molecules in such a way as to produce intense heat in certain substances. The higher the liquid content, the greater the heat. Insects were literally cooked on the wing."

"Dot is how my bug banisher worked, too," Maximus Lavender added, his lungs laboring like bellows. He ran as if different portions of his anatomy were bound for different points on the compass.

"But the waves did not differentiate between insects and other things," Long Tom added sourly. "In higher concentrations, they could harm animals, even people."

"I fixed dot clunker," Lavender snorted. "I fixed up what you call a reflector, like on a bulbflash."

"A what?" Monk asked.

"Bulbflash. Like on camera."

"Oh. Why didn't you say so?"

"Did. Dis reflector focused der radio waves, like gun."

Long Tom continued, "The heat generated could literally cook a man, or whatever part of a man the radio waves affected. In high concentrations, death would result. It would not be a very pleasant death, either."

Doc lifted a hand for silence. Everyone came to a stop.

"Listen," the bronze man cautioned.

The others' ears, less sensitive, picked up the sound of airplane engines some seconds later.

"The gold plane," Ham moaned. "We're too late."

"Come on!" Doc rapped. He dropped sleeping Harmon Cash and rushed ahead.

The airfield was not far distant. It was smack in the middle of the cane field, where unwanted eyes would not stumble across it.

Doc plunged out of the thick cane, saw a big transport plane make a low, preliminary pass, dragging the field.

It was a very modern field. Blacktop. Well-illuminated. The sun was starting to sink and the field lights were already ablaze.

Doc was spotted almost as soon as he emerged from the cane.

"There he is!" a hoarse voice slammed out.

Bullets snarled in the bronze man's direction.

He reversed course so quickly that it appeared to the gunman that he had simply vanished.

"Bring up that Blind Death gadget!" another voice crashed. "We'll get him that way."

"But what about the chief? He gives the orders, don't he?"

"Hell with the chief! If that transport don't land, we're out all that gold!"

Hearing this, Doc Savage gathered up his band.

"They are about to unleash the Blind Death," he explained. "Listen carefully. We will form a circle around Miss O'Fall. There is a good chance this will deflect most of the radio waves."

"What about mine friend, Cash?" bleated Maximus Lavender.

"We will form the circle around him, as well," Doc said.

They went in search of Harmon Cash.

They found the place where he had been. The impression of his body in the rich, red earth was plain.

"Now what?" Monk grumbled.

"Form the circle," Doc said quickly. "Pull your hoods over your heads, and cup your gloves over the hood eye holes. Face away from the airfield. It is essential that none of the radio waves strike exposed surfaces, especially the eyes."

They formed a tight circle around frightened, white-faced Dana O'Fall.

Doc started off.

"Where you goin'?" Monk called anxiously.

"To find Harmon Cash."

XXXII

THE MILL

Harmon Cash left a clear trail in the soft red earth.

Doc Savage followed it, cutting between stands of flexible sugar cane with such dexterity that the long, drooping leaves were undisturbed by his passing.

Soon, he hove into view of the fleeing crook.

Doc's voice lifted.

"Cash!"

Harmon Cash whirled, as if at the sound of a marauding jungle cat. He took one look at the silvery tower that was the pursuing bronze man and his disoriented eyes went rolling around in his head in fear. He plunged on.

Doc lunged after him, calling, "The criminals are about to unleash the Blind Death! They do not care who is harmed, their gold fever is so great."

Harmon Cash kept running. Even in the failing light, Doc Savage could see the droplets of blood he left on the sickle-sharp cane leaves.

"Your only chance is with us!" Doc warned.

Then, wall-eyed Harmon Cash abruptly came to a halt. His back was to Doc Savage, but the bronze man saw his arms jump up suddenly.

Cash staggered backward. His moans were terrible.

"No!" he wailed. "It's got me! The Blind Death! It's got me!"

Doc came to a wary halt, as if uncertain about whether to proceed.

He watched as the smooth crook corkscrewed around, his hands clamped to his eyes. Harmon Cash was moaning inarticulately now. His fingers plucked and dug at his eyelids, as if he were intent upon pulling his very eyeballs out of their sockets.

Teetering, Harmon Cash gave a final gulp of terror and his hands simply fell slack from his eyes.

They were the disconcerting orbs of Harmon Cash no longer. Instead, the blank white gaze that had marked the faces of previous Blind Death victims stared sightlessly.

Without ceremony, Harmon Cash pitched face-first into the red soil. He did not move again.

Doc Savage had by this time donned his protective silver hood. He started creeping toward the unmoving form of Harmon Cash.

A cry from behind him caused him to reverse direction abruptly.

It was Monk Mayfair's voice, high and frightened. *"Doc! It's startin'!"*

The bronze man put on speed. No weaving among the cane stalks for him now. Those that happened to be in his way were snapped and flattened by his mad rush to reach his companions.

He smelled the smoke first. Standing cane is akin to tinder in its flammable qualities. And there were windrows of piled cuttings all around them.

By the time he had returned to his tiny band, he could hear the crackle of cane afire. It made snapping, spiteful sounds, like a crawling animal of flames.

They were standing in a circle around exquisite Dana O'Fall. The lady private detective wore an expression such as Joan of Arc might have evinced upon being tied to the stake.

Doc joined the circle.

"They must have a more powerful broadcaster," Long Tom said, stealing a look at the bronze man, "for the cane to go up like that."

"Vere's Cash?" Maximus Lavender asked huskily. Fear was a violin string playing in his voice.

Doc Savage described the grisly scene he had witnessed.

It had an immediate effect on big, bald Maximus Lavender. He stepped from the circle.

Doc, one hand across his eyes for protection against the invisible radio waves, reached out with the other to snag the man.

"No!" Lavender said, angrily. "Too many have died because of my invention. No more!"

"We need you to protect the girl," Doc returned.

"Dot is what I am about doing," Lavender shot back. "I am a thief mabbe, but crooked like a string I am, too."

He began shucking himself out of his protective-foil suit like an oversized ear of corn.

When he was done, he handed the garment to pretty Dana O'Fall. Wordlessly, the girl accepted the offering. She drew it on, stepped into the spot that her benefactor had vacated.

"The middle of the circle," Maximus Lavender said bravely, "she is for me." He took his place.

The nature of radio waves is that they are invisible. Other than the nearby fury of blazing cane, there was no sign of the Blind Death agency in the air about them.

It took Maximus Lavender to alert them to the danger.

"Heller than hot, I think I am," he muttered nervously.

"Better bend down, Lavender," Doc warned. "Your height may expose you to the micro-waves."

Lavender bent his knees.

A popping sound like a dime-a-pack string of fire-crackers let go, not far from them.

"What's that?" Dana asked fearfully.

"Exploding ammunition," Doc Savage explained. "I left my machine gun where it would not injure us if this happened."

The explanation did nothing to reassure the clus-tered group. Standing with their eyes covered, they were completely blind, unable to judge what was happening to them. It was an altogether unnerving position to be in.

Minutes passed. Nothing seemed to change. Fire still crackled here and there.

Then a voice cried, "Here comes the gold plane!"

The thunder of the transport loomed overhead. It seemed to pass over their very heads.

"Lavender!" Doc rapped. "Do you still feel the heat?"

"What I feel," Maximus Lavender said in a strange and subdued tone of voice, "is deep in the marrow, and warm she is hot not."

"Eh?"

"You hear of the Three Blind Mice, mabbe? I am the fourth rodent, I think."

"Oh no!" breathed Dana O'Fall.

"You are blind?" asked Doc Savage.

"She's hard to tell in this darkness," Maximus Lavender offered, small-voiced, "but a minute ago I could see sparks from the fires. They are no more."

Doc Savage removed his foil gloves from his flake-gold eyes. He looked around.

Fire glare had taken the cane. Sparks shot skyward. A wall of flames was drawing near to them, hungrily.

The bronze man took Maximus Lavender by one shoulder and lifted his face to the glare. The man's features worked, his squint more pronounced. In front of each eye was a thin cloud. Doc had seen such a phenomenon once before. It had obscured the eyes of the Harmon Cash underling, Blackie Doyle.

"Link hands!" Doc directed. "We have to escape this blaze!"

They joined hands, Doc in the lead, squinting Maximus Lavender in the center.

"Where we going, Doc?"

"The mill, if we can reach it."

"Are you really blind?" Dana O'Fall asked Lavender in a thin voice.

"If I am not," the other said thickly, "mine peepers are doing a good job of fooling my poor brain."

"I don't get it," Monk snorted. "How come he ain't dead?"

"For the same reason that Blackie Doyle survived his brush with the Blind Death," Doc Savage explained. "The devices which White Eyes has employed up until now were limited in their range and power. Those caught square in the path of the focused waves were struck dead. Others, depending on their position, suffered only mild effects, such as heat discomfort, fever, facial burns like those Maximus Lavender experienced when his steel-rimmed glasses, which were highly conductive, were warmed during his own experiments."

"That don't answer the question," Monk reminded.

"In every case," Doc went on, "victims of the Blind Death were literally poached by the radio waves. Due to its liquid content, the human eyeball was most easily affected. Other victims, like Jim James Garben, also suffered broiled brains and metal teeth fillings that had expanded."

"I get it now," Monk said. "The eyeballs just clouded over the way a fried egg turns white on a fry pan."

"The condition," Doc Savage added, "is known as cataracts. Normally, the clear protective membrane of the eye—the cornea—can cloud over due to extreme old age. Surgical removal is the only recourse to restoring the sight."

"Dot mean I vill see once more, yah?" asked Maximus Lavender.

"If we survive," the bronze man told him.

Behind them, the sugar-cane field was aroar with hellish red light and leaping flames.

"This stuff's worse than tinder," panted Long Tom Roberts, who had been conserving his voice—not to mention his strength—throughout the ordeal. Despite Doc Savage's miraculous healing powers, he had not fully recovered from his torture and long imprisonment.

Over the roar, came a familiar thunderous voice.
The booming tones of White Eyes. They were charged
with anger.

*"You men on the ground! Shut the Blind Death
device off! The fires are scaring off the transport! If
you do not obey me at once, a terrible fate will befall
you."*

Above, the transport was circling. White Eyes
shouted thunder anew.

*"One of you get on the tri-motor radio! Tell them
it's all right to land!"*

"If it lands, they'll slaughter the transport crew,"
Ham conjectured. "We can't let that happen!"

Doc Savage brought the fleeing band to a halt. His
bronze head—he had removed the protective hood, as
had they all—swiveled about like a fine bust on a
rotating pedestal. His weird flake-gold eyes were bright
with reddish reflections.

"Cut lengths of cane where you can find them," he
ordered.

They moved to obey, all but big Maximus Lavender, who stood like a forlorn lost soul, blinking his
clouded eyes.

The machetelike blades swung and hacked. First,
they sickled off the sharp, thin leaves. Then they felled
the long stalks, reducing these to handy lengths.

They rejoined, fists full of green cane.

Seeing Monk sucking brown juice from one of his
lengths, Doc said, "Monk has a good idea. We'll need
all the energy we can derive. Come."

Imbibing the thin, brownish sucrose juice as they
ran, they followed the bronze man. He took them to
the advancing edge of the fire.

"Make firebrands," he ordered.

It was as simple as plunging the raw cane into the
flames until they caught. They ignited easily.

"Spread out," Doc ordered next. "Our aim is to
start as many fires as possible."

"Why?" Ham asked.

"Don't be a dope," Monk snapped. "That airfield's

like an island in all this cane. We surround White Eyes
and his mob with fire, and they're licked."

They set to work. Dana remained with unhappy
Maximus Lavender. Up until now, she had been a very
sassy specimen. The sass appeared to have been knocked
out of her by the lumbering radio inventor's sacrifice on
her behalf. She watched Doc Savage and his men
disappear into the cane.

The sky was already alight. In less than five minutes, it seemed ablaze. The furious roaring and crackling of consuming cane intensified.

High in the night, the transport's landing lights
continued to sweep in a wary circle.

One by one, Doc Savage's men returned, their
metallic garments a wavering hell red as they walked.
Doc was the last to show himself.

"That will buy us time to get to the sugar mill," he
said.

They set off.

"What's at the mill?" Dana O'Fall demanded.

"A short-wave radio was recently installed there for
convenient communication with the plantation office,"
Doc explained. "We may be able to raise the local
authorities from there, as well as warn off the plane."

"You," Dana said pointedly, "seem to be a walking
encyclopedia of Cubama facts."

"Doc happens to possess a remarkably trained
memory, young lady," Ham Brooks interjected.

"I'd like a gander at the study book he read before
he got involved with this matter," she said, not a bit
satisfied. By that, the others took it that the chestnut-
haired detective's spunk was returning. Her violet eyes
threw off sudden sparks. "And where do you get the
idea these crooks haven't taken over the mill as well?"

"Because it is five miles distant from here," Doc
replied.

At that, Dana O'Fall came to a sudden, skidding
stop. Hapless Maximus Lavender happened to slam
into her, upsetting them both. Dana evidently forgot
she had been leading the bald inventor by the hand.

As she helped the big man to his boatlike feet, she said, "Five miles is a long run at full tilt, if you ask me."

"We are not going directly to the mill," Doc told her, "but to the rail line that feeds the mill. It is a short distance from here."

Dana opened her pretty mouth to speak, and clamped it shut with defeated finality.

They resumed their jogging trot through the cane.

The railroad was a toylike, narrow-gauge line. It snaked through the cane as if laid down by industrious children. In either direction, there was no sign of engine or train.

Doc selected a direction, and they walked, single file in the fashion of Indians filtering along a woodland path, due north.

They had not gone far when a short siding presented itself to them. Balanced on the rails was one of those flat cars that is motivated by a two-handled rocker crank mounted on a low hump of mechanism.

Giving vent to a howl of pure pleasure, hairy Monk jumped aboard, laying claim to one end of the motivating mechanism.

"A go-devil!" he exclaimed. "This'll cut the hike some."

The others got aboard. There was not much room. Dana had to help blind Maximus Lavender climb up and hold on.

Doc Savage took the other handle. He and burly Monk initiated a seesaw pumping rhythm.

Soon, the little conveyance was squeaking and toiling along the main line. They picked up speed. It was a bumpy ride. Behind them, geysers of sparks occasionally roared heavenward, created by toppling, blazing cane stalks.

Here and there, they spotted more bodies sprawled in the cane. Their mood darkened.

The mill was a long building that might have been an oversized barn or warehouse, except for the squat evaporator tanks that stood in a row along the flat roof.

It was of brick, an unusual building material in rural Cuba.

At the terminus, a small train of cars laden with stacked cane was lined up at one end of the great mill. One car had its cradlelike bed tipped into an aperture high in the side of the mill.

The moving end of a conveying belt could be seen through the maw. A great humming and clanking of machinery filled the night—which had arrived with the startling suddenness of the tropics.

"We're in luck," Ham exclaimed. "The mill is still in operation."

The dapper lawyer's optimism was unfounded, they discovered upon disembarking from the creaky go-devil.

For the immediate vicinity of the mill was littered with the bodies of many native workers.

A respectful silence fell upon them then.

Doc Savage went among the sprawled forms, seeking signs of life. He found none.

While the others hung back, the bronze man reconnoitered the mill, whose mighty stacks were throwing black smoke into the night sky.

Doc eased into a side door.

Almost at once, a harsh voice said, "Do not move or I will shoot you dead."

XXXIII

CATARACT

Doc Savage caught the gleam of light along the double barrel of a long shotgun that was pointed at his face. It was impossible to tell if the weapon was loaded with stinging birdshot or lethal buckshot—a significant difference under normal circumstances.

But buckshot or birdshot, if the triggers were pulled at such a close range, the bronze man would be in a bad way, regardless.

It took nerve to twist the dual maws up and away. Doc accomplished this feat as if he did it every day of his life.

He had luck. The man behind the shotgun, for whatever reason, had neither of his fingers on the triggers. Nothing happened except that the bronze man ended up holding the rifle.

Doc swapped ends, pointing the weapon at his erstwhile ambusher.

"You might," Doc suggested, calm-voiced, "show your face in the light."

The man complied. He got a good look at Doc Savage in the same instant the bronze man discerned his features by the gory light of a firebox.

"Senor Savage!" he gulped. He was a brown-skinned man of short stature and morose countenance. He wore the thin coatlike shirt of white gauze known as a *guayabera*, which makes the sweltering tropical days bearable.

"Chino," Doc said. "Are you alone?"

"*Si, si!* The bad *hombres*, they came and killed everyone. Even my poor brother, he is——"

Doc quieted him with a reassuring hand to the man's shoulder.

"I am sorry, Chino. Have you other weapons?"

"*Si!* I came from the fields where I heard the shootings. I hid them. Over here." He pointed toward a stack of machine parts in a dark corner of the mill.

Doc called to the others.

Much to Dana O'Fall's perplexity, all seemed to be acquainted with the small brown man named Chino. Monk explained that he was an overseer on the plantation. The hairy chemist declined to say how he had come into possession of this article of trivia.

They uncovered a cache of weapons, ranging from modern rifles to an assortment of pistols.

It was off to one side of the long mechanism that somewhat resembled a steam locomotive laid upside down. At least, there was quite a row of turning cast-iron wheels on one side of the machinery. The wheels—they were gears really—were easily fourteen feet in diameter. They revolved steadily. They were the motive force impelling the conveying belt that ran the length of the cane-milling machine—for that was what it was—and kept it turning relentlessly.

It began at the railroad loading aperture at one end. Set along the train were a series of tandem crushing rollers, constantly turning. The other end seemed to consist of a line of boilers and open vats. There were stacks of dried, pressed cane—the obvious by-product of the milling process—situated at this end. A lot of the dead-looking stuff was stacked by a roaring firebox, indicating that it was used to fuel the cumbrous works.

This made it very hot in the shadow of the mill machine. The close air was so heavy and sweet Dana imagined she could taste sugar with each indrawn breath.

Distributing the weapons, Doc asked Chino, the overseer, "Where is the short-wave set?"

Chino replied, "I hid it in the bagasse, senor."

Doc followed the man to one stack of dried cane—
or bagasse—unearthed the set, and warmed it up.

He rapped out quick words in a strange tongue. A
student of languages would not have recognized it,
except to realize it was the same dialect the bronze man
had used several days ago when he had ordered the
mysterious shipment by the short wave in his skyscraper headquarters.

Doc disconnected, turning to the others.

"The transport understands the danger," he reported.
"They will not land."

"*Bueno,*" breathed Chino. It was like a prayer of
thankfulness.

"What are you waiting for?" Dana asked as they
stood about.

"The tri-motor also has a short wave," Doc explained.
"Doubtless White Eyes has been using it in an attempt
to coax the transport to land. He will have recognized
my voice, if not my words. We will hear from him
soon."

It was not long. The carrier wave gave a squawk
and the voice of White Eyes boomed out.

"*Savage!*" he snarled. "*I don't know what lingo
that was, but you did a fine job of scaring off that
plane!*"

"That was my intention," Doc Savage told him.

"*And mine,*" White Eyes threatened, "*is to seize
your gold. Those fires you started were pretty clever,
but it's dying down in spots. We're coming for you. And
we will find you, wherever you are.*"

"Try the mill," Doc said.

Dana gasped.

"*What?*"

"I said," Doc repeated, "we are at the sugar mill.
It is five miles north of the field."

"*I know where the damn mill is. We're on our way.
And if you don't get that transport on the ground by
the time I arrive, you're going out the same way Harmon
Cash did.*"

Doc switched off the set.

"We will make our stand here," he said calmly. "Miss O'Fall, I want you to take Lavender behind the cane-milling machine until this is over."

"What happened to calling the local marines?" Dana snapped.

"The Havana authorities cannot hope to reach us in time to affect the outcome," Doc explained. "Besides, this is our affair. We will settle it in our own way."

Carrying a cane knife, Chino escorted Dana and Maximus Lavender to a position behind the milling machine that could not be penetrated by bullets.

As they walked, Dana asked the brown overseer a question.

"What is Doc Savage to you, anyway?"

"Doc Savage," Chino said simply, "is a great man."

"Phooey!" Dana spat.

The attack was not long in coming.

When it came, it was short.

Doc, Monk, Ham, and Long Tom each stationed himself at different points of egress.

The sound of the big conveyor stifled their ability to detect stealthy approach to a marked degree. But there was nothing stealthy about the way White Eyes announced his arrival.

"*Savage!*" he boomed. "*We're here! And you know what we're after.*"

Doc raised his voice only slightly. The degree to which it carried over the rumbling machinery was striking.

"The gold is beyond your reach," he called. "You might as well give up on that score."

"*I went to a lot of trouble, spent too much money and killed too many men to throw my hand in now,*" thundered White Eyes.

Doc did not reply.

"*Last chance!*"

Doc maintained his silence.

"*All right, boys. Go in and get them!*"

"But, chief," a rough voice complained, "they're

barricaded inside that thing. Why don't you just use your Blind Death on them and save us maybe getting shot?"

"Because, you dolt, dead they are of no use to me. Only Savage can call back that transport plane. Now get in there or I will strike you all thoroughly blind!"

There was no more argument after that.

Doc had stationed himself at the mill's main door. The portal was open a crack.

He put one golden eye to the crack, withdrawing instantly.

The door shivered under a hail of lead. It whanged back on its hinges. Doc shoved it shut with the barrel of his shotgun.

"That was the bronze devil himself!" White Eyes roared. *"I do not want him killed! Don't you fools understand that?"*

"You want us to get shot first?"

"What I want," White Eyes said wrathfully, *"is that damned gold."*

White Eyes's orders gave Doc and his crew a certain tactical advantage. They used it.

Doc gave vent to his trilling sound now. He sometimes used it as a signal.

From their positions, the others began shooting through cracked doors and windows.

"Aim for their legs only!" the bronze man warned.

Suiting action to words, he stepped up, dropped the double barrel, and pulled one trigger.

An advancing gunman went down, his legs riddled with birdshot. The birdshot came as a relief to the bronze man, and it did the job.

Doc Savage did not have to uncork the other barrel. The man's companion retreated, howling, a few pellets having nicked him with stinging rebuke.

Here and there, other shots sounded.

"Got one!" Monk howled gleefully.

"Bagged the blighter," Ham joined in. He had selected a fowling piece of antique vintage. He was using it to good advantage, however. Each time he fired, a few gunmen broke and ran. The weapon sounded unnervingly like a small cannon.

The attackers beat a hasty retreat to positions of safety.

The withering abuse White Eyes's amplified voice inflicted on his hapless cohorts caused huddling Dana O'Fall to clap her hands over her ears. It was very profane.

At length, Doc Savage ventured an observation.

"Taking this building may be more than your gang can handle," he called out.

"I'm not beaten yet!"

"Think about this," Doc warned. "We are well armed."

"Your concern for our well-being," White Eyes called acidly, *"is touching in the extreme!"*

Doc's alert ears caught a sudden exclamation from one of the surrounding gunmen.

"Chief! I just thought of something. That bronze guy—everybody knows he's got some code against killing people. He don't have his trick pistols on him, either."

"Yeah, that's right!" came another voice. "We've been playing this wrong."

The voices dropped to whispers. Doc strained to hear, but over the clanking of machinery nothing could be gleaned.

He signaled in the dimness to Monk.

Moving low to avoid a lucky shot coming through the thin clapboard doors and windows, the hairy chemist drew alongside of the bronze man.

"We may have to change our thinkin', sounds like," Monk suggested. His pleasantly homely face was worried.

"The only way in that we do not have covered is the conveyor opening," Doc pointed out. "Keep an eye on it."

"Gotcha," Monk said, returning to his station. It was the door nearest to the maw, and the apish chemist kept a weather eye on the square opening. It was cut high in the wall, and could not be entered without scaling. Even then, the constantly moving conveying belt, which fed raw cane through a succession of revolving blades and other pulverizing processes designed to milk the cane of all its sweet juice, presented a hair-raising obstacle.

This was the main reason the bronze man let the machinery run untended.

Doc let several minutes go by. When he felt it was reasonably safe to do so, he eased the door open a crack and, kneeling so his head showed at an unexpectedly low elevation, peered out.

He saw nothing in the warm murk, despite the moon having come up.

"Ham!" Doc rapped. "Check for skulkers!"

Ham reported none. Long Tom poked a pale eye out from a keyhole and said, "No sign."

Monk Mayfair, his gaze divided between his door and the conveyor machinery, gave the latter a hasty glance and then tried his door.

A single bullet blew a hole not an inch from his mashed-down nose and the simian chemist fell backward, landing on the seat of his pants. He scrambled around on his hands and knees and cocked his pistol. It was a big Webley.

One bullet went through the clapboard door—and a voice emitted a satisfyingly distressed howl.

"No wild shooting!" Doc warned.

"Lucky shot," Monk muttered, stifling a grin of pleasure.

The next sound that came puzzled them all.

It was the noisy commotion of the tiny locomotive engine huffing and clattering to life.

"What are they up to?" Ham wondered.

The cars outside rattled into life, briefly. The upended car that had blocked the loading aperture slide aside, letting in moonlight. Steam brakes engaged. The train stopped.

Then, to their surprise, the conveyor entrance went dark again as the next rocker car in the train outside was upended and a sliding, scraping rustle of raw cane shoots came tumbling out.

"Diversion!" Ham wailed, answering his own question.

He was wrong. The cane went into the whirling steel blades, creating a grinding racket like a million brooms being chewed to pieces.

Then, clambering over the upended car, a man appeared. Monk Mayfair shot him promptly dead.

He followed the cane into the blades. An ugly snapping sound was produced.

Others appeared. They seemed bent on scrambling in all at once, obviously fearful of being picked off.

"Monk!" Doc rapped. "The mill! Switch it off!"

"Huh!"

"Those men will be killed!"

Monk moved then. He made a dash to a series of levers in the machine's base. He grabbed one at random, threw it.

It seemed only to make the conveyor move that much faster.

White Eyes's men were pouring over the entrance like ants from an anthill now. A few warning shots rang out from their weapons. They went into the roof, mostly.

The men went into the blades. Bones broke. Screams lifted. They were horrible, blood-curdling. A few gunmen, seeing the carnage before them, attempted to turn back. But others, anxious to get through, and mistaking the screams for those of Doc Savage and his men, urged them forward roughly.

"Monk!" Doc shouted, his bronze voice a great crash of a sound.

"I'm tryin'," Monk howled, throwing levers. He shoved several more than once, as if losing track.

"Ham!" Doc said. "Guard this door!"

Doc moved in, shouldered Monk to one side, and grabbed a lever that the hairy chemist had not yet thrown. It was the only one he had missed.

With both hands, Doc hauled back on this.

And with a shudder, the conveyor apparatus clanked to a jerky halt. The mill went deathly quiet.

Doc looked up. The entrance was bereft of raiders now. All was still.

Along the conveyor train, thin brown sucrose juice foamed in a rushing cataract along the sluice run. It began to run pink, then red, then very, very red.

Here and there in the hideous stew, body parts bobbed.

Doc Savage fixed sheepish Monk Mayfair with his stern regard.

"This lever is plainly marked 'Stop,'" he pointed out.

Monk peered at the sign. It was white, and quite prominent.

"Whaddya know about that?" he squeaked. "It was so dang gloomy in here, I never even noticed!"

XXXIV

EYES THAT TOLD

A great silence descended over the gloomy sugar mill after the cane-grinding machinery had gone quiet.

Chino, Dana O'Fall, and gawky Maximus Lavender emerged from the shelter of the mill machine.

A few of White Eyes's minions had not fallen into the revolving blades and succession of great rollers, there to be rendered into unrecognizable chunks. They had managed to squeeze through the narrow spaces on either side, to land instead on the floor.

Doc examined these. None had survived. Their wounds did not match any of the weapons carried by Doc Savage's men. They were more on the order of long, ghastly gashes.

Doc's compelling gaze went to Chino, noticing the crimson-streaked, cleaverlike *mocha* hanging loose in one brown fist.

"These *hombres*," Chino explained weakly. "They killed my brother, Paco. I could not be a man and let them live."

Doc said nothing.

Through the walls, a voice like thunder penetrated. *"Is everything all right in there?"*

"White Eyes!" Long Tom gritted. "The coward hung back!"

Doc moved to a door and twisted his voice into a passable imitation of one of the criminals he had overheard. The bronze man was an excellent mimic.

"It's O.K., chief!" he shouted. "We beat them!"

White Eyes's voice came cautiously.

"*Is Savage alive or dead?*"

"Alive. And he's talking a blue streak!"

"*I'm coming in, then,*" White Eyes called.

Doc Savage retreated from the door.

"He may still have control over the Blind Death," Doc explained, waving his men to find cover.

The door that Doc Savage had quitted creaked inward slowly, spilling a fan of ghastly white moonlight.

The figure in the moonlight might have been a congealed glassful of lunar phosphorescence, as he stepped in. Even his shadow appeared pale.

"*Where is every one?*" he demanded of the gloom. The ever-present velocity microphone was clutched in one hand. A bulky radio receiver lay in the crook of the opposite arm.

In the murk, a short *swish!* of a sound split the last echo of the amplified voice. The swishing stopped abruptly, punctuated by a meaty *chuck!*

The howl that the being who called himself White Eyes emitted then was all the more terrible for being reproduced through the radio diaphragm. It cut through the darkness like a keen blade.

He stumbled back from the door—back into the night.

Moonlight glinted off the worn half of the *mocha* knife that had buried itself into the thick portion of his right thigh.

Chino's voice came then, choked, embarrassed, saying, "I am sorry, Senor Savage. I could not help myself. That *diablo blanco*, it was he who gave the order to kill my brother, Paco."

Doc pitched forward. He got to the door, flung it aside, and saw the stumbling form of White Eyes twist on the run. There was something small and dark in one hand. It went *whoom!*

Doc backpedaled madly, one step ahead of the lead pellet that clouted the space where he had stood.

He plunged out again, his men following.

White Eyes was running as if for his life, the bronze man saw. He was making fair time, considering that his right leg was virtually skewered by a twelve-inch blade. He favored the leg badly, taking one crippled hop for every two steps his good leg essayed, like a rabbit that had lost a foot to a trap.

The left leg of his trousers was turning more crimson with each loping leap.

Hearing the sounds of pursuit, the white-clad criminal wheeled. He had dropped his microphone somewhere along the line, but oddly, retained the bulky radio.

He brought the radio—it was of the table-top variety popularly styled a cathedral set—up before him and an audible sound, like a switch being tripped, came distinctly after he plunged a hand into a coat pocket.

Doc jerked on his hood, turned about in one motion.

"He's activated the Blind Death!" the bronze man clipped, clapping silver-gloved hands over his hood eye holes.

Behind him, his men followed suit. Dana tripped Maximus Lavender and threw herself protectively over his long, awkward body. Chino found shelter behind a boulder.

Nothing seemed to happen for an eternity of moments.

Doc Savage waited until the clumsy hopping sounds the master criminal made were faint enough to suggest safety before he dared to turn around.

The radio had been placed on the ground. Doc maneuvered around it, claiming Monk Mayfair's Webley revolver along the way.

When he judged himself out of range of the deadly micro-waves, he took aim, firing once.

The cathedral radio jumped apart, disgorging a profusion of shattered tubes and capacitors. In the midst of the entanglement were the remains of a compact dry-cell battery and a device like a cross between a sound horn and a camera flash-bulb reflector.

Doc claimed this, signaling for his men to follow.

They soon approached the outermost extent of the cane field, which was ghostly in the moonlight. They, themselves, resembled phantoms of flexible steel in the tropical effulgence. It forced them to keep their distance, inasmuch as they made excellent targets.

A little farther along, another shot volleyed back at them. It went chopping harmlessly through the cane.

"He's in the cane," Monk complained. "Otherwise I could nail him." Monk had taken possession of his Webley once more.

Doc Savage pointed to a spattering trail of scarlet running along the ground, as if a paint bucket had sprung a leak in a man's hands.

"He is losing blood rapidly," the bronze man explained. "He cannot get far."

Noticing the curious sound horn of a device in Doc's hands, Dana O'Fall asked, "Is that it? The Blind Death focuser, that is,"

Doc nodded. They were in the cane now. It forced them to move slowly, and with care. They spread out in a line.

The trail of blood was like a messy arrow showing them the way.

Another shot rang out, forcing them to duck and wait. The top of a cane stalk near Long Tom's head jumped loose.

"That Luz," Monk Mayfair said with hard vehemence, "is gonna rue this day, I'll tell a man!"

Crouched nearby, Doc Savage said, "Eduardo Luz is not White Eyes."

"What!" Monk exploded. His incautious yell brought another warning shot. It seemed quite distant now, owing to the acoustical peculiarities of the thick cane.

"Come on," Doc said, coming to his feet.

"Doc," Ham Brooks said. "Much as I hate to agree with this missing link, Eduardo Luz must be White Eyes. The man who kidnapped me while I was staking out Miss O'Fall's office set-up wore white clothing, as every one says Luz did."

"You were what?" Dana snapped, hot-eyed.

Doc interjected, "Did you ever see your captor's face?"

"Well, no," the dapper lawyer admitted.

"I did," Dana put in. "It was Eduardo Luz! He burst in on Mr. Lavender and me while I was pumping—I mean asking—him about his association with Harmon Cash."

"Nice time to start tellin' the truth," Monk growled. "A few days ago you were protestin' that Luz was as innocent as a newborn babe."

"I had my reasons," Dana sniffed.

Doc said, "Ham, what have you to add to this?"

"Not much," Ham admitted. "When my captor pushed me to the door, this Lavender fellow stepped out, with a gun. There was a fight. I was shot with my own mercy pistol. When I woke up, I was being wrapped like King Cheops and bundled to that speedboat, along with Miss O'Fall and another man."

"Lavender," Doc prompted.

"Like he say," Maximus Lavender responded. "This man in white, he barge into my poor shack. Deliberately, I shoot him by accident. Next comes the monkey man. Him, I conk on head. Then, all hell, she break free. The men from the speedboat arrive. I lose track from there. A bad time, she was had by all."

"The man who brought Ham to Lavender's Long Island estate was indeed Eduardo Luz," Doc Savage continued. "No doubt he, too, was on the trail of Harmon Cash, for his own reasons. However, Luz never left the building. Wounded, he was taken prisoner by White Eyes and his men, who had come in the speedboat."

"So where's Luz?" Ham asked.

"The Long Island fire department reported the discovery of a body in the ruins of the burned house," Doc Savage said. "It was burned beyond recognition, of course, but there is no doubt that the body was his."

"But, Doc," Ham said in a doubtful voice. "That makes no sense. White Eyes must be Luz. What about his white clothes? His bitter enmity toward his partner,

Harmon Cash, which resulted in so many deaths? And the cigarette stubs that fell from his pockets? Good grief, he was financing his criminal army with the bonds we know he stole from Cubama."

They were drawing close to the spreading cane fire. Soot and a strange smoke—bitter and sweet at once—attacked their lungs.

"We know from the testimony of the pickpocket, Benny the Bust, that White Eyes was indeed financing his enterprise with stolen Liberty bonds," Doc admitted. "But the missing Cubama securities were not Liberties."

"But—" Dana started.

Doc cut her off. "As for the cigarette-stub clue which Harmon Cash apprised us of, I myself noticed several spilling from White Eyes's pockets back at our Hidalgo warehouse. It struck me then as deliberately done, which matched my impression of White Eyes. He was no cigarette smoker."

"How do you know that, Sherlock?" Dana demanded tartly.

Doc stopped suddenly. Moonlight glinted on a sliver of steel up ahead. Doc surged for it.

The others caught up with him as he was lifting a *mocha* knife to the light. It was a slick wet red except for about a foot in front of the haft.

"We must hurry!" Doc said, tossing the blade aside.

"Why are we in a rush again?" Dana wanted to know.

"The man who calls himself White Eyes has made a bad mistake," Doc rapped. "The blade pierced a leg artery, but the blood trail indicated the blade sealed the severed ends, stanching the flow somewhat. Removing it means quick death."

"How come we are all for saving this crook's whiskers all of a sudden?" big Maximus Lavender thumped.

"Doc don't like killing," Monk said in a tone that carried a hint of disagreement.

"What I want to know," Ham sputtered, "is if

White Eyes is not Eduardo Luz, who is? There are no suspects left alive."

They discovered the truth a moment later, when they stumbled across White Eyes sprawled in a welter of his own gore. His immaculate suit was now very red below the waist.

He was not moving. And voracious red ants were already crawling over him, like living drops of blood.

They approached the body cautiously. Doc Savage watched for telltale signs of respiration—risings and fallings of the chest—and noting their utter absence, knelt down.

"Dead," he said, testing the wrist for a pulse. His tone was disappointed.

"It's early for Christmas," Monk Mayfair said jauntily, "but I say we unwrap this present anyway."

"To answer Miss O'Fall's question of a moment ago," Doc said as he reached for the porcelain mask, "I knew that White Eyes was not a cigarette smoker simply because his person was redolent of a particular blend of pipe tobacco."

"Yeah," Long Tom said, sniffing the air. "I smell it now." It reminded him of something. "Hey!" he began. "That means—"

Doc Savage lifted the mask, exposing to the moonlight a face that was contorted in agony, eyes open but unseeing because they were as blank as polished bone knobs.

A chorus of gasps and exclamations went around the group.

"Who?" Maximus Lavender bleated, squinting in all directions. "Nothing I can see. Who it be?"

"Harmon Cash," breathed Dana O'Fall. "And he's still clutching his derringer in one fist."

"How that be?" Lavender demanded. "The Blind Death already got him. Doc Savage tell us so."

"No," Doc said. "I described what I saw—Harmon Cash falling over in agony, his eyes as white as you see them. It was a ruse intended to keep himself out of our hands."

Doc dug bronze fingers into the man's eyelids. They came away with white shells, revealing the askew, lizardlike true orbs of the man who was, in truth, White Eyes—Harmon Cash.

Monk grabbed one of these shells, held it up to the moonlight. It was glass, painted white.

"Blazes!" he squeaked. "These are just like the ones you sometimes wear to disguise your eyes, Doc! Only bigger."

Ham took one. "There's a pinhole in the thing!" he announced.

"Enough to allow sight after a fashion," Doc added. "Harmon Cash was a clever man, but he was the logical suspect from the very start. He built himself up as a man who disdained killing. White Eyes never killed directly, you will recall. His deadly radio devices did that for him. Too, all who died, from Nug Hassell to C. Perley Swain and the other supposedly respectable businessmen, were either Cash henchmen or those who stood in his way."

"But he was killin' off his whole mob!" Monk protested.

"It was part of his master plan," Doc said, his bleak eyes on the leonine features of the dead master criminal. "He was determined to build a criminal army, yet throw suspicion away from himself. Annihilating his own mob served those ends, as well as allowing him to hog more of his ill-gotten gains."

"Yeah," Monk said. "Like double-crossing Topper Tweed and his bunch after they did all his dirty work for him."

On the ground, the red ants were swarming over the dead master criminal's horror-struck features. His dark eyes seemed to goggle in terror before the advancing army of insects. Even in death, the orbs appeared to look everywhere at once and at no point in particular.

Now, the latter was literally true.

Maximus Lavender cleared his throat noisily.

"One thing I do not yet get," he said. "I know Cash come to my house that time when I was prisoner. I hear his voice from other room. But three mummies were taken away before the shack go blooie! Who vas third man?"

"No doubt a Harmon Cash minion," Doc explained. "Since two white-coated men had entered the house but only one left, Cash had to cover up the fact that he was leaving in his White Eyes disguise."

Lavender's face contorted in a massive pucker.

"I thought der third bloke was Cash," he grunted.

"Exactly what he wished," Doc vouchsafed. "No doubt he was forced to reveal his true identity to more than one of his men during the sleight of hand involved in that trick, but it was a risk he had to take. Just as he risked letting them imprison him in the Cubama vault with us in order to pump us for the truth about the gold shipment."

Just then, the roar of the transport came again. One engine was sputtering badly.

"They are low on fuel," Doc said, looking up. "We must be on hand when they touch down."

They took the easy way to the field, by backtracking to the mill and taking the cane-carrying locomotive. Monk shoved the useful go-devil off the tracks and out of their way by main strength.

The plane was dropping its wheels for the landing when they came into view of the field. The surrounding cane was a devastation of blackened and flattened stalks.

"A shame," Dana said. "The crop is ruined."

"No," Doc said. "Cane is sometimes harvested by burning it to the ground. If it can be brought to the mill within a few days, little sucrose will be lost."

"Humph!" Dana said. "Know-it-all."

They expected resistance at the field. There was none. Evidently, White Eyes's mob had all gone to the mill—and their deaths.

The plane landed, lumbering up to the operations shack with only one propeller spinning. A hatch popped open and armed men piled out. They were a mixture of white men and brown. The latter had a primitive look about them, like jungle Indians.

Doc Savage walked up to them. Low words were exchanged. In a matter of minutes, the plane crew was unloading heavy wooden crates. One happened to slip, and break on the ground.

It spilled a clatter of gold ingots. Monk and Ham raced forward to pile them back into the receptacle.

"I take it," Dana O'Fall said to no one in particular, "that this is the mysterious gold shipment no one wants to talk about."

No one, evidently, still did.

In frustrated silence, Dana watched the shipment come off the plane and the refueled transport depart. Nothing she said or did could bring Doc Savage or any of his men to explain the gold.

It was, in actuality, one of Doc Savage's deepest secrets.

The Man of Bronze was a person of immensely more wealth than was popularly supposed; this, despite the fact that newspapers often referred to him as a multimillionaire. The bronze man was rich as Midas, but it was a strange sort of wealth. He had access to a lost valley in Central America, where was hidden the master gold mine which had supplied much of the fabulous wealth of the Incas. The valley was presided over by a lost clan which was composed of pure descendants of the ancient Mayas, who had no wish to mingle in the so-called civilized world. This little fragment of lost people remained in the valley and supplied the bronze man with incredible quantities of gold in return for a favor which he had once done them—a favor which was responsible for the majority of them still being alive.*

The wealth, Doc used in his strange work of righting

---

*The Man of Bronze

wrongs and aiding the oppressed. And the strange tongue which he had twice resorted to—understood by only him and his five men in all the civilized world— was pure Mayan.

Dana got an inkling of the truth as Doc and his men began loading the golden trove into their tri-motored plane.

When they were done, a general search of the plantation was conducted. They found a few stray Harmon Cash underlings. These were easily subdued, and loaded aboard the tri-motor, to be turned over to Doc's crime college for retraining. Eventually, they would enjoy new identities and no memory of their wicked pasts.

They buried Harmon Cash in a shallow grave, in the white raiment that had been his downfall. A simple length of cane was set in the ground and the dirty Panama hat set atop it. No tears were shed.

Later, Doc Savage took big, blind Maximus Lavender aside to tell him about the college.

"Your drift I don't think I catch much," Lavender muttered nervously after Doc had finished speaking. He shifted his feet like a race horse in a stall, squint eyes blinking splashes of white.

"You are not an evil man, but you have a crooked streak," Doc explained. "Your theft of Long Tom's patent led to many deaths, even if you were not, strictly speaking, part of Harmon Cash's scheme. I can offer you a new life and restored sight."

"Where I bane end up?"

"You will have a choice of opportunities," Doc assured him. "Those men who flew the transport, for instance, were graduates of the institution I spoke of."

Lavender chewed on the inside of one cheek, cudlike.

At length, he asked, "Can you mabbe straighten out my poor twisted tongue, likewise?"

"Yes."

And that settled that.

*   *   *

As they prepared to leave, Doc Savage spent some time at the tri-motor's radio in communication with the governor of New York. Monk was with him.

The situation at their skyscraper headquarters had resolved itself without further loss of life. When the Army had surrounded the building, the minions of White Eyes, understanding dawning on them that they had been abandoned by their criminal boss, simply laid down their weapons and turned themselves over to the Manhattan police peaceably.

"Sounds like the Army scared the tar out of them," Monk grinned. "Wish I coulda been there to see it. Musta been a sight!"

The bronze man seemed not to share in the jubilance. The tragedy that had befallen the Cubama Sugar Exporting Company and its workers weighed heavily on his mind.

"We no doubt will have a great deal of repair work to do at our headquarters," Doc said without pleasure.

Monk spanked a wooden crate. "No problem there. But I guess our Cubama set-up hasn't panned out too well, huh?"

"We will have to make new arrangements for transferring the Mayan gold into our hands in the future," Doc Savage agreed. "Cubama will revert to being a sugar plantation, and no more. It is too dangerous to continue as it has."

"Too bad," Monk grunted. "This is a swell spot to get away from it all."

It was dawn by the time final preparations to depart had been completed.

Long Tom Roberts drifted up to Doc Savage.

"There's still one problem," he said sourly. "I spent weeks working with Sigmund Holmes trying to find those missing bonds. Where the heck are they?"

Dana O'Fall perked up when she heard that question. "Why, I have them."

Even Doc Savage's normally impassive face betrayed a flicker of surprise when he heard this.

"You?"

Dana grinned. "Sure, I found them in Sanchez's hideout. I shot a picture off a wall so I had some glass to untie my hands with. There was a secret panel behind it. The bonds were in there, along with one of those Blind Death projector things—although I didn't know what it was until to-night. I took them both, and put a different picture up on the wall to cover the hole."

Monk snapped his fingers. "That explains how the Blind Death got Sanchez! No wonder that big radio of his was strictly a department store model. The thing that killed him was in the wall all along."

"And Dana survived only because she was lying bound on the floor, and under the focused microwaves," Long Tom said.

Doc nodded. "No doubt Harmon Cash, as he represented to us, did provide some of his henchmen with what they thought were simply samples of Maximus Lavender's bug banisher. These were in the nature of insurance policies for when he had to get rid of unwanted accomplices. Further investigation should show us that in instances where he employed hidden devices, he had spies on hand to tell him when his intended victims were in range of the deadly contrivances."

"Probably triggered by radio control," Long Tom added. "Slick."

Doc addressed pretty Dana O'Fall.

"None of this explains your strange behavior throughout this affair," he said sternly.

"Sure it does," Dana countered. "I was hired by Sigmund Holmes to recover those bonds and nab the thieves. I got the bonds, and was well on my way to getting the goods on Luz and that Harmon Cash before you barged in."

"Not true. I made a call to your agency, and the man in charge assured me you were not working on a case at present."

"That," Dana retorted, "is because Sigmund Holmes

insisted upon absolute confidentiality. I got the impression he was very embarrassed by the theft."

"Makes sense, Doc," Long Tom ventured. "Holmes thought he was going to lose his job if the bonds didn't turn up. He might have hired this girl before fessing up to—er—Cubama's owner."

"I distinctly recall your suggesting that Luz had nothing to do with the Cubama theft," Doc pointed out, not mollified.

"Luz was my catch," Dana sniffed. "If you think I was going to allow you to chisel me out of the finder's fee Mr. Holmes promised me, you're very much mistaken. And once I get back to New York, I intend to pull those bonds out of my bank deposit box, hunt up Mr. Holmes's replacement, and collect!"

"You," Doc Savage told her, "will not have to go that far."

Dana narrowed her violet eyes, saying, "What do you mean?"

"I own Cubama Importing," Doc said. "And if you had played square with us in the beginning, considerable trouble might have been avoided."

"Is that so!" Dana flared. "Well, Mr. Know-it-all Doc Savage, if you had told me that *you* owned Cubama, I wouldn't have held anything back. So put that in your pipe and smoke it!"

Monk howled. "She's got you there, Doc."

Doc colored slightly. It was the truth.

"And if you want your bonds back," Dana added, "it's going to cost you triple." She jerked a thumb at the gold-laden transport. "And don't you dare tell me you can't afford it, either. I've seen how loaded you are."

"I think," Doc Savage said sheepishly, "that the time has come to depart."

"I'll take that to be a yes," Dana said firmly.

As the bronze man went off to warm up the plane's engines preparatory to take-off, Monk and Ham fell back into their latest quarrel, as if the entire bloody ordeal they had just experienced was no more than a flat tire encountered in the course of a Sunday afternoon drive.

"There are no pirates, buccaneers, freebooters, or corsairs in my line," Ham was insisting. "Actually, I've got the most wonderful family tree."

"Is that so?" Monk snorted derisively. "And what are you—the sap?"

Continue the all-new series written by Will Murray, writing as Kenneth Robeson, with an adventure story based on a plot proposed by Lester Dent.

A mad scheme to ignite a Third World War begins with the mysterious disappearance of all sea life in the fishing grounds off New England. Called in to solve the problem, Doc Savage uncovers a terrifying scientific secret that leads him to intrigue in Occupied Japan in 1949, a woman he thought he'd never see again, and an old enemy he'd long believed dead.

A sequel to THE RED SPIDER and THE SCREAMING MAN, here is the exciting first-chapter preview from THE FRIGHTENED FISH.

The man was tall, with sand for hair and a hide whose raw color and abraded roughness suggested that he had spent some time around the sea. The tips of his sunburned ears were red and peeling in spots. He was an ordinary man except for one particular: Fear rode his rubbed-by-sandpaper features, twisting them with unnerving harshness.

It was that harshness of expression which made the headwaiter of the restaurant nervous as he conducted the man to a corner table by the window. The sunburned man had specifically asked for that table in a tense voice. His tone added to the headwaiter's unease. After ascertaining that the man didn't desire a cocktail, the headwaiter hurried off, leaving him to peruse his menu in tight silence.

The restaurant was one of those peculiar establishments that can be found in Greenwich Village. Innocuous on the outside, it was decorated with disquieting gaudiness within. It was the lunch hour, but the restaurant wasn't crowded. One table over from the sunburned one with sand-colored hair, three men sat huddled in earnest conversation. They looked like typical New York businessmen, which made them overdressed for the casual Bohemian atmosphere.

Presently, a waiter—it was the table waiter—rolled an aquarium up to the table where the three businessmen sat. He presented each customer with a pair of tongs, which they employed to extract the fish of their choice from the tank. One man had some difficulty snaring his intended meal—a butterfish—causing him to remark aloud, "I'm not so sure I like this any better than ordering from a menu. I can't seem to trap the little beggar."

"At least you can be sure that you're eating fresh fish," a companion laughed.

That last comment caused the sunburned man seated nearby to look up from his menu in shock. His shock turned to near-panic when he saw the man finally tong a flat silver fish from the portable water tank.

"No! No!" he screeched. He bolted to his feet, upsetting his table. "Take it away!"

"Here, now, fellow. What is this?" the man with the fish demanded. It squirmed and flopped between the tongs, its gill flaps fluttering with delicate urgency.

The sunburned one, a picture of utter and complete panic, tried to run. He tripped over his own chair. The commotion caused patrons all over the restaurant to stand up and gawk. The trio at the water tank followed suit. One of them, still clutching his tongs tightly, made a move to offer his free hand to the fallen customer. As he leaned down to help, the flopping silver fish eeled from the loosening tongs. It landed on the agitated man's chest.

The man's eyes riveted on the fish, now in the final convulsions of death. With a last weak squirm, it lay flat. Only its puckered mouth worked after that.

"Take it away! Take it away!" the sunburned man bleated, his eyes pleading. "I can't stand the look of fear in its eyes!"

"It's all right, friend," the helpful man said soothingly as he tonged the fish up, leaving a damp smear on the prostrate man's shirt-front. He brought it up to the other's nose. "See, it won't harm you."

Instead of producing the expected calming effect, the gesture had the opposite result. In a frenzy, the sunburned individual grabbed from the floor the knife which had bounced from his overturned table setting, and jumping back into a corner, applied it to his own throat.

"Hey! That guy's trying to kill himself!" one of the three businessmen yelled.

"Somebody stop him!" another howled. "No, I'll

do it." He jumped the man, who was sobbing horribly, but otherwise accomplishing little. A bread knife is not quite the instrument with which to cut one's own throat.

There was a brief tussle, with the result that the would-be suicide landed back on the floor, the victim of a Judo throw.

The man who had done the throwing stepped back and asked of the gaping restaurant clientele, "Did you see that? He tried to kill himself when he saw me pick out the silver fish! Why would anyone be frightened of a little silver fish?"

The silver fish in question, meanwhile, gasped for air on the floor, but no one paid it any attention, and it died there. In death, it wore a scared, round-eyed expression not unlike that of the man who had been terrified by it.

The would-be suicide found his feet momentarily. He looked dazed. He ran one shaking hand through his shock of sandy hair. No one tried to stop him when he stumbled from the restaurant like a hagridden old man.

The other patrons slowly resumed their seats. The waiters busied themselves with their duties, deflecting questions with bored shrugs and murmurs.

Not long after, the three businessmen filed out of the restaurant without a word, their meal forgotten.

An hour later, the same sunburned man walked down a lower Manhattan side street near the Battery, his face warped with ugly tension. His progress appeared aimless until he came abreast of a run-down corner market. There was a large fish in the window, lying on its side in a tray of ice. The fish was silver. Even its flat dead eye was silvery. The eye looked uneasy, as if even in death it feared its eventual fate.

The man noticed it with a stride-stopping start. He panicked again. He screamed. High and shrill, the sound was something to chill the bone marrow. It attracted attention up and down the street. People came out of doorways and leaped from passing cars. A few converged on the sound.

"They're everywhere!" he shrieked. "The frightened fish are everywhere! I can't escape them! No one can escape them!"

The man looked around wildly. He spied an approaching taxi. He started toward it, and his intention to hurl himself in the path of the machine became obvious to passersby.

Two men jumped him before he got twenty feet. The taxi braked hard, slowed, and struck a lamp post. The impact banged the cab's grille out of shape, but the driver emerged unscathed.

"What the blankety-blank is going on?" the cabby demanded, not using quite those words.

One of the rescuers yelled back, "I don't know, dammit! This guy lyin' here took one look at a fish in that market window and went crazy. I think he was tryin' to get himself run over."

The man in question lay dazed in the street. A crowd gathered.

"What's so damn terrifying about a fish?" the cabby wanted to know.

"Nothin' that I can see," the second rescuer put in. "It's just a fish, a common silver trout. Looks more scared than that guy, if you ask me."

They went over to the window to look at the fish. The whole street went over to the window. Some squeezed into the tiny market itself, causing the proprietor to have fits. No one was buying.

While all this attention was being focused on a storefront fish, the one with the suicidal inclinations picked himself up and ran off.

A few minutes later, his two rescuers entered the slightly damaged taxi. The cabby was already behind the wheel. He drove off. Not a word passed between them.

The Parkside-Regent Hotel, overlooking Central Park, was quiet as three well-dressed men entered the lobby, ostensibly to secure rooms for themselves. They wore overcoats and carried luggage, which made them look like out-of-town visitors.

They were the same three men who had tried to

prevent the suicide of the man who had been frightened by a fish in a Greenwich Village restaurant earlier in the day. Dressed differently, they were also the same trio who had been involved with the near-suicide in front of a Manhattan market. One of them had been driving the taxi. They were preoccupied now with details of registering at the Parkside-Regent.

They didn't appear to notice that the man with the ungodly fear of fish had quietly entered the lobby to purchase a newspaper from a cigar stand. He paused at a rack of postcards, casually turning the spinner to examine the display.

Abruptly, he let out a howl that produced a sympathetic squeal of fright from the counter girl. He knocked the card-spinner to the floor. His eyes were wild. He kicked at the fallen rack as if it were a vicious dog. Cards scattered all over the floor. Several of these fell faceup to reveal the picture of a mounted swordfish. The swordfish was silver. Its profile suggested wide-eyed, gape-mouthed terror.

The sight brought renewed screams from the man, and from the counter girl. The man stamped at the postcards frantically, but to no avail. "Get them away! *Get them away from me!*" he wailed. "They haunt my dreams, those frightened fish!"

He ran then. Not for the revolving door, which was clogged with a matron pulling a small dog on a leash, but for the big plate-glass hotel window. Head lowered, he butted the glass like an enraged bull. The glass was stout. He bounced back. Sobbing, he then picked himself up to try again. He bounced a second time, which brought tears of frustration to his eyes, but no willingness to give up. His object, it was plain, was to dash his brains out against the glass. But he was unable to build up enough of a head of steam to complete the task. It was a horrendous sight.

The three men at the lobby desk went into their act—it was not obviously an act to bystanders—once again. Yelling, they piled on the other man before he could smash his skull against the lobby window a third time. They wrestled him to the ground as the manager frantically called the police.

By the time the police arrived, minutes later, the suicidal man had vanished. So had his rescuers. The manager, who was almost entirely speechless, professed to understand none of it.

The counter girl, considerably calmed down now, gave her version of what happened.

"He didn't act crazy, at first," she explained, chewing gum nervously. "He came in, bought a paper, and started looking through the postcards. Then, well, he just turned into a maniac. Fella destroyed the rack for no reason."

That much was obvious to the two cops. "Did he say anything?" one asked.

The girl thought. "It was mostly yelling, but he did say something about fish haunting him, or something like that. I remember him stamping on the ground like a crazy man. You know, kinda the way you'd step on a poisonous snake. Except I didn't see any snake. Just postcards."

The two cops looked over the rug. They found several postcards scattered about, all bent and scuffed, and all bearing the identical photograph of a mounted swordfish. There were other postcards strewn on the rug, the usual Manhattan skyline portraits intended for the tourist trade, but these were undamaged.

"This is screwy," one of the cops remarked, puzzled.

"It sure is. Why would he be scared of a swordfish?"

"You ask me, the swordfish looks darned unhappy, too."

"I never heard of a scared swordfish," the second cop remarked.

"Well, we'd better call the boys at Bellevue. Could be one of their inmates is loose."

"An escaped lunatic. Sure, I'll bet that's who he was."

They left the hotel with their shared opinion unchanged.

The skyscraper was New York's tallest. For that matter, it was the tallest in the world. It rammed up from the pavement over one hundred stories in height from its busy modernistic lobby to the needle point of its dirigible mooring mast—a ludicrous adornment in an age of jet aircraft. It boasted more offices than some small cities. The skyscraper was famous for another reason, too. Its eighty-sixth floor was the headquarters of Doc Savage, an individual whose avowed profession was no less Galahadian than that of righting the wrongs of the world and bringing malefactors to justice, where normal law-enforcement agencies could not do so.

Almost everyone—including Doc's enemies, who were many—knew of Doc Savage and his work, and knew, also, that he operated out of this midtown Manhattan skyscraper. That was why the elevator operators in the building received instructions to report any unusual occurrences in the busy lobby.

Doc Savage was in his laboratory—his suite consisted of laboratory-library-reception room set-up—when the phone rang.

"Mr. Savage? This is Henry, one of the elevator operators."

"Go ahead, Henry." Doc's voice was quietly powerful, like the engine of an expensive limousine as it idles.

"There's somethin' funny goin' on down here you might want to know about."

Interest lifted the controlled timbre of Doc's tone. "What is it?"

"There's these three guys hangin' around out front."

"Describe them."

Henry did so. The descriptions meant nothing to Doc Savage.

"Continue, Henry."

"Well, they were just hangin' around, like I say, but as soon as they thought on one was lookin', they got down and drew a fish on the sidewalk."

"A fish?"

"I know how it sounds, but that's what they did. I watched them from the lobby. They drew a fish outline in chalk. I think it's a sunfish. It's very round."

"What's unusual about that?" Doc asked. "College pranksters perpetrate these sorts of stunts every day."

"That's my point," Henry said excitedly. "These guys weren't frat boys. None of them looked under thirty. After they drew the outline, they filled it in with silvery paint."

"What did these men do after that, Henry?"

"They ducked around the corner. They're still there, too. Like they're waiting for something to happen. But don't ask me what."

"Anything else to report?"

"Yes. I don't know who looked more frightened, them or the fish."

"Eh?"

"The fish," Henry said, "is wearing the most terrified expression you ever saw."

"Thank you, Henry," Doc Savage said after a pause. "You did the right thing to call." He hung up.

The information had both puzzled and intrigued Doc Savage. The altercation involving the man whose fish phobia was so great that he would try to take his life had made the afternoon editions, and Doc had read an account of the matter. He had thought little of it until a television news broadcast of the incident at the Battery market came over the air. The Parkside-Regent incident was too recent for him to have heard about.

Swiftly, Doc shucked off a laboratory smock discolored by the chemicals of an experiment he had been performing on the molecular stability of polymers. He strode across the huge laboratory.

Doc Savage was a spectacular man. He had a reputation as a combination scientific genius, mental marvel, and physical giant, which he more than lived up to. He lived up to his reputation, as a matter of fact, the way the atom bomb lives up to its reputation as an explosive weapon. In person, Doc was a giant bronze man with hair a little darker than his skin, and a pair of compelling flake-gold eyes that could calm you down or lift you out of your seat—whichever effect Doc desired. He was a man of immense physical strength whose intelligent face ended any suspicion that he might be all muscle and no brain. It was a face whose handsomeness was made tolerable, to Doc's way of thinking, by its angular regularity.

All in all, the giant bronze man was too conspicuous to investigate the mystery of the fish-drawing pranksters without taking precautions. Doc was a genius at taking precautions. Truth to tell, he was a genius at most of what he did.

Doc dug a cab driver's uniform and cap out of a clothes locker, changed into it, and took his special pneumatic elevator to the secret garage he maintained in the skyscraper's basement. There, he left the establishment in an old taxi, exiting through a secret door activated by a radio signal from the cab, which happened to be bullet-proof, among other not-very-obvious wonders.

Doc turned the corner, spotted three men answering the elevator operator's description loitering by a telephone booth, and hit a dashboard button. The left front tire of the cab let go like a shot. The car veered wildly. Making a show of the struggle, Doc fought the wheel to the curb opposite the three men. He got out and proceeded to go through the motions of changing the tire, seeming not to pay any attention to the loitering trio.

The three men were huddled in conversation. The two doing most of the conversing more or less faced Doc, which was fortunate because it enabled him to read their lips with a gadget consisting of a mirror attached to a telescopic rod, somewhat like the examining tool dentists use. Doc was a skilled lip-reader.

"This is ridiculous," one of the trio was saying. "Here we are practically camped on his doorstep. And who says this goofy stunt is even going to work?"

"I don't hear any better suggestions," growled the other. He possessed a hard, weather-beaten face with light-colored eyes that brought to mind carpet tacks. There was absolutely no warmth in them. "And where the hell is George? I told him two o'clock. It's ten past."

"I'm more worried about Savage, dammit. He's big stuff."

"So is this, brother," the second speaker said fervently. "So is this."

"I keep hearing that, but I still don't see how any of these fish shenanigans are going—"

"What do you want we should do?" the second man—he seemed to be the group's leader—remarked with strained exasperation. "Go up there and ask him? 'Excuse us, Mr. Savage, but we're with Max Wood's outfit, and we were wondering, before we get too deep into our activities, whether or not you have been warned about us and intend to put a stop to these activities?' Is that what you want us to do? Is it?"

The first man shifted his feet. He rolled a well-chewed toothpick from one side of his mouth to the other. All three were watching the street, searching approaching faces.

"But this fish thing is screwy—"

"Sure, but if Savage knows anything, he'll be getting ready to tear off for Quincy. We have to find out now and head him off. He's the only one who could queer the whole plan. He's exactly the type, too; this is just his damn meat." The man stepped away from the others and peered around the corner toward the skyscraper's main entrance. Seeing nothing more than the usual New York pedestrians unconcernedly trampling the silver-paint sidewalk fish, he returned to the others.

"Now we've pulled this scared-fish gag in enough places all over town to get his attention, but he hasn't made a move so far. One last try in front of his headquarters should do it. He'll grab George. George will tell him a fable and pump him. And there you have it. We either skrag Savage or make tracks, depending on how close to being a monkey wrench in our well-oiled works he is."

The third man, away from the mirror, suddenly pointed north toward a man crossing the street.

"Here comes that damn George now," the straw boss muttered without pleasure.

"About damn time."

They gathered themselves into a close-knit knot, straightened out their clothing as if it would smooth out the nervous lines of their faces as well, and turned the corner, the straw boss man taking the lead.

Doc, on the opposite sidewalk, abandoned his flat tire and took up a position in a phone booth where he could better keep an eye on the others.

A sunburned man with sandy hair and a grim face was striding toward them, Doc saw. He did not appear to recognize the trio, nor notice the round silvery fish on the concrete until he stepped on it. Then he definitely took notice of the design.

His head went down. His face went slack.

He leaped a foot in the air and his blood-curdling yell bounced along the street. "The fish!" he screeched. "The frightened fish! It means the end of civilization!" He began pulling at his hair. He beat his chest, his head, his sides, and presented a convincing portrait of a demented and terrified person.

The trio, acting the part of bystanders, fell upon him, wrestling him to the ground, and otherwise made a big show of protecting the screaming man from himself. They eyed the skyscraper entrance at every opportunity.

Doc Savage walked up from the opposite side of the street.

"You can cut the acting," Doc told them all.

One of the trio looked up in bewilderment. "What— what did you say?" he gulped.

Doc removed his driver's cap. "I said you can drop the act," he repeated. "I know everything." Nothing on his face indicated this last was a fib.

Open-mouthed astonishment transfixed the quartet of men, a tangle of bodies on the sidewalk.

"You do?" one spoke in a hoarse croak. It was the sunburned newcomer. George.

"I do," Doc told him.

"Then I guess it's all over," George muttered, staring down at the silver sidewalk fish that looked as if it were frozen in terror.

Then one of the men pulled a pistol and shot the bronze man twice.

Doc Savage was driven backward three steps by the force of the bullet. He kept his feet, as if fighting to hold onto his balance against a hurricane-force gale, not a sudden flurry of .38-caliber slugs. With the third step, he twisted at the knees and ankles and collapsed on the curb. He did not rise again.

The quartet of men took off in a flock, knocking through the gathering crowd like football linemen. A waiting car carried them away.

Doc Savage picked himself up. His breathing was red agony. Both bullets had hit him in the solar plexus, a particularly bad spot, even with the bullet-proof chain mesh undershirt protecting it. He fought for air, as he shook off the solicitous hands of the gathering crowd. He made for his cab.

A press of a dashboard button reinflated the supposedly flat tire, and the cab got under way.

Doc caught sight of the fleeing car almost immediately, reasoned out its general direction and kept abreast of it by running down parallel streets on either side. Manhattan's gridlike street layout made this simple. Meanwhile, he concentrated on getting his wind back and mentally berated himself for allowing himself to be shot. The zaniness of the man-terrified-by-frightened-fish lure had caused him to underestimate his opponents.

The trail led north to the Queensboro Bridge and then to Long Island. Doc was calculating his best next move—whether to follow at a distance or cut his quarry off and confront them—when they turned onto an abandoned flying field near Patchogue, and he knew with a sinking certainty that the quartet of suspicious men would have had a plane standing by for just such an eventuality as this.

He was right. Floats bumping along the rutted, weed-choked ground, a small yellow seaplane took off moments later and moaned northward.

Doc Savage watched it with unwavering metallic concern etched on his bronze mask of a face.

THE LEGENDARY MAN OF BRONZE—IN A THRILLING NEW ADVENTURE SERIES!

DOC SAVAGE

❑ PYTHON ISLE, Kenneth Robeson

29357-5 $4.50/$5.50 in Canada

After more than forty years, Doc is back in an all-new novel based on an unpublished outline by Doc Savage's original creator. When the mysteriously vanished aviator Tom Franklin returned as if from the dead, he brought a mysterious woman in a battered plane that had been repaired with plates of pure gold. Franklin and his charge fall into the clutches of a diamond smuggler, and Doc Savage becomes embroiled in a raging battle for control of one of history's myst closely guarded mysteries, the lost secret of Python Isle.

❑ ESCAPE FROM LOKI, Philip José Farmer

29093-2 $4.50/$5.50 in Canada

A brilliant supervillain has dreamed up the ultimate secret weapon...a desperate masterstroke that will assure victory for the Kaiser—or obliterate mankind from the face of the earth! Hugo Award winner Philip José Farmer, superstar of speculative fiction and author of biographical studies of Doc Savage and Tarzan, now adds to the legend of the Man of Bronze in this riveting adventure of Doc's early days.

■■■■■■■■■■■■■■■■■■■■■■■■■■■■■■■■

Available at your local bookstore or use this page to order.

Send to: Bantam Books, Dept. FL 8
414 East Golf Road
Des Plaines, IL 60016

Please send me the items I have checked above. I am enclosing $_____ (please add $2.50 to cover postage and handling). Send check or money order, no cash or C.O.D.'s, please.

Mr/Ms._____

Address_____

City/State_____Zip_____

Please allow four to six weeks for delivery.

Prices and availability subject to change without notice.   FL8 12/91

"CALLING DICK TRACY! CALLING DICK TRACY!"

Max Allan Collins brings America's favorite
detective to life in an all-new series.

❑ **DICK TRACY** 28528-9 $4.95/$5.95 in Canada

Five of the city's deadliest hoods lie dead in a downtown garage.
"Big Boy" Caprice is on the rampage. He plans to destroy his
gangland opposition and unite all the tough guys in town in an
organized reign of terror. Just one man stands in Big Boy's way:
Dick Tracy. Based on the screenplay by Jim Cash & Jack Epps,
Jr., and Bo Goldman & Warren Beatty. Now a major motion
picture from Walt Disney Pictures.

❑ **DICK TRACY GOES TO WAR**
28890-3 $4.95/$5.95 in Camada

A wave of wartime racketeering has the city in its deadly grip
and Tracy rushes into battle with his tommy gun blazing. Yet
between the town's toughest gangsters and a slinky seductress,
the crime-stopping hero may find himself distracted from the
real danger: foreign agents who are zeroing in on a top-secret
weapon that could destroy the world.

❑ **DICK TRACY MEETS HIS MATCH**
28891-1 $4.99/$5.99 in Canada

Tess Trueheart is enthralled when Dick Tracy agrees to marry
her on national TV. But when their show is interrupted by a
bullet, Tracy leaves his bride at the altar to pursue the sniper.
One thing is certain: with the next wedding airdate set, ratings
and tension soar as Tracy's enemies try to cancel him midseason.

Available at your local bookstore or use this page to order.

Send to: **Bantam Books, Dept. FL 21**
         2451 S. Wolf Road
         Des Plaines, IL 60018

Please send me the items I have checked above. I am enclosing
$_____ (please add $2.50 to cover postage and handling). Send
check or money order, no cash or C.O.D.'s, please.

Mr./Ms._____

Address_____

City/State_____Zip_____

Please allow four to six weeks for delivery.
Prices and availability subject to change without notice.   FL 21 2/92

INDIANA ————
———— JONES

Bold adventurer, swashbuckling explorer, Indy unravels the mysteries of the past at a time when dreams could still come true. Now, in an all-new series by Rob MacGregor, officially licensed from Lucasfilm, we will learn what shaped Indiana Jones into the hero he is today!

❏ **INDIANA JONES AND THE PERIL AT DELPHI** 28931-4 $3.95/$4.95 in Canada
Indy descends into the bottomless pit of the serpent god of the Order of Pythia. Will Indy find the source of Pythia's powers— or be sacrificed at their altar?

❏ **INDIANA JONES AND THE DANCE OF THE GIANTS** 29035-5 $4.50/$5.50 in Canada
Indy takes off on an action-packed chase from the peril-filled caves of Scotland to the savage dance of the giants at Stonehenge—where Merlin's secret will finally be revealed.

❏ **INDIANA JONES AND THE SEVEN VEILS** 29334-6 $4.99/$5.99 in Canada
With his trusty bullwhip in hand, Indy sets out for the wilds of the Amazon to track a lost city and a mythical red-headed race who may be the descendants of ancient Celtic Druids.

❏ **INDIANA JONES AND THE GENESIS DELUGE** 29502-0 $4.99/$5.99 in Canada
Indy sets out for Istanbul and Mount Ararat, fabled location of Noah's Ark, when various forces try to bar him from finding a certain 950 year-old boat-builder...

Available at your local bookstore or use this page to order.

Send to: Bantam Books, Dept. FL 7
2451 S. Wolf Road
Des Plaines, IL 60018

Please send me the items I have checked above. I am enclosing $_____ (please add $2.50 to cover postage and handling). Send check or money order, no cash or C.O.D.'s, please.

Mr./Ms._____

Address_____

City/State_____Zip_____

Please allow four to six weeks for delivery.
Prices and availability subject to change without notice.   FL 7 3/92

A TOP-SECRET MISSION—AND THE PRICE OF FAILURE IS
MORE THAN THE WORLD CAN AFFORD

THE FLIGHT

by C.F. Runyan

"A high-pressure adventure by the newest
master of the craft." —Clive Cussler

1942, the Philippines: Corregidor falls to the Japanese, and
the Americans who survive will face brutal POW camps.
Many will die, including a brilliant young army doctor who
has just discovered a miracle cure...for cancer.

1994, Washington, D.C.: The most popular president since
FDR has only weeks to live. His deteriorating condition
must be kept secret, for his presence at an upcoming Summit
meeting is vital to bolster precarious East-West accords. But
as time runs out, a cryptic letter found in General Douglas
MacArthur's archives offers the only hope. And from the
president's deathbed a desperate mission is launched...

"Enticing and original...I'd be hard-pressed to conceive a
more intriguing plot."—Barrett Tillman

"Brilliant...Mixes adventure with bloody intrigue in a
desperate race against the clock. A great read."
—Martin Caidin, author of *The Final Countdown*

Available at your local bookstore or use this page to order.
❏ 29610-8 THE FLIGHT $5.99/$6.99 in Canada
Send to: Bantam Books, Dept. FL 19
2451 S. Wolf Road
Des Plaines, IL 60018
Please send me the items I have checked above. I am enclosing
$_____ (please add $2.50 to cover postage and handling).
Send check or money order, no cash or C.O.D.'s, please.

Mr./Ms._____

Address_____

City/State_____Zip_____
Please allow four to six weeks for delivery.
Prices and availability subject to change without notice.   FL 19 2/92